VIOLET EYES

I hesitated at the top of the stairs, uncertain whether to retreat to my room or to try to salvage the evening. But even as I stepped on the first stair, I became aware of Rafe, waiting for me, looking up at me. My heart lurched, and as I descended I found myself unsteadied by the intensity of his regard.

"Like pansies," he murmured.

I stared at him. What on earth . . . ?

"Your purple eyes, Vi." He stepped closer. "They're like huge velvet pansies. A man's cautions could drown in their soft depths."

He held out his hand to me. "I'll make you a bargain, Violet. I'll try not to blame Ned if you will try not to blame me."

I hesitated, then reached down to seal the pact with a traditional shake of the hand. I intended to do no more than grasp the tips of his fingers, but the moment my hand touched his, I knew I was lost.

Did I walk down the step that separated us? I felt as if I had floated into his arms, and for a long delicious moment all that mattered was the warm urgency of his mouth on mine . . .

MORE THRILLING GOTHICS FROM ZEBRA BOOKS

THE MISTRESS OF MOONTIDE MANOR (3100, $3.95)
by Lee Karr

Penniless and alone, Joellen was grateful for the opportunity to live in the infant resort of Atlantic City and work as a "printer's devil" in her uncle's shop. *But her uncle was dead when she arrived!*

Alone once more, she encountered the handsome entreprenuer Taylor Lorillard. Danger was everywhere, and ignoring the warning signs—veiled threats, glances, innuendos—she yearned to visit Moontide Manor and dance in Taylor's arms. But someone was following as she approached the moon-drenched mansion . . .

THE LOST HEIRESS OF HAWKSCLIFFE (2896, $3.95)
by Joyce C. Ware

When Katherine McKenzie received an invitation to catalogue the Fabulous Ramsay oriental rug collection, she was thrilled she was respected as an expert in her chosen field.

It had been seven years since Charles Ramsay's mistress and heiress had mysteriously disappeared—and now it was time to declare her legally dead, and divide the spoils. But Katherine wasn't concerned; she was there to do a job. *Until* she saw a portrait of the infamous Roxlena, and saw on the heiress' finger the very ring that she herself had inherited from her own mysterious past.

THE WHISPERING WINDS OF
BLACKBRIAR BAY (3319, $3.95)
by Lee Karr

Anna McKenzie fulfilled her father's last request by taking her little brother away from the rough gold mining town near City. Now an orphan, Anna travelled to meet her father's sister, whom he mentioned only when he was on his deathbed.

Anna's fears grew as the schooner *Tahoe* reached the remote cove at the foot of the dark, huge house high above the cliffs. The aunt was strange, threatening. And who was the midnight visitor, who was whispering in the dark hallways? Even the attentions of the handsome Lyle Delany couldn't keep her safe. For he too was being watched . . . and stalked.

Available wherever paperbacks are sold, or order direct from the Publisher. Send cover price plus 50¢ per copy for mailing and handling to Zebra Books, Dept. 3700, 475 Park Avenue South, New York, N.Y. 10016. Residents of New York and Tennessee must include sales tax. DO NOT SEND CASH. For a free Zebra/ Pinnacle catalog please write to the above address.

WHITE ROSES OF BRAMBLEDENE

JOYCE C. WARE

ZEBRA BOOKS
KENSINGTON PUBLISHING CORP.

For my mother:
always there for me;
always dear to my heart.

ZEBRA BOOKS

are published by

Kensington Publishing Corp.
475 Park Avenue South
New York, NY 10016

First printing: March, 1992

Printed in the United States of America

CHAPTER ONE

It may have been a trick of the light. A passing cloud, perhaps, or the lengthening twilight shadows. A mere trick of the light, coupled with my reluctance to return to that unhappy place. Whichever it was, viewed at a distance through the small carriage port fogged with my breath, Brambledene resembled, huddled blind-windowed under that cold February sky, nothing so much as a malevolent toad, its square gothic tower a weighty crown upon its warty squatness.

Yes, it must have been a trick of the light, for no sooner had my shabby conveyance from the Lenox station rounded the sweeping hemlock-hedged drive than the huge oaken door opened wide and Flora, Freddie, Wink, and Iris came running out to meet me, gilded by the golden lamplight that spilled out after them.

They were my oldest and dearest friends. We had shared the happiest hours of my girlhood; together we had endured the horror of the worst, here at Brambledene. In the year since, the circumstances of our changing lives had kept us apart, but the warmth of their greeting dispelled my fear that the bright bonds forged in the springtime of our youth might have tarnished during the long months of separation.

"Vi! Vi! We thought you'd never come!"

Freddie Latimer waved away the coins I dug from my

purse to tip the driver, and proffered with a slightly pompous flourish a bill from his own pocket. Dear Freddie! How he yearned to be thought a man of substance.

"You travel light for a girl, Vi," Wink McEldowney said as he effortlessly swung my bags down from the luggage rack. Wink, who didn't give a fig about substance, commanded automatic respect by virtue of his height and erect carriage.

"Vi isn't a girl anymore, Wink," Iris Blanchard chided in her rich contralto. "She's a woman." The contrast of Iris's voluptuous voice with the austere, almost fierce look of her strongly sculptured face never failed to startle me.

"And a very cold one at that, I wager," Flora said. "Come along, do!" So saying, Freddie's twin linked her plump arm in mine and we all scurried, laughing, up the steps, across the terrace, and into the house.

A few minutes later, divested of my outdoor wraps, I pressed as close as I dared to the birch logs crackling in the baronial fireplace in the large oak-paneled parlor. It was a somber room at best. In summer its dimness might lend the illusion of coolness and provide a welcome escape from the blaze of sunlight, but at this twilight hour of the cruelest of the winter months Brambledene seemed as coldly barren inside as out, although there was in fact no tomblike chill, no sour odors of disuse or rising damp.

The oak floors and panelled walls were stained a dismal brown ebonized by the shadows; the chairs and couches had been clothed in a plum-colored brocatelle and midnight blue velours more suited to a medieval cathedral than a country house in the Berkshire hills of Massachusetts, and the luxurious pile of the dark Sarouk carpet underfoot offered scant relief from the funereal effect. One could almost imagine the smoke wisping fitfully up the face of the granite fire-surround as issuing from the censer of a remorseful, renegade priest.

I shivered and edged even closer to the flames, drawn

by the play of light and shadow among grape-laden vines deeply incised in the dark gray stone. From a blazon centered at the top, the horned head of a goat-eared Pan leered maliciously. I wondered, not for the first time, why these ancient symbols of a cruel and lustful pagan era were so commonly employed as decorative accessories in the parlors of the solidly respectable. Fanciful depictions of erotic flight were particularly admired, and cloven-hoofed fauns chased many a scantily attired marble maiden through late Victorian ferneries.

I traced one finger through the carvings swirled through the quartz-flecked granite. The warmth the stone had absorbed from the flames helped to dispel my uneasiness. Despite its having been the setting for the tragic event that had affected the lives of all of us reassembled there, I told myself there was nothing inherently shuddery about Brambledene itself, certainly nothing to warrant comparison with a toad. Its darkness? A cheerful Gothic structure would be a contradiction in terms! Its mortuary air? It was mid-February! I daresay at this time of year even Delmonico's splendid dining rooms must seem lugubrious before the lamps were lit and the doors opened to admit the anticipatory chatter of the evening's clientele.

Nevertheless, even with all allowances made, this house compared ill with my father's spacious New York apartment where I resided still and which, I prided myself, I had made invitingly homey, in defiance of my father's chronic and dispiriting illness, through the use of floral chintzes and crewel-embroidered linens in unfashionably sunlit colors. I sighed and closed my eyes, wishing for an Aladdin's lamp to rub and a genie to whisk me back home.

"Violet! The moment I caught a glimpse of that black gloss of hair I knew it must be you."

The sound of Ned Poole's voice behind me shattered my musings.

"Just see how it captures the firelight, Rose."

I turned slowly to greet my host and hostess, hoping

the blush I sensed spreading across my cheeks would be ascribed to the leaping flames.

"Welcome to Brambledene, Vi, dear." Rising on her toes, Rose darted a cool greeting kiss upon my flushed skin. The icy blueness of her taffeta dress was softened by a spreading collar of creamy lace repeated in a high ruff that lent her neck a swanlike grace, and the sleeves were so airily puffed that the slightest breeze might have carried her delicately boned body aloft.

"Pay no mind to my incorrigible husband," she continued. "If it were summer, he'd remark upon the sunlight dazzingly reflected by your crowning glory—or by mine, or for that matter, by any pretty woman's."

Another man might have chided her plainspokenness, but Ned was far too self-assured for that sort of pettiness. "Where's the harm in letting a pretty woman know she's admired?" he said, his bright blue eyes sparkling with amusement. "After all," he continued, winking at me as he bestowed a kiss on the top of Rose's tidy blond head, "didn't it win me the prettiest of them all?"

Pretty, yes, I thought, but not the prettiest. Lily had been that.

As if she had been reading my thoughts, Rose turned her face up to her husband's and searched it consideringly. "Did it, Ned?" Her voice was so low I'm not sure she meant me to hear. "Did it really?"

Both blond, both slender, Lily had been as playful as a kitten, her whole being animated with a sense of fun; Rose seemed as contained and sleekly catlike as ever. Even in the midst of the most riotous of our childhood games, she had been watchful, oddly remote. I liked Rose, but I had loved Lily.

A sudden commotion in the foyer—the yelping of an excited dog and commands to hush in a well-remembered deep voice—riveted everyone's attention.

"Ah, Violet! The last of my beautiful blossoms has arrived! Now my bouquet is complete."

I reached out my hands to grasp the welcoming ones extended to me. "Oh, Victor, how grand to see you! It's very bad of you to remain so handsome, though." I marveled that his dark chestnut hair remained untarnished by gray. "Fathers are supposed to be stuffy and pompous and sport bay windows draped with gold watch chains."

"My word!" Ned interjected, "that sounds like our Freddie, bay window and all—could it be you have a missus and kiddies you haven't told us about, old chum?"

"I may have a bit of a pot," Freddie retorted, "but I certainly don't—"

"Oh, hush, you two," I broke in laughing, "what I'm trying to say is that fathers have no business being trim and dashing. It's altogether counter to the natural order of things. Why, if Victor were *my* father I wouldn't at all mind still being a LOPH!"

"Sorry, Vi!" Rose hurried over to link her arm through Victor's as if to renew her rightful claim, "I'm afraid he's spoken for even if I'm not technically a member of the L.O.P.H.'s anymore."

Count Stirbey's brown eyes regarded his blond daughter warmly. Although their coloration was in striking contrast, the look they exchanged was in perfect accord. How I envied them. Although my father had never been at a loss for words at his patients' bedsides, he had been almost inarticulate in his love for my mother and me, and his illness—he was at the midpoint of a long, slow, inevitable decline—made him querulous as well as remote.

"And what, may I ask, is a LOPH? Calm yourself, Bruno!" The last was addressed to an exuberant liver-and-white spaniel who bounced in, red tongue lolling, at the speaker's heels.

Victor laughed. "He knows he shouldn't be in here, Rafe. Bruno's place is in Jack Stark's quarters, above the stables. You'll be giving him ideas above his station."

The stranger exaggeratedly arched fine dark eyebrows. "Well, now, that would never do, would it? Nothing worse than a canine social climber."

Flora giggled and rolled her china-blue eyes at me appreciatively as he clucked at the excitedly circling dog and issued him back out through the hall and front door.

He was a moderately tall, well-proportioned man, in his early thirties I guessed, for although his dark hair was liberally laced with silver—notably more so than Victor's, his senior by a score of years—his olive-toned skin was unlined. The fine quality and impeccable cut of his tweeds hinted of Savile Row, but his English accent, although unmistakably upper-class of the public-school variety, was less clipped and lower-pitched than that of a native of those sceptered isles. An educated man, I guessed, no doubt well mannered, and undeniably attractive, but why would Rose include a stranger in this reunion of old friends linked with Brambledene by tragedy? And yet, as he surveyed the room with amused speculation, something about the cool arch of his black eyebrows above pale gray hooded eyes nudged at my memory.

"Well? Cat got your collective tongues?" the stranger drawled. "Victor has been telling me about his beautiful blossoms: Rose, Flora, and Iris I already know, so you," he said with a smiling nod of greeting to me, "must be Violet. Tell me, does one have to have a floral name to qualify for the mysterious LOPH?"

"Hardly, for that would have eliminated Wink and Freddie, yet both are, rather *were*, bona fide members. As for you, sir, since I don't know who you are, I can't say whether you qualify or not, although something about you, a certain *je ne sais quoi*, tells me not."

"Sorry, Vi, I'd forgotten you hadn't met Rafe," Rose said. "May I present my cousin, Rafael Taliaferro, lately removed from Paris to New York, who fails to qualify as a LOPH on two counts: his father is no longer living, and he's an architect. Presumably self-supporting—or about to be," she added in a murmur.

It was impossible to tell from her cousin's contained expression whether he considered Rose's rather curious qualification slighting. Had it come from anyone other than Rose, it could have been interpreted as a sly tweak, but Rose had never been the teasing sort. As they stood there looking at each other, I sensed a certain wariness that made me suspect that their relationship was neither close nor particularly trusting. They were so unlike in looks and coloring it was hard to believe that Thornbush blood ran in both sets of veins, but perhaps I was merely observing an exercise of the same sort of circumspection I had myself felt as a child when urged to join the games of cousins seen only on widely spaced holiday occasions. After all, if Mr. Taliaferro had only recently arrived from Paris . . .

I stiffened. All at once I remembered well who Rafael Taliaferro was, and deeply regretted my rather coy response to his query. It had been in Paris nine years earlier, in August of 1887, that I had first met Rose's cousin at his mother's grand house in the Plaine Monceau, where he and a friend were enjoying an infrequent holiday from their studies at the Ecole des Beaux Arts. Awed and fascinated by their sophisticated banter and smartly turned-out good looks and urbanity, I had followed them as fawningly as Victor's spaniel until cruel words and a thoughtless action broke the spell of my infatuation and blighted my budding vanity. It was not a happy memory. I frowned and turned away.

Sensing a rebuff, Rafe addressed the room at large. "Since Miss Grayson seems unwilling to supply an unqualified answer to my question, may I call for a volunteer? Unless, of course, it would mean exposing dark secrets best left unrevealed." His voice had taken on a dramatically hushed timbre intended, I thought, to make me look foolish. The years had not improved his character.

Rose laughed. "Sorry to disappoint you, Rafe. L.O.P.H. stands for nothing more sinister than Left on Papa's Hands. You see, the five . . . that is, the four of us now," she hastily amended, "Violet and Flora and Iris and I, became friends at school. Then, finding ourselves temporarily at loose ends after we graduated, lacking employable skills and eligible suitors, we filled our time as ladies-in-waiting with the planning of holiday houseparties—family vacation affairs for the most part."

"But we cleverly managed to stretch the definition of family to include every personable male cousin and brother's college friend who could be cajoled into joining us," Flora cheerfully confided. "Isn't that so, Vi?"

I nodded reluctantly, regretting Flora's unwitting portrait of what, to an outsider, might seem a rather giddy, ongoing conspiracy.

"What larks we had!" Flora's voice was breathy with remembered excitement. "Horseback riding at Poland Springs and ice skating at Mohunk—"

"And once, at my dyspeptic father's insistence, we even took the waters at Saratoga Springs," Iris added, "although we girls found it exceedingly boring."

"You girls can be grateful you never actually drank those Saratoga waters," Wink broke in. "They taste like seepage from a rusty drainpipe. Ugh!"

"Don't forget Lake Placid," Freddie said. "I never will, because Flora and I always ended our stay there with dreadful cases of poison ivy."

"Poor blistered twins!" I exclaimed, forgetting for the moment my displeasure at renewing Rafael Taliaferro's acquaintance. "No one would share a cabin with either of you on the night boat back from Albany because your scratching and moaning made it impossible to sleep!"

We all laughed, even Flora and Freddie, although the discomfort I made light of now had been very real at the time. "It was at Lake Placid where Wink taught me to row properly," I said. "We used to sneak off together because my father thought rowing was much too strenuous a sport for ladies." I smiled as I recalled those long, sweet summer days. "Oh, how I loved that trim little cedar-strip skiff! Remember, Wink?"

"Our guilty secret, Vi. I can't quite look your father in the eye to this day."

"Say, wasn't it at Lake Placid where we met Ned?"

Freddie inquired. "Yes, now I remember! There he was, rocking on the porch along with a hundred others, most of 'em of our parents' vintage, except that Ned was the only one with cowboy boots propped up on the railing and a wide-brimmed Stetson hat pulled down over his eyes. Then he looked up, tipped back his hat, and flashed that outlaw grin of his at the girls . . ."

Freddie broke off with a rueful smile and shook his head. "Well, I knew right then that us college fellows didn't stand a chance! Tell us, Ned, aside from breaking every female heart in sight, what brought you to Lake Placid? Pretty tame stuff after the wild west you'd just come from, I reckon."

A sudden, awkward silence descended as Freddie's tactless words reminded us that although Ned had indeed broken many hearts that summer, including mine, it was Lily's heart, not Rose's, at which his cupid's bow had taken very precise aim that summer, and by the end of it had won.

As the silence lengthened, Ned slid his arm around Rose's slender shoulders and drew her close, as if to defy our unspoken thoughts.

"Tameness was what I was looking for, Fred." Ned's eyes, bereft of their sunny glint, grew as darkly opaque as the sea clouded by a sudden squall. "If you'll recall, I'd just lost my partner to the west's wildness you speak of so lightly. Croquet greens and pretty girls with parasols were just what the doctor ordered."

Chagrined, Freddie muttered an apology. A moment later Ned's reproachful expression surrendered to the grin his admiring friend had so accurately described, and looking at him now, his high spirits revived, Ned's slouchy grace and roguish charm did indeed seem more suited to a gold town gambler than a member of the socially prominent Van Renssalaer family tree, albeit a modest branch of it. His father, I knew, was a prominent pathologist about whose studies of the essential nature of disease my father had often spoken admiringly. One of his older brothers was a clergyman, the other an importer of coffee and tea. Both considered him, Ned had once told me, a bit of a black sheep.

I thought his so-called blackness became him. He had indeed once broken my heart, and my unhappy and unwelcome realization that I yearned for him still, brought with it the sour taste of jealousy. Rose was but a pale copy of Lily: if I were blond, might it have been my shoulders he embraced? My lips that offered solace? *My bed he shared?*

Given the envious tenor of my thoughts, I was startled to see Rose twitch herself out from under Ned's encircling arm like a cat eluding an unsolicited pat. I had thought it ironic that Rose, the only one of that summering flock of girls who had seemed immune to Ned's devil-may-care charm, had in the end been the one to accompany him to the altar. I wondered now just how eager her passage down the aisle had been, and if she had since come to regret it.

I hoped she had, I thought bitterly. I hoped they both had. Considering the grief-stricken hours Ned and I had shared in the aftermath of Lily's death, had it been so unreasonable of me to hope he would one day ask me to share his life?

I blinked as Victor suddenly clapped his hands. "Come, come, my blossoms! Dinner is at eight, and we will gather in the library for sherry, a splendid Amontillado, at seven-thirty, which leaves barely an hour for you to work the magic that will make you even more enchanting than you already are."

Victor's deep voice was as honeyed as his words, and although he had left his native Romania many years before, there was still a hint of the Balkans in his speech. "Off with you," he commanded, shooing us out with sweeping motions of his long aristocratic hands. "No exceptions, Violet," he said to me with mock sternness as I paused irresolutely at the parlor door.

"But I don't know which room I've been assigned, Victor. I arrived only shortly before you and Mr. Taliaferro returned from your walk."

He looked at me in consternation. "Dear me. I can't be much help to you, I'm afraid. Rose?" But Rose and Ned had already gone up to their room. "Nothing for it but to ring up Mrs. Devlin . . ."

A brisk pull on the bell rope soon brought the housekeeper gliding in from the kitchen. Her tall figure swathed in black combined with her dark visage and grave expression gave her the look of someone in perpetual mourning.

"You rang, Count Stirbey?"

"We were wondering which room this young lady is to have, Mrs. Devlin."

"Such a nuisance to disturb you in the midst of dinner preparations," I said.

Mrs. Devlin regarded me impassively. There was no way of telling from her expression if she remembered me from the house party that had ended so tragically the year before.

"Not at all, Miss Grayson."

She *had* remembered. In fact, as her eyes took stock of me, in no more than a sliding glance, I was suddenly, uneasily, certain that she intuitively perceived more about me, about everyone, than one might have cared for her to know.

She turned toward the stairs and mounted them with a firm step and straight spine, looking neither to the left or right, assuming I would follow obediently in her wake. Even if I had had another choice, I doubt I would have dared to exercise it.

As we entered the spacious hall at the top of the stairs, Mrs. Devlin's footsteps slowed upon the worn but handsome Oriental carpet that stretched from one end to the other. To my bewilderment, she reached out to open the first door on the left, then turned and beckoned me to enter. Not this room, surely! My heart began to pound. I stepped back, colliding with Victor and Rafael Taliaferro, who had followed with my bags.

"Victor, oh, Victor! I can't—truly I cannot stay in this room . . ." Panic quickened my breath.

Rafe at once put down my things and offered me the support of his arm. "Miss Grayson! You are suddenly so pale! Victor?" He turned urgently toward the older man, seeking an explanation for my odd behavior. Was I ill? Hysterical? It was not difficult to imagine his speculations.

"There, Violet. Of course you can't stay here. Whatever were you thinking of, Mrs. Devlin? Had you forgotten Miss Grayson shared this room with Lily Forrester?"

"I'm sorry, sir. I thought . . . that is, I assumed the passage of time—"

"The passage of time does little to ease the pain and shock of finding one's closest friend murdered, Mrs. Devlin!"

"Good God!" Rafe exclaimed. "Murdered, you say? I knew something unpleasant had happened, but—"

"Oh, do stop going on about it!" I cried. "Please, is there another room I could have? It needn't be as large or fine as—"

"You may have my room, Miss Grayson," Rafe offered. "I haven't unpacked yet; it would take no more than a moment to make the trade. What do you say?"

I hesitated, loath to be beholden to a person who had so carelessly bruised the sensibilities of an impressionable child. The years may have toughened me, but my resentment smouldered still.

"Good of you, my boy," Victor said heartily, without waiting for my assent. He led the way down the wide hall and entered the room that opened off the inglenook at the end of the corridor. "I think you will be quite happy here, Violet. This room overlooks the rose garden. Pity it's February instead of June."

I stood quietly to one side as Rafe collected his belongings. At the last minute, just as he stepped through the doorway, I murmured my obligatory thanks with a lack of enthusiasm which caused him to slant a coolly disapproving look in my direction. Clearly, another favor would not soon be forthcoming.

* * *

I crossed the room to the bank of oak-framed casement windows, dark bands against the white plastered walls. I stared into blackness, the moon having not yet risen. I cranked one of the windows open just a crack and took a deep breath, relishing the frigid, reviving rush of air. I could hear the creaking of the branches of the great beech tree I knew stood between the house and the rose garden, beyond whose formal hedge-guarded beds rambled the riot of wild roses which had given Brambledene its name. Within that dense bramble a roughly mowed rectangle of pasture grass had been grudgingly yielded by the thorny tangle of sweetbrier to the Thornbush family cemetery.

I had always liked the idea of a simple burial ground marked with mossy stones which would themselves be buried in turn by virtue of nature's verdancy. My own family lay in a pair of miniature Greek temples set side by side in a formally landscaped Bronx cemetery that overlooked the bustling city developed by the barons of banking and industry interred there. One Greek temple was tolerable; two such follies, the second built to receive my poor mother's fragile remains, seemed ridiculous.

A sudden spreading glow turned the windows into mirrors. I saw Mrs. Devlin's reflection behind me, adjusting the wick of the lamp on the table next to the bed. The smell of kerosene, though strong, I found pleasanter than the headachy sweetness of city gas. She brushed by me to close the window with a firm click.

"Mr. Devlin says the wind is falling and the mercury along with it. There is another down-filled coverlet in the chest at the foot of the bed, should you need the extra warmth." She paused. "I'm sorry if I upset you, Miss Grayson."

I smiled. "It's forgotten, Mrs. Devlin."

She stood beside me a moment longer. "She's buried there, you know. Your friend, Miss Forrester." She gestured toward the rose garden and the graves beyond.

I hadn't known. I turned away to hide my distress. Aware that Lily had had no close relatives, I had presumed that one or another of her second cousins, having been notified of her death by Lily's lawyers, had assumed familial responsibility for her interment in some distant cemetery. Overwhelmed by my grief for Lily and burdened by the duty owed my father, who had fallen ill soon after my return from Brambledene, I hadn't questioned what seemed the inevitable disposition of her remains. At the time, having already bid farewell to Lily in my heart, it hardly mattered. What *did* matter was that no one had thought to tell me otherwise.

I felt a hand on my arm. Startled, I turned to find Mrs. Devlin's dark eyes, shiny as jet, only inches from mine. "She's still here, you know," she said in a hushed voice.

Her conspiratorial air offended me. "Yes, you just said that she was—"

"Oh, not just her body, Miss Grayson. Her poor, restless spirit."

I laughed, but the sound that emerged, high and thin and shaky, had little mirth in it. "Surely you aren't suggesting . . . come now, Mrs. Devlin, Brambledene is much too down-to-earth for a haunting!" Yet as I spoke, my earlier, unwelcome image of it as a malevolent toad flashed unbidden through my mind.

My eyes challenged hers, but it was I who looked away first. There was something dismaying about Ada Devlin's fathomless dark gaze.

"Perhaps," she conceded politely, her voice yielding no hint of uncertainty. "Now, if you have everything you want, I must return to the kitchen. The girls we brought up from the village mean well enough, but if left too long on their own . . ." She shrugged.

"I'm in charge of my father's household, Mrs. Devlin, so I know well the mischief untrained girls can do. I've taken too much of your time already."

"Not at all, Miss Grayson." She turned back at the door. "Mind you draw the curtains across the windows before you come down to dinner. The moon will be full tonight, and the light can be . . . disturbing."

By the time I unpacked, there was barely time enough to wash my hands and face, tidy my hair, and pinch my cheeks, much less change out of my gray merino, whose leg-of-mutton sleeves had become sadly creased during the long day of jostling travel. On impulse, I draped around my shoulders the lovely paisley shawl my father had given me for Christmas.

A hasty twirl in front of the wardrobe's mirrored door confirmed that the finely patterned accessory not only disguised my traveling costume's shortcomings, but provided the silvery gray wool with a welcome accent of color. The frown the mirror reflected eased. No one need know how impromptu my choice had been, and if the night turned as cold as Ada Devlin's husband had predicted, I would be warmer in the merino outfit than anything else I had brought with me.

Before leaving, I turned the lamp down low. As I did so, I became aware of a silvery glow spreading up behind the black leafless tines of the beech tree. I remembered Mrs. Devlin's suggestion—an instruction, really—to draw the curtains, lest the full moon's brightness disturb my sleep. Nonsense! I decided, as I hastened to join the party whose chatter and cheery bursts of laughter I could hear issuing forth from below. It had been a long and tiring, somewhat trying day; after a hearty dinner accompanied by good wine and lively conversation, what could be more peaceful, more reassuring, than to drift off to sleep bathed in moonlight, watched over by that great tree and the enduring Berkshire hills beyond?

CHAPTER TWO

The evening began festively. Upon entering the library, I inhaled the mingled, wonderfully pleasing aromas of polished leather, wood smoke, and lemon oil. By far the most welcoming room in the house, the library's dark woodwork was enlivened by row upon row of leather-bound volumes in a variety of textures and colors—warm tans, burnished golds, rich reds and blues—brightly lettered in gold.

The sherry Victor generously poured for us—and it was indeed as good as promised—smoothed away the slight shynesses, the hint of awkwardness, that often mark reunions of old friends after months of separation. Although these particular circumstances were far from ordinary, enough had happened since last we saw each other to allow us to avoid convincingly the most extraordinary happening of all.

Freddie Latimer, whose days as a pale, frantically overworked law student at Columbia University had once made us fear for his health, had been whisked into the family firm immediately upon his admission to the bar. Judging from the faintly porcine look Ned had remarked upon earlier, his snug new niche agreed with him.

"Daddy and Uncle John have decided to open another office, in Albany this time," Flora announced, "and Carter and Freddie will be in charge!" Her plump cheeks pinked with pride.

"At that rate there'll be Latimer lawyers blanketing the state," Ned said. "You'd better find yourself a wife and set about ensuring the supply, Freddie."

"No need to rush on *that* score," Freddie said. "My brother, Carter, has five sons already—"

"And from the look of her, Marjorie is in the family way again," Flora finished.

"Besides, Flora's already agreed to keep house for me, and I doubt if anyone else would suit me as well."

"We've found the dearest house, Vi," Flora burbled. "Do say you'll help me choose fabrics for the upholstery and draperies. We'll be doing a lot of entertaining," she amplified importantly, "and I want to send all those Albany politicians' wives home green with envy, convinced everything in their own parlors is terribly old hat. It'll be such fun shopping together!" she exclaimed, taking my aquiescence for granted. "Your eye is so much better than mine."

"If you want your new quarters looking smart as paint, I may prove a disappointment, Flora. I'm not *au courant* with interior fashions; besides, do you really think envy is the best basis on which to build a clientele?"

The Latimer twins exchanged looks of smug assurance. "Count on it, Vi!" Freddie said. "There's nothing like a tip-top meal served in a fashionable house to establish a man's reputation. Appearances do count, you know."

"Of course they do," Flora firmly agreed. "My goodness, Vi, you really are an innocent when it comes to the ways of the business world."

Although I couldn't help wondering if sibling affection would prove to be enough over the long run, as the twins continued to beam at each other—fond Tweedledum to doting Tweedledee—I thought that in this case perhaps it would. Flora had had her share of schoolgirl crushes, but her talk of them had always been in airy-fairy, hearts-and-flowery terms. In fact, my recollection of her opinion of the physical expression of love as described by me, a doctor's daughter, to my enthralled friends, was an uncharacteristically firm, "It doesn't sound very nice *at all.*"

At the time I might have agreed with her, but upon reflection, and despite my lack of personal experience, I suspected that when it came to lovemaking niceness was irrelevant. I reconsidered. No, not irrelevant . . . *inappropriate.*

All at once, images of the juxtapositions of bodies and intertwining of limbs that would justify my startling amendment began flashing unbidden through my mind, and a moment later I became aware of having caught Rafael Taliaferro's attention.

He was standing under the library balcony, one long hand resting on a mahogany tread of the graceful little spiral staircase, chatting with Victor and Rose. Their conversation must have had something to do with the room's architectural detail, for he pointed with his free hand at the windows and the high ceiling, his fingers tracing curves and angles in the air. As he spoke, his glance traveled toward me, hesitated, and stopped. I can't imagine why; surely he couldn't have read my very private thoughts.

His intent eyes were the palest of gray, almost crystalline, as light and clear as spring water. When they met mine something flashed in their depths, suddenly reminding me of a deep, gin-clear pool I had come upon years before while paddling up the inlet stream of a wild woodland pond near Lake Placid. I remember staring down, fascinated by the pebbles that seemed to undulate in the slow, sunlit current. All at once a huge trout, which had been masquerading as a long sliver of rock, revealed itself in a silvery glitter of fin and tail as it fled the menacing shadow of my little skiff's hull. It had been so unexpected, so wonderfully . . . *mysterious,* I had caught my breath, as I did again now. But why? And what did that flash in those hooded gray eyes, that glint of silver—hardly more than a flicker, really, but it *had* been there—what did it signify?

A hand warmly grasped my elbow. "A penny for them, Vi."

I looked up into eyes as blue as a sunny June sky. Nothing lurked there; the only danger Ned Poole posed was if I dared to venture beyond my depth. I looked hastily away. "I fear my thoughts are hardly worth even a penny, Ned. I was merely reflecting on the changes in our lives since last we met."

He squeezed my arm comfortingly. "This is neither the time nor place to try to explain what happened," he said in a low voice.

He was referring, of course, to his whirlwind courtship and marriage. All of a sudden I realized that not only did I not want to know why he had chosen Rose over me, I wanted even less to learn that he had been unaware he had had a choice to make. The deep hurt I had tried to suppress welled up hotly. Since I couldn't bear to hear about Rose, I focused my resentment instead on my exclusion from Lily's burial arrangements.

"I was Lily's closest friend!" I hissed. "How could you have left me in ignorance about her burial here at Brambledene?"

Ned stared at me, as near nonplussed as I imagine he ever allowed himself to be. Although this was obviously not what he expected me to question him about, he did not attempt to deny his knowledge of it. "It never occurred to me . . . I assumed that Rose, that somebody—" He broke off in consternation.

"That 'somebody' turned out to be Mrs. Devlin, who mentioned it to me today, not more than an hour ago, in passing. *How could you!*" I repeated brokenly.

Ned's blue eyes darted toward where the others were gathered in groups of two and three to see if anyone had noticed our emotional exchange. Only Rose seemed to be looking our way, and although that didn't necessarily signify any particular interest on her part, Ned was taking no chances. He bent his head toward my ear, his bronze curls brushing along its rim. "*Later*," he promised, then, referring to my earlier remark, added, "Not all our changes have been happy ones."

I stared at him, recalling Rose edging away from his embracing arm. Surely the bloom couldn't have faded so soon. "Haven't they?" I asked warily.

"Apparently Iris was informed in no uncertain terms by a Madame Bleska-something-or-other that her desire for a singing career was futile." He grinned. "We could have told her that long ago, couldn't we?"

I laughed. Out of relief, I suppose. The blighting of Iris's unrealistic hopes was, after all, hardly as serious a matter as the foundering of a marriage. Although Iris was the proud possessor of an unusually lush voice, she had, poor dear, been cursed with a tin ear. As a result, her friends had suffered from years of her resoundingly contralto, off-key recital selections.

"She accepted a position to teach music at that school you girls went to, but finds it more painful than rewarding. A constant reminder of her dashed hopes, I guess. She's taken up marching for women's suffrage—as a way to vent her frustration, Rose thinks."

How tiresome of Iris! She was a dear girl, but the least excitement scattered her wits, rendering her incapable of organizing anything more demanding than a tea tray. She would likely be more nuisance than use to the worthy cause she had espoused. I looked over at her and sighed. There she stood in all her wide-hipped Wagnerian splendor, created for motherhood if ever a woman was, her great dark eyes fixed on Victor, whom she idolized, resolutely ignoring Wink McEldowney, who, their second-cousinhood notwithstanding, adored her.

Wink, it turned out, was in the process of exchanging rowing on the Harlem River of Manhattan for the Rangeley Lake district in Maine.

"Your club must be very sorry to see you go," Victor said. "I understand you are a capital oarsman."

"I can vouch for that," I volunteered, "but why so far away, Wink? Imagine choosing bears and moose for neighbors!"

"It *is* far," Wink said with a mournful look at Iris. "But the family had an opportunity to enlarge our Maine timberland holdings and Father needed another manager. I rather like trees, you know," he added earnestly, then looked bewildered when we all laughed.

The truth was that Wink looked rather like a tree himself: tall, muscular, with a neck that always seemed about to burst the confines of collar and tie, and auburn hair as coarse as shredded cedar bark. Although more at home on Yale's playing fields than in the forestry school's lecture halls, I doubted he needed more than his gentleman's *C* to become a responsible lumberman. Wink might be a bit dim, but he was a noble elm of a man.

"Speaking of living far away, you might as well be living in Maine, too, Vi, for all anyone ever sees of you," Freddie said. "Whatever possessed your father to move to the west side, and to the Dakota Apartments of all places?"

"Considering your distinguished alma mater has lately removed itself to Morningside Heights, Freddie, you needn't look down your nose at our west side address! We find it very convenient. My father is not well, and he wished to be relieved of the responsibility of our midtown house."

"But what on earth do you do with yourself up there?" Flora asked.

"I'm helping my father with his book. Although he's still associated with Roosevelt Hospital in an advisory capacity, his health forced him to retire from private practice. My combined duties as scribe and housekeeper leave me little time to wonder how to fill my days."

In truth, my father's book had become his obsession. The only way I was able to wangle time for myself was to maintain a regular schedule of walks in Central Park, an activity he deemed suitable for young ladies, unlike the rowing he once feared would enlarge my heart. Father was not aware that my walks more often than not ended at the Metropolitan Museum where my interest in historical textiles had allowed me to be accepted by the curatorial staff as a harmlessly obsessed person in my own right.

Rafe Taliaferro stepped out from under the balcony. "Am I correct then in assuming that you, Miss Grayson, are the last of the LOPH's? Strictly defined, that is."

I cared neither for the reminder nor the arch manner in which he delivered it. "As strictly defined," I began stiffly, "you are indeed correct, Mr. Taliaferro. But then I'm used to being left behind," I added deliberately, "at least I *should* be, don't you agree?"

He stared at me. "If you say so," he murmured.

He started to edge away from me at the same moment Ada Devlin arrived to announce dinner. Left with little choice, Rafe offered me his arm and we followed wordlessly in the wake of our laughing companions as they passed through the cheerless parlor into the dining room.

Facing us as we entered was a French-windowed, north-facing wall that I remembered Rose telling us opened in summer upon a shady fernery. Tonight, the only thing the windows offered was a draught that made me uncomfortably aware that the night, as Milo Devlin had predicted, had grown markedly colder. I shivered involuntarily and drew my paisley shawl close. Seeing me do so, Victor considerately seated me to his right, where a fire hissed comfortingly behind me on the wide, marble-manteled hearth, and directed Rafael Taliaferro—whose twist of lip was as eloquent as a groan—to the right of me.

Iris, seated on Victor's left and greedy for his attention, began plucking at his sleeve. Victor, after flashing an apologetic smile at Horatio and me, bent an attentive ear to Iris's eager recital of the wonders that granting women the vote would accomplish.

Rafe and I addressed the creamy soup in silence. It was

lamb-based, enriched with egg yolks and enlivened by a hint of curry. I hoped it foretold more lamb in the offing. I seemed to recall that Ada Devlin had a flair for its preparation.

Conversation buzzed around us. Candlelight glinted off polished silver and the elegant celadon-green porcelain service that complimented both in theme and color the gorgeously robed Mandarin elder who contemplated us in two-dimensional silence from a very old scroll hanging behind Victor upon a wall painted so dark a green it appeared almost black. His ancient, inscrutable expression made me edgy. Seeking distraction, I raised my wine glass to my lips.

When he had spooned the last of the soup from his plate, Rafe cleared his throat. "Tell me, Miss Grayson, what is the subject of the book you are transcribing for your father?"

"Tight-lacing," I replied.

"Tight-lacing," he repeated under his breath.

I decided to wait him out, assisted in my endeavor by Victor's carving of the anticipated lamb, pinkly rare and deliciously redolent with garlic. My father would have disapproved of my partiality for its pungent flavor, which he thought smacked of the teeming masses that he, unlike Lady Liberty, did not welcome to the city of his birth.

As the juicy slices of lamb were apportioned I continued to sit in contented silence, seemingly oblivious to the restless shifting of my companion as he attempted to contain his curiosity.

"The tight-lacing of what?" he muttered at length, as if to himself. "Of boots, perhaps? A limited subject for a book, surely . . ." His murmured speculations trailed off as a serving dish heaped with braised celery and carrots was unceremoniously thrust between us by one of the girls Ada had brought up from the village to serve.

"Not boots, Mr. Taliaferro," I said in a firm, clear voice, as I spooned buttery juices over my helping of vegetables. "Corsets. My father's book is about the tight-lacing of women's corsets."

He looked at me askance. Obviously, he considered corsets a dubious choice for discussion at the dinner table.

"The title my father has chosen is *The Fatal Fashion.* He is convinced," I continued, "that corsets not only impair female health and childbearing capacities but threaten the entire social order."

"Oh, Vi," Flora protested, "not tight corsets again!" Her eyelashes fluttered with indignation. "Why won't your father grant that sensible women don't do that sort of thing?"

I smiled. Flora had conveniently forgotten that she had once, when dressing for a long-anticipated cotillion, exhorted her friends to lace her almost to the point of insensibility. "My father won't grant that there is such a creature as a sensible woman."

"Hear! hear!" Ned called from across the table, his eyes alight with mischief. "Good sense is rare among my own sex, and downright dreary in a woman. Besides, I rather fancy a waist a man can span with his two hands."

"The list of things you fancy grows ever longer, Ned dear," Rose said with unexpected asperity.

"Actually, in Europe even some men wear corsets," Rafe added, now assured that, at this table at least, the subject was not taboo.

I blinked at him. "*Men* do?"

"Military men of high rank, usually. To maintain the illusion of the trim waist and erect posture of their active service years, I suppose. True, Victor?"

"Alas, yes. In fact, I understand such foolish vanity is not uncommon in my native country." He shook his dark aristocratic head.

"No such foolishness for you, though, eh, Victor?" Ned spoke carelessly enough, idly twirling his wine glass, the candlelight sparking off the great rough nugget of gold on his finger, but the glint in his eyes had cooled and his teasing tone seemed edged.

Victor's hand clenched upon the heavy linen cloth. A muscle twitched in his jaw. "No, Ned, most assuredly not for me."

Rose turned quite pale. The curious little depression that perpetually dimpled her right cheek, regardless of whether her expression was a happy one, marked her fine-grained complexion like a dark smudge. Not knowing where to look or what to say, I drank more wine. It had been a long and wearing day, but the fruity Beaujolais was light and fresh and comforting. Victor, always the attentive host, refilled my glass and I continued to sip, perhaps more than I intended, for when the dinner service was cleared, and I turned my head to follow the progress of an elaborate cake borne in with much ceremony from the kitchen, the room tilted.

Victor slowly rose to his feet, and tapped his wine glass. The gesture was unnecessary, for all attention was riveted upon the cake, aswirl with snowy curlicues and pink roses, set down before Rose and Ned. It was a wedding cake. I was appalled.

"As you know, six months ago Rose and Ned were married in Paris at her aunt's home," Victor said. "It was a very quiet ceremony, for reasons I need not explain. But now it is time for their union to be not only formally announced, but validated . . . *blessed*, if you will, by the dear friends who shared with them the anguish occasioned by the tragic passing of Lily Forrester, here at Brambledene, one year ago."

The passing of Lily Forrester? Lily hadn't passed on or crossed over; neither had she departed this vale of tears or shuffled off its mortal coil. She had been *murdered.* Brutally, senselessly murdered by a ragged stranger who had vanished like a wisp of smoke into that cold February night. Lily had been my dearest friend, and Ned had been her fiancé. I had forced myself to accept his marriage to Rose—what choice had I?—but I could not find it in my heart to bless it. I drained my glass in a long defiant swallow.

Ned shoved back his chair. "Thank you, Victor," he said with a nod in his father-in-law's direction. His gaze, solemn now, moved around the table, pausing briefly at each of us in turn. "My friends," he began, "I have, I think, been the unhappy witness to more violence than any of you here tonight. During my years in Colorado, hardly a day went by without a miner being killed in a fall or the cave-in of a carelessly dug shaft, or a foolhardy attempt to recoup gambling losses with a gun. But I never grew used to the killing; not there, and certainly not here, for Lily was . . ."

Ned's voice faltered. I saw him grope for Rose's hand. Her fingers whitened in his strong grip. "If I learned only one lesson during my search for gold in those cruel Colorado mountains, it is that life must go on. It will not wait for us to recover. Lily is forever lost to us, my friends, and Rose has taken her place in my heart."

It seemed a curious phrasing, but there was no time to ponder it, for Ned turned immediately to the doorway where Ada Devlin was waiting, and nodded. The sturdy hired girls carried in a tureen filled with ice, out of which poked the heads of wire-caged corked bottles. Ada followed with a silver tray of crystal champagne saucers.

Ned smiled down at Rose. "Dearest, if you will cut the cake, I'll do the honors with the champagne . . ."

Corks popped as the cake was served. As soon as our glasses were filled, Ned lifted his in a toast. "To the fairest Rose that ever bloomed at Brambledene, and to her talented cousin, who I hope will help bring our plans for it to fruition!"

I joined in the toast, albeit with reservations. So that's why Rafael Taliaferro had been included in this gathering of old friends! I couldn't help wondering what plans Ned and Rose had in mind for Brambledene. I knew Rose had never spent much time here, regarding it more as a vacation retreat than a home. Could Ned have tired of his role as black sheep of his family? Did he yearn for the respectability being a settled country squire would bring him?

I suddenly found myself resisting the notion with a fervency that surprised me. I drained my glass of champagne. *Don't give in, Ned! not yet . . .*

"Off with the old and on with the new," Rafe murmured beside me.

"I beg your pardon?" I peered into his face. It seemed . . . blurred. It must be the smoke from the fireplace, I decided.

"For all his solemn words, Ned Poole seems in a bit of a rush to get on with it, Valentine party and all."

"Party?" What was he talking about? I allowed my glass to be refilled, and captured the bubbles as they rose to tingle my tongue.

"Brambledene's traditional Valentine costume party on Saturday. Poole's dead keen on it, although I must say Rose seems less than enthusiastic. Can't think why. I remember my mother telling me about them. She said when she and her sister, Rose's mother, were growing up, the only thing that made the bleak weeks after the first of the year bearable was planning the costumes and games for the Valentine party. Everyone for miles around was invited, and friends came up on a special train from New York. We were talking about it at lunch today . . . but you hadn't arrived yet, had you?"

I put my glass down very carefully, and sat there, stunned.

"Hurrah for Rose and Ned!" Freddie caroled. "For they're a jolly good couple, for they're a jolly good couple, for they're a—"

I rose unsteadily to my feet. "You're planning a Valentine party for Saturday? You can't be serious! Rose? Ned?" Seen across the table, their faces wavered indistinctly in the candlelight. Victor was the closest. I leaned toward him, my hands splayed upon the cloth.

"Tell me, Victor," I cried, searching his stricken face imploringly. "Whose body will I stumble upon this year?"

I covered my face with my hands, trying to shut out the memory of Lily's sightless, bulging eyes and blackened tongue, the cruel bruises on her throat, but how could I erase what was printed indelibly upon my mind's eye? Worst of all was the odor which surged up out of memory to clog my nostrils with its vileness. "The smell!" I cried. "Oh, dear God, that vile, vile, smell . . ."

I sensed my consciousness drifting away and heard a tinkle of crystal as my champagne glass overturned, a victim of my trembling hands.

Victor's arm circled my collapsing shoulders. "Come along, Violet," he gently urged. "Iris? I'll need your assistance."

As I left the room, half-walking, half-carried, I heard Rose's voice, high and thin, exclaiming behind me. "I told you she would take it badly, Ned."

"It was the shock, Rose," he said angrily. "You should have told her earlier!"

"It was also the effect of too much wine." Rafael Taliaferro's voice, cool with disdain, followed me up the stairs. "Tell me, is your pretty little friend always this . . . flighty?"

When I woke in the middle of the night with a pounding headache and raging thirst, Rafael Taliaferro's opinion of me is what first sprang to mind. *Flighty*. How Lily would have laughed.

"Our good, gray Grayson," she'd tease affectionately when I expressed doubts about some lark she proposed. "You think too much, Vi," she used to say, and once, when I replied primly that prior thought had saved me many regrets, she chucked me under my stiff chin and said, "Ah, but sometimes the doing is worth the regrets."

Not this time, I thought, as I massaged my aching

temples with my fingers. Moonlight streamed through the windows, encouraging me to slide out of bed and make my way toward the stand where the water pitcher—filled with fresh, cool water, I prayed—was housed. I gasped as a shapeless form on the chaise longue stirred and sighed. Dark hair spilled over the coverings. It was Iris. Watching over her intoxicated friend, no doubt. I wondered self-pityingly whether she had volunteered or merely drawn the short straw.

Not wishing to disturb her, I moved carefully across the unfamiliar room. The moon was high now, very bright in a sky so clear I fancied I could almost see around to its dark side. The big beech was a spiky silhouette against the silvered hills, and the garden hedges cast moon shadows on the rosebeds.

As my gaze swept back through the windows to plot my progress to the water pitcher, I caught out of the far corner of my eye a flicker of white in the tangle of sweetbrier beyond the hedges. I blinked. There it was again. Larger now, a cloud of white rising up from the Bramble—no, beyond the Bramble from the clearing, oh God, from behind the mossy headstones I could not see but knew were there . . .

Draw the curtains, Ada Devlin had said. *She's still here, you know . . .*

Silent as the grave from which it came, a drift of whiteness rose up and up across my fixed and wide-eyed field of vision, lasting but a moment, no more, but a moment that stood outside time.

It must have been then that I screamed.

CHAPTER THREE

"Oh! Oh, my Lord! Oh, my dear Lord, what's happening?"

Iris tumbled off the chaise, tripping over her nightdress in her haste to escape whatever had been responsible for the scream that had wrenched her from her dreams. With the moonlight streaming across her disordered hair and her panic-stricken eyes big as headlamps, she looked more like Medusa than Isolde. "Vi, oh, Vi, was that *you?*"

My mouth worked uselessly; I couldn't seem to find words to tell of what I had seen.

"Violet!" she implored, "Speak to me!"

"I saw . . . I thought I saw . . ." My voice was a whispery rasp. "There was something out there, Iris. Something white that floated up from . . ." I shuddered, and pointed a trembling finger toward the Bramble. But there was nothing there now; nothing but moonlight.

"Something where, Vi, in the rose garden?"

I shook my head.

"In the graveyard, then? You saw something . . . *white?*"

Iris's widening eyes met mine. "A ghost!" she gasped as her overwrought imagination leaped to the same terrifying conclusion mine had a few moments earlier. "You saw Lily's ghost!"

Her lusty scream made my earlier cry seem the piping of a small bird. My temples throbbed in protest.

"Do hush, Iris! Whatever I thought I saw is gone now. *Please,* dear," I implored, "you'll wake the entire household!"

My warning came too late. The muffled sounds of hastening slippered feet and questioning voices preceded an urgent knock on the door, which then flew open to admit what appeared to be the entire company.

Flora flew to her old friend's side. "There, there, dear," she soothed, but despite the worthiness of her intention, it is difficult to comfort someone who towers over you by a foot or more.

"Victor? Where's Victor?" Iris whimpered plaintively as she looked over Flora's head to search the assembled faces. She began to cry in great gulping sobs.

"He's in the tutor's room downstairs where you and Flora would be if he hadn't insisted on giving you his larger room up here," Rose said flatly. "Although how anyone could sleep through this racket I really don't know," she added in a fretful undertone. "Wink? Can't you do something?"

Rose's suggestion was all it took to set Wink into eager forward motion. In less time than it takes to tell, Iris's dark head was cradled upon his broad, flannel-robed shoulders.

"You neglected to draw the curtains," Ada Devlin said. I resented her smug tone and the satisfied little twitch of her lips.

"I *chose* not to draw them, Mrs. Devlin," I corrected stiffly. "I rose in the night for a drink of water, I was very thirsty, you see, and when I passed by the window I looked out . . . at least I think I looked out, I was only half-awake . . . It's so hard to remember exactly, but I saw, I *thought* I saw . . ."

Iris's quavering moan stilled my meaningless stammer

of words. As one, all eyes glanced toward the leaded panes. Beyond them, the beech tree's great arms stretched blackly across the silvered landscape.

"Moon shadows," murmured one voice. I think it was Rafael Taliaferro's. "Moon shadows playing tricks. Nothing unusual about that."

His cool amusement was lost on Flora. "Doesn't this room overlook the Thornbush burying ground?" she asked in a hushed voice.

"It does, Miss Latimer," Ada Devlin replied in measured tones. "It does indeed," then hurriedly, a bit anxiously, added, "I told her she should draw the curtains, Milo . . . the moon is full now, as it was *then* . . ."

"Now, Ada, m'dear, I think that's enough of that sort of blather," said a deep new voice from behind me. "I don't imagine you remember me, Miss Grayson, I'm Milo Devlin. I look after things here at Brambledene for Miss Rose as I did for her grandfather before her. D'ye think you're up to telling us yet what this is about?"

I couldn't make out the features of the broad figure that blocked the light from the door, but I remembered the full head of white hair, and the Irish lilt of his speech. I found his sympathetic good sense reassuring.

"I'm sure Mr. Taliaferro was right, Mr. Devlin. Whatever I saw was probably only the moonlight playing tricks on me. I'm sorry for the commotion, disturbing everyone's rest—the blame rests more with me than poor Iris."

"There's no blame attached to seeing things, Miss. It's what we *think* we see that sometimes takes a bit of interpretation, if you take my meaning."

Someone lit the lamps. I found myself looking into blue eyes roofed by tufted black eyebrows. Serious eyes, yet something about his creased ruddy cheeks suggested a smile. Curious.

"Yes, I think I do," I replied slowly. I closed my eyes, willing the image to appear upon the inner surface of my lids. "It was white, that I know, and . . . wavery. Not indistinct, like mist or fog but . . ." I paused, trying to find just the right words.

"You're doing just fine, miss," he said encouragingly.

"Fluttery," I said finally, "but not like a butterfly, more . . . *purposeful,* and it rose right up from the . . . from the graveyard, up and up . . ." I could feel the terror begin to rise again. "That's when I screamed." My voice began to quaver. "Then Iris screamed, and then it wasn't there anymore," I finished in a rush.

Milo Devlin nodded. "This white fluttering thing, did it rise up like this, would you say?" He lifted his arms from his sides and propelled them slowly up and down, hands outstretched, in a powerful sweeping motion. I suppose under different circumstances this burly man standing there flapping his arms, surrounded by solemn onlookers garbed in nightclothes, might have cut a ridiculous figure. As it was, he seemed almost . . . majestic.

I watched, as solemn as the others, and nodded. "Yes," I whispered. "Like wings." *Like the ghost of an angel.*

"I think what you saw, Miss Grayson, was a snowy owl. Jake Parsons over at Oakwoods on the other side of the valley mentioned seeing one. They come down this far some years, when hunger drives 'em. Big birds they are, four feet or more across in flight, and quiet, too. Quiet as the—" He broke off abruptly and cleared his throat. "Snowy owls are ground-perchers, you see, and like all hunters have their wits about 'em. I imagine a clearing in the middle of a sheltering bramble's a grand place to spend the winter."

So my ghost was a big white owl! I smiled, and the sense of relief that overswept me bubbled up into the chuckling laugh Lily used sometimes to tickle me to hear.

"Good Lord, how could I have forgotten?" said a deep wondering voice. "You were that wispy little girl with the purple eyes! I thought I'd probably never see eyes that color again; I was sure I'd never hear that laugh."

Rafe Taliaferro's words seemed to have issued out of

the shadows. I turned abruptly; my searching eyes spied him standing near the windows, out of the lamplight.

"If I had had any say in the matter, you wouldn't have," I said coldly.

The moon shone in upon his well-formed head, transforming his graying hair to gunmetal. He looked almost otherworldly with his olive skin burnished by the silver light that traced along the hollow of his taut cheek and the strong line of his jaw. His quicksilver eyes were masked in shadow, but the thought of them watching me . . .

I was suddenly very aware of my dishabille. Clutching the ruffled vee of my nightdress close to my bared throat, I turned back to the others.

"I'm sorry we disturbed you," I said. "Iris and I will be fine now. Please, you need not delay returning to your warm beds."

"Not very warm by now, I reckon." Ned's tone was teasing, but I sensed an undercurrent of irritation. At least he had someone to help warm his, I thought resentfully. Across my mind flashed a disturbing image of loosened nightclothes and intertwined limbs.

The party trailed out, and I was more pleased than sorry when Flora, seeing I had recovered from the effects of the wine, urged Iris to return with her to the room they shared. It was wrong of me, I know, but I was relieved to be spared spending the rest of the night calming Iris's palpitations; I had more than enough agitations of my own.

The house was very quiet when I entered the dining room the following morning. I had deliberately delayed my descent, hoping to be able to eat my breakfast in silence—my head still chided me for my overindulgence at dinner—but as I crossed with my plate into the morning room beyond, where small tables had been set for the morning meal, I found I was not alone after all.

Hidden by the partly opened folding doors, Rafael Taliaferro sat sipping coffee. One tweedy leg was crossed over the other; his polished booted toe gently wagged to the tune he was humming. It was "Three Little Maids" from Gilbert and Sullivan's tuneful operetta, *The Mikado.*

Victor had taken all five of his "beautiful blossoms" to the opening of the D'Oyly Carte production in New York, and Lily had promptly claimed the song for ourselves, adding two maids to the original three.

"There are, of course, only four of us now," I commented by way of greeting.

His toe stilled. "I beg your pardon?" he asked, rising to his feet.

I waved him back into his seat. "Rose and Flora and Iris and I, Mr. Taliaferro. Four little maids from school."

He shook his head. "I'm sorry, is this some sort of riddle? If so, the answer escapes me."

This had gone on longer than intended; my eggs were growing cold. "The Gilbert and Sullivan tune you were humming became our theme, Mr. Taliaferro."

He contemplated me consideringly. "I seem to remember you addressing me as Rafe when we met in Paris—please join me," he added politely as I continued to stand looking down at him. "You were passing through, on a Grand Tour with your mother, I believe."

"I was." I sat down opposite him; it would have been churlish to refuse. "And you were on holiday. You called me Violeave."

I met his questioning gaze directly, challengingly. A frown creased the smooth skin between the elegant, well-remembered arch of his dark brows. Although he could have been no more than twenty-two at the time, he had been the man of my thirteen-year-old dreams, a story-book hero to sigh over: proud, audacious, gallant when it suited him, and not above an occasional flirtatious wink that could turn my knobby young knees to water. Even his name had thrilled me. Tal-i-a-ferro. Like the purling of a mountain brook. And then, on the third morning of our visit, his voice had floated up to my bedroom window from the courtyard below.

I do wish Violet would let us alone, poor little wretch. Those great yearning purple eyes are a constant reproach.

Leave, Rafe, his languid blond English friend had corrected.

H'mmm?

Leave us alone, not let.

A moment's silence, then a hoot of laughter. *Violeave! How funny!*

They had called me Violeave for the rest of my brief stay, and I hadn't thought it funny at all.

A dark flush stained his olive cheeks. He remembered. "So you overheard," he muttered.

"Oh, yes."

"And have you never, honestly now, have you never said any careless thing about someone you would not have wished them to overhear?"

Daisy Graham. The name leaped out of the recesses of my memory. A newcomer to Miss Peeble's, a younger girl who assumed her floral name would gain her admission to our exclusive coterie. I recalled a few of *our* careless words, and averted my eyes.

I was too late. Rafe smiled. "You see?"

"But it was more than that," I said. "You abandoned me."

He looked disconcerted. His cool hooded eyes flared briefly wide. "I'm sure we never—"

"In the menagerie in the Bois de Boulogne. A new steeplechase course had been set up at Auteuil and you wished to 'give it a go'—"

"'Give it a go,'" he murmured. "Yes, I might have said that."

"It wasn't far, you said."

"It wasn't."

"But you were gone hours." *Hours,* I repeated to myself softly, recalling the thinning of the crowds as the afternoon light faded into evening, the laughter of children replaced by the grunting and snarls of unfamiliar animals pacing in their cages. "I was terrified."

"Yes, now I remember. We ran into . . . acquaintances and forgot all about you. Good Lord, how horrified your poor mother was! The horses were in a lather by the time we returned to the Bois to retrieve you, and there you were, huddled on a bench, your pansy eyes dark with tears. I also remember thumbing their tracks from your dusty cheeks," he added softly, "and all the way home I tried to tease out that funny little laugh of yours." He shook his head. "I failed miserably."

Because I was so miserable. I abandoned my plate of half-eaten eggs, walked across the pale-colored room—in its listless way as dispiriting as the gloom encountered elsewhere at Brambledene—and poured myself a cup of tea from the service set upon a table beneath the windows that looked out upon the sweeping drive and hemlock-hedged lawns beyond.

I pushed aside the ashes-of-roses linen drapery with one finger to admit the morning sun upon my upturned face. It felt warm upon the cheeks that Rafe had wiped of tears those many years ago.

I recalled that when we arrived back at the Taliaferro residence, my frantic mother had confronted her hostess. "She's still a child, Rosamund! It was cruel to treat her so carelessly!"

"Yes, yes, Althea, I admit it was very bad of them, but the Beaux-Arts demands so much of its students, and they *are* on holiday—"

"Anything might have happened!"

"But it didn't, did it?" Mrs. Taliaferro's tone had hardened. Two lionesses protecting their cubs. It was one of the memories I most cherished of my usually timid mother.

"Violet's a sweet little thing, my dear, but she is a wee bit persistent, wouldn't you say? Youths of Rafe's age prefer young women older than themselves. *Experienced* young women," she added with a knowing smile whose meaning had escaped me. Then, her smile fading, she said almost as if to herself, "It will be many years before they develop a taste for pretty little girls."

"Rosamund!"

My mother's scandalized exclamation had startled me, but at the time I hadn't a clue what that meant, either. Now, wondering, I slanted a look back at Rafe. There had been, I recalled, no suggestion of Mr. Taliaferro having been in residence during our visit, either in person or in spirit. I had seen no homely evidences of husbandly occupancy—no humidor or rack of pipes; no aromatic cedar boxes of cigars—nor were there any walking sticks or an outsize black umbrella in the stand provided in the vestibule. I guess I assumed he was off somewhere on "business"—which was something I knew fathers who were not doctors, did—and he did not seem at all a family man in the sense that mine and the fathers of my friends were. Perhaps it had been her husband's taste for pretty little girls to which Rafe's mother had been referring. If so, an estrangement was hardly to be wondered at.

I sighed. It had all been so long ago. "Tell me, Rafe, did you win the race at Auteuil?"

His smile reached his gray eyes and glimmered there, making me glad I had extended my olive branch, even if obliquely. "Do you mean the one on the new course I neglected you for? As a matter of fact, I did. My last race as it turned out . . . a good one to bow out on."

"What a pity!" I exclaimed. I never saw him ride, but I had admired the rosette-and-ribbon-bedecked silver cups proudly displayed in mother's sitting room along with photographs taken of him through the years astride a score of mounts from tubby Shetlands to tall sleek thoroughbreds.

He shrugged. "Family reverses. According to my mother, it isn't *comme il faut* for a gentleman jockey to require his winnings to maintain his horses."

I detected an undertone of bitterness. I wondered how

I would feel if I learned *my* father had become financially as well as morally bankrupt? Would my filial loyalty outweigh my resentment and distaste? My mind balked at an answer, largely I suppose, because the situation was so unimaginable. My father had his shortcomings, but he was as solid as the Rock of Gibraltar.

Rafe had fallen into an abstracted silence; his eyes were again hooded, his expression hard and withdrawn.

"But surely you haven't given up riding altogether?" I prodded gently.

He gave a start; his grimace relaxed into a wry smile. "These days, I ride only for pleasure."

"Then we must see what Milo can turn up for you," Ned said as he sauntered in, catching the last few words. He grinned and winked at me. "The Arkham bloodlines of the Brambledene horses are well thought of here, although they may not meet your lofty standards."

"Lofty? I would hardly call them that, Poole. Perhaps it's the measure one chooses. A good honest country hack is always preferable to a nervy outlaw, no matter how good the breeding is said to be." Rafe rose to his feet in a fluid motion and deposited his empty cup upon the serving table. "Is Rose up and about?"

"She's out on the grounds somewhere, but if you're planning to—"

Rafe nodded curtly, cutting Ned short. "Good morning, Violet."

He strode out of the room, all but colliding with Freddie, who stared after him indignantly. "I say! He's a haughty sort, isn't he? Morning, Vi, seen any owls lately?" Without waiting for an answer, which was just as well, he headed purposefully for a table with his heaped, steaming plate, his eyes alight with anticipation.

"What on earth was that all about, Ned?" I asked in a low voice.

"All what?" Ned's blue eyes were as wide and guileless as a baby's.

"You don't care much for Rose's cousin, do you?"

"No more than you, Vi."

"That's different," I demurred. "Our . . . misunderstanding goes back a long way, and . . ." I broke off with a shrug. "I didn't realize you two knew each other."

"We don't, not really. He was in and out during those days we spent at his mother's house in Paris when Rose and I were married, and we've seen him a few times lately in New York. He got all excited about some chap's newfangled building at the Chicago Exposition—when was that, '93 or '94? Came to the States expressly to see it, can you imagine? Then he went back to Paris and brooded about it for a few years—he's a great one for brooding, that one—before deciding to seek his fame and fortune in New York. Maybe it was seeing Rose again that tipped the balance, knowing there'd be a family member to turn to in a pinch . . ." Ned's words trailed off, his eyes narrowing in response to an unspoken thought.

"And?" I prompted.

His bright blue eyes snapped back into focus. "Anyway, I thought that since no New York architectural firm had given him the nod yet—at least none that suits *him*, to hear him tell it—I thought he might be interested in drawing up my ideas for Brambledene."

"Yes, you mentioned that last night, Ned. What plans have you?"

Ned's eyes danced. "Wait here until I get my breakfast, Vi," he said, pulling back for me the chair I had recently vacated. He leaned close. "I could use a sympathetic ear, especially one as pretty as yours," he added in a teasing whisper that stirred the loosened tendrils of hair on my neck.

I knew that Ned flirted as naturally as he breathed, even Rose had mentioned it, but I could feel heat rising in my cheeks. To cover my confusion I handed him my plate of congealed eggs. "Here Ned, if you'll do something with this and bring me a piece of toast to have with the rest of my tea, my shell-like ear is at your service."

"To begin with," he said when he rejoined me, "I want

to add a guest wing, with a proper bath adjoining each room. It's annoying to have to wait one's turn and downright embarrassing for gentlemen and ladies to have to share the same facility."

I strongly doubted anything embarrassed Ned, but I could see his point.

"Capital notion!" Freddie cried from the adjacent table.

"Furthermore," Ned continued, "in my opinion Brambledene hasn't enough space for proper entertaining. We need a hall for large dinner parties, but instead of cold stone underfoot, I was thinking of a tightly set wooden floor—I've heard maple is best—suitable for dancing. Yes, a great beamed room with a dais for the musicians—you know, a pianist, a couple of fiddlers, and a horn or two. We could have concerts, even give plays . . ." His eyes danced as he sketched his notions in the air.

It all sounded very grand to me. "Good heavens, Ned, wherever will you find enough people to fill it?"

"Up from the city, of course. These country yahoos' idea of a good time is to eat and drink themselves into a stupor and be home and snoring before midnight."

Freddie laughed delightedly. In fact, he greeted almost anything his adventurous friend did with admiring approval. A conservative sort himself, Freddie had adopted Ned as his alter ego. If I weren't so fond of him, I might have said he fawned, but who was I to cast stones?

"The grounds need work, too, of course. I thought we might grub out the bramble and put in a maze—not boxwood, of course, that would take ages, but hemlock or privet. Yes, I think a maze would be jolly! A tennis court, of course, and perhaps croquet beyond the beech tree, although the lawn there needs reseeding. And—listen to this, chums!—out to the north, commanding that grand view of the Berkshires, a polo field! The real thing, mind you, not just a rough pasture full of groundhog burrows. We could have a regular schedule, enlarge the stables to accommodate the ponies of visiting players during the season . . ."

Ned's blue eyes lost their focus again. Caught up in his visions of Brambledene's transformation, he leaned precariously back in his chair. His wide, mobile mouth curved into a satisfied, almost sensual smile as he hooked his thumbs into the pockets of his leather waistcoat and stretched out long western-booted legs. The rough, scuffed leather contrasted strongly with the pale arabesques of the faded Aubusson carpet into which his broad high heels heedlessly dug.

I was stunned. I knew Ned had struck it rich in the Colorado gold fields and that Rose was wealthy in her own right, but his plans seemed so . . . so *lavish.* Brambledene's five or more hundred acres of superbly scenic Berkshire hills and meadows qualified it as an estate, I supposed, but although the Tudor style of the dark, oak-timbered house was carefully detailed, the impression it gave, crouched upon its hilltop, clinging there like some huge amorphic creature, was hardly that of a Newport showplace. As for grubbing out the brambles, one might as well attempt to hold back the tide.

"What does Rose think?" I ventured.

The smile faded; his lips pursed. "She'll come around."

"And Victor?"

"It's none of Victor's business," he snapped. "As for Taliaferro," he said, forestalling my next question, "I wish I'd never brought him into this, but I thought that being family he—" Ned stopped abruptly. "I'm not a patient man, Vi, and you know how architects are," he continued, "slow as molasses. So I thought, being family, he might give us better service."

"And, seeing he's not yet found employment, a lower fee, too, I warrant," Freddie supplied cheerfully. Ned shot him a murderous look. "Oh, well now, I didn't mean to imply . . ."

Ned recovered rapidly. "Quite right, Fred, old boy,"

he said with a disarming grin. "How does that old saw go? Count your pennies and the dollars will take care of themselves."

Later, after we dispersed, and I, gloved, coated, hatted, and wound with scarves, prepared to go out the front door for a stroll, Rafe burst in, looking stormy.

"You look suitably outfitted for a journey to the North Pole, Violet. It's gotten quite a bit milder; you may want to discard some of your wrappings. If you're looking for company," he added, "you'll find Rose in the bramble."

He moved on, but my curiosity got the better of me. "Is it true you're here to undertake an architectural commission?"

He paused and turned back, frowning. "I'm here to decide whether I wish to undertake a commission, which is very far from certain."

"What do you think of Ned and Rose's plans?"

"Not Rose's," he muttered. "No indeed, not hers." He started to move past me again, then, grabbing my arm, turned me to face him. "You're fond of that fellow, aren't you?"

I hesitated. *What right had he to quiz me?* "I . . . well, of course! Ned is an old and dear friend."

I met his gray searching gaze. His eyes were dark as thunderclouds. I could tell he knew I had not told him what he wanted to know.

"That afternoon in the Bois? Alone in the menagerie? Remember how frightened you were?"

I nodded. His grip on my arm tightened painfully.

"Those animals were caged, Violet. Ned Poole is roaming free."

I wrenched my arm free of his cruelly encircling hand.

"You know nothing about Ned and me!" I cried. "After Lily died it was Ned who listened to me, held me, and comforted me . . ." Sudden tears blurred my vision.

The others, even Victor, had been unequal to the

occasion—not that I blamed them! It was a horror for all of us. But Ned and I, who had loved Lily best, clung to each other, and he encouraged me to tell, over and over, the details of that dreadful night, sensing somehow that in the telling my heart would eventually find peace.

"The most I will ever have received from *you* is the wiping away of a few tears you were the cause of! Ned Poole's warmth and affection saved my sanity."

His grimace told me I had struck home, but as I opened the great oak door, his voice followed me out into the cool, bright February day.

"Perhaps so, but he married Rose, didn't he?"

CHAPTER FOUR

Tears continued to well up into my eyes, making it difficult for me to see where I was going, but they were tears of anger now, the fruit of Rafael Taliaferro's cruel truth.

How dare he! I strode across leaf-strewn perennial beds, dry flower stalks snapping beneath my heedless feet, and swept through the hedgerow into the wildwood beyond. My headlong progress slowed as I caught sight of Rose standing alone in the cemetery clearing, her bowed blond head silvered by the pale bright February light. A soft woolen cape in an autumnal russet shade billowed out behind her. The gentle curve of her slender body and sheaves of evergreens clasped in her arms lent her the air of a Pre-Raphaelite maiden. No wonder Ned had chosen her.

"Why is your cousin here?" I demanded.

Rose whirled, her cape describing her movement like the flaring skirts of a dervish. Her startled rounded eyes and mouth reproached me. The frown that followed told me more clearly than words that my bluntness was easily a match for Rafael Taliaferro's.

"Forgive me, Rose," I blurted. "It's really none of my business." I turned to leave.

Rose reached out toward me. "Wait! I think perhaps I should be begging *your* pardon, Violet. I thought it . . .

inappropriate to introduce an outsider into our melancholy reunion, but Ned insisted. I guess it never occurred to him Rafe might be unsympathetic to his plans. I think Ned hoped he would be intrigued by the challenge and would in the end win Victor and me over. But of course it's much more complicated than that . . ."

I thought it curious that Rose described as melancholy the reunion that Ned had gone to such pains to characterize as a celebration of their marriage. It was obvious that communication was not a strong suit here at Brambledene.

"Families." Rose did not so much pronounce as exhale the word in a long regretful sigh. She stooped and placed a sheaf of greens on each of two graves marked with a single white limestone headstone. "My grandparents," she said. "And they were indeed very grand, Vi," Rose added with an uncharacteristic touch of irony. "Grandfather built railroads. His railroads opened the west to settlement and commerce and made him a fortune in the process. With it, he bought himself a lovely present, my grandmother, Althea."

Sensing my shock, Rose raised one slender hand in an apologetic gesture. "At least that's what my mother told me. You see, my grandmother, who was famously beautiful, had embarked with her parents upon a Grand Tour in the hope of snagging a titled husband, but she hadn't reckoned on a ripsnorter like Roswell Thornbush being a fellow passenger. By the time the Baltic docked at Liverpool, they were engaged." Rose smiled. "Apparently the enormous size of Grandfather's holdings compensated for his lack of a title. But it was a true love match, and Brambledene was the love nest he built for her."

An expression like "love nest" was too unlike Rose to have originated with her; in fact, this entire conversation—more monologue than dialogue, actually—was unlike Rose. She had never been a confiding sort. Even Lily, who was an accomplished teaser-out of secrets, had failed to penetrate her lovely, seamless facade, although not for lack of trying.

"I hadn't realized they built Brambledene, Rose. I always assumed, from the look of it, that it had been in your family for generations."

We turned together to look at the weighty dark Gothic crown that reached above the treetops save for the venerable beech which rivaled its height. Judging from the immense girth of its silver-skinned trunk, it had preceded by a hundred years or more this house sprawled along the hilltop.

Rose smiled and nodded. "Grandfather planned it that way. He came from simple stock, the kind the English call yeomen. His ambition took him far from his humble beginnings, and he wasn't shy about displaying the material possessions his industry provided him, but he never lost the Thornbush love of the land. He was offered this property in settlement of a debt, and instead of refusing it out of hand—with cash he could have bought land of his own choosing—he decided, on impulse, to take a look at it.

"It was love at first sight, just as it had been with his beloved Althea: the big beech tree, the Ashley river winding through the meadows, and especially the sweetly perfumed pink and white cloud of sweetbrier roses.

"It was the merest chance they were in flower the day they first visited here, Vi. Sweetbrier blooms all at once, you see, the blossoms soon withering. My mother said their tiny petals scattering on the wind had the look of a snowstorm in summer. Given his name, Grandfather thought the roses a good omen."

I raised my eyebrows. "It's hard to imagine a captain of industry like Roswell Thornbush heeding omens."

Rose smiled. "Ordinarily, he would have scoffed at that sort of thing," she agreed, "but in this case . . ." She shrugged. "The family story is that Grandmother Althea claimed it was written in the stars. The name they chose for the estate, even the names they gave their daughters were inspired by that tangle of sweetbrier, which has since laid claim to most of the hilltop."

"But didn't they also have a house in New York?" I asked. "Isn't that where you and your father lived while you attended Miss Peebles?"

"They lived there during the season and when Grandfather had to be in town on business, but it was never more than a lavishly appointed convenience for them. When we were in Paris last fall my Aunt Rosamund told me she dreaded what she used to call the retreat to Brambledene after the social whirl of the winter season in New York. From Thanksgiving until New Year's there was one grand and glittering party after another. All the best people were in attendance, of course—the Astors, the Morgans, the Whitneys, and the Vanderbilts—but of far more interest to Aunt Rosamund were the young men home on holiday from Yale and Harvard and Princeton. Her dance card was always filled. She said she loved dancing more than anything in the world. There wasn't much dancing at Brambledene."

"But the summers here must be heaven!" I protested.

"Not for Aunt Rosamund! She told me the bramble reminded her of a hostile army, and that she fully expected one day to be 'swallowed up in its thorny advance.' She left home at the first opportunity—marrying without her parents' consent—and settled abroad in Italy with Rafe's father's family. My grandparents never quite forgave her."

"She still lives in Paris?"

"Yes. She moved there with Rafe when he was still a boy. For his education, or so she says."

"And Mr. Taliaferro . . . ?" I was curious as to how much more of her family's history Rose was willing to share with me.

She took momentary refuge in a close inspection of the stitching on her elegant kid gloves, which, as far as I could tell, were flawless. At length, she granted that their marriage was, as she put it, "complicated."

"And yet, in spite of his business dealings keeping

them apart much of the time, Aunt Rosamund told me the only thing she truly regretted about her elopement was leaving my mother to fend for herself in that 'dismal, bucolic love nest.'"

It was obviously a direct quote, satisfying my earlier curiosity about where the term 'love nest' had originated.

"My aunt claimed it was unhealthy for my mother, but I never understand why. Rosalind adored Brambledene. No one knew it better than she: she knew where the foxes had their dens and the trees the owls favored for nesting. And the horses! Milo says she was the gamest rider he ever saw. She scared her parents half to death, he said, but nothing on four legs ever scared her."

"But what about people her own age?" I asked.

"What about them?"

"Wasn't she lonely, Rose?"

Rose frowned, and turned her face away. "She didn't need anyone else," she said stiffly. "She was free here to do whatever she wanted . . . imagine how glorious that would be!"

I was startled by the intense, almost fierce note in her voice. "But surely her parents—"

Rose turned back to face me. "They had their world, and she had hers. Oh, Vi, the stories she used to tell!"

The corners of Rose's lips lifted in a smile of fond reminiscence, and her head inclined to a listening tilt. I sensed my own ears straining to hear the voice she appeared to be attending. It was a strange, uncanny sight.

"She's buried over there, beyond the stone bench in the west corner." Her voice dropped to a melancholy whisper. "Mother didn't want a headstone. 'Let my grave be embraced by sweetbrier,' she wrote at the end. Such a sad, short life . . ."

I decided it was time to turn the conversation from this morbid talk of death and graves. "I believe your Aunt Rosamund was a classmate of my mother's—did your mother attend Miss Peebles, too?"

"Yes. Poor Rosalind! She was expected to follow in her

clever sister's footsteps, but she hadn't the knack for studies and she missed Brambledene dreadfully. By her third year there she gave up altogether, and Miss Peebles sent her packing. My grandparents were incensed: at Miss Peebles, of course, but at my mother, too. Grandfather couldn't understand how any child of his could be so lacking in ambition."

No more than I could understand Miss Peebles taking such drastic action because of mere scholastic ineptitude. Why, Flora and Iris would have been prime candidates for dismissal on *that* ground. Might Rosalind Thornbush have been dismissed for another reason? Miss Peebles tolerated dullness, but dealt severely with conduct she considered unladylike, as my high-spirited friend Lily had ample reason to know.

It's only the vast Forrester fortune that saves me from being sent packing, Lily had once said. *Old Peebles hopes that when I come to my senses—Oh, Vi! I hope I never do!—I'll make my gratitude for her forbearance manifest in the form of a very large contribution* . . . I wondered why the same line of dollars-and-cents practicality had not been applied to Rosalind Thornbush.

"Aunt Rosamund had settled in Paris by then," Rose was saying. "Her husband was forever off chasing business opportunities in faraway places, or so she claimed, and she invited my mother to come and stay with her. I don't know why my grandparents consented. Maybe they hoped some of my renegade aunt's social polish would rub off on her.

"I'm sure the last thing anyone expected was that within the year she would have become Countess Stirbey. Grandmother was thrilled! Much as she loved my grandfather, a title, even a penniless one, still had the power to impress her. As for Grandfather, since a distinguished marriage was as much as he expected of a daughter in the way of ambition, she moved back into his good graces, and when they died in a boating accident she inherited the bulk of the Thornbush estate. Countess

Stirbey was considered more worthy than the daughter they never forgave for deserting Brambledene and eloping with an Italian nobody."

"Are you saying your Aunt Rosamund was disinherited?"

Rose's pretty lips twisted wryly. "You see, Vi, Grandfather believed in a strictly applied system of reward and punishment, but it didn't work as well with daughters as it had the hunting dogs he trained in his boyhood. Aunt Rosamund knew what she was risking when she ran off with her lover; unfortunately, it's Rafe who ultimately paid the price. All he can hope for is Brambledene, and only if I die childless before him. It's an uncomfortable situation for both of us."

Uncomfortable not only for them, I realized. "You mean Ned can never possess Brambledene in his own right?"

Rose hesitated, then shook her head. "Not by inheritance. My grandparents wanted their beloved home to remain in the family even if it might mean putting the Taliaferro name on the gatepost."

This was indeed startling news.

I nodded absently as Rose excused herself to place her last sheaf of greens on her mother's grave. Considering what she had told me, it was no wonder Ned and her cousin were at odds! If Ned could not inherit Brambledene, his grandiose schemes must seem to Rafe an architectural desecration he might someday be forced to undo at great expense.

I glanced toward Rose. Despite her confidences—if that is really what they were; I'm more inclined now to think I was merely a convenient receptacle for an accumulation of *mementos mori*—she remained an enigma. As I watched, she sank down with a sigh upon the weathered stone bench near her mother's grave.

According to the deeply incised dates on the headstone, Rosalind Thornbush Stirbey had been not much older than Rose and I when she died. The feathery tips of the hemlock Rose clutched quivered as she leaned to place her tribute. Its satin ribbons, of a green so dark it seemed black in its shadowed turnings, contrasted somberly with the straw-colored grasses through which they trailed. Her emptied hands lay limp upon her lap. I could not see her face but I could guess at its pensive expression, a match for that carved upon the bowed head of the stone angel, the cemetery's only funerary sculpture, which kept watch, eternally grief-stricken, over the Thornbush graves.

Unwilling to intrude, I turned and walked slowly toward the rustic trellised entrance. As I did so, a square of crystalline whiteness off to one side caught my eye. It was a small slab of marble, set flush into the rough-mown meadow grass, bearing two sharply incised initials, *L* and *F*. This must be Lily's grave! There were no dates, no epitaph, no ribboned offering of hemlock and blue-berried cedar. It was almost as if Lily had been hidden away there, awaiting the weathering that would soon dim the betraying luster of the marble and erode the letters beyond easy recognition.

I felt a sudden hot rush of protective anger, and when Rose spoke behind me I whirled upon her, accusing words at the ready.

"I'm so very sorry, Vi, I meant to show you where we buried Lily rather than have you happen upon it like this." She gestured toward the little square of marble. "It's only a temporary place marker, of course," she said. "Ned and I placed the order for a headstone before we left for Paris, but the man who was to do the carving fell gravely ill and has only recently been able to resume work on it."

Although Rose's well-meant words blunted my initial anger, nothing could ease the hurt I felt now upon learning that Rose had sought only Ned's advice about a memorial.

"Why did no one tell me about the decision to bury Lily here at Brambledene, Rose? As her closest friend, closer to her in some ways that even Ned was, I wish that someone had thought . . . that someone . . ." I averted my face to hide my tears.

"Oh, Vi, I assumed that Ned—" She broke off. "Lily had no family to speak of. We finally located a couple of distant cousins, but when they learned there wasn't even enough money left to bury her properly they refused to take any responsibility. It was awful, Vi; you can't begin to imagine how awful it all was."

Rose's voice was tight and high, her face white as chalk. How could I have forgotten how terrible it had been for her, too? I reached out impulsively to take her small hands in mine.

"I just didn't think," she continued brokenly. "It was Victor who suggested we lay Lily to rest here in the Bramble, and by that time we thought it best for everyone if it were done as quickly and quietly as possible."

"And you were right, of course. Lily would have been very touched by your kindness; it was petty of me to complain. Let's say no more about it."

"Thank you, Vi. Of course, when the headstone is finished, we will want you to be here when it is put in place. You may wish to say a few words."

"Yes, I'd like that, Rose. I'd like that very much."

We strolled together out of the Bramble through the opening in the hedges. Rose gave me a sidelong look. "I imagine you were surprised when you learned Ned and I had been married in Paris."

I felt the breath catch in my throat. "Rose, please, what difference does it make how I felt?"

We fell silent. Rose and I had never been close; her cool, sweet serenity had always presented an invisible barrier to intimacy. Now, for the first time, I sensed currents swirling in unsuspected depths.

On the heels of Lily's cruel death we had all been jolted anew when we learned that Lily's guardian had bled her inheritance dry, and in the many consoling hours I had spent with Ned in the aftermath of the tragedy he had spoken often of his wish to memorialize her. Her spirit had been too bright, he had said, to be allowed to slip out of the world unnoticed.

Surely Ned must have known that Rose had made a place for Lily in the Thornbush family cemetery: had I been deliberately excluded from the decisions I felt I should have been party to, or merely overlooked? The most grievously hurtful of all of them, of course, had been Ned and Rose's decision to marry.

It was Iris who had told me.

"No one ever said a word of it to me, Iris, why should they tell you?" Shock had made me blunt.

"They didn't, Vi. It was all to be a secret until afterwards. A classmate of ours—remember Patsy Albright?—saw Ned and Rose and Victor embarking on the same boat her parents were sailing on, so she knew something was in the air."

Iris reminded me what a bulldog Patsy was, and how she finally got them to admit they were off to Paris to be married.

"It surely must have been a whirlwind romance!" Iris had enthused. "After what happened to poor Lily at Brambledene that awful weekend, who could ever imagine a happy ending? Lucky Rose!"

A whirlwind for them, perhaps, but an ill wind bearing no good for me. *Ned and Rose and Victor.* Always Victor. I wondered meanly if Victor had accompanied them on their honeymoon.

"I've always thought how unusual it was that you call your father by his first name," I said idly.

Rose stopped short and stared at me. "What on earth makes you say that?"

"Why, nothing really, Rose. We had been talking of his consideration for Lily and—"

"I very much resent your implication, Violet."

I stared back at her open-mouthed.

"I've always called my father Victor, just as I called my mother Rosalind. She encouraged it. She didn't like thinking of herself and Victor as parents—she was so young and pretty . . . I find nothing unnatural about it."

"Good heavens Rose, I intended no criticism, it's just that I can't imagine addressing *my* father as Clarence, can you?"

Deliberately, I puffed out my cheeks and stomach in cariactured emulation of my portly parent's somewhat pompous bearing. There were probably no more than ten years difference in age between my father and Count Stirbey, but in every other particular they were eons and worlds apart. I could only hope that Rose, who was well acquainted with my father, would see the humor in it.

To my relief, she began to smile, and the next moment found us giggling together like schoolgirls. The tension having eased, I asked Rose if I might have some flowers from the conservatory to place on Lily's grave. Her face grew pinched and pale.

"It would mean a great deal to me, Rose."

When Rose finally spoke, her words were measured, her tone remote. "I assigned the responsibility for the conservatory's upkeep to Mrs. Devlin; perhaps she can help you make a suitable choice."

"If you don't want me to go there, Rose—"

"What I want has nothing to do with it!" She clutched my wrist. Her blue eyes darkened with dread. "I *can't*, don't you see? *I cannot cross that threshold.*" Her voice dropped, and her eyes slid away from mine. "I wonder that you, of all people, can. If it had been up to me, none of us—"

Rose stopped abruptly. Her mouth clamped shut on the inhospitable words she had obviously been about to say. Poor Rose! Had the reunion been Ned's idea, then? Victor's?

"It's all right, Rose. If truth be told, I very nearly

didn't come, and I'm afraid that last night I allowed my . . . misgivings too much rein. I behaved badly. This morning I determined I would see the weekend through, and so I shall. So shall we both." I smiled—resolutely, I hoped—then started off toward the conservatory without allowing Rose time to fret about whether or not she should, after all, accompany me.

When I rounded the corner of the lawn beyond the beech, breaking free from the shadow cast by the dark, squat ramble of the house and the screen of garden sheds clustered along the edge of the Bramble, I was stopped by the sight of the glassed octagon of the conservatory shining in the morning sun. Jewel-like insets of stained glass glittered in the cast-iron crownlet surmounting its delicate glass and iron construction. An addition to the original house, it had been built for Althea Thornbush, Victor had told us, by her penitent husband by way of recompense for some brash deed or words that had displeased her. I recalled Lily standing there, hands pressed to her breast, her eyes wide with awe. "Imagine being given that instead of a box of chocolates!" she had said enviously, and we all laughed.

My footsteps slowed as I crossed the intervening ground. It was going to be harder, I now realized, than I had thought. The interior had, I recalled, been furnished rather like a leafy lounge, with wicker chairs and tables, and even a Turkish rug upon the bricks, where one could enjoy a friendly chat over a cup of tea or the solitary contemplation of blossoming plants set among an astonishing variety of ferny fronds. Lily could often be found there during that fateful February house party, drinking in the rich aroma of the warm damp earth like a flower seeking nourishment.

I hesitated in front of the outside entrance. Tenting my eyes with my hands, I tried to peer inside, but the glass walls fogged this cold morning by the warmth and moisture trapped within, were all but opaque. I placed my hand upon the doorknob. I took a deep breath, turned the knob, and entered.

It had changed almost beyond recognition. The cleared place, Lily's leafy retreat, was no more. Gone were the sheltering palms and bamboo, the luxuriant, tropical ferns. The wicker furniture, piled higgledy-piggledy in a cobwebbed corner, was blotched with mildew; the bricks underfoot were slimed with moss. Gone, too, the bright Turkish rug and the musical splash of the pretty fountain rimmed with fanciful gaping fishes. The fetid liquid encrusting its basin—one could hardly think of it as water—accounted, perhaps, for the reek of decay. I shivered. Despite the well-tended benches bright with flowers, I felt as if I had entered a tomb.

I sensed movement across from me. I peered through the frizzy strands of sprengeri suspended in pots from the ornamental iron roof bars. Ada Devlin stood no more than four feet away, her back to me, dressed in her usual black, poking at a bed of glowing coals in a small stove whose black chimney snaked up through the steeply pitched glass roof where a pane had been removed to accommodate its exit. A tight-drawn knob of ebony hair swelled like a huge boil upon the nape of her neck. I cleared my throat.

She turned quite slowly, almost as if I were expected. She wiped a charcoal-blackened hand on her apron; the geraniums in the pot she clutched with her other hand to her inky bosom were of a red so intense they seemed to cast a bloody glow upon her sallow cheeks. Her smile, I told myself, was welcoming.

"Miss Grayson! I hope you haven't been looking for me long."

"No, I came here directly. You see—"

"Hardly anyone comes here anymore. I never thought that you . . ."

Her words trailed off as her eyes slid over and down to the spot where Lily had been cruelly attacked and left to die. Tears pricked my eyes; a bitter taste filled my mouth. I turned away, swallowing hard.

"I find it peaceful," she continued in a softer tone, "and I enjoy working with living things." I thought her choice of words unfortunate. She smiled again. "May I be of service?"

I explained my errand. Mrs. Devlin regarded me in silence for a long moment, as unblinking as a cat. I returned her gaze resolutely.

"You do understand that nothing grown here can take this wicked cold for long," she said, turning to lead me through the rows of benches. "The begonias would turn black at once," she said, gesturing toward a bench crowded with pink and white belled plants. "But these chrysanthemums will do quite well, if we choose the darker colors . . ."

She reached out to clip some stems, but my eye had been caught by a cloud of yellow lilies beyond.

"No, thank you," I said. "The lilies, please."

She frowned. "Miss Grayson, I don't think—"

"The lilies," I repeated firmly.

She gave a little whuff of disapproval—even the sharp click of her secateurs seemed to reprove me—but soon supplied me with an armful of the glorious golden blossoms.

"You will want some hardy ferns," she started. The implication, unmistakably, was that if I didn't, I was even more foolish than I had already demonstrated. "I potted up some for the holidays . . ."

As Ada Devlin scurried through the conservatory peering under benches for the errant ferns, my uneasiness engendered by the sour-sweet odor of rot was heightened by the discovery of a flat of thickly mossed peaty soil on a nearby bench. Slender stems topped with dainty pink and red flowers rose out of whorls of flat glistening leaves rimmed with sticky hair-like protuberances of unequal length. As I watched, a small flying insect, perhaps propelled by the whirlwind of my exhaled breath, blundered onto one of the shiny leaves. Presently, the hairs began to undulate like tiny demon fingers, gradually bending inward, trapping its feebly struggling victim. I felt suddenly faint.

"I found the ferns," said Ada Devlin, coming up beside me. She thrust leathery dark green fronds in amongst the lilies. "At least these will survive." When I failed to respond, she followed my dumbstruck gaze. "Ah! You found the sundew. This one's having a little snack, I see, but try as they might, they're no match for the nasty little bugs that thrive here. I really must fumigate."

I wondered if any insect could be nastier than this . . . what did she call it? Sundew? What a pleasant name for such a horror.

"I don't remember these from . . . before," I muttered.

"I brought them from Lake Miskatonic, near where I lived until I was married. They grow in the bogs along the lakeshore there, only much larger. I potted them up snugly in bog mosses to make them feel more at home here, so it must be the water that accounts for the difference in size. Next time I go home, I'll fill a jug from the lake."

I glanced at the leaf whose tentacles had now completely enfolded its prey. The thought of these predatory plants two or three times larger in size made me shudder.

"It smells almost like home here now," Ada said, taking a deep contented breath of the dank air, "and just you wait and see—" She broke off. "Milo doesn't like me to talk about Arkham."

Arkham. I seemed to remember Ned saying something about Arkham, but in what connection . . . horses! That was it.

"Isn't Arkham famous for its horses, Mrs. Devlin?"

"Indeed it is," she said proudly. "My father raised especially fine ones. That's how I met Milo. Most of the horses in the Brambledene stable have Arkham blood."

My curiosity got the better of me. "Then why does he not—"

Ada Devlin leaned close, anticipating my question. Her black dress smelled musty, her breath sour. "Arkham's known for other things, too, Miss Grayson. It's only thirty miles east from here, in the lowlands—the Ashley River that bounds Brambledene begins there at Lake Miskatonic—but it's a very old place, Arkham is, and the old ways are respected there. There have always been rumors, about the clan of witches that came over from England, bringing their wisdom with them. When the British soldiers came to search them out, my great-grandmother told me she hid away under the gambrel roofs with the others even though she never had the gift." She laughed scornfully. "Outsiders talk of ancient beings summoned from the deeps of the lake by the Arkham witches, but the truth is simpler, Miss Grayson. Simpler and stranger."

I began sidling away, but Ada clutched at my arm, sending the lilies and ferns tumbling to the moss-slimed bricks.

"Never forget what happened here!" she commanded in a harsh whisper, as if I ever could. She retrieved the fallen bouquet and thrust it into my trembling hands. "And do not linger alone at her grave. For all my Milo's talk of snowy owls and such, the Thornbush cemetery is an uneasy resting place."

CHAPTER FIVE

I returned to the cemetery and placed my bouquet of golden lilies on the small white slab marking Lily's resting place. It was very peaceful. No moaning wind, not even a sighing breeze, disturbed my equanimity. The only evidence of habitation of any sort was the wintry chatter of a chickadee as it hopped perkily through the dense tangle, unscathed by the sharp little thorns that clothed the intertwined vinelike branches.

Despite Ada Devlin's warning, I lingered in the sunlit clearing. I told myself that what I had seen the night before had probably been nothing more than a moonbeam reflecting from the gleaming surface of Lily's marble marker. But in my mind's eye I saw again that rising whiteness, those silent spirit-wings. *Had it really been an owl?*

A cloud dimmed the sun. Suddenly chilled, I turned abruptly away. As I did so my foot scuffed a pile of seedlike husks mixed with white fragments that I realized on closer inspection were small bones, of mice and shrews most likely. An owl's traces? Milo Devlin would know.

I went to the stables in search of the estate manager, and found there instead Jack Stark, Ada's brother, whose long, narrow-jawed head and unremarkable features were limned in shades of a grayish yellow, including his close-set eyes. It was as if his older sister's bold dark coloring had used up all the colors in their parents' palette.

He was wiping the coat of a very large and restive horse, whose bay coat where the dust had been removed was as glossy as patent leather. Those rolling eyes and impatient hooves would have persuaded me, no horsewoman, to keep a safe distance, had it not been for the fragment of crazy quilt being used as a dusting cloth. Jack acceded to my request to study it. Unlike the garish silk and velvet crazy quilts currently in mode, the fragments of cloth used in this one's finely stitched construction were very old and quite remarkable: toiles de Jouy, damasks, brocaded silks, linen embroideries, lustrous flowered calamancoes, and a twill tapestry the like of which I had seen only in the Metropolitan's textile holdings. It seemed an extravagant choice for a grooming tool. I was reminded of a reclusive great-aunt of mine, long deceased, whose Persian cats drank from Waterford crystal.

I must have frowned, for Jack volunteered, more than a bit defensively, that he had found it under the hedges after Lily was murdered.

"Sodden it was, miss. Those bits you're admiring would be nothing but threads and dust by now if I hadn't seen it, and it suits me, it does."

I returned the piece to him wordlessly.

He gave the big bay a final, flourishing swipe and made an elaborate show of shaking the dust from the fragment while crossing to the tack room where, with calculated ostentation, he draped it over a wall peg. "Better me than that Raggedy Man, miss. I respect pretty things."

I cared neither for his sly insinuation nor the thin-lipped smile that accompanied it, and yet I remained standing there, irresolute, reluctant to abandon my search for answers that seemed less and less important with each passing moment. Just then Milo Devlin entered.

"Good morning, Miss Grayson!" he greeted me heartily, as one might a timid child. "Come to see the horses, have you? They're worth your admiration, thanks to Jack here. He's got the Arkham way with horses."

"I'm sure they're very fine, but that's not why I've come." I described what I had seen.

Milo nodded. "Owl pellets for sure." His broad reassuring smile deepened the oddly placed dimple on his cheek. "You may rest easy tonight, Miss Grayson."

"There's more'n owls in the Bramble," Jack muttered. "Ada knows, Ada—"

"That'll be enough of that sort of talk!" Milo thundered. "Begor, I could do without some of your Arkham ways." Anger had thickened his brogue.

We stood in uneasy juxtaposition, like pieces on a chessboard awaiting the next move. And then the knight strolled in.

"Is that you, Milo?" The voice, cool and resonant, was Rafael Taliaferro's. "I hoped I might find you here." He paused just inside the large stable doors to allow his eyes to adjust to the dimness; his well-shaped head and trim frame were silhouetted against the bright day beyond. "I wanted your opinion about the feasibility of adding to the stable."

Jack Stark's spaniel, which I had noticed dozing in the tack room on an old horse blanket, came bounding out, apparently attracted by the sound of Rafe's voice. Rafe stooped to give the dog's feathered ears a ruffle and received for his modest attentions a look of slavering adoration that made Jack's sallow face darken.

"Back to your bed, Bruno!" he commanded. "The silly mutt don't rightly know which side its bread is buttered on," he muttered as the dog reluctantly obeyed, its stumpy tail held sideways, the tip aflutter with guilt as it cast a remorseful red-eyed glance over its retreating shoulder.

Rafe laughed. "My mother once had a terrier that took an inexplicable fancy to the laundress who came to our house once a week on Thursday mornings. She was a large, silent, rather disagreeable woman, but that little dog thought the sun rose and set upon her. He would take up his station near the service entrance a good hour before she was due and wait there, hardly moving a muscle—'Patience on a monument' was how my mother described it—until his goddess arrived."

Rafe thrust his hands into his trouser pockets and smilingly shook his head. "She paid him even less attention than I have Bruno. Dogs, it seems, sometimes have no more sense about their attachments than people do." His eyes sought mine meaningfully, but I declined to share his amusement.

"You see, Jack?" Milo said, laughing, "Isn't that what I've been telling you?" He turned to Rafe. "About the stables, sir, if it's more stalls you're meaning, Mr. Poole's already spoken to me about that. No reason it can't be done, but it's not adding stalls that's the problem, it's finding the lads." He shook his big white head regretfully. "Lick and a promise, that's all you get these days."

"My brother's boys would come, Milo," Jack volunteered.

"The twins? With but a half a brain between them? Thank you kindly, no. Besides, I'd never be able to tell which of the pair was slacking off, would I?" His tone had softened, and we all laughed, even Jack.

Hearing my laugh, which he had said he found so distinctive, Rafe stepped toward me. "Did you come to admire the horses, Violet?"

I shook my head. "I'm ashamed to admit that horses frighten me. They have such large teeth, and one can never be sure what they'll do with those sharp hooves of theirs. One stepped on my foot once, and although I was assured he had meant no harm, that didn't help my poor bruised toes. If it were up to me, I'd make the stables smaller, not larger."

Rafe laughed. It was a nice sound, deep and warm. "Your loss, Violet. There's a fine lot here."

"Arrah, that they are," Milo agreed, "but you should have known Tindalos. There was nothing that horse couldn't or wouldn't do, isn't that so, Jack?"

"Paw said he was the best he ever bred," Jack said. "'Course, by the time I knew him he'd been put out to pasture."

Milo's eyes lighted with reminiscence. "He'd fly over fences too high to see over, then put a child up on him and he'd plod around the ring gentle as any old dobbin. We even tried him at polo."

Ned had mentioned polo, I recalled. That was why he wanted the stable enlarged, to house visiting ponies.

"He was too big to be handy," Milo continued, "and he never did get used to the mallet swishing under his tum, but we had some good times. Then one day, one of the horses stepped into a woodchuck hole. Not much harm done, a bit of a limp was all, but Rosalind put up an awful howl and that was the end of it. Animals was all the world to the girl. Always ready to help the stable cats with their kittening, whether or not they wanted it! Anyway, the gear's still here, over in that corner. I should have got rid of it long ago, but it was custom-made in Dublin and fashioned as pretty as a bride's trousseau.

Rafe stepped across to inspect the dusty pile of leather and mallets. He gave a low admiring whistle. "Lovely stuff. Where did they used to play?"

Milo gestured with his head toward the stable door. "Other side of the wall out there, in the pasture on the crest of the hill. Nice stretch of level ground, and the view down the valley with the Ashley looping through it like a silver ribbon . . ." He paused; his voice hushed. "Sometimes, in summer, when the land's at its greenest I can think meself back in Lismore as a lad, settin' out at dawn, fish pole in hand, to lure a fat Irish trout out from under the Avondale's grassy banks."

He laughed and shifted his feet. "Wisha, listen to me carryin' on as if you had all the time in the world to listen." He turned to Rafe. "This is a good place for all its sadness, Taliaferro, and I mean to keep it that way as long as I'm able. But whether it's bigger or smaller—" He broke off with a shrug. "That's not up to me."

A cautious man, Milo Devlin. Clearly, he loved Brambledene, and wasn't about to say or do anything that might jeopardize his position.

Rafe looked at the older man in silence for a long moment. I could almost feel his keen intelligence considering, questioning, and finally accepting Milo's neutrality. He nodded, then held out his hand for Milo's brisk shake, a gesture of respectful good will exchanged between two men who were, for the moment at least, equals. I felt a sharp twinge of envy for the male straightforwardness that social convention largely denied to women.

Rafe turned to me. "Since the horses hold little attraction for you, would you be willing to quit this equine hotel and accompany me to the conservatory?"

I was about to offer my regrets—I had no wish to return so soon, if ever—but the pressure of his fingers as they closed in a warm, light grasp around my arm made me feel, just for a moment, almost dizzy . . . no, to be honest, *quite* dizzy. It was so unexpected the excuse I had in mind to make dispersed unspoken from my mind.

"I rather fancy your company among the ferns," he continued, smiling down on me. The light in his gray eyes shimmered like quicksilver. Could this be the same man I had fled from in tears only a few hours before? What was he really like, this man who so long ago stole, then broke my heart? Intrigued, I found myself trailing along beside him toward the stable doors.

My return visit to the conservatory proved to be less unsettling than I had feared. Ada had left, and except for her carnivorous plants, which I carefully skirted, there was little about the glass house's present arrangement to cause me unease, or remind me of Lily's fatal enchantment with its leafy bowers. I was even able to appreciate, if not wholeheartedly share, Rafe's enthusiastic interest.

"What a delightful structure this is!" he exclaimed as we toured the airy glass octagon. "Elegant in design, yet entirely practical. Private conservatories were all the rage on the continent in the '60's and '70's, but they were more often great glass temples than pretty little chapels like this one, and the cost of maintaining them proved too much once the initial novelty was past. Rust, rot, and corrosion always won over time."

"It is pretty, isn't it?" I agreed. "The jewel in Brambledene's crown—except, of course, for Rose."

"Except for Rose," he agreed, but only after a moment's hesitation.

I couldn't help wondering if the resentment Rose had hinted at in the Bramble extended beyond the unfair disposition of his grandparents' estate to encompass Rose herself. How often might he have said to himself upon seeing her that there but for an unforgiving grandfather go I? And if, as Rose had said, all he could ever hope for was Brambledene, Ned's schemes must be like salt in his wounds. No wonder Rose felt uncomfortable having him here. Perhaps he could do with a reminder that despite appearances Rose's life had not been, as they say, all beer and skittles.

"I hadn't realized until Rose showed me her mother's grave in the Bramble this morning how young Rosalind Stirbey was when she died. Why she was barely thirty! I don't think Rose has ever entirely recovered from her loss. Thank God she has Victor—and now, of course, she has Ned, too."

"Of course," Rafe echoed drily. I could have guessed the sardonic twist his mouth took without seeing his face. Then on the verge of speaking again, he frowned, hesitated, leaned down as if to sniff at a pot of fragrant narcissus, then turned back to face me, still unsure whether or not to say what was on his mind. When he did, his words were hardly above a whisper. "She took her own life, you know."

My hand flew to my mouth, stifling my distressed cry. *Rose's mother a suicide?*

"According to my mother," Rafe continued, "Rosalind was a very troubled child."

"She was? Rose said she adored Brambledene and had wonderful stories to tell about growing up here. It sounded like a wonderful childhood to me."

Rafe raised his eyebrows. "Wouldn't that depend on whether they were true stories or fantasies? She was always subject to erratic changes in mood, Mother said, and when she came to stay with us in Paris . . . I was only a child, but I can recall the tears and the rages. And she was sick a lot of the time, too. Physically sick, I mean."

"So might I if I had gone away from all that I loved best and sailed across the ocean to stay with a sister I hadn't seen or heard from for several years. From what Rose said, I gather they were quite unlike."

"That's true," Rafe conceded, "but Mother loved her. She said it was hard not to love someone so vulnerable, and she was quite beautiful. Rose looks rather like her, but Aunt Rosalind had this . . . special magic. She'd smile at me and off I'd trot, to do her bidding best I could. I recall Mother scolding her about it. But when she was in the room there was always this sense, this anticipation of something about to happen: something wonderful and, sometimes, something dreadful, but always *something.*

"She was hard to resist. Victor couldn't. As you may have sensed by now, my uncle is somewhat less dashing than he looks."

I frowned. "He's very kind. That counts for rather more in a father than dash, it seems to me."

"I grant you his kindness, but he hadn't the least idea how to cope with a volatile girl like Aunt Rosalind. It all happened so fast! There was no courtship to speak of; they met, and three weeks later were married. Mother tried to talk some sense into her sister, but she said she was tired of people telling her what to do. I guess she already knew Victor wouldn't—or, more likely, couldn't.

"Mother said they traveled with a lively set. Rosalind became known as the beautiful American who drank too much and caused scenes in the cafes along the boulevards. It's a wonder Rose survived the pregnancy—my mother has always been very tight-lipped about that—and after she was born, Aunt Rosalind's behavior grew even more outrageous. Victor tried to protect Rose from her excesses as best he could, but he began looking to other women for comfort.

"It all became too much for Aunt Rosalind. Soon after Victor's . . . defection, she began to avoid the company of her dissolute companions. She became reclusive, spending long hours in her darkened suite of rooms, dreaming of Brambledene, spinning tales of it to her daughter, not sure when, if ever, she would be able or welcome to return. One day, left alone again in their Paris apartment, she smashed all her hidden bottles. Then, when her craving returned to overwhelm her, she slashed her wrists with a fragment of the shattered glass. Rose found her lying on the floor in a pool of alcohol and blood."

I found it hard to imagine the agony of despair that had driven Rosalind Stirbey to such a dreadful act. I thought of Rose finding her mother dead, clothes sodden with blood and liquor. I took a deep breath to keep my tears at bay, but the smell of the conservatory's warm damp earth overwhelmed me, causing my image of Rose's mother to give way to the more vivid one of Lily Forrester whom I had myself found dead near where we stood.

Huddling in upon myself, I began to cry. No wonder Rose refused to enter the conservatory. Earlier, I had thought it somewhat self-indulgent of her—it was I, after all, who had found Lily there—but to have been faced with two such tragic deaths while still so young . . .

Rafe gathered me in his arms and allowed my tears to fall unchecked upon his shoulder. Presently, I stammered out the grim tale of Lily's cruel death and my discovery of her body. The tensing of his embracing arms told me it was the first time he had heard the particulars.

"I had no idea, Vi. Your outburst at dinner . . . the cries in the middle of the night. I confess I found it difficult to take you seriously. You seemed so . . . so . . ."

"Flighty," I supplied.

"Oh dear. You do have a way of overhearing things you weren't meant to." He looked stricken. "But you're really not in the least flighty, are you?" He held me out at arm's length, regarding me earnestly. "Under the circumstances, I can't imagine why Rose planned this house party. It seems, at the very least, insensitive. I wouldn't have thought it of her."

"I don't think the idea originated with Rose," I said, "and I'm sure its purpose was to lift the shadow cast on Brambledene, not darken it."

"But if the murderer has never been found . . ." Rafe's sentence trailed away as he belatedly realized what his words had implied.

"The person the police have reason to suspect of the crime, a derelict known locally as the Raggedy Man, must be long gone by now," I protested. "There's no reason to think he may return."

I looked at him, seeking reassurance, but Rafe shook his head doubtfully. "Derelicts rarely roam aimlessly, Violet. The very fact that this one has a local sobriquet—what do you call it here, nickname?—is proof of that. They need to know where they can shelter in bad weather, and which farms will barter food for chores."

I shivered at the possibility of him being out there, somewhere. "He was like something out of a monstrous fairy tale, Rafe. A bundle of rags cinched in the middle with a leather strap. And the smell of him! It was unspeakably vile." I closed my eyes, seeing again that crazy jumble of quilted pattern crouched over Lily's body, then fleeing the scene looking more like a nightmarish scarecrow than a man. "He was holding something, a knife I think. I have this impression of something metallic in one of his hands as they pulled away from her throat, something that glinted like steel . . ."

The hazy memory came into focus, nudged by my nearness to the place where I had first seen her sprawled form. "It must have been a knife, Rafe, because I remember wondering what awful things, if I had not come just then, he might have done with it . . . have done to *her.*"

I found myself wishing fervently that the ugly detail which had plagued me so during my repeated recountings of it to Ned had remained buried in my memory, and as my tears began again to flow, Rafe drew me close.

"Lordy, Lordy, what a touching sight. I guess you and Rafe have made up your little differences, eh, Vi?"

At the sound of Ned's voice, Rafe and I sprang apart like guilty lovers.

"Be warned, my girl," Ned continued in an exaggerated drawl, "these Paris fellers are mighty slick hombres."

"It's not what you think, Ned," I cried, trying in vain to wipe the evidence of tears from my eyes.

"It doesn't matter what he thinks, Violet," Rafe rebuked me. "He has no claim on you. In my opinion, he has little claim to anything."

Ned bristled. "What's that supposed to mean, Taliaferro? By God, I wish I'd never shown you any courtesy!"

"If you're referring to my invitation to Brambledene, since when has an attempt to trade on family connections to use someone's professional training become a courtesy?"

Ned's hands closed into fists as he lunged forward. I moved quickly between the two men in an attempt to forestall physical violence, but as I did so I nudged a pile of clay pots set precariously near the edge of a bench. They toppled onto the brick floor with a deafening clatter, shortly followed by Victor's alarmed entrance through the double doors leading into the house.

"What on earth . . . ?" His puzzled expression became a frown as he assessed the belligerent tableau frozen into place before him. There was a moment of startled silence, then, as Rafe and Ned began speaking at once, each accusing the other and none of it comprehensible, I vacated my position between them and escaped to Victor's side. It was thus that Rose found us a few minutes later.

"I guess you didn't hear the gong announcing lunch," she said stiffly as her eyes traveled from Rafe to Ned to Victor and then to me, who by my chance position appeared to be at the center of the hubbub and under Victor's solicitous protection.

"I don't know what the problem here may be, Victor, but may I remind you Violet is a grown woman now? I doubt you need act as a proxy father whatever her wish in that regard."

Victor withdrew his hand, which had been resting on my shoulder, as if from burning coals. I gaped at Rose. Gone was the gracious hostess and confiding companion of this morning. Her narrowed blue eyes bright with hostility, but the reason for it utterly escaped me. Although it made no sense, she seemed more jealously concerned about her father's role in the little scene she had come upon than her husband's. Was it because she was unable to relinquish the saving link to sanity Victor's love had forged in the aftermath of her mother's suicide? Yes, that might explain it.

I attempted a smile. "Rafe and Ned and I had a . . . misunderstanding, Rose. It was all quite silly and unnecessary, really. Then I knocked over a stack of clay pots," I added, indicating their littered fragments, "and the noise summoned Victor only moments before you arrived."

Rose looked at me consideringly. "Well, then," she said, with her usual cool courtesy, "Shall we join the others?"

We fell in obediently behind her. Victor began talking to Rose in a low, urgent tone. Ned, who was still bristling, preceded me, and Rafe brought up the rear. I turned once, to see if I could gauge his mood, but his eyes betrayed no lingering hint of hostility, and his smooth olive-skinned face might have been a mask for all the expression it showed.

Ned had called him a slick hombre; the idiom my father favored for men he judged untrustworthy was "slippery customer." I hoped neither term applied. From what he had told me Rafe had reason enough to be resentful, but devious? I would not have thought it of the carefree, attractive youth I had known, too full of himself to bother to dissemble. And yet, although Rafe was still attractive, compellingly so, what kind of man had he become, really? His rancorous exchange with Ned seemed to indicate he had no intention of helping Ned translate his notions into architectural reality, but if that were the case, why had he come?

I had no way of knowing, and it was probably unwise to guess.

CHAPTER SIX

The arrival of the five of us, one after the other in a silent Indian file, alerted the others awaiting us in the dining room. Four pairs of eyes curiously followed our progress, for all the world like a litter of kittens presented with an intriguing but somewhat alarming new toy. As we took our seats Iris opened her mouth to speak, then thought better of it. It was left to Freddie, not known for his sensitivity to nuance, to end the lengthening lull in conversation.

"Your cheeks are red as roses, Vi," he said, beaming at me across the table. "To what do you owe their becoming bloom?"

I frowned. "Don't you think holly berries a more apt comparison than roses this time of year?"

Freddie received my undeservedly snappish answer in silence, pursing his lips as he spooned a generous portion of creamed chicken onto the biscuits previously served.

I heaved a put-upon sigh. "If you must know—although I can't think why it would interest anyone—I expect my ruddiness is the result of my morning spent exploring the grounds. Nothing like a brisk walk to counteract pallor and pudginess, I always say."

In fact it was the first time I had ever said it, but my rather mean-spirited barb had the desired effect of turning the company's attention from prickly me to more general subjects.

"Have you any jigsaw puzzles, Rose?" Flora inquired. "We could clear the table in the library, light a fire, and—"

"What? Spend this beautiful day indoors going blind over odd-shaped bits of wood?" Wink cut in. "Not me, thank you very much! I say we all go down to the river and try to find a bend broad enough for skating."

"Sorry, Wink," Victor said. "The Ashley's current is too swift to allow ice strong enough to safely bear a person's weight."

There was a discouraged silence punctuated only by the clink of cutlery on the gold-banded porcelain.

"If it were April instead of February," Rafe commented idly, "I'd propose a round of informal polo. I suspect the horses need exercise as much as we do."

Ned smiled. "And what do you suggest we'd hit the ball with, croquet mallets? You'd need either awfully long arms or very short ponies." His darting blue-eyed glance invited the rest of us to share his amusement. Flora obligingly tittered.

"Not a bit of it," Rafe replied mildly. "In fact, there's a good lot of proper gear out in the stable, isn't that so, Violet?"

I nodded, albeit reluctantly. I had no wish to encourage an activity that involved horses' flying hooves.

Ned leaned forward alertly. "You don't say! Why, that's capital! Sport for the chaps and entertainment for the ladies! As Wink said, it's a beautiful day today, not much wind, a bright warming sun—Victor?" His coaxing smile was dazzling.

"I don't know, Ned, we'd have an ill-matched set of mounts . . ."

Though Victor's words were hedged, Ned seized upon his use of the conditional as signaling the kindling of his interest and turned abruptly to Rafe.

"Taliaferro?"

Rafe met Ned's challenging gaze directly. "Count me in." Then, grinning, he leaned back in his chair and folded his arms. "But I'll not be the one to inform Milo of this balmy enterprise."

Ned raised a lordly eyebrow. "Leave Milo to me. But we need one more player. Freddie?"

Freddie threw up his hands in alarm. "I was city born and bred. Never been on a horse, old boy, and I value my noggin too much to start now!"

Ned scowled. "Wink? Surely you're game for a little friendly competition!"

All eyes turned expectantly toward the only one among us whose credentials as an all-around athlete were unchallengable. Wink shifted uncomfortably. His playing fields had not included ones with horses cavorting on them. "I'd rather put my trust in my own two legs . . ." He paused. Iris's huge brown eyes radiated disappointment. "But I guess I can stick on long enough to give you a game."

"Hurrah!" The relieved whoop was Freddie's. "I'll volunteer as referee—"

"Actually, we should also have umpires," Victor commented, "but under the circumstances, we'll be lucky if we can come up with something to use for goal posts. At least we'll have an audience to cheer us on—"

"With champagne for the winning team!" Rose announced spiritedly.

"And how," I asked, "shall we console the losers?"

Rose met my searching gaze. Although her blue eyes were unreadable, her soft pink lips curved in a slow smile that accentuated her deep dimple and raised my spirits. I interpreted it as her way of kissing our bruised friendship and making it well. "Champagne for them, too, Vi."

After lunch we adjourned to the parlor where dessert and coffee were consumed amid a rising buzz of conversation involving, on the men's part, what regulations should apply, English or American, and how rigidly they should be observed. Since Freddie was unfamiliar with both sets of rules, the game, like the discussion, seemed destined to become a free-for-all.

The ladies, meanwhile, debated the burning question of costumes appropriate for a sporting event on this deceptively springlike day, bearing in mind the mid-February reality and our inactive role as admiring spectators. Our debate ended in a draw: Iris and Rose chose style over practicality, but Flora and I thought the need for warmth more persuasive.

The men soon dispersed to the stables to acquaint Milo with their plans. I did not need to be a proverbial fly on the wall to be sure that Milo's verbal reaction would be peppered with many a "begor" and "begod." Nevertheless, by the time Flora, Iris, Rose, and I had changed our clothes and began making our way down the gentle rise above the broad flat pasture adjacent to the stables, we saw below us much coming and going with gear and what looked to be short sections of fencing.

"My guess is that they will be using the fencing to mark the goals," Rose said. "The ground is much too hard to drive poles into."

I eyed Rose's hunting outfit enviously. Her knee-length flared tweed skirt swirled above well-polished leather gaiters, and the exaggerated puff of the sleeves of her leather-belted jacket emphasized the slimness of her waist. Perched on her sleek blond head was a jaunty suede hat sporting a plume of irridescent feathers. She looked, much as it pained me to admit it, adorable.

Iris's forest green wool walking suit had a mannish, smartly cut Norfolk jacket also eminently suitable for rural pursuits, although I thought her soft-crowned wide-brimmed cap unbecoming to her classic good looks. As for Flora and me, thanks to Rose's loan of mohair shawls in bright tartan plaids we would at least be warm.

The sun, too, would be a welcome source of warmth for another half hour or so. I threw back my head, the better to capture its gentle heat upon my cheeks, enjoying the crisp exhilarating scent of the cold, clear air. Wink was right, it was indeed too beautiful a day to spend indoors!

Arms outstretched, I pivoted slowly in place as the crests of the winter hills traced around me a lovely irregular line against the glowing blue of the sky. Brambledene itself, its narrow diamond-paned windows set aglow by the declining sun, seemed more like a curled-up cat blinking yellow eyes in snug content than the squatty unwinking toad that I, fevered by dread, had imagined upon my arrival. Even the unexpected appearance on the slope above me of the housekeeper's tall, somber figure failed to dampen my spirits.

Nevertheless, although I told myself there was no reason why Ada Devlin should not also choose to enjoy this uncommonly fine afternoon, I turned my back upon Ada's distant approach, and urged the others to a faster pace.

"Come along, girls!" I cried. "Look! They're bringing the horses out!"

Ignoring my own apprehensions where horses were concerned, I bravely led a breathless scamper down to where a rough bench had been created from a wide plank supported by blocks of stone wrested from the nearby wall. The men mounted as we took our seats; then, after our chatter subsided, assured of our undivided attention, they paraded before us, all the while pretending they were doing nothing of the sort.

They *did* look splendid. The horses snorted great bursts of steam and sidled nervously as the weight and swing of the mallets were tested, much, I imagine, as the thrust of lances were in the days of tilts and jousts. I wondered which of these latter-day knights I might have chosen to wear my colors.

Victor's mount was the tall dark bay I had seen earlier in the stable. Its ears flicked back nervously to catch Victor's foreign-sounding soothing murmur and the glossy muscular neck maintained a tense, bowstring arch.

"You needn't fear," said a voice beside me as I drew

my legs away from the restive animal's high-stepping hooves, "Count Stirbey and Aleppo are old friends."

I looked up, startled, to find Ada standing beside me at the end of the bench. Her uncannily silent arrival made me wonder if the black cloak enveloping her had been fashioned from raven's wings.

"He's one of the Arkham horses, isn't he?" I asked.

Ada nodded proudly. "Tindalos was his sire, and Aleppo sired Lunette, the mare Mr. Taliaferro's on." Ada turned to her brother, who had joined her after adjusting the placement of the fences serving as goals. "Lunette's as quiet as a little gray lamb with him, isn't she? No firecracker high-jinks today."

"Never saw the like of it," Jack admitted grudgingly.

Rafe and the pretty dapple gray mare he sat astride were a matched pair of neatly boned aristocrats. A current seemed to flow between man and horse, and as he put her through her obedient silky paces it was like watching a centaur. His signals, whether conveyed by gloved hand, booted leg, or subtle shifts of tweed-trousered thigh, were quite invisible to my untrained eye; nevertheless, I was suddenly, very acutely aware of the power in his flesh. I bit my lip and turned away.

A whoop and a whinny echoed across the hillside as Ned raced by, heedless of the bits of icy turf sent flying by his mount's galloping hooves. Grinning, he waved his wide-brimmed hat around his bright, tousled head.

Flora clapped her hands together. "Why, Ned could be Buffalo Bill himself," she crowed delightedly.

Ned pulled up his horse with a flourish and trotted him over to where Wink sat, resigned but brave, upon a stalwart, benign-looking, gray-muzzled barrel of a horse. "C'mon, Wink, race you back on down!" Ned's speech seemed to have acquired a western twang since lunch. "Looks to me like that old *cayuse* you're on could use a little firin' up."

Wink looked alarmed. Rose came to his rescue. "Don't be such a tease, Ned," she admonished. "Besides, it looks to me as if that creature *you're* on needs calming down more than Sergeant-Major needs firing up. I don't recall seeing him in the stables—does he always roll his eyes like that?"

Jack tittered. "Billy's better'n he looks, Miss Rose . . . I mean Miz Poole, beggin' your pardon. He sure's come a long way since I got him. Still a little crazy, mebbe, but he's strong and fast. Mr. Ned knows how to handle 'im, Ma'am."

I eyed the grizzled horse doubtfully. His mulish head, long neck, and powerfully developed hindquarters had little in common with the other Brambledene horses. "He's not of Arkham breeding, is he?" I inquired.

"Good heavens, no!" Ada Devlin cried indignantly.

"And what an odd color!" I exclaimed.

Milo joined us. "A strawberry roan he is, Miss Grayson. An ugly brute, but Jack has the family liking for a horse, and I guess you could say he rescued this one."

Somehow it was hard to think of Jack Stark as a good Samaritan.

"The farmer who had him tried to beat manners into his hide," Milo continued, sensing my skepticism. "That way never works, of course, just makes'em worse. The beast cornered the foolish man in the barn one day, and if Jack hadna come along might of killed him. He was supposed to be a temporary boarder here, just until his cuts healed and we fattened him up some, but Mr. Poole took a fancy to him, so he'll be staying on." Milo frowned. "He's young yet, so it'll be a long stay. I just thank the good Lord he's a gelding," Milo added in a mutter.

I looked up at Ned. He had fallen silent, his lean frame relaxed into slouchy grace, but I sensed that the reins loosely drawn through his long hands maintained a controlling contact with his restless, head-tossing mount whose bit, as he worried it, jangled like discordant bells.

Ned replaced his worn hat on his head at a rakish angle, then tugged the wide brim low over his eyes, almost as if to conceal the direction of their intently directed attention. From my angle, however, it was not hard to figure that it was Rafe.

He and the trim gray mare continued to cut elegant figures through the ragged tufts of grass. His finely chiseled face reflected the pleasure he found in riding an animal capable of responding so well to his skilled direction. He looked relaxed and in control.

As he watched Rafe, a muscle quivered in Ned's set jaw; a fleeting grimace pulled taut the lines between his long nose and wide mouth. I had always found Ned's insouciant charm enormously appealing, but this new and unsuspected side of him, intense and a bit dangerous, was . . . exciting.

I sighed. These challengers wore no armor and no banners adorned our rough lists, but I would have been pleased to have either Ned or Rafe wear my colors. I looked from one to the other, unable to make a choice, and sighed again. Then, as the foolishness of my nonexistent predicament overcame me, I laughed aloud. Hearing me, Ned's head jerked around in my direction, his expression still grim and unreadable. An instant later, he flicked his hat brim up with his thumb, winked broadly, and saluted me with his mallet before gathering up his reins.

"Time's a wasting, boys!" he cried. "If the ladies sit here much longer they'll freeze their dainty toes off, and then what will we do for dancing partners Saturday night?" He spurred Billy into a brisk trot and rallied the other players. "Victor, we'll be the red team; Rafe and Wink can be the white."

Rafe raised a dark eyebrow. "Like the War of the Roses? I thought this was to be a friendly game, Poole."

"Game of the Rose, then," Ned acceded with a sunny smile, "in honor of my lovely wife."

The four players walked their horses to the middle of the field where they met with Freddie, their referee, to decide on which rules of play should apply to the match.

Considering the lack of proper goal posts, the indistinctly marked foul line and the insufficient number of players, there were ample grounds for argument. Voices rose as makeshift adaptations were proposed and rejected, and judging from the bewildered expression on Freddie's face, he would, once the game was underway, be about as capable of making informed decisions as the tattered scarecrow atilt in the adjacent cornfield. I was soon proved right.

Rafe was the first off the mark. He pressed his horse forward boldly, hit the ball smartly, and shot it cleanly between the Red team's gates before the others could collect themselves.

"*Damn!*"

Ned's exclamation rang in the clear cold air. Rising in his stirrups like a jockey on a race course, he urged his ungainly mount into a neck-stretching gallop, but his wild swing at the ball failed to connect. Victor, wheeling in from the side, saved the day with a backhander, knocking the ball out of Rafe's reach and delivering it to Ned who had pounded up in time to drive it down the field toward the White goal with a resounding whack.

Rose jumped to her feet and began to clap, but Freddie rushed forward, frantically waving his arms, to declare Ned's play offside. The horses, eyeing him nervously, tossed their heads and shied. Ned gave an exasperated snort and murmured something that sounded uncomplimentary.

"The American game has no offside, Fred," Victor said, "and that's what we're playing . . . trying to play, I should say."

"Oh." Freddie's pink cheeks grew pinker. "I thought it was the other way around. Sorry about that, chaps."

Rafe was again the first to set the ball in play, but his straight shot was deflected by a tussock of grass, and it fell to Wink to complete the play. Iris began to giggle as Sergeant-Major lumbered forward, Wink's heels beating a brisk tattoo on his barrel-like sides, but just before he got within mallet's reach of the willow-root sphere, Ned deftly winkled it out. Laughing, he began nudging it criss-cross down the field in a series of short, oblique shots while Freddie stalked up and down the sideline demanding to know if what he was doing was cricket.

"Wrong game, old boy," Ned called, "This is polo, not cricket."

"Begor, the daftest game of polo I ever saw," Milo muttered beside me, "And the ground's a menace. There's no one to do proper scything now. Just look at it, all tussocked with weeds! That old Raggedy Man was the last of the good hands."

I looked at him sharply.

"At scything's what I meant, miss!" Milo exclaimed, his eyes widening in dismay.

I acknowledged his amendment with a nod of my head. "The game does seem a bit much for that poor horse," I said as Sergeant-Major barged down the rough field in vain pursuit of Ned's taunting, twisty course.

"Aye, he's too old now for this kind of nonsense, Miss Grayson, but in his day he was the steadiest, bravest hunter in all the Berkshires. Mr. Thornbush was a big man, you see, and I bred and trained Sergeant-Major to order, you might say. There wasn't a fence too high or stone wall too broad for them to take in stride." Milo frowned as the old horse faltered. "Mr. Poole should know better than to lead him such a chase," he added under his breath. "Wisha, sunset will soon put an end to it."

Victor patted Aleppo's glossy neck as he waited patiently for Ned to finish his foolishness, but Rafe's mare, who had been temporarily blocked by Sergeant-Major's slow-moving bulk, sprang forward at her rider's urging the moment an opening presented itself. As she sped down the field, a gray zephyr in the fading light, Rafe leaned low, mallet at the ready. They overtook Ned just short of the goal. Rafe swung strongly back, but Ned wheeled Billy broadside to block Rafe's access to the coveted ball and, brandishing his mallet triumphantly, braced himself for the inevitable collision if Rafe failed to give way.

It was all quite idiotic, really; nevertheless I found myself admiring Ned's daredevil challenge, and when Rafe, usually so cool-headed, accepted it, no one was more surprised than I. It may be, of course, that he was simply unable to pull up in time, but whatever the reason—and I confess to preferring the former—once met, their mallets connected like lances in a medieval tourney. But instead of the clang of bright steel we heard the shattering crack of dry wood, and when Ned raised his stick to hit the ball home he found its cigar-shaped end had broken off, leaving a useless bundle of splinters.

He gaped at it, turning it this way and that as if willing it to become whole again. Rafe began to laugh; we all did. Not at Ned, but at the game that had begun as an entertainment and ended in farce. Ned, however was not amused, and when Rafe, still grinning, reminded him in a cheerful shout that he who laughs last laughs best, he spurred Billy into a headlong, bucking run to the end of the pasture.

Milo stamped his feet and beat his mittened hands against his thighs. "It'll be dark soon, gentlemen. I'd appreciate it if the horses were cooled off and bedded down before the light fades. Besides, that mallet of Mr. Poole's has ended up looking more like broom straw than something to hit a winning goal with, eh?"

There was a general murmur of assent, the cold having long ceased to be exhilarating. The men turned their horses toward the stable, and allowed them to pick their way home over the frozen ground at their own pace. I rose, stretched, wrapped my borrowed shawl closer around me, and prepared to follow my companions up to the welcome warmth of the fire sure to be ablaze on the parlor hearth.

Suddenly, a piercing whinny knifed through our quiet chatter, followed by the sound of pounding hooves. Billy loomed up out of the gloaming with Ned clutching the pommel of his saddle with one hand as he tried with the other to regain the reins swinging loose around the galloping horse's extended neck. The shattered mallet, held tight between Ned's upper arm and side, protruded like an arrow from a drawn bow.

Aghast, we watched helplessly as the panic-driven horse raced on a beeline toward the other riders on their ambling mounts. Rafe, who had already entered the narrow passage between the east pair of fences turned idly to see the cause of the commotion, only to find himself the likeliest target of the rapidly approaching menace. Victor and Aleppo were ahead of him blocking the exit; there was nowhere else for him to go.

Wink, who was waiting off to one side for the others to pass through, sensed Rafe's danger before the rest of us. Acting with cool courage, his reflexes honed by years of athletic competition, he urged Sergeant-Major forward, directly into Billy's path. The two horses collided with a fearful impact, pulling each other down in a squealing flail of hooves.

Ned was thrown clear, his splintered mallet catapulting harmlessly onto the verge of the field. Billy struggled up and stood shivering a short distance away, head down and reins dangling. Freddie and Flora hurried past the exhausted animal to where Ned sat, head in hands, and helped him regain his feet. Rose joined them a moment later. After a brief exchange of words, he limped away assisted by the solicitous twins. Rose started after them, hesitated, then turned back, ever the dutiful hostess, to where Wink lay groaning, his right leg trapped beneath Sergeant-Major's bulk.

The big horse tried to rise. Shuddering, he fell back, causing Wink to cry out.

"Isn't there some way we can get him up, Milo?" Victor implored. "I don't like the look of Wink. We must get him up to the house out of the cold."

"If Sarge *can* get up, he will," Milo replied grimly,

"but you fellows better be ready to pull Mr. McEldowney clear when the old boy has another go at it."

The next time Sergeant-Major attempted to struggle up, they dragged Wink free. It was too dark to tell the extent of his injuries, but there was no doubt of the pain he was suffering. Iris knelt beside him and rubbed his hands with hers as the men improvised a litter from the plank we had used as a bench. Jack helped ease Wink onto his rough stretcher, then turned back to where Milo stood tall and silent over the old horse's bulk.

Victor, hearing the animal's labored breathing, hesitated before lifting his end of the plank. "Milo? Is Sergeant-Major . . . ?" His words trailed off questioningly.

Milo shook his big silver head. "There's nothing can be done, Count Stirbey. Broke his leg, he did." Milo called to his brother-in-law. "Jack? Fetch my revolver from the tack room, there's a good lad." Jack nodded silently and sped off up the slope. "And Ada, you had better go up to the house with the others. The young man will need looking after and you know where the supplies are."

Ada got up reluctantly from where she was kneeling beside the stricken horse. She pressed her husband's hands to her heart. "Oh, Milo!" I heard her say in a low, broken voice. Then she turned, and her black cloak soon melted into the shadows.

"Milo, if it would be easier for you," Rafe began, "What I mean is, given the circumstances . . . I could . . ."

Milo squared his shoulders. "'Tis a kindly thought, sir, but seeing as how I helped bring Sergeant-Major into this world, and a fine big lusty colt he was, the duty of easing him out of it belongs with me."

Rafe nodded, and turned back with Victor to where Wink lay moaning. When Jack returned, the three men and Iris, who was as strong as any of them, carefully lifted their awkward burden and started the slow journey back to the house. As they departed, I could hear Iris murmuring reassuring words to her stricken, newly found hero.

Rose and I brought up the rear. We had taken only a few steps when Rose turned and darted back to where Milo stood hunched, his arm stiffly down by his side, the revolver clutched in his big, rawboned hand. She stood in silence, obviously searching for something comforting to say. At length, words having failed her, she sighed, curled her fingers on his sleeve, and stretched up on tiptoe to kiss his cheek.

He looked down at her, startled, then patted her shoulder softly with his other, mittened hand. "Go along, now, Miss Rose," he said. "Go up to where the fire waits to warm you and your friend. There's already been enough sadness for you to remember here at Brambledene."

As Rose rejoined me, I reached out to capture her hand. The impulsive kindliness of her gesture toward Milo had touched me, and I welcomed this uncommon opportunity to share in her warmth. Alas, it was short-lived. When the expected, dreaded shot rang out a moment later, Rose's hand tightened convulsively in mine, then wriggled free. She darted away without a word, and by the time I topped the rise her slim figure was nowhere in sight.

I paused to catch my breath. Brambledene's massive crown loomed above me, inked in broad curving strokes across the purpling sky. The narrow windows flanking the door, lit unwaveringly from within, reinvoked a slit-eyed reptilian image. Not the rustic stone-and-plaster-warted toad I had conjured up on arrival, but an altogether more horrific and alien creature scaled with slate and slicked with the watery sheen of the vanishing light. I shivered and trudged the last few yards alone in the gathering dusk, wishing I could escape the unwelcome ambiguities Brambledene presented me at every turn.

CHAPTER SEVEN

By the time I arrived at the house, Ada had determined that although Wink might find walking painful for several days, he had suffered nothing more untoward than severe bruising.

He lay in state on one of the big parlor sofas: Iris, his self-appointed Florence Nightingale, had seated herself at his head, from which vantage point she alternated coseting him with periodic commands for warmer blankets, softer pillows, and fresher, hotter tea. In the intervals between tucking and plumping and pouring, she described to each of us in turn the grievous harm done his poor leg, the extent and fearful coloration of which grew larger and more dramatic with each telling. Judging from Wink's contented expression as he gazed up at his ministering angel, the accident had ended up doing him more good than harm.

Flora and I, who stood side by side as close to the blazing fire as we dared, exchanged knowing glances as Iris stroked his brow.

"Do I dare fancy wedding bells in the not-too-distant future?" she whispered.

"I fancy you do," I replied as I stepped back from the crackling logs, expecting at any moment to see smoke issuing from my skirt. I loosened the warm shawl Rose had loaned me and drifted it across the end of Wink's temporary sickbed. Iris scowled at me reprovingly. I sighed. "And let's hope they ring sooner than later, Flora, otherwise we may all drown in the syrup of this burgeoning romance."

Flora giggled. "What a dreadful cynic you are, Vi. I think it's sweet."

"Exactly my point!"

We laughed, but were soon sobered by Rose and Ned's entrance, Rose frowning as Ned gesticulated. "I told you I've already spoken to Rafe," he was saying testily, "but I'll see Milo in the morning, Rose, not now."

"Better sweet than sour," Flora murmured. I shot her a sidewise look. So she had noticed, too.

As they approached Wink, Ned stopped short at the sight of Iris tending her wounded hero. He turned back to Rose. "You seem to have forgotten, my darling, that I was in the accident, too." His voice was barely audible, and if he had not been facing us as he addressed Rose, I doubt I could have made out his words. "It didn't take long for your undying gratitude to give up the ghost, did it?"

His tone was abrupt, almost cutting, but his meaning—gratitude for what, I wondered—escaped me. A moment later, as he leaned forward to commiserate with Wink, Ned's broad warm smile and his cheery beckoning to Rose to join him there, persuaded me that I had witnessed nothing more than an ordinary instance of the disagreements experienced by every young married couple during the period of adjustment. This was to be expected, wasn't it? Nothing to worry about. Nothing to raise one's hopes about, either, I amended enviously as Ned's arm encircled Rose's slim waist.

". . . poor old Billy," Ned was saying, "off I went, barreling down the field hell for leather, and by the time I got there I could feel my saddle—which had felt none too secure during that little dust-up Rafe and I had—begin to slip sideways. Damned uneasy feeling when you're aboard an unpredictable brute like Billy! Anyway, when I lifted up the flap to get at the girth buckles, an awkward business at best, I completely forgot about that damn mallet until it stung into Billy's tender belly like a hive of hornets. He'd like to have headed for the moon! I don't know how I managed to stick on as long as I did; I just wish I hadn't lost the reins. If there's anything I can do . . ."

"I got hit worse playing football my last year at Yale," Wink said. "At least you're not a Harvard man."

Iris thought that was the funniest thing she had ever heard. In fact, it cheered everyone up to see Wink in such good spirits. Well, not quite everyone. Rafe chose not to join our truncated sherry hour—Ada announced the roast could not be held any longer—and although his arrival at dinner was punctual, I had the distinct impression, due perhaps to the slight disarray of his usually well-groomed hair and the bits of straw clinging to his sleeve, that he had been outdoors again since returning from the makeshift polo field.

Dinner was an uninspired affair. Iris and Wink had theirs on trays in the parlor; Rose seemed distracted, and Ned and the Latimer twins gossiped idly of people and places I knew little and cared about even less. Victor's conversation with Rafe, which concerned the architecture of other estates in the area, was of more than passing interest to me, but was conducted in tones too low to be shared effectively with anyone else.

Coffee was served in the parlor, where Iris's played-to-the-hilt role as nursemaid was fast becoming an embarrassment. Victor soon retired, pleading fatigue. I put my cup on the tray, intending to follow his lead, when Freddie called spiritedly for a game of cards.

"Poker!" cried Ned.

"It was my idea," Freddie challenged. "I say Euchre."

Rose, Flora, and I looked at each other. "Whist!" we said, almost as one voice.

Ned shrugged. "Whist it is," he conceded. "But surely you'll agree to a modest wager."

"Please, Ned!" Rose remonstrated.

"A few cents a stake," he wheedled, his blue eyes alight with anticipation. "Man is a gaming animal, my love, and what could be a safer outlet for his passion than a game of whist with only a few cents for the stake?" His smile tilted roguishly awry. Who could resist him?

"Take pity on the lad, Rose," Freddie implored. Even Rafe smiled.

The corners of Rose's mouth relaxed. She reached up and ruffled her husband's gently curling hair, burnished by the firelight. She shook her finger under his nose. "A few cents a stake!"

He captured her finger and kissed it. "A very few," he promised, then, rubbing his hands briskly, he called for a deck of cards.

Freddie suggested we have our game at one of the tables in the library, but Rafe, saying that he and Rose had business to discuss, asked that we remain in the parlor.

"I *am* sorry," he said smoothly, "but the matter had quite slipped my mind. Actually, that round table under the window will serve your game better."

Ned eyed Rafe narrowly. He slammed the new box of cards Rose had given him upon the mantel. "If there's family business to discuss—"

"*My* family's business, Poole," Rafe cut in, "the Taliaferros," he amplified, belatedly acknowledging that Ned was, in fact, a member of Rose's family. "It concerns my mother's . . . situation." At least he had the grace to sound apologetic.

"Oh." Ned shifted from one foot to the other. "Well, in that case . . ." He looked from Rafe to Rose. No help there. He opened his mouth to speak, then, suddenly aware of the audience interestedly observing this domestic exchange, Ned picked up the cards and, as his wife and her cousin crossed to the library, presented them to me with a flourish to shuffle.

The hours spent with my ailing father, who when not

engaged in his treatise on tight corsets enjoyed relaxing over a game of cards, had allowed me to perfect a rather showy shuffle. A minor skill, to be sure, but it had the desired effect of diverting everyone's attention from the recent contretemps. Freddie gaped as I carelessly waterfalled the crisp cards from one hand to the other.

"My word, Vi! If I didn't know better I'd take you for a riverboat gambler!"

Ned laughed. "I'm certainly glad my suggestion of poker was outvoted. Why, I've seen no better than that in the gold field saloons." He winked at the others, twirled an imaginary mustachio and leaned close. "Tell me, little lady, what other unsuspected talents do you possess?"

Even though it was meant to be overheard, the suggestive tone of his teasing whisper sent Flora into a fit of giggles and the blood rushing to my cheeks. My safest course was to take him literally. "If you gentlemen will be so kind as to set up the table and chairs for our game, I will be happy to demonstrate."

The task I assigned gave me time to collect myself. Once seated, I cut the cards, fanned them into a wide arc, folded it, then cut and recut them in an elaborate, very fast shuffle of my own devising before spreading them out for the draw.

"You're the second woman to give me a double shuffle today," Ned muttered as he picked a card. "But I think I prefer your variety."

I colored again, even more deeply. The term was sometimes used as a metaphor for deceit, and the only other woman he could be referring to was Rose. "You picked the low card, Freddie, so it's your deal," I prompted briskly, pretending I hadn't heard Ned's aside. It was one thing to be attracted to Ned, but quite another to be tempted to take advantage of what was probably only a temporary failure in marital communication.

The rigor of the game soon absorbed all our mental energies. Flora's grasp of the play was uncertain, but

Freddie was a surprisingly shrewd player and Ned predictably daring. I held my own, proving in the end that slow and steady wins the race.

As I smugly collected my modest winnings—to Ned's credit, he had held to his promise to Rose—Freddie pointed an accusing finger at me.

"We've only your word that you've been living up on Central Park West this past year, Violet Grayson. I'll bet you anything an investigation would find you've been fleecing unsuspecting passengers all up and down the Mississippi!"

"Stop fussing, Freddie," Ned advised. "There'll be no more bets tonight, and no more losses, either." He stretched and began putting the room back in order. "My muscles are complaining about this afternoon's ride, and besides, Violet's cleaned me out." Ned turned his pockets inside out and eyed us forlornly.

I smiled complacently. "I have indeed, and with my winnings I'm going to buy an estate on the Hudson, or perhaps a chateau in France and a palace in Venice with a Canaletto view." Yawning elaborately, I got up. "I'll be happy to play cards with you again any time, my dears," I offered condescendingly as I plucked at my moire leg-of-mutton sleeves to revive their puff.

My words were greeted with a clamor of derision soon hushed by Iris, who had been nodding in a wooden chair at Wink's side.

"Do be quiet!" she hissed indignantly. "Can't you see Wink is trying to sleep? You're as noisy as a pack of red Indians."

We glanced guiltily at our friend. He lay dead to the world in his nest of blankets, mouth open and gently snoring.

"Oh, for heaven's sake, Iris," Flora said testily. "I doubt if John Philip Sousa and all his bands could rouse Wink. I suggest you come upstairs with us. You won't be much use to him tomorrow after spending the night in that chair."

Iris hesitated, then began to unfold herself out of the straight-backed chair. "I am a bit stiff," she confessed.

"Of course you are," Flora agreed. "Come along, now," she commanded. "You, too, Brother!"

Ned and I exchanged amused glances as Iris and Freddie fell meekly into step behind Flora's plump figure. Flora might be a bit silly, but she had a talent for practical organization Freddie lacked. I decided they would make a good domestic team after all, and that any paternal yearnings on their part could no doubt be satisfied by the burgeoning supply of Latimer nieces and nephews.

Ned soon followed the others upstairs. I lingered, hoping to find some diverting reading matter in the library. The popular novel I had brought with me was fraught with betrayal, heartbreak, and doom, which was hardly conducive to a restful night. Shortly, the library door snicked open. Rose, looking rather pale, glided by me unseeingly; Rafe paused as I turned to enter.

"I hope you haven't been waiting long," he said in an apologetic whisper, in deference to Wink's stuttering snore. "Had you anything particular in mind?"

"Thank you, no. I was hoping for amusement—light essays, a collection of stories . . ." I peered in at the shelves filled with set after set of handsomely leather-bound volumes, and sighed. "But I guess I'll have to settle for something either uplifting or fearfully literary."

"Not a bit of it," Rafe said. He pulled out one of a number of magazines he had wedged under one arm and held it out to me. "Would St. Nicholas do?" He colored slightly, as if embarrassed to be offering a publication edited for juveniles. "Or Punch, perhaps? The only issues I found were over a year old, but I doubt if it matters."

"Oh, Punch, please! I know St. Nicholas well, and still love it dearly, but my father thinks Punch smart-alecky. Won't have it in the house."

"Which is why it appeals to you, of course," Rafe shrewdly guessed.

"Ah! You've found me out!" I said, laughing.

He lifted an eyebrow. "Have I? Somehow I doubt it. You're not an easy woman to read, Violet."

His silvery gray eyes held mine in a gaze so searching I turned away, as if to hide depths he appeared about to penetrate; depths whose contents even I hesitated to explore.

The magazines tumbled to the floor. As Rafe stooped to gather up the slippery pages, Wink stirred in his sleep, his snore skipping a beat before resuming its rhythmic rumble.

"I guess poor Wink will be lame for some time to come," I murmured as we tiptoed toward the stairs. "By the end of the evening Ned was feeling the effects of the accident, too. How lucky you were to escape it!"

"Lucky?" Rafe shot me a sardonic glance. "Assuming it was an accident, I suppose one could say that."

I stopped dead halfway up the stairs. "'*Assuming* it was an accident'?"

"For the sake of argument." His tone was steeped in irony. He cupped his hand under my elbow and exerted a gentle, upward pressure. I shook free angrily, and marched up to the landing, where I turned to face him standing on the step below me.

"I resent your attempt to herd both my movements and my thinking," I said in a furious low voice. "Ned explained to us what happened. If you had deigned to join us over sherry and heard his story, perhaps you wouldn't be so quick to think the worst. Although where Ned's concerned, you always do, don't you?"

"Your loyalty is admirable, Violet, but your judgment . . ." His head moved from side to side in a slow, mocking shake. "As it happens, I heard Ned's explanation before you did."

I dropped my eyes. Even as he spoke, I recalled overhearing Ned informing Rose he had spoken to Rafe. I bit my lip, determined not to apologize.

"He went on at great length, all about a loose girth and

the splintered mallet and pricking Billy's undersides. He even apologized, although he couldn't resist implying I had set him off in the first place."

I thrust out my chin belligerently. "Well, if you hadn't laughed at him when his mallet broke—"

"Good God, Vi! We all laughed. I distinctly remember hearing you. Am I to be held responsible everytime Ned Poole's nose goes out of joint? If so, I might as well lay in a good supply of sackcloth and ashes." He frowned and began plucking irritably at the bits of straw on his sleeve. Rafe had arrived for dinner with that straw on his sleeve, and it suddenly dawned on me where he must have been.

"You went out to the stable to check Ned's story, didn't you?" I didn't wait for an answer. "Of all the cheek!" I was so angry my voice trembled.

Rafe stepped up onto the landing, but wisely kept his distance. He thrust his hands into his pockets and rocked back and forth on the heels of his well-polished boots. "That splintered mallet did a lot more than sting Billy, Vi, it punctured him. Deep enough to leave clotted trails of blood on his hide. I imagined myself astride, lifting up the saddle flap, the broken mallet protruding down from under my arm, just as Ned described it, but no matter how I tried I couldn't make those wounds fit that steep, slanting angle." He looked at me directly. "I did try, Violet."

"Don't bother trying to convince me your eye wasn't prejudiced!" I cried. "I imagine you can't wait to tell Rose—" I broke off as an unpleasant suspicion presented itself. "Or maybe you already have. Maybe *that's* what that hurried conference was all about. No wonder Ned wasn't welcome!"

"It would be nice if you could spare me a fraction of the benefit of the doubt you lavish on Ned Poole! I have told Rose nothing; I very much wish I had said nothing to you, and for the moment I'm *sure* of nothing more than that Ned intended to scare me."

His implication was monstrous; my expression must have reflected my incredulity.

"Oh, yes, Violet," Rafe said. His voice harshened and red flushed the hollows of his cheeks. "He resented being made a fool of, resented even more my laughing at him and, as is so tiresomely often the case with Ned, in the end he went too far. Even you will admit he can be dangerously hotheaded, which, for reasons that utterly escape me, you appear to find exciting."

"Perhaps because his willingness to express his feelings is such a refreshing novelty! All of us here have been so steeped in gentility I doubt we even know who we are under our societal wrappings." I laughed derisively. "As for you and Rose, even Salome wore fewer veils than you Thornbushes!"

Rafe's eyes flashed. I stepped back as his arm shot out. "I am a Taliaferro first!" he proclaimed, his finger stabbing emphatically, "and a Thornbush—"

"Only when it suits you?"

"Not at all! I have a duty toward Rose and this property, but most of all to my mother, who expects my allegiance to my duties to be unfailing."

"How very manly of you," I drawled. As he stood there challenging me—challenging the world!—his lithe figure taut as a bowstring, his voice choked with emotion, I succumbed to the temptation to provoke him further. "And how pompous," I concluded with a regretful sigh. "You seem to have forgotten that Ned is, after all, the master of this house."

Rafe's arm fell to his side. His dark-lashed eyelids dropped to mask the lightning. "Only by virtue of his marriage to Rose." Coolness again enveloped him. "My mother has no interest in returning to Brambledene under any circumstances. She has appointed me to look after her . . . *our* interests here. If that seems pompous to you, so be it."

He nodded stiffly and strode to his room. The only

remaining sign of his emotional outburst was the harsh rhythmic slap against his thigh of the periodicals he held clenched in his hand.

I undressed mechanically. The night was again very cold, and I slipped gratefully into bed with the issue of Punch borrowed from Rafe to distract me. I soon put it aside. The cartoons failed to amuse me, the humorous essays seemed labored, and the lamp on the table beside the bed flickered unevenly. I turned it out, resolving that tomorrow I would ask to have it adjusted.

The house was very quiet. The only noises were the expected creakings of an old house's bones adjusting to a drop in temperature. A down comforter kept my body warm, but a frigid breath of air seeping through the frames of the leaded windows laved my cheeks. I turned my head to look through the panes at the moonlit sky. I wondered if I might see the owl again, rising on ghostly wings. I wondered, too, how the flowers I had placed on Lily's grave had fared. Succumbed to the cold by now, no doubt. Another of Brambledene's innocent victims.

Victims. Could Rafe possibly be right? Had Ned truly intended to frighten him? Had this house party become a genteel counterpart of Ned's storied Colorado gold camps, famous for the rough pranks of men unable to peacefully contain their fierce jostling? Was Brambledene itself the prize coveted by both Rafe and Ned? *But think of the price!* I shuddered. The price was Rose herself.

It was a dreadful thought, *truly* dreadful, and yet—I'm loath to admit it even now—I found myself idly wondering in which corner of the Bramble's clearing Rose would be laid to rest.

I sat up in bed, heart pounding, hating myself. I'll never know why I did what I did then: was it an unconscious need to punish myself? Did I somehow think I could compensate for the coldness of my thoughts by exposing my flesh to the cold night air? Whatever the motivation, I tugged on my slippers, wrapped my comforter closely around me, and fled down the stairs, out into the icy, lambent night.

As I neared the Bramble, I fancied I saw a glimmer of white through the dark barrier of hedges, and wondered if the owl had returned. I stole through the opening, hoping to come upon its roost before it glided up in susurrant, snowy-winged flight.

But when I entered the clearing I knew no bird emanated the glow I saw wavering before me. It was pale, insubstantial, twisting like a wisp of fog, surrounded by a pulsing shimmer. It hovered, its indistinct outline shifting, above the small square of marble marking Lily's grave. The flowers I had placed there that morning looked as fresh as summer, the quilled yellow petals bright against their nest of ferns.

I sensed the warmth before I felt it, and my approach was unafraid, unquestioning. I stooped and extended my hand wonderingly toward the bouquet. As my hand passed through, the misty column seemed to curtsy, and the warmth I had sensed became palpable. It touched my hand, and then, in a caressing glide of sensation, enveloped me. I felt a faint trembling pressure, like a dreamed kiss, upon my forehead.

I closed my eyes, the better to capture this astonishing moment. When I opened them, the aura had begun to fade, and as it swirled away into the shadows the cold crept in to reclaim its domain. Its icy fingers clutched me and the frost-ravished lilies in my hand quivered like live things as their bright petals curled and blackened in its cruel, unrelenting grip.

"*Lily!*" I cried, but the glowing shape without form, the shade without color, had gone beyond my recall.

CHAPTER EIGHT

Somehow I managed to return to my room and into my bed without rousing anyone. I continued to shiver despite the extra down coverlet I pulled from the chest at the foot of the bed, chilled as much by the eerie recollection of that graveyard vision as by the cold night air itself. What I thought I had experienced was not possible; it *could* not be possible, yet Ada's words continued to reverberate in my mind: *she's still here, you know.*

I lay awake until dawn. Finally, just as first light spread in a widening rosy stain across the horizon, I fell into exhausted sleep. When I awoke with a start a few hours later, only disjointed fragments remained of the dreams responsible for my disordered bed clothes and crumpled pillow: I recalled an armored knight leaning stiffly down from a great black horse to give me a bouquet of golden lilies. As I reached up to raise his battered visor, the lilies in my hands transformed into a monstrous Arkham sundew, its sticky, leafy jaws dripping blood. Suddenly, both the mysterious knight and I were overtaken by a roiling cloud of dust from which issued the relentless pounding of horses' hooves.

"Violet?" The noise came from my door. The pounding hooves, I realized, was someone urgently knocking. "Violet! Are you all right?"

The door opened a crack. I saw one round china-blue

eye and a lock of strawberry-blond curls.

"Come in, Flora," I said. "I'm fine now, but I . . ." I decided to keep the night's uncanny happenings to myself. "I had difficulty going to sleep, and I guess I overslept." Flora's fresh, smiling, *normal* presence, soothed my jangled nerves. "Keep me company while I dress. I suppose I've missed breakfast."

"And about to miss lunch, if you don't hurry."

"Oh, my, that would never do. I'm absolutely starved." I poured some water into the basin on the washstand. It felt like ice water on my warm skin. Flora laughed as I gasped with the shock of it.

"Heartless girl!" I cried. "Hand me my shirtwaist, please—the striped one hanging in the wardrobe—and bring me up to date on the lovebirds."

"Well, Wink is ever so much better this morning. Victor has lent him a big knobby walking stick—with that red hair of his, all he needs is a kilt to look like a proper highland laddie—and he's hobbling about with one hand on the cane and the other on Iris's supporting arm."

Flora paused. "And here's a funny thing, Vi," she said, cocking her head considerably to one side. "Rose seems thrilled to pieces by it all. Why, I believe she'd tie the knot for them herself if she could. I've never seen her so . . . so *animated.*"

"I suspect she's pleased to have something nice happen at Brambledene for a change, poor dear." I fastened my blue tweed skirt and smoothed the seams into place. "I guess, too, that she's relieved Victor will be spared Iris's moonstruck yearnings."

Flora sighed. "I sometimes wish *my* father were more like Victor."

"I said much the same thing to Rose myself."

Flora looked puzzled. "Why would you wish my father was like Victor?"

"Not *your* father, Flora, *mine.* Rose wasn't thrilled about *that.*"

"Why ever not? I would think it a compliment."

I thrust my unbuttoned cuffs under Flora's pert nose. "Be a dear and do these up for me—I should have thought to do it before I put it on. To answer your question, all I can do is guess. According to Rafe, Rose and Victor grew very close after her mother died." I didn't know if Flora was aware Rosalind Stirbey was a suicide, but I saw no point in mentioning it. "I think she resents anyone who appears to attract his attention."

"But Victor wasn't attracted to Iris, he was merely being kind. Why, he's old enough to be her father!" she added indignantly.

I laughed.

Flora looked sheepish. "Well, he is, Vi."

"I know, Flora, but I'm not sure Rose thinks that makes much difference." Now that I thought of it, my parents had a May and December marriage, which made my youthful mother's death ironic as well as sad.

"That's ridiculous!" Flora exclaimed. "Besides, if I were lucky enough to be married to Ned Poole I wouldn't care what anyone else did or didn't do."

Neither would I, I thought as I slipped into my jacket and pinned on my lapel watch. "There! Finally ready."

The pleasure of the lunch I had been looking forward to was considerably lessened by the plans Rose had made for the afternoon. She had already dragooned Flora and Iris and Freddie into helping her with the decorations for the Valentine party, and Wink volunteered to offer encouragement and advice from the chair Iris promised to provide for him.

Rose addressed me from across the table. "Vi? You always had original ideas for this sort of thing when we were at school."

I averted my eyes and wordlessly twiddled my spoon in my soup. I tried to respond as I knew I should, but I found repugnant the very idea of a repeat of a party that had ended so tragically. The thought of assisting in the preparation of decorations, especially in light of what I had experienced in the Bramble during the night, made me feel physically ill.

"I'll help with the preparation of the buffet," I pleaded as Rose waited expectantly for my assent, "I'll even do the lion's share, but right now I really do feel the need of fresh air."

"She does look peaked," Wink said, peering at me concernedly. "I say we let her off. A walk will do her good."

Bless him! Although Wink himself had never suffered from vaporish sorts of ill health, he had always been sensitive to the needs of those who were. Many were the brotherly pattings he had bestowed on my quivering shoulders as I wallowed in adolescent doldrums of despair.

The cold air felt good on my face. I avoided the Bramble. I couldn't remember what I had done with the flowers reduced last night in one shocking moment to blackened slime, and I had no wish to come unexpectedly upon their ugly remains.

A pale and dispiriting shade of gray, yielding no breaks or substantial clouds of darker gray, veiled the sky as far as the eye could see. The landscape's austere winter palette, pleasing in sunlight, had been drained of all emphasis by the neutral light. In spring, purple crocuses, the golden horns of daffodils, and here and there a blaze of tulips no doubt softened the bleak, unrelieved joining of the sprawling house's foundation to its wide lawns. Today, the dirty white sky, moisture-darkened stucco, and parched, straw-tipped green of the frozen grass seemed a scene from Purgatory, well suited to a listless soul like myself.

Was it a lingering, half-submerged memory of my clash with Rafe about Ned that guided my footsteps toward the stables, or just the need for uncomplicated company? If the latter, the warm pungency of the aroma that filled my nostrils, together with the horses' contented snorts and straw-muffled stampings, seemed made to order to ease a troubled mind.

Aleppo tossed his handsome glossy head as I passed; the gray mare Rafe had ridden extended her neck and snuffed at my hands with flared nostrils, seeking the treat I had neglected to bring. A shaggy Shetland peered up at me from the next enclosure, followed by numerous stalls housing animals of similar size and bay coloration. Arkham-bred horses, no doubt.

Ned's favorite mount, Billy, was across the corridor, separated from the rest. His stance, hindquarters facing me, and a flash of his wide white blaze as he turned, briefly, to roll wall-eyes at me, signaled the hostile broodiness of an outsider. The largest stall of all, adjoining the tack room, was empty.

"Sergeant-Major's," said a gruff voice from the tack room door.

Startled, I looked up to see Milo Devlin. I opened my mouth to ask how they planned to dispose of the horse's massive bulk, then thought better of it. Instead, I gestured toward Billy. "I understand his mallet scratches were rather worse than expected."

Milo shot me a sharp look from under his bushy eyebrows. "They are that, but it wouldn't be Mr. Poole telling you of it."

It was a statement, not a question.

"No-o-oo," I began cautiously, "according to Ned—"

"What's done is done, Miss Grayson, and sometimes it's better to believe what suits the situation than to go looking for the evidence."

Milo had moved, surprisingly deftly for such a large man, to block my return to Billy's stall. "D'ya hear what I'm saying, miss?"

I looked up into his piercing blue eyes. "I . . . I think so, Mr. Devlin."

"I was sure you would." His broad smile transformed his oddly placed dimple into a wide fissure. "You know,

Miss Grayson, should you want a bit of a canter, I have a sensible pony might suit you. Comfortable as an armchair and dependable as an alarm clock."

"If you're referring to the Shetland next to Aleppo, I fear my toes would drag on the ground."

Milo laughed. "No, not little Nonny, he's Aleppo's pet. I'm speaking of the Welsh pony Jack's out on now."

I stared at Milo. "Aleppo's *pet?*"

"Sounds daft, doesn't it? But sometimes a horse will become attached to another animal the way we do to a dog or cat. I had a racehorse once that wouldn't run if his pig was left at home." Milo shook his head. "Can you imagine hauling a sow along to the courses? There was a lot of sniggering about *that,* I can tell you."

We laughed together. "Thank you for the offer, Mr. Devlin, but I prefer riding behind a horse than on one, and to tell you the truth, I'm not always happy about that, either. Now, these new automobiles—"

Milo looked at me aghast. "Saints preserve us from those noisy monsters, miss. Why, I'd as soon drive a dragon!"

"Well, I'm sure it will be a long time before you'll see any up here in the Berkshires," I said soothingly.

"Wisha, my God, let us hope so," he said fervently. "To my mind, 'tis only a small step from here to heaven. We have no need for hell raisers, beggin' your pardon, in horseless carriages."

I took my leave of Milo at the stable door. His values had been fashioned in a simpler world, and no amount of gold or promise of worldly prestige could induce him to desert them. I hoped my prediction about motor cars would prove to be right. No matter the convenience, I hated the notion of Milo's Garden of Eden being invaded by them.

I entered the house through the great front door. The parlor's gloominess was accentuated by an oppressive stillness and the sour smell of charred logs awaiting kindling and the strike of a match to bring the cold, dark fireplace back to life. The group in charge of party decorations was, I knew, in the old classroom off the corridor leading to the conservatory. Victor and Ned had taken a carriage to collect props for a Valentine tableau from a neighboring estate.

"Violet?" Rafe stood in the library doorway; he seemed to be at loose ends, too.

"Hello, Rafe. How did you escape being pressed into Rose's service?"

"Duty first," he said. "No, really," he added as I looked at him askance. "I promised to list the more important of Brambledene's furnishings, room by room, and what with one thing and another, there's been precious little time. Perhaps you'll accompany me? I could use another knowledgeable eye."

I raised my eyebrows. "What leads you to believe my eye is any more knowledgeable than, say, Flora's?"

"Because it was Flora who told me about yours," he replied. "'Vi loves nothing better than pawing through dusty old relics.'" The light, quickened inflections of his falsetto captured Flora's speech pattern perfectly. I laughed.

"According to her," Rafe continued, quick to press his advantage, "you spend 'whole afternoons' in that 'dreary museum,' and worse than that, you think too much. That's why you get headaches."

"The gospel according to Saint Flora."

He grinned. "Which museum?"

"The Metropolitan," I said. "It's across Central Park from where I live. My father thinks—" I broke off. Why should I share my childish deceptions? "My father thinks I should spend more time outdoors."

"He and Flora should get on very well."

"Flora has a weakness for tight corsets."

Rafe looked utterly at sea, until he recalled what I told him at dinner the night before about my father's work in progress. "In that case, we must keep them apart."

We smiled agreeably at each other, our disagreements temporarily in abeyance.

"Shall we get started?" I suggested. "I should warn you, my knowledgeable eye becomes rapidly unknowing once removed from textiles."

Rafe looked up from the lists he held. "Textiles? Really? Why, that was my mother's first love. The collection she assembled in her youth is stored here at Brambledene. Amusements of the sort a lively girl enjoys were lacking here, so she became an accomplished needlewoman. Saved her from being bored to death, she said."

"She must have a wonderful collection by now," I said enviously.

"Actually, she doesn't. Mother has become a true Frenchwoman: thrift now heads her list of virtues, and she's become more interested in storing her gold against comforts for her old age than acquiring pretty things." He gave a very Gallic shrug. "A lot of the thrill of collecting is in the hunt, you know. These days, whenever Mother chances upon anything special in the way of a tapestry or embroidery, she notifies other collectors better situated to preserve it."

"Few connoisseurs are that generous," I murmured, saddened to think of Mrs. Taliaferro's keen eye and discerning taste lying fallow because of a lack of funds.

"Mother's a grand old girl," Rafe said. "You two would get on famously."

Maybe we would now, but recalling the sharp exchange between his mother and mine all those years ago, I just smiled.

Although I would have been reluctant to admit it at the time, the hours Rafe and I spent together that afternoon were delightful. When we weren't at odds, Rafe could be a stimulating companion. He was never at a loss for either a keen observation or a witty aside, and the attention he paid my comments was all the more flattering in light of his own expertise regarding Brambledene's interior style and furnishings. He soon identified several fine old pieces overshadowed by the preponderance of overly ornate, velours-upholstered vulgarities, and I was impressed by his familiarity with American cabinet-makers.

"They came from my grandmother's family, a more refined lot than Roswell Thornbush's," he said.

When I admitted to having completely overlooked the better pieces, he smiled wryly. "It is a gloomy old pile, isn't it? I think, though, that ivory paint and some of the colorful old fabrics Mother collected would work wonders. I must ask Mrs. Devlin where her boxes are stored. If there's time to spare, would you care to look at them with me before you leave Brambledene?"

"Oh, yes!" I said. Outside of the Metropolitan staff, he was the only person I'd ever met who accepted my interest in textiles as normal, even commendable.

But there was more to it than that. As we made the rounds, our heads in close juxtaposition as we inspected the joinings in a block-front chest and the graceful turned and reeded legs on a Duncan Phyfe card table, I became acutely aware of the smooth olive curve of his cheekbones and the crisp texture of steel-threaded hair, as glossy as Aleppo's, that invited the smoothing touch of my hand.

Once, unexpectedly, he turned to share a smiling remark and caught my eyes upon him. His smile faded and I saw a knot of muscle tighten in his jaw. "Violet?" he murmured. The breath caught in my throat. Then, before anything could come of it, a burst of merriment floated in from down the corridor.

My perspective restored, I moved away to a safer distance, once again unsettled by the shifting perceptions that had plagued me since the moment of my arrival at Brambledene. Nothing stayed the same. It was like being trapped in a huge kaleidoscope in which people, instead of bits of colored glass, were reflected in an endless variety of patterns. Even the house itself was a changeling.

"I wonder if there's anything of interest in Victor's room," I called back over my shoulder to Rafe as I started down the corridor.

"Since that was where the tutor was housed, I expect it was largely furnished with discards," Rafe said, following in my wake.

"Ah, but one generation's discards often seem like treasures to the next."

The door was standing ajar. I opened it wider the better to see the crazy quilt folded across the end of the narrow bed. Reminded of the fragment Jack used as a polishing cloth, I stepped forward, eager for a closer look.

Rafe hung back. "I'm not sure Victor would appreciate our invading his quarters without permission, Violet, treasure or no."

I huffily disregarded his cautionary words, but the sound of approaching footsteps—it was Ned and Victor, returned from their errands—forced a hasty retreat.

"What's this talk of treasure?" Ned's voice caroled cheerfully. "I doubt there's anything worth a second look here. When Freddie and I were assigned this room last year, our steerage status put our noses quite out of joint; this year it's poor Victor's honker that's been dislocated."

Victor winced at the vulgarism, but Ned just grinned. They smelled of horses and woodsmoke. A pleasant odor, but it reminded me of my conversation with Milo in the stables and his rather obliquely phrased suggestion that I turn a blind eye in regard to the extent of Billy's injuries. Just why, I still wasn't altogether sure.

I looked up into Ned's smiling blue eyes. He looked about as devious as a spaniel puppy.

"Sorry, Ned, but the treasures I seek are fashioned from cotton, wool, linen, and silk. The only gold to be found is in an occasional thread of embroidery."

"How awfully womanly of you, Violet." How boring, is

what he meant, of course.

Rafe scowled. In the interest of avoiding another clash, Victor suggested we go to see what progress had been made with the decorations. I trailed along reluctantly, and as we entered the schoolroom my spirits fell further at the sight of a row of frilled hearts, newly refurbished, that Lily had fashioned for last year's ill-fated party from a length of red flannel and intricately cut papers.

The sight of them recalled to my mind the bone-chilling rawness of the weather that afternoon. A mixture of snow and sleet had been falling since dawn, but I had grown bored with the preparations for the party and had wandered into the schoolroom hoping to coax Lily into taking a walk with me. I can remember her saying, as she continued to snip away painstakingly at the stiff, parchment-like sheets, that she would rather cut paper inside than capers outside on a day like that. How I had laughed! I gave in and joined her, of course, and I recognized the next-to-last heart in the row, the cock-eyed one, as my handiwork.

It was too much. I left abruptly, and as I retreated back up the corridor toward the parlor I heard footsteps behind me, and then Ned's voice calling my name. Catching up with me, he linked his arm through mine and began murmuring comforting words. Grateful at first for this revival of the solicitousness he had shown me in the weeks after Lily's death, it only gradually dawned on me that Ned hadn't the faintest idea why I was upset now, and when Rafe came striding up a moment later to suggest in a challenging tone that a revivifying walk around the grounds would do me a world of good, I sensed with dismay that I had unwittingly become the rallying point for an exercise in male domination. As the two men glared at each other over my head, I expected any moment to hear them snort and paw at the Sarouk rug in lieu of a dusty patch of ground.

Undecided whether to be insulted or amused, I turned

my back on them both, and as I climbed the stairs I was aware of them, deprived of their symbol, going their separate ways.

Once upstairs, I closed the door of my room, lay down on my bed, and stared up at the ceiling where the shadows of the wand-like ends of the big beech's leafless branches crisscrossed restlessly. I felt achy and irritable and my gritty eyes complained of lack of sleep. Perhaps, I mused, being left on Papa's hands had its compensations, not the least of which was being spared buffeting by the emotional currents I sensed swirling through Brambledene.

Questions thronged my weary brain: questions about Rose's relationship with Ned, Rafe's with Rose, and Victor's with any and all of us. Yes, I decided, Victor was the most puzzling enigma of all. Undeniably charming, unfailingly patient and yet so . . . elusive. He seemed always ready to bend to the needs of others, and yet I could grasp no real sense of him as a person with needs of his own.

Rafe had suggested that by now I probably realized that Victor wasn't as dashing as he looked, as if it were somehow Victor's fault. But surely his wife's suicide must have marked him as it had Rose; the misery it caused them both was enough to dampen anyone's dash, and yet . . .

A picture of Ned, jaunty as ever, flashed into my mind. If Rafe thought Victor's lack of dash a fault, why did he have such a poor opinion of Ned's resilience? I mentally shrugged. One might as well compare apples and oranges. Ned had once told me his father had wanted him to follow in his footsteps. "Being a doctor is bad enough," he had said, "but a *pathologist?* Imagine being the kind of man whose notion of a suitable Saturday morning outing for a father and his young son is a visit to the mortuary!" His exaggerated shudder had made me laugh in spite of his expression of distaste for my father's profession. "I want to practice the art of living, Vi," he had said. "I don't really give a hoot about how people sicken and die!" Ned didn't give much of a hoot about other people's opinion of him, either. "I'd rather be envied than respected," he had once declared to me.

I sighed as Milo's words echoed in my head: *sometimes it's better to believe what suits the situation.* I wondered if it wasn't even better to believe what suited *me.* I would, after all, soon be gone from this uneasy house, separated once again from the old friends from whom I had already begun to drift apart, leaving behind the glowing, undulating shape in the Bramble . . .

Enough. It was clear that no easy answers were forthcoming. My eyelids fluttered shut, and I escaped for a while into blessed sleep.

CHAPTER NINE

I awoke from my nap feeling much refreshed, and when Rose suggested after dinner that we play charades I responded enthusiastically.

As we sipped our coffee, served by Ada in the parlor, I noticed with amusement that several of our number had fallen into the staring silences that to a practised charades player like myself signify the effort to devise original, clever, and fiendishly difficult categories with which to confound the opposition, even though in practice it was usually the simplest notions that proved the hardest to convey.

Rose appointed Iris and me team captains and prevailed upon our lame duck, Wink, to serve as timekeeper. No sooner, however, had he gallantly retired with his cane to the sidelines than Victor was pounced upon as Iris's first choice for her team.

Iris's energetic capture of her father brought a frown to Rose's brow. Her annoyance, vented in a snappish marital exchange, served to goad Ned into an unseemly display of flirtatiousness with me as its object, whereupon I, resentful of being used again as a means to someone else's end, chose Rafe for the place on my team that Ned had expected to fill.

The pleasurably anticipated entertainment, already off on the wrong foot, soon deteriorated further. Wink, deciding he could not bear to be separated by so much as a room's length from his beloved, and perhaps a bit jealous of the handsome Count's polite attentions, lumberingly displaced Victor. Rafe, after muttering uncharitable comments about Ned's crudeness and Wink's besottedness, announced to the company at large that he had no intention of playing a game that had provoked such childish clashes of temperament before it had even begun.

This blanket indictment did not sit well. Taking advantage of my team captaincy, I arbitrarily assigned Rafe to Wink's abandoned post as timekeeper, which in charades is equivalent to being sent to Coventry, and ended my foray by hauling Victor bodily over to my side of the parlor to fill Rafe's involuntarily vacated position. Rose, whose prerogative as hostess I had high-handedly usurped, was not pleased.

"Really, Violet, sometimes I think you've been left on *your* papa's hands too long."

I prudently decided to let her ill-tempered remark pass without comment, but Flora's curiosity got the better of her.

"Whatever makes you say that, Rose?"

"Ever since she arrived she's been flitting about from one man to another in a way rather typical of someone about to enter the ranks of confirmed spinsterhood."

Flora stared at her hostess openmouthed, clearly appalled at having innocently invited the opening of this unsuspected Pandora's box.

Rose turned to me. "I really think you should get out more, Violet."

Although she may have hoped her unsolicited advice would dilute the acid of her earlier remarks, the result was quite the opposite; nevertheless, I held my peace. What can you say when an old friend publicly equates you with a neurotic butterfly?

"Come now, Rose," I heard Rafe say from behind me. "Spinsters are never confirmed, only bachelors are."

His drawl expressed amusement more than reproof,

but when I turned, surprised, to look at him, the watchful look in his gray eyes told me that his disarming, seemingly offhand remark had been carefully calculated.

"Besides," he continued, "I think the foolishness we've all been prey to this evening has been enough to drive anyone to desperate measures. I say we vote to disband before our swords' points result in further bloodletting."

"Hear! Hear!" Freddie exclaimed. "What d'ye say then, all in favor?"

"Aye!" The response was resoundingly unanimous.

The company drifted away in smaller groups of twos and threes, but although I longed to join the Latimers and Ned, from whom I heard Flora coaxing tales of his adventures in the gold camps, I thought better of it. I had no wish to present Rose with another opportunity to distort my motives.

I passed by Rafe on my way into the library. "Thank you," I murmured.

He raised his eyebrows questioningly.

"It was decent of you to attempt to rescue me."

"I was 'rescuing' Rose as well, Vi. I'm afraid her attachment to Victor sometimes overrides her better judgment. Besides, you had good reason to be annoyed with my boorish remark about a pastime everyone else here obviously enjoys."

I inclined my head thoughtfully to one side. "I think boorish is too strong a term," I said solemnly. "Priggish, perhaps?"

Rafe winced. "I'd rather be thought a boor, if you don't mind. Prigs are so . . . nasty-nice."

"Very well, then. I promise to tell anyone who asks that Rafael Taliaferro is not to be mistaken for a prig. He is a boor and proud of it."

Grinning, he extended his hand; grinning, I took it, but instead of the brisk shake intended, my hand lingered in his. The feel of his warm skin against mine was almost sensual, and as his fingers slid caressingly across my knuckles my hand pressed closer still, as if to capture an image of his palm in mine. I stared down at our clasped hands, an ordinary amalgam of skin and blood and bone, and yet the sensation that swept through me could not, I think, have been more intense had we been joined, flesh to flesh, head to toe. Dazed, I lifted my eyes wonderingly to his, and looked into molten silver. He had felt it, too.

I pulled my hand free and hurried past him into the library. I could feel his hot eyes on the back of my neck as I tried to choose a title from among the rows of leather-bound sets, but the gilt-lettered spines were a meaningless blur. I didn't discover until later, just before getting into bed, that the volume I finally in desperation chose, largely because of its scarlet binding, was a collection of sermons on the seven deadly sins. Resisting the impulse to hurl the offending tome across the room, I turned to the windows and stood staring out at a scene made luminous by moonshine.

"Oh, Lily," I breathed. "What is happening to me?"

But tonight there was no glow wavering in the bramble beyond the hedges, and even the memory of it seemed to cast doubt on my sanity.

Spinster. A disappointed, desperate woman given to queer notions, that's what the word signified didn't it? Was Rose right? Was I on the verge of that fateful transition from a girl who had not yet found Mr. Right, to spinsterhood? The worst of it was that deep down I knew that Rose's suspicions were founded in truth. I had no romantic interest in Victor Stirbey, of course—the jealousy of a fiercely devoted motherless daughter had created that particular fantasy. But there was no point in pretending that my feelings in regard to Rafe Taliaferro and Ned Poole conformed to what young women of my class had been told was the maidenly norm: one man at a time, preferably at arm's length until the marriage trap had been sprung; married men, never.

I recalled Lily reading me a line from Ouida's *Under Two Flags*, a deliciously florid novel passed surreptitiously from book bag to book bag the term before we graduated. Lily, who was in one of her convention-defying moods at the time, had held it in her lap at lunch, right under Miss Peeble's long nose.

"Listen to this, Vi," she had hissed. "'There will always be millions of commonplace women ready to keep up the decorous traditions of their sex . . . one little lioness here and there in a generation cannot do overmuch harm.' There! What do you think? Shall we practice roaring?"

Our redoubtable headmistress, observing our whispers, had favored us with one of her famously steely glares. "If one hadn't ample reason to know better, Lily," she had remarked from the head of our table, "one might assume from your bowed head that you were praying. Kindly attend to the conversation of your lunch companions. You might learn something."

"Speaking of lionesses . . ." I had hissed back.

The memory of that incident made me achingly aware of the extent of my loss. I sighed and trudged back to my bed, feeling hardly capable now of anything more than a halfhearted, domesticated meow, but if Lily had lived . . . oh, yes, if Lily had lived even Ned might have been taken aback by the lustiness of our roars.

Lily had, of course, been aware of my feelings for Ned. She had had a sixth sense about the romantic yearnings of all her friends, but she was especially sensitive to mine. Lily, however, had never taken me to task about it, as Rose had done.

"I know you won't believe me, Vi," she had said once, when I had given way to tearful self-pity, "but Ned's not for you. You could never keep up with him."

"What makes you think you're so much fleeter of foot than I?" I had cried.

Lily had smoothed back the hair from my tear-streaked cheeks. "What I should have said was that you wouldn't *want* to keep up with him." I remember how sad and knowing her expression was as she chucked me under the chin. "Dear, sweet Vi," she had murmured.

It was Lily who had given the timorous girl I had been the courage to hope for an interesting, fulfilling life. Since her death, I had allowed myself to be captured by my ailing father's needs at the expense of the dreams Lily had nurtured.

On impulse, I pulled the bedclothes over my head and gave an experimental roar. It was feeble and uncertain, a soprano snarl more suited to a house cat than a jungle predator, but with practice and determination perhaps I might one day give the bars of my cage a mighty rattle.

At breakfast next morning, Rose offered an apology for her remarks to me the previous evening, which I of course accepted, although I knew its hurtful traces would remain to cloud our relationship. Judging from Victor's sad, anxious expression as he hovered in the background of our brief exchange, he shared my unhappy certainty.

How I regretted the gradual disconnection of our relationships! In its heyday, news of the LOPH's frolics spread well beyond our little group. Our envied outings were the models for others in our New York set, but finding just the right family mix was apparently as difficult as producing a perfect soufflé. It took only one parental breath of cold air to collapse the best laid plans of youthful larks. There wasn't any recipe for our success; it had been serendipity, pure and simple. Alas, nothing was pure and simple anymore, save, perhaps, for Freddie Latimer.

I couldn't help but smile as I watched him refill his plate from the breakfast buffet. His eyes sparkled as he spooned creamy scrambled eggs into the nook created by three links of sausage, but when he realized he had no room left on his plate for the crisp bacon next in line his round face radiated distress. I stepped into the breach.

"Open wide, dear," I commanded as I plucked a strip of bacon from the platter. Freddie did so, and I fed it bite by bite into his eager mouth.

Flora, who was next in line behind her brother, giggled. "Good heavens, Vi, just like a mother bird! Next thing you know you'll be gathering twigs and building a nest."

"I rather doubt it, Flora," I said drily. "Not unless a father bird comes along in the meantime. Besides, Freddie is growing much too tubby to fit into any nest I might build."

"There you go again, Vi!" Freddie exclaimed. "I do wish you wouldn't make my person the butt of your jokes."

Freddie looked bewildered by our burst of laughter, then grew flustered as he realized what he had said. It was like old times.

"I've an idea!" I impulsively proposed. "What d'ye say we walk off our breakfast bacon? I haven't been down to the river yet, and a tramp through the meadows would do us all a world of good."

Rose and Victor begged off on the grounds of domestic responsibilities. Freddie, clearly weighing the comparative advantages of staying warm indoors or, by coming along with me, escaping further party preparation chores, chose the latter course. Flora, Iris, and Wink, who was eager for fresh air and a chance to exercise his sore muscles, made up the rest of the party, Ned and Rafe having not yet put in an appearance.

In deference to Wink, we decided to take the wagon path that wound down through the pastures and around a willow-bordered bit of swampy ground before ending at the river. As we passed the stables we waved at Milo and Jack, both of whom were on horseback and heading for a fenced ring where another rider was already putting a bay horse through its paces. It was Rafe. The distinctive set of his shoulders and elegant shape of his dark head was unmistakable even at this distance.

"That Taliaferro's a good rider," Freddie conceded

grudgingly. "Ned's just as good, of course—a different style, but just as good."

"He'd be even better if he weren't such a wild Indian," I suggested with a nod in Wink's direction.

"Oh, now, Vi, that's not fair!" Freddie protested. "It was just that one time. You can't condemn a man for that. Ned's a jolly good sort! Didn't he promise to look after Lily when he learned her fortune was almost certainly gone?"

My steps slowed. I had thought that Ned had been no more aware than the rest of us of Lily's disastrous financial situation until after she died. "Are you sure about that, Freddie?"

"Of course I'm sure!" Freddie returned indignantly. "Our firm handled the legal end of her affairs, and I don't mind telling you that my father had suspicions early on about the probity of Lily's guardian. Unfortunately, by the time we had proof it was too late." Freddie hesitated. "It may not have been my place to tell Ned," he confided, "but they were engaged to be married, after all. If anyone could've cushioned the blow, it was Ned."

"I'm sure I would have done the same in your place, Freddie."

He shook his head sadly. "It was a bad business, Vi. A bad business all around."

I sighed. "Well, at least Lily went to her grave not knowing she was a pauper."

Freddie, grasping at straws of comfort, brightened. "She would have hated that, wouldn't she?"

I squeezed his arm. "Yes, she would." Actually, I thought it more likely that Lily, once the first shock passed, would have considered it a challenge. I could almost hear her excited chatter. *Not a typist, Vi, that would be too dreary, but maybe an actress or a Paris artist's model or—I know! I'll buy a caravan and become a Gypsy!* . . . A blond Gypsy. Yes, that would have suited Lily's style admirably.

Flora trotted up to join us. "If ever there were proof of three being a crowd," she sniffed.

I smiled. "I can't imagine Wink deliberately making anyone feel unwelcome."

"Oh, not Wink, Vi. It's Iris. She acted as if I weren't there at all."

I had a sudden mental picture of a stork overlooking a chickadee. "She'll come around in time, Flora."

"But we've been friends *heaps* longer than she and Wink have been . . ." Flora colored and shrugged. Lovers, is what she had been going to say.

"And you will be again," I promised. But it won't be the same, I thought. Nothing will be, for any of us. "Can you imagine Iris discussing the latest Paris fashions with Wink?"

"I can't!" Freddie hooted. "I doubt Wink can tell a fichu from a furbelow."

"No more can you, Brother!" Flora retorted, much restored.

We went on together, arm in arm, chattily exchanging nothing of consequence, but Flora's spirits took another plunge as the road dipped through the brambly hummocks edging the low marsh that lay between us and the river.

"Ooooh, I'm ankle deep in ice water!" she cried, as her pretty kid boots broke through the thin glaze that masked the depths of the ruts. She lifted her skirt and inspected her sodden, muddied footwear with dismay, then looked up at Freddie and me expectantly.

"We're so near the river, Floss," Freddie said apologetically. "I hate to turn back now."

"Vi?" Flora looked at me imploringly.

"I borrowed stouter boots than mine from Rose, and as Freddie said, we're so near—"

"Suit yourselves, then," she cut in. "All I know is it's too far for me, no matter how near it may be." She turned away with a toss of her head.

"Where are you off to, Flora?" Iris inquired cheerfully as she and Wink overtook us. "The river's just a hop, skip, and a jump from here."

"Oh, bother the river," Flora snapped. "I've done all

the hopping, skipping, and jumping I intend to do for the rest of our stay. I've already ruined my boots."

"If you'd packed what I suggested—"

"Not everyone takes a steamer trunk along on a country weekend, Iris!" Flora glared at her friend and started back up the hill, her strawberry-blond curls bouncing with every indignant step.

"Whatever is the matter with Flora?" Iris asked plaintively. "She's been out of sorts all morning."

"We're all a bit on edge, Iris."

"We are? I can't imagine why."

Iris's great brown eyes looked blankly from Freddie to me. Such beautiful eyes! As soft and moist as a Jersey cow's, and about as perceptive. I sighed. "It's of no consequence, Iris. Come along, the river beckons."

As we stood side by side on the frosty bank, Wink grinned at me. "The river's not doing much beckoning today, Vi."

As Victor had predicted, the Ashley wore a thick shawl of ice as it meandered through the meadows. Further up, where the hills began to break up out of the valley in rocky thrusts, one could hear the distant chuckling of water falling too fast to freeze. The steep slopes were clothed in hemlocks whose dark branches were iced by the spray where the river, broken by ancient, glacier-borne boulders, tumbled into a myriad of streamlets before rejoining in a single silent glide. It would be a lovely place to explore in summer, but today . . . I shivered.

Freddie stamped his feet and crooked his arm for me to grasp. "Home, Violet?"

I turned away regretfully, somehow knowing I would not return to Brambledene in any season. For good or ill, this weekend would mark the end of a chapter in my life. It could have been worse; it had, God knows, been worse for Lily, but I couldn't help wondering what might have been.

"Freddie, I know you said that Ned vowed to look after Lily, but did he still mean to marry her?" I paused.

Knowing Freddie, I suddenly regretted my idle question. "It's not *quite* the same thing, you know."

Freddie stopped short. "Of course he would have married her, Vi! You've been listening to Victor and that Taliaferro chap, haven't you?"

"Oh, Freddie, please don't—"

He waved his hands. "I don't want to hear any more about it, Vi. I don't care if they *are* Rose's family. They've never liked Ned, never thought him good enough. Damned foreigners! That high muck-a-muck cousin of Rose's sniffing around after Lord knows what and looking down his nose at everyone."

Freddie began to pace back and forth; I'd never seen him so agitated. He shook his finger under my nose. "First Ned loses his partner in that frightful accident, then his fiancée is murdered—Good God, Vi, hasn't he suffered enough without being accused of fortune hunting, and by you, of all people! There was a time when Flora and I thought that you and Ned—" He stopped abruptly, reddening.

I knew what he and Flora had thought; so had I for a time, which made Freddie's tirade all the harder to bear.

"I never accused him, Fred!"

"Suspected him, then."

"Not even that!" I searched his unyielding face. He looked years older; years . . . *harder*.

"I see Flossie's paused at the brow of the hill. I'll try to catch up with her, if you don't mind, Violet. She seemed so upset earlier."

Meaning, of course, that he knew the order in which loyalties should rank even if I did not. "Go along, Freddie. As a matter of fact, I'd enjoy some time alone."

Correctly interpreting my remark to mean that I was dismissing him, rather than the other way around, Freddie stalked off huffily.

I soon discovered I wasn't too keen on being left alone with my thoughts just then, so I waited for Iris and Wink to catch up. Iris's curiosity turned out to be stronger than her desire for a twosome.

"What on earth is going on, Vi? First Flora, now Freddie rushing up the hill like mountain goats."

Wink burst out laughing. "More like two of the three little pigs, sweetheart, all huffing and puffing. Who's the wolf, Vi? Not you, certainly!"

I shrugged and smiled wryly.

"Well, if you ask me," Iris offered in a conspiratorial tone, "it could have started last night. You know how Freddie loves charades, Vi, then Rafe made that cheeky remark about us acting like children, remember, Wink?"

"Quite uncalled for," Wink murmured dutifully, but his sheepish look made me suspect he shared Rafe's opinion.

We continued our walk at a regal pace, in deference to Wink. His limp was more pronounced now than when we started, but knowing how he would hate any mention of it, I searched out opportunities to give him a moment's rest.

"Really, Violet," Iris said as I paused yet again, "I don't see why every leafless tree and narrow vista we pass is worthy of remark."

Wink leaned on his borrowed stick as he surveyed the scene I had indicated. "It is a capital place though, isn't it?" He took a deep breath of the crisp, clean air. "It's no wonder Ned has such plans for it. Grander than I would make, but Ned always was a bit of a high-flyer."

"Your brother was a classmate of his at Yale, wasn't he?"

"He was, and he had some stories to tell about him, too. Not all of them fit for ladies' ears, girls. Ned was a big man on campus, full of plans even then, and whenever there was a town-gown rowdy-dow he was sure to be in the thick of it. Popular as all get-out." Wink paused consideringly. "Funny he was never tapped for Bones. My brother never would say why, sworn to secrecy and all that. It may have had something to do with the Pooles. Worthy people, mind you, but . . ." He shrugged.

"I would have thought his Van Renssalaer blood would have out-blued the lesser varieties."

Wink looked uncomfortable. "The secret societies are a tradition kind of thing, Vi. There's not always sense to it, but there you are."

There you are, indeed! That was the trouble with the world: too many standpatters like Wink. "But he did graduate with his class."

Wink looked shocked. "A man's club has nothing to do with his diploma, Vi! He graduated, and then, just as everyone else was settling in down on Wall Street or some family bank or business or other, Ned went West." Wink scratched his auburn head. "To my recollection, Ned was the only Yale man in my day who actually followed Greeley's advice. 'Course, it was pretty old hat by that time."

"It proved lucrative for Ned, though."

"Lucrative?" The word seemed to puzzle him at first, then recognition dawned. "You mean the strike in Colorado! Yes, to hear him tell it, I guess it was lucrative, all right. Regular wild west stuff."

"His partner was killed, Wink."

"I know, Vi, it's just that . . . well, I seem to store away only the good memories. Take Brambledene, for instance. To me, it will always be the place where Iris and I fell in love." He looked at me shamefacedly. "I guess you think I'm a pretty shallow fellow."

I put my hand on his arm. "No, Wink, what I think is that you're very dear, and if Iris doesn't take good care of you I'll . . . I'll punch her in the nose!"

"You'd have to catch me first, Vi!" Iris taunted, her dark eyes flashing.

We gathered up our skirts and sprinted up the hill, followed by Wink's delighted shout of laughter. It was the last truly lighthearted moment I can remember enjoying at Brambledene.

CHAPTER TEN

Lunch was a quiet affair. Flora, pointedly ignoring Iris, questioned Rose about the local gentry who had been invited to the Valentine costume party; Freddie, avoiding my eye, joined Wink and Ned's lively discussion about the probability of the automobile displacing the horse as a means of private transportation.

Flora's conversation with Rose soon attracted Iris's attention, and before long the two old friends were chattering away together as animatedly as ever. I smiled, pleased to see the morning's frictions smoothed away. Although Iris's marriage to Wink would create a certain distance between them, their friendship need not be much affected unless Flora chose to magnify the inevitable lessening of its girlhood dimensions.

"I'm pleased to see all my beautiful blossoms abloom again, Violet," Victor said to me in an avuncular tone. "Your smile has been a rarity of late, although I must confess that all this talk of horseless carriages is enough to rob me of my own."

I laughed. "You and Milo Devlin are birds of a feather when it comes to automobiles, Victor, but although I appreciate your feelings about horses you must admit that the streets of New York would be pleasanter without them."

"Ah, so you share Rafe's opinion on that score!" he

said with a rueful smile. "At least you have the excuse of not having much fondness for horses."

"I wasn't aware Rafe and I agreed on the subject." I was, however, very much aware of his absence from the table. "He appears to have missed lunch," I said as one of Ada's helpers came in to clear the sideboard. "I trust nothing is amiss."

"When last I saw him, he was deep in a discussion of the Arkham bloodlines with Milo and Jack, so I asked Ada to send a packet of sandwiches out to the stable. Rafe's very impressed with the breed."

"Didn't I see him exercising one of them in the ring this morning?"

"Yes, that would have been Rafe," Victor confirmed. "He's a splendid horseman, undaunted by anything on four hooves, regardless of temperament. Milo says he takes after my late wife in that respect . . ." Victor's eyes dropped. His slowly exhaled breath was almost a sigh. I waited in silence as he visibly pulled himself together.

"That's why I think him more traitorous than you, my dear," he continued lightly, tapping the back of my hand with his forefinger, "when he dares speak well of conveyances that do without horses altogether."

His teasing smile animated his long thin face, smoothing away the fine lines that had begun their tracery during the last year.

Aware of Rose's pale blue eyes slanting toward us, I quietly withdrew my hand and placed it in my lap. "It's a different generation, Victor."

His fine-drawn face clouded. "Yes. Yes, it is. I keep forgetting . . ." He looked troubled, almost haunted, but he wore his years well. The few signs of age—a touch of gray, the furrows fanning from the corners of his eyes and the slight pouching beneath them—lent character to a face that when young was probably so handsome as to lack interest.

"Violet? Could I impose upon you to supply a new centerpiece for the table? The holly's looking a bit worse for its long wear."

I looked across at Rose speculatively, suspecting her request was intended to separate Victor from me and my spinsterish wiles, but a closer look at the holly leaves revealed disfiguring spots of black fungus, and then, to my further chagrin, I recalled Rose's reluctance to enter the conservatory. "I'll be happy to, Rose. Something bright and springlike might be nice for a change."

"It would indeed, Vi. If you have any questions about a suitable selection, I'm sure Mrs. Devlin will be happy to advise you."

Not if I can avoid it, I resolved as, sweetly smiling, I took my leave.

I had no sooner taken stock of what the conservatory had to offer in the way of spring flowers than Mrs. Devlin came gliding in, almost as if she had been waiting in the wings for her entrance cue.

"Mrs. Poole said as how you might be wanting to speak with me about flowers."

She nodded as I explained my purpose and handed me the secateurs she had used to cut the bouquet I had placed on Lily's grave. "Are you enjoying your stay?" she asked as she picked up a short, curved pruning knife from the bench top for herself. It seemed an odd question considering that the last time I had seen her was at the polo game that had ended so disastrously. "Milo says he saw you young people strolling down toward the river this morning. A pretty walk, isn't it?"

"Yes, we found it so," I agreed. "I was especially taken with the view of the hemlock grove from the river. It was too far away to see the falls clearly, but I would imagine it's a lovely picnic spot in summer."

Ada's hands clenched around a pot of daffodils she had selected for me. Their sunny blooms contrasted sharply with the dread that overspread her face.

"Not in the Cobble, Miss Grayson. Never in the Cobble."

"Why ever not?" I asked, perplexed by her alarm. "Even though steep, and in places slippery no doubt, there must be any number of inviting shady nooks next to the falls, and on a hot August day—"

"There are caves in the Cobble, too, Miss Grayson. My Arkham ancestors blocked many of their dank, foul-smelling openings scores of years ago. But there are many more that no one will ever find."

"But what is the worst one might encounter there, Mrs. Devlin? A fox, or perhaps a bobcat? I doubt the caves are large enough to accommodate something truly fearsome." I turned away, hoping to end the conversation, and picked up two pots of hyacinths, one white, the other blue.

Ada moved closer and clutched at my arm.

"They needn't be big," she confided. "The Old Ones practiced many shapes and sizes while they waited in Lake Miskatonic, out beyond where the weeds grow thick along shore."

The Old Ones? The hyacinths quivered as I tried to pull away; their sweet, cloying perfume wafted into my nostrils, making my head swim.

Ada's grip tightened.

"One day long ago, long before the memory of humankind, the earth's very foundation cracked somewhere far below us." She glanced warily down at the moss-slimed bricks as if expecting them to shift beneath our feet. The pot of daffodils in her hand tilted perilously. "No one knows the how or why of it, though some have their guesses," she added in a harsh whisper, "but after a while—years beyond counting by our reckoning—the lake fingered down into those cracks and began to pry. It pried here and scrabbled there, searching out a path to the sea, and in the doing of it provided the Old Ones with watery paths to new hunting grounds."

"Surely you can't believe that, Mrs. Devlin!" I scoffed. She blinked at my disbelieving tone, and I took advantage of the momentary relaxation of her grip to wrench my arm free of her bony clutch. "It's superstition, nothing more. A legend told small children, lest they wander too far from home."

Ada stood intimidatingly erect, her arms falling by her sides. "A legend? Ayuh, I grant you that, miss, but d'ye not know that legends mask the truths we cannot bear to see? I learned this one, as all Arkham babies do, while still suckling at my mother's breast, and it will be a part of me"—she thumped her own breast fiercely—"until the day I die!" She laughed harshly. "Milo says I'm moonstruck, but I know what I know!"

Her jet eyes, staring down at me from her commanding height, were mesmerizing. I felt as helpless as a rabbit caught in the beam of a hunter's lantern.

Assured of her audience's continued, if unwilling, attention, Ada uttered a grunt of satisfaction before resuming her strange narrative.

"Long before the river's course was set, the waters oozed here and there through crannies in the Cobble, gnawing runnels that can be entered from beneath its present banks."

She paused to give me time to reconcile my image of shallow dens of woodland creatures with the far more sinister picture emerging from her words. She took the hyacinths from my nerveless hands and placed them with the daffodils on the bench beside me. She leaned closer.

"They move through water, the Old Ones do, and when the rivulets supplied by summer storms and melting snows trickle down to those ancient passageways far below, as they sometimes do, when the rain is heavy and the snow deep . . ." She paused to let me absorb the portent of her words. "The Old Ones are good at waiting, Miss Grayson. They've had such a very long time in which to learn, you see. Time beyond imagining by the likes of you and me."

The smile with which Ada Devlin concluded her corrupt tale was more suited to a Sunday School homily, which made me all the more anxious to escape her malign presence. But she continued to block my path, and the look in her black eyes, an almost furtive watchfulness, filled me with dread, for I sensed—no, more than that, I *knew* that she had not yet finished with me.

"Mrs. Devlin, please let me pass . . ." I despised the quaver in my voice.

Pretending she had not heard me, she cocked her head to one side in a caricature of sudden recollection. "It had snowed that day, hadn't it, Miss Grayson? And all the previous day, too. A terrible depth of snow followed by a sudden thaw. I remember the water running in the drains. Poor Miss Forrester . . ."

I clapped my hands over my ears. *My God! What horror was she suggesting!*

Her eyes were alight with an intent I could not begin to fathom. A rage of frustration took possession of me.

"Are you completely mad? I saw who killed Lily! It was a creature of flesh and blood, like you and me! I saw that quilt-shrouded figure; I heard those running feet! The police said, they told me . . ."

As the words tumbled out I was dismayed to find I could no longer make sense of the jumble in my head. I thought of the hours Ned had patiently devoted to helping me untangle the twisted strands of my tormented memories—yet here I was, again unable to separate my recall of what I had actually seen from what I had been led to believe. Tears stung my eyes. I bit my lip and tasted the warm saltiness of blood. I would not give her the satisfaction of seeing me cry.

"*What do you want from me?*" I rasped.

"*Want* from you, Miss Grayson? I want nothing! I only mean to warn you that there are things here . . ." Her shoulders slumped, and all at once she looked tired and worn. "You're all so young and fresh, and Mrs. Poole . . ."

"What about Mrs. Poole?"

"She plans to stay, her and Mr. Poole. I'm not sure it's wise, Miss Grayson. Perhaps if you tell her—"

"Tell her what, Mrs. Devlin?" I masked my alarm with contempt. "That there are demon creatures here, ancient beings oozing down from Arkham to Brambledene, wrapping themselves in quilts, glowing in the Bramble—" I broke off, appalled. I had not meant to say that; I had not suspected I was even thinking about it.

"What did you see in the Bramble, Miss Grayson?"

She leaned toward me, her avidly searching black eyes penetrating mine like shards of obsidian. I cried out, and as I pushed past her, my flailing, heedless arms sent the pots we had selected clattering to the moss-slimed bricks.

I fled down the corridor, dim after the bright flat light of the conservatory, and ran headlong into Victor as he opened the door to his room. I clung to him, my tears released by the comfort of his familiarity, and he led me in, the better to calm me.

Rose found us there, perched on the edge of her father's bed, my head on his shoulder, his hand gently smoothing my hair as I sobbed in great, gulping gusts.

"Aren't Rafe and Ned enough for you?" Rose drawled scornfully.

"Come, Rose!" Victor protested. "The girl's had a frightful shock of some sort . . . she came bolting out of the conservatory as if the devil himself—"

Rose laughed. It wasn't a pleasant sound. "Her sly scheming doesn't fool me! Tears and fears are a tried and true way of wooing male attention and sympathy, isn't that true, Vi? But it won't work this time, because I'll never let him go!"

I stared up at Rose out of tear-blurred eyes. Her face was distorted; her mouth thinned and ugly with hate. *Had everyone in this odious house gone mad?*

"Rose! Think what you're saying!" Victor said in a low, tense voice.

I wiped my eyes with the backs of my hands. "I have no designs on anyone, Rose. The blame for the sorry state you found me in belongs to Ada Devlin and her accursed tales, hinting of things too horrible to repeat. The woman's steeped in superstition; I should have known better than to let her—"

"*What* horrible things?" Rose demanded. "Ada has never been anything less than an admirable housekeeper, as good in her domain as Milo is in his. I suspect these 'horrible things' you speak of are a product of your own devious imagination."

I sprang to my feet and began to pace. I twisted my hands. She had left me no choice. "Rose, Ada Devlin doesn't think the Raggedy Man killed Lily. She thinks someone . . . some *thing* else was responsible. She says—"

I broke off, alarmed, as Rose swayed and turned a chalky white. "She's wrong, of course," I cried, trying to convince myself as much as Rose. "I know what I saw!"

Rose slumped into Victor's arms. "She's been under a strain," he said quietly. "She doesn't really mean what she said." He nodded toward the door. "Leave us, Violet, please."

I left them, of course, what else could I do? Rose's increasingly erratic behavior worried me, but she had a husband and a father to look out for her. I hadn't appreciated Rose calling me a spinster, and I liked even less being thought a schemer; I would be better employed looking out for my own well being.

There was something very strange going on at Brambledene. It was nothing I could put my finger on, but my senses responded, like the quivering of a tuning fork, to a kind of feral undercurrent that had been causing me unease ever since my arrival at that afflicted place. Heightened now by Ada Devlin's malignant tales, it threatened to overwhelm what remained of my customary good sense.

CHAPTER ELEVEN

Shaken, I headed toward the stairs. As I mounted them, I met Freddie coming briskly down. Taken by surprise, he blurted a clumsy apology for abandoning me on our morning walk. Unfortunately, my distracted reception of his attempt to make amends came across as disregard.

"Don't give it another thought, Violet!" he huffed. "*I* certainly won't."

I looked after him as he stalked into the parlor, but I couldn't summon up the energy to follow him and smooth away the hurt. As I trudged up the stairs knowing I had inadvertently placed another old friendship at risk, I could feel tears sliding down my cheeks.

"Violet? Is anything the matter?" It was Rafe, just entering the corridor above. He closed the door to his room and walked toward me. "Why, you're crying!"

"I seem to be doing a lot of it these days . . ." I sniffed and attempted a watery smile. "You know how women are." It was a cheap subterfuge, but nothing better came readily to mind.

He arched one black eyebrow. "I know how *some* women are, but I don't think you're the type to cry without good reason." He reached out to gently wipe away the wetness with his thumb. "For one thing, it makes your eyes puffy." He sounded like an indulgent uncle. "Would it help to talk about it?"

I hesitated. I was as much concerned about Rose's well-being as distressed by her attitude toward me, but I wasn't sure I should say anything about it to Rafe. Although she was his cousin, I sensed a certain strained formality between them that I found puzzling.

"It's Rose, isn't it?" he guessed shrewdly.

I nodded.

"Did you run afoul of her daughterly devotion again?"

"I'm afraid so, but it's more than that. She seems so . . . so tightly wound, like a clock spring. I'm afraid for her, Rafe. I think this house party was a very poor idea."

"I expect that seeing Brambledene as anything less than the idyllic haven her mother painted for her might seem to Rose to be an act of betrayal. According to my mother, Aunt Rosalind could be very seductive. Think how confusing being alternately smothered and ignored by a parent like that must have been for her."

"Do you think that could be why Rose resists Ned's plans?" I asked, carefully picking my way. "Might she feel trapped between her loyalty to her dead mother's illusion and his intent to change it?"

"Indeed she might," Rafe said. "In fact, I think if the decision were hers alone, Rose would close Brambledene."

Abandon Brambledene? Even granting her present distress, surely that was unlikely.

"But she has a family obligation here that I'm sure she doesn't begrudge," I protested. I told him of the touching exchange I had observed between Rose and Milo after the polo game.

"As to the first, Brambledene is, as you said, a *family* obligation, not just Rose's; as for her expression of regard for Milo Devlin," he shrugged and smiled wryly, "I guess she shares her mother's weakness."

I eyed him sharply. "If you're implying that Rose's gesture was alcohol-induced sentimentality—"

"Good Lord, Vi, I never meant you to infer anything of

the kind! I was referring to her mother's excessive fondness for animals. You were in the stables yourself when Milo mentioned it."

I had a vague recollection of something of the sort being said, but all of us were saddened by Milo's having to destroy the old horse he had raised and trained, not just Rose. Nevertheless, I was troubled, for although Rafe seemed sincerely shocked by my faulty interpretation, if Rose's emotions suffered from excess in one area of her life, why not others?

No matter how planted, a seed of that sort is quick to take root, yet I was loath to suspect Rafe of fostering deliberate misconceptions. Rose was clearly not the serene girl her friends had always thought her. I had ample reason to know that unsuspected currents swirled darkly beneath her fair, placid surface, but did that justify my wondering if Rafe hoped his cousin's mounting distress would drive her to seek solace in drink as her mother had before her? On the other hand, even if he might regret her descent into self-destruction, it could rebound to his benefit . . .

"If Rose should die," I asked, "who would inherit Brambledene?"

Rafe looked puzzled by my apparent nonsequitur. "My mother would, in the ordinary course of events, but she has already had papers drawn up—" He broke off. His eyes darkened and his finely sculpted nostrils flared, as he plunged straight to the heart of the matter.

"I won't pretend I wouldn't like to be in a position to rescue Brambledene from Ned's grandiose pretensions, but the price you seem to be proposing is one that no decent human being would ever consider paying. It deeply saddens me to learn you think I might be prepared to do so."

"I'm so sorry if I offended you," I said, "but I think the inference you unhesitatingly chose to draw from my question is interesting."

His eyes narrowed. "Tell me, Violet, how far would

you go to escape your father's growing dependency?"

"How dare you!" My rage flamed all the hotter for the guilt I perceived flickering beneath it. "I love my father! Our relationship has nothing to do with this!"

"Except to demonstrate that all relationships harbor elements of gain and loss, even loving ones." He gave a humorless bark of laughter. "Has it never occurred to you that Ned has more to gain than I? He stands to inherit the bulk of the Thornbush estate upon Rose's death."

"But not Brambledene!"

Rafe waved his hand dismissively. "He could buy another Brambledene. A bigger, better Brambledene. All he has to do is keep that marriage going just long enough—"

"Then why his attentions to me?" I demanded. "Even you remarked upon them!"

"If Rose loves him, wouldn't you say his playing at Don Juan at the least opportunity—don't think you're the only one, Violet!—amounts to putting up signposts to Lethe?"

Lethe. The river of forgetfulness. I stared at him.

"And if she doesn't love him," he continued, "if in fact Rose feels trapped in a failed, loveless marriage, I'm sure she's quite capable of finding her own way to those seductive river banks. Alcohol, ether, opium, the waters of Lethe . . ." He shrugged. "They all amount to the same thing, don't they?"

I uttered a cry of protesting disbelief. "What could Rose possibly know of such things? I've read of the Parisian taste for decadence: your new face of Eros would not dare show itself here, and neither would your vices!"

"You think not?" He looked at me incredulously. "You think because Rose played so sweetly and calmly at croquet at your . . . how do you call it, your Placid Lake, she forgets how her mother died? Your blind innocence does not become you, Violet! Beware it does not one day bring you harm."

Anger had broken the Anglicized pattern of Rafe's speech. As he stood glaring at me, an arrogant thrust to his chin, I was reminded of a novel Lily once lent me, *The Picture of Dorian Gray*. Wilde's monstrous creation might have looked thus: that sleek polished helmet of hair, smooth, unlined olive skin, and black arcs of brows over hooded eyes.

"Better innocent than corrupt!" I cried as I turned to escape into my room.

I was too agitated to rest. My room proved too small to contain my pacing—barely six steps separated the Gothic paneled bed from the similarly styled marble-topped bureau—and my throbbing temples threatened to burst the confines of my skull. I needed space and fresh air!

The day had turned colder. Clouds scudding in from the west muted the faint warmth the sun had provided on our morning walk. I plunged my hands deep into my pockets and headed for the stables seeking comfort in the warm presence of the undemanding animals housed there. Their needs, like my father's, were known and easily satisfied. Unpredictable creatures like Ned and Rafe had no place in my tidy, well-ordered life, and yet . . .

I paused, suddenly recalling Lily's exasperation when I had expressed reservations about participating in one of her adventuresome expeditions.

"That prune-faced grown-up attitude of yours is really very tiresome, Vi," I can remember her saying.

How shocked I had been. To my sixteen-year-old mind, being thought adult was my fondest wish.

"We're young, Vi!" she had countered spiritedly. "We're *supposed* to be giddy, even reckless if we've a mind to. We have the rest of our lives to act like stuffy old adults, for heaven's sake!"

Lily's life had ended before she had had to come to terms with the realities of adulthood, but I found myself wondering if perhaps she hadn't been wiser than I in her perception that cinched-in emotions could be as injurious as the tight-lacing of corsets my father deplored.

As I stood, bemused, in the wide, straw-littered passageway, I heard the sound of approaching voices. It was Rose and Victor!

Unwilling to meet them so soon after our recent unsettling encounter, I pressed back into the shadows, hoping my outline would be confused by the tangle of harness hanging from the stout post I sheltered behind. The odor of that soaped leather will forever recall to my mind the ensuing fragments of desperate dialogue never meant to be overheard.

At first it was no more than a low, undifferentiated mumble; then, rising out of it, I heard Rose's clear voice, pitched high with urgency. "We'll never be free of him, Victor! We're bound with ties of blood . . ."

I suppressed a gasp of dismay. She could only mean Rafe—who else here, other than Victor, was related by blood to Rose?

Nourished by suspicion, the seed planted earlier began to grow; its tendrils pushed through my mind, unfurling poisonous leaves. Rafe had said his mother no longer collected fine antique textiles because she was, as he put it, 'storing up gold for her old age,' but suppose his light tone masked a grimly penurious reality? Suppose Rafe wanted, *needed,* more than Brambledene? If Rose and Ned's marriage dissolved before she had children, wouldn't that place Rafe next in line for the entire Thornbush estate? Cousins can't be divorced—no wonder Rose despaired of being free of him! I had a sudden ominous image of a sleek, gray-eyed vulture patiently circling on noiseless wings in ever decreasing circles.

Their mumbled conversation slowed, then hushed. I heard a sigh and the sliding sound of feet on straw. Were they leaving? I stole a look from behind the massive post that concealed me and saw Victor take Rose in his arms.

She responded to his embrace with an eagerness that perplexed me until I saw her face. Love shone in her eyes and tenderly curved her lips, a love so strong and bright it defeated the shadows, but of a kind more expressive of a woman's yearning response to her lover than a daughter's devotion to her father.

Shocked and embarrassed, I averted my eyes and withdrew to my former position. When their murmuring resumed, I edged cautiously backward into the tack room I knew was close behind me. I had no wish to eavesdrop further lest my odious suspicions be confirmed.

The shelter I had chosen was cramped, dim, and cold. The long narrow bench set against the wall beneath a row of saddle racks was thick with dust. Without thinking, I reached for the piece of quilt Jack Stark used as a grooming cloth to wipe the surface clean so I could sit. It might be a long wait.

Idly, I picked at the ravelings along the fragment's frayed edges. Despite what Ada had darkly hinted at, I clung to the notion that Lily's killer had been all too human and wearing, perhaps, the very quilt from which this piece had been torn.

Clung to the notion . . . How very odd, I thought as the words repeated themselves in my head. Why should I feel more comfortable with the flesh and blood reality of an undoubtedly deranged derelict than the frightening and forbidden possibilities that Ada had conjured up for me, making me doubt my own sanity? Although in truth, it was hardly more difficult to accept Ada's lurking, loathsome Old Ones than to admit, even privately to myself, that Rose and Victor Stirbey might be lovers.

"That old bench'll be just as dusty again tomorrow, miss."

I looked up, startled, to see Jack Stark grinning at me from the doorway. Rose and Victor must have left.

"You seem to have taken as much a fancy to that bit of quilt as the Raggedy Man hisself." Apparently Jack did not share his sister's dreadful theory.

"You're convinced, then," I began, "that somehow it got torn away that night from—"

He didn't bother to let me finish. "Not 'somehow,' miss," he exclaimed as he moved toward me, still grinning. His breath had the rancid odor of decay. "Caught on a bramble, it did. No trick for them sharp little thorns to rip through old stuff like that. Had to be that nasty old bugger, din' it? Such a pretty girl she was . . . alive one minute, and then . . ."

Jack held out rough, chilblained hands. He turned his palms upward; thick ridges of scars jagged across them, livid against his grimy skin. His fingers bent into claws as he slowly revolved his hands and squeezed them shut.

His clutching hands vividly recalled to mind the bruises on Lily's white throat. Repelled by his cruel gesture and the sly smile that accompanied it, I sidled towards the doorway.

"My cloth, please, miss?"

Unwilling to chance the touch of his hand, I replaced it myself on its peg. His little grunt of satisfaction as I did so, as if it were a keepsake, a sort of morbid souvenir, made me shudder. I wanted nothing more than to quit the company of this unsavory fellow, but a bedeviling question remained.

"You and the police seem so sure this tramp you call the Raggedy Man killed my friend, but where has he gone? Why can't he be found and taken away?"

Jack brayed with laughter. "I never sided with the coppers on anything before, miss, but on that score I'm as sure as them. I never seed that old gaffer again after he done his wickedness. No one hereabout has, and that's a fact. But he's sure to be out there roamin' the byways, or holed up in one of his hidey places . . . or maybe prowling nearby, waitin' for another pretty girl . . ."

He clawed his hands at me again, and then, in a burst of malignant invention, he thrust out his arms and wriggled fingers that hideously mimicked clusters of long white worms.

I turned and fled, his high, excited giggle ringing in my ears.

I burst from the stable, my steps propelling me upon a collision course I failed to see until a shouted warning pulled me up short.

"Whoa, there, Vi! Where's the fire?" Wink and Iris loomed red-cheeked above me, snorting steam like a pair of Percherons.

"Do either of you have a train schedule?" I urgently inquired.

They looked at each other, then back at me, shaking their heads.

"What on earth do you want a schedule for, Vi?" Iris's huge dark eyes were as round and uncomprehending as a Persian cat's. "Aren't we all taking the same train back to New York on Sunday?"

"Come now, Vi," Wink said, giving my shoulder a brotherly pat, "I know things aren't going quite as we all had hoped. Even Iris has remarked on how nervous Rose has been acting, isn't that so, dear?"

If I had been less agitated, his remark would have made me smile. If 'even Iris' noticed something, then it must indeed be obvious to everyone else. But only I had overheard that shocking exchange between Rose and Victor; only I knew that Rose was more than nervous. She was desperate, and desperate attitudes often spur desperate actions.

I felt grievously burdened by disclosures I had never sought. How I wished Rafe had never told me that Rose's mother had taken her own life! I wondered now why he had: had he been preparing me to accept any . . . accident Rose might suffer as springing from a similarly suicidal impulse? I had often heard my father ascribe patients' ailments, even premature deaths, to "a family tendency"; was that to be Rose's fate? Would she be consigned to the earth in the Bramble with nary a question or backward glance? It hardly bore thinking about.

My anguish must have been visible on my face. "I know it's been particularly hard for you, Vi," Wink added, "but I think Rose needs us. All of us," he added pointedly.

"'All for one; one for all,'" I said automatically.

"That's always been the LOPH motto," Wink said.

"And there's the party," Iris chirped. "Don't forget the party!"

Wink allowed a trace of irritation to crease his brow. His intellect may have been nothing to brag about, but he had more capacity for empathy in his outsized little finger than Iris could muster from her entire being in a lifetime.

"Do stay, Vi," he urged. "It'll only be a few more days, after all." He grinned and waved the knobby cane Victor had lent him. "I don't really need this anymore, and what else can happen in a few more days?"

CHAPTER TWELVE

I waved Wink and Iris on ahead of me. I needed time to think. Not about what else could happen in the remaining days of our visit—for my own peace of mind it was better not to think about that at all—but about my obligation to my fellow LOPH's, especially Rose.

In the end, of course, I decided to stay. I expect Wink knew I would when he asked me. What else could I do? I had no wish to desert a ship that, although generally perceived to be in dangerous waters, no one but me could feel sinking beneath them. Even rats wait until the very last minute.

And yet I had to tell someone of my misgivings concerning Rafe and my more recent dark suspicions about Jack Stark. That odious scene in the tack room had made me wonder if Jack might not have been overlooked in the rush to assign guilt. Sometimes, as in that clever story Poe wrote about a purloined letter, we fail to see what's right under our noses.

I had only Jack's word for it that he had found his precious bit of quilt under the hedges. A pad of old sheeting would have served as well for the purpose he claimed it served. But if, as I suspected, he kept it as a kind of ghastly souvenir, like those miniature gallows hawkers used to sell at public hangings, then perhaps it was a memento of his own villainy rather than some passing derelict's. The very thought made me shudder. Imagine flaunting it like that!

Anger revived my spirits and swept away my remaining doubts. Ned was the logical choice for a confidant. Considering Rose's prickly attitude toward me, I felt shy about exchanging anything more than perfunctory courtesies with her, particularly in light of the disquieting conversation I had overheard. Her husband was the only one other than she who had the authority to send anyone packing.

After searching high and low, I found Ned in the library, the last place I expected to find him, as he was not the contemplative sort. He was seated alone at one of the long tables practicing my waterfall shuffle. Judging from the collapse of the arc before the cards completed their slide into his receiving hand, he wasn't having much success at it.

He looked up at me sheepishly. "Come, Vi, take pity on this poor clumsy wretch. My father always said I'd never amount to anything, and look at me! Even a simple shuffle is more than I can manage. Teach me your secret, and I'll be in your debt to the end of my days."

A simple shuffle? Like most skills of that sort, the easier it looked the harder it was to make it appear so. If he only knew the hours I had devoted to perfecting it! Some might say they were wasted hours, but illness had made my father querulous, and I had learned from frustrating experience that intellectual pursuits did not prosper when subject to frequent interruption.

In other circumstances, Ned's beseeching eyes and smile would have coaxed from me the answer to the Sphinx's riddle, but I was in no mood for games that afternoon.

"Later, Ned. Please, I must speak to you, and it's so difficult to find a private moment."

His smile faded. He searched my face, then satisfied that I was in earnest, he beckoned me to follow him to a heretofore unnoticed windowseat tucked in behind the spiral stairs, overlooking the Bramble. "Rose likes to curl up here sometimes with a favorite book," he said.

I could understand why. It was an inviting nook, whose long narrow Gothic-arched window had been angled so as to capture the big beech tree in the vista it overlooked. I wondered if Roswell Thornbush had planned it as a special treat for his beloved Althea. Yet I hung back from joining Ned there. Was this wise? If anyone came upon us together, all but hidden from view, might it be misinterpreted?

Ned's attentions to me could be considered excessive for a newly married man—Rafe certainly thought so—although in Ned's case, flirting was as natural as breathing. All his old friends knew that; even Rose had granted as much. As for the brash impulsiveness that had caused Wink—and poor Sergeant-Major—injury, I was sure he had not deliberately set out to cause harm, Rafe's dark hints to the contrary. As far as I was concerned, Rafe's opinions about anything could be considered suspect.

Ned patted the cushion. "Come along, then, Vi."

I hesitated no longer. Yes, Ned was brash and impulsive, but he could be wonderfully loyal and tender, too. Hadn't he proved that to me in the months after Lily's death? Of course I could trust him!

I began with Jack Stark. Ned heard me out, listening intently, nodding when I made a point he agreed with, but in the end he dismissed Jack's performance in the tack room as wholly characteristic.

"I grant you he has a very queer sense of humor—"

"It's more than queer, Ned!" I protested, "It's downright morbid. And those awful scars!"

"Apparently the result of trying to impress his father with his skill at horseshoeing. He was only a lad at the time, and mistook a white hot tool for cold. His father just stood by and watched him do it. Miserable old sod. Jack's not a violent sort, Vi; he's too cowed for that, but he's a good worker—a wonder with horses, according to

Milo—and hard though it may be to credit it, I understand he has a girl back in Arkham who's devoted to him. Can hardly wait to tie the knot, in fact."

I expressed my disbelief in no uncertain terms, but Ned merely smiled. "Now, Violet, you really must allow for different tastes. 'One man's meat,' you know."

I shuddered. What kind of taste was it that would allow a woman to let a man like Jack Stark touch her?

"Besides, the police are still convinced, based largely on what you yourself told them, that the Raggedy Man was the killer. He's probably gone to ground, just as Jack said."

A picture of the hard ropes of scars on Jack Stark's disfigured hands flashed through my mind. Yes, they could have caused the odd bruises on Lily's throat, but so might the horny callouses that scything can cause to build up over time. According to what Milo had said, the Raggedy Man's skill with a scythe was legendary and much in demand, which made it likely for him to have intimate knowledge of the grounds of every estate in the area.

Suppose, caught in the snowstorm while tramping his accustomed route, he was drawn by the glow in the conservatory. How warm and inviting it would have appeared to him, and even more inviting would have been the pretty blond girl within, alone in the candlelit greenhouse glade she loved so. Perhaps he had watched her dancing with an imaginary partner, as I had often seen her laughingly do. He might have yearned to be that partner—holding her young, sweetly scented body in his old arms, whirling her around to the music floating in from the party—and he would have known the location of the outside door . . .

"Violet? A penny?"

I blinked. "Sorry, Ned, I was just thinking . . . you're right, of course. Just because Jack looks like a weasel and laughs like a hyena dosn't mean he's capable of murder. But Jack's not the only one who concerns me . . . I . . ."

I turned away, unable to continue. My insides roiled. I

wished—oh, how I wished!—that Rafe was as unattractive as Jack Stark, and yet to even think such a thing made me feel akin to the foolish women who forgive in the morning the handsome brutes who beat them the night before.

I took a deep breath. "It's Rafe, Ned. I think he covets Brambledene much more than he allows."

"Well, yes, I'm aware of that, Vi. His reaction to my plans made that clear. But even if Rose predeceased him, her Aunt Rosamund, Rafe's mother, would inherit Brambledene, and from what I saw of her in Paris when Rose and I were married, she's got a good many more healthy years ahead of her."

"Ah, but you see she's already signed over her interest in the Thornbush estate to Rafe."

Ned eyed me skeptically. "Are you quite sure of that, Violet? Rosamund Taliaferro struck me as the sort of woman unlikely to relinquish control of her affairs short of her deathbed."

"Rafe let slip a hint of it, quite inadvertently, but it was Rose who confirmed it, Ned. This very afternoon, in fact, out in the stables." I looked directly into Ned's blue eyes. "I was not meant to overhear what was said, and I want you to understand I will not repeat it to anyone else, but I feel you should know. We've already been through so much together . . ."

Ned gathered my hands in his. "It's all right, Vi. Anything that concerns Rose, concerns me as well. You are right to share it."

When I repeated to him Rose's desperate words to Victor about the blood ties that bound her, Ned turned quite pale. He got to his feet and began pacing the narrow space like a tiger in a cage.

"Don't you see, Ned? Rose is afraid of Rafe. She's afraid for her safety, and so am I. Rafe has told me more than once about her mother's tragic illness and death, how can we be sure he's not setting the stage for an encore? They may be cousins, but how well does Rose know him? How much does she really know about his character, or what's more to the point, about his needs and wants? The two aren't necessarily the same, you know."

Ned paced a moment longer, then, plunging his hands in the pockets of his tweed trousers, he looked down to meet my troubled gaze. "Vi, it may be true that Rafe is planning to take advantage of the situation to suit his own selfish ends, and it's no secret I don't like the fellow, but murder planned to look like suicide? No, no, put any such thought out of your mind."

Ned looked genuinely shocked, and until he put my fears into words, I myself had not traced the tangled threads of my suspicions to their grim end. *Murder.* Such hideousness on Rafe's part was unthinkable! Yet hadn't my own suspicions led to thoughts of fatal accidents? And in this context what else might such an "accident" be *but* murder? My sinking heart told me I dare not ignore the possibility, and I wondered if Ned would have so quickly dismissed it if he were aware of the Taliaferros' dire financial straits.

I opened my mouth to speak, then thought better of it. What proof had I aside from what I had inferred? Would mention of Rafe's supposed financial distress serve only to deepen Ned's distrust of him to no purpose?

Ned broke the lengthening silence with a resigned sigh. He sat down again beside me. "The truth is, Vi, that Rose is not the same sweet girl I married. That sweet serenity that all of us admired is slipping away. Her dependence on Victor has become . . . unhealthy. I've tried to keep her love and her trust—I've tried every way that a husband can." His meaning was unmistakable. "But my beautiful bride would rather be her Daddy's girl." He laughed bitterly. "She's taken to treating me like an interloper, and when I . . . touch her, she . . . she . . ."

I held up my hand. "Ned, please, you needn't tell me this." I was distressed by Ned's unwitting confirmation of my suspicions about Rose's feelings for her father, but

I decided not to tell him what I had witnessed between them in the stable. It would serve no purpose except to hurt him even more.

"Who else is there?" he muttered. He avoided meeting my eyes. He began plucking distractedly at the cushion cover. "Afterwards, she's remorseful, of course. She weeps and begs for my forgiveness, but once I've given it, as I always do, it starts all over again. At first, only Victor was my rival, now it's alcohol as well. So you see, Rafe wasn't so far wrong."

I sprang to my feet. "Ned, you can't be serious! I never saw Rose take more than a sip or two of wine. She always said she hated the taste. Why, Lily and I used to tease her about it!"

"This is hardly something I'd joke about, Vi! She still doesn't *like* it, but when she's alone, those sips soon add up to dozens, and she's very clever about hiding her supply. She refills patent medicine bottles—even her perfume atomizers." He shook his head sadly. "Sometimes she loses track of which is which, and ends up smelling like a distillery."

I guess it was that last homely detail that convinced me. "Then she needs treatment, Ned, and she needs to get away from Brambledene." And from her father and cousin as well, I thought but did not say. If Rose's mental stability was in question, perhaps her hostility to me and what I had seen and overheard in the stable were no more than symptoms of the madness that shadowed her.

I sighed. Whatever the truth of the matter, there was nothing more I could do. I had discharged my responsibility by making Ned aware of the situation; Rose's protection was now in his hands.

I took those long, strong hands in mine, and leaned over to kiss his cheek. We could never be more than friends, I knew that now. To make Rose well again would take most of his time and energy and all of his love.

"We could leave in the morning, Ned. All of us LOPH's, that is: Iris, Wink, the twins, and I. Just say the word and I'll—"

"Oh, no, Vi!" Ned pulled back from me in alarm. "Rose would never hear of it." He looked almost angry. "The preparations are well underway for the party; we have guests coming from all over the county, old family friends Rose hasn't seen in years. I think it will be good for her."

His face relaxed in an apologetic smile. He patted my hand. "Here I am, snapping at you, of all people. We'll go ahead as planned, Vi. We'll muddle through somehow; it would only agitate her if she suspects she's being coddled." He raked his tousled mop of honey-gold hair with his fingers. "She's been so difficult lately . . . you can't imagine how much your being here means to me."

He gently tugged a lock of my hair. I pressed my palm softly into the hollow of his cheek. I could have drowned in the warm blue sea of his eyes.

"Oh, Ned," I murmured. "I—"

He placed a cautionary finger across my lips. "Hush, dear girl. It will do us no good to wish for what might have been."

"Ned? Ned, old boy, where are you hiding yourself?"

It was Freddie's high voice, full of bonhomie, caroling in from the parlor. Ned got up without another word, and as he loped across the library to forestall his admiring friend's entrance his lean grace revived the yearning I had tried so hard to suppress.

What was it Miss Peebles had once said to Lily, our little clique's most indomitable dreamer? *Remain open to your fantasies, my dear, but don't allow yourself to be consumed by them.* Yet as I looked after Ned I could feel the flames licking at my toes.

CHAPTER THIRTEEN

As I looked around the dinner table that evening it was easy to pretend that nothing was amiss. Rose had seated Rafe and Wink on either side of her, and the three were listening attentively to what Iris, on Wink's left, had to say about the women's suffrage movement in New York City, with which she had lately become involved.

Actually, it was difficult to tell from Rafe's expression whether he was impressed or incredulous, but no matter if her remarks were wise or half-witted, Iris was indeed magnificent to gaze upon: her huge brown eyes were aglow and her cheeks flushed with the fervor of her commitment. Even her chestnut hair seemed to throw off sparks.

"Your other blossoms will be hard put to match Iris's gemlike flame tonight," I remarked sotto voce to Victor.

He smiled. "Wink's a lucky fellow."

I looked across at my besotted friend. As far as Wink was concerned there *were* no other blossoms. *Imagine spending the rest of one's life listening to Iris . . .* "Wink's a *happy* fellow," I corrected dryly.

I was not surprised at the puzzled expression my amendment elicited. An appreciation of irony was not among Count Stirbey's many virtues, if indeed it were a virtue. I sometimes wondered if my taste for it was, if not quite a vice, at the very least unfeminine.

". . . I don't know how Rose puts up with them, Neddie. A regular pair of witches, those two."

Freddie Latimer's carrying voice attracted our attention.

"To which two witches do you refer?" I solemnly asked.

Bewildered by my question, Freddie slowly repeated it under his breath. "Oh, Violet!" he scoffed at length, pleased by my teasing that signified an end to the strain in our relationship. "I was referring to those Starks. Ada Devlin and her brother, Jack. Ned's been telling us about Jack's baiting you in the stables. Damned impertinence, I call it!"

"It's more than that though, Vi," Flora confided, leaning across her brother. "Ada thinks Brambledene is haunted. I ran into her in the corridor as she was coming out of their quarters, and I asked her about that owl you saw. I wondered if it had been seen again. But it was just something to say . . . I mean I really didn't care one way or the other."

"Oh, Flossie, do get on with it," her brother prodded.

"Well, she warned me not to go into the Bramble—not that I had any such intention. That's when she said it was haunted."

"Which? The Bramble or this house?" Freddie asked.

"*I* don't know, Brother. Bramble . . . house . . . What difference does it make? They're both Brambledene, aren't they?"

"Ada said as much to me, too," I said quietly, effectively putting an end to their bickering. I was not, however, about to mention the phenomenon I had myself experienced in the Bramble. "Arkham, the village where Ada and Jack were born and raised, is a queer place. To hear her tell of it, the Mayflower people were newcomers compared to the Starks."

"Surely that can't be so," Flora said.

"I'm not saying it's true, Flora, but the impression she gives is of an ancient mist-shrouded hamlet, huddled on the boggy shores of a lake whose waters are so murky no one has dared plumb its depths, although I expect the truth of it is that the Arkhamites aren't very good swimmers. Rural folk seldom are."

My attempt to make light of Ada's arcane tales elicited a giggle from Flora, but I found it difficult to expunge altogether the uneasiness I, too, felt about her and her brother. "But I do recall mention of witches. Something about them hiding away under the gambrelled roofs to escape British troops determined to root them out. Ada told me her grandmother hid away with them, even though she didn't have the gift."

"'Gift'?" Freddie repeated. "That's a rum way to put it. More of a curse, I'd say."

"Superstition," Victor amended flatly. "I should know. My native country seethes with it."

Ned looked at Victor with interest. "Romania, isn't it? Prince Vlad Dracul's castle is in Romania . . . Dracul means devil, doesn't it? And wasn't his son known as Dracul the Impaler?"

"Transylvanian upstarts," Victor said stiffly. "I fail to see what that has to do with Ada Devlin, Ned. Whether or not Ada's grandmother had this so-called gift, or even if Ada inherited it, for that matter, Milo is worth putting up with an entire coven of witches."

"I think that's the point Ned was trying to make, Victor," I put in, wishing this entire subject had never been introduced. "That is, that certain traits have a tendency to run in families. At least that's what medical science leads us to believe," I concluded lamely.

I regretted my words the minute they left my mouth. I knew insanity ran in families, perhaps addiction to alcohol did, too. I could tell from Ned's narrow-eyed look at me that he had caught my unintended implication; I prayed Victor had not.

"Do you suppose Ada can call up spirits?" Flora inquired in a hushed voice.

"Oh, Flora, all that sort of thing is nonsense!" I felt

back on solid ground. "My mother used to go to seances; in fact, our parlor was the scene of one of them. I was quite small at the time and very curious, especially about the noises I heard from where I was crouched on the stairway above. My curiosity finally got the better of me, and I remember sneaking down the stairs and crawling on my hands and knees into the darkened room and under the table through a forest of stangers' legs.

"I couldn't see a thing, of course, but I headed toward the funny noises and the next thing I knew a screen fell over on top of me and I got tangled in a web of wires and silvery things that glowed. I was terrified! I began to scream, and a large stout person covered head to foot in dark veils sprang up from the table and began waving her fists at me. So of course I screamed even louder.

"Afterward, when everyone had left and my mother had recovered from her mortification, I think she was grateful for my inadvertent unmasking of the medium. As far as I know, she never attended another session. They're all frauds, you know."

"Who are, Vi?" Iris called from the other end of the table, the suffragettes having run out of steam for the moment.

"Mediums, Iris."

"You mean like Mrs. Piper of Boston? I hear she's quite amazing. Someone I know was acquainted with that young author who became her control after he died. She said his spirit manifestation was utterly convincing."

"Does she levitate furniture, too? Like that Neopolitan peasant woman, Eusapia something-or-other?" Flora inquired.

"Eusapia Palladino," Rafe supplied. "She's even alleged to have levitated herself."

"I have a great aunt who does automatic writing," Wink offered hopefully.

There was a sudden guilty hush as Ada Devlin entered to announce that coffee would be served in the parlor. All eyes were fixed upon her back as she exited, and when she suddenly twitched her shoulders and turned back to sweep the company with an alert, hawklike gaze, Flora gave an audible gasp.

Ned quieted the ensuing nervous babble with a rap of his dessert fork on his water glass. "It appears to me that the redoubtable Mrs. Devlin has just satisfied any remaining doubts about her potential as a sensitive." The solemnity of his tone was belied by the sparkle in his blue eyes. "I therefore propose that we ask her to conduct a seance for us this very evening. If there really are spirits roaming Brambledene, now's the time to discover if they mean us good or ill. All those in favor?"

My protest, as well as Rose's and Victor's, was drowned out by the titillated chorus of ayes. Nothing like the prospect of a good scare to promote jollity, I thought cynically.

Rafe, who had listened expressionlessly to Ned's injudicious proposal, strolled from the dining room, as maddeningly aloof as ever, either unaware of or unaffected by his cousin's stricken expression. Indeed, if my suspicions of him were justified, why should he care? Why should he lift a finger if the rest of us insisted upon doing his job for him?

As for Ned, whatever could he have been thinking of! The answer, of course, was that he had been thinking of nothing; he had once again allowed his brash impetuosity free rein. The collision on the polo field flashed through my mind. I prayed that Ada Devlin would resist his importuning.

As we waited for Ned to return from the kitchen, Rose poured our coffee. Ada's rich, strong brew, which I usually enjoyed, left a bitter taste in my mouth that night, and when Ned rushed in to say that she would meet with us at ten o'clock in the old schoolroom, its dark acidity coiled into my stomach.

"The schoolroom is next to the conservatory, Ned,"

Rose said. I had noticed the look of apprehension she had exchanged with Victor, but the only hint of it in her voice was a slight rasp, as if her words had been drawn out over fine sandpaper.

"Yes?" Ned stood poised, his eyes beaming loving attentiveness as he waited for the rest of her statement.

How could he not have already made the connection? If he had, did he think the juxtaposition of murder scene and seance site inconsequential? Could he possibly imagine it might enhance the entertainment? Lend an extra *frisson*, as it were?

I could make no sense of his seeming insensitivity, and neither, apparently, could Rose.

"I don't think Ada should be encouraged," she said, changing tack. "You know how Milo disapproves of this sort of thing."

"*I* don't think employees should be allowed to dictate what their employers should or shouldn't do," Ned returned sharply. "You've got to stand up to fellows like that."

"It's a gamble Rose shouldn't be asked to take," Victor admonished. "Milo's one in a million."

"Life is a gamble, Victor. You of all people should know that."

Rivalry between a father and son-in-law was nothing new under the sun, but I was perhaps the only one aware of the fuse sparking just below the surface.

"Speaking of gambling," I said briefly, "while we're waiting, why don't we build up the fire and enjoy another cup of Ada's coffee along with one of Ned's stories of his adventures in the Colorado gold fields."

"Cracking good tales they are, too!" Freddie seconded enthusiastically.

"Perhaps we could even toast some marshmallows," Rafe drawled. "I understand they're a popular treat around American campfires."

"Only for children," Iris explained helpfully.

Rafe raised his eyebrows, "Oh, well, in that case . . ."

I gritted my teeth and hurled a log on the fire, creating a veritable explosion of sparks that diverted everyone's attention to the stamping out of embers on the carpet.

Ned relieved me of the poker, and when the logs had been rearranged to his satisfaction he remained standing there, quietly at ease, one foot up on the fender, his features bathed in the flickering golden light. Like all good storytellers, he waited until he had his audience's complete attention.

"It was raining hard the day I rode into Cripple Creek," he began. "Water streaming down from the mine-pocked tree-stripped hills had turned the main street into a mire. On both sides of it, ranged along the broken-down wooden sidewalks, was the saddest, soggiest collection of ragtags, roughnecks, yokels, and Yahoos you ever saw. There was no way to tell the winners from the losers, and the sorriest, most woebegone specimen of all was Willard Syms—"

"Syms is the fellow who became Ned's partner," Freddie blurted.

"D'ye want to tell this, Fred?" Ned said, inviting him up beside him with an elaborate sweeping motion of his arm.

"Sorry, old boy. Mum's the word."

"As I said, it was raining hard. Too hard to work a claim or prospect for one. But the saloons were as noisy as the Fourth of July, what with men drinking and gambling and buying the ladies' favors when they won." He grinned and rubbed his jaw. "'Ladies' being a highly complimentary form of address in this setting, you understand."

"I forgot how Willard and I got into conversation, but I bought him a drink, and somehow a pack of cards got produced, and next thing I know we're sitting at a table dealing them. Syms pulls this greasy little pouch out of his pocket and plunks it down in front of him. I can still see the rainwater trickling down on that old leather sack from Willard's hat brim."

Ned paused to take a sip from his cup, smiling as we stared up at him as expectantly as a nestful of baby birds.

"It was half full of gold dust, that sack was. The first genuine Colorado placer gold I'd seen, and the minute I saw that gleaming color I understood why men endured what they did in their search for it."

At first, Willard seemed typical of the breed to Ned. The kind that no sooner stake a claim than they either lose it in a poker game or to rascals whose legal-looking partnership papers end up leaving them with little or nothing.

"Poor old Syms," Ned said, shaking his head. "He was even worse off when I met him than most gold town vagabonds, but he had interesting stories to tell and when I pieced what he said together with what others said about him, I sensed he was somehow different from the rest. Was it possible, I asked myself, for a man to have a nose for gold the way those French pigs do for truffles? His nickname was Eureka, by the way; I figured that must count for something."

Ned leaned over to poke up the fire. "Well, I thought about it a *whole* lot over the next few days, and when he called on me at my hotel the following week to tell me he was hot on the trail of a bonanza, I took a gamble."

"Right then and there?" I asked. It seemed rash even for Ned.

He laughed. "On the very spot, Vi. I can still see him standing there, expecting the worst, twisting that moth-eaten old hat in his grimy hands, then trying to keep himself from throwing it up in the air when I told him I'd stake him. Best investment I ever made."

Ned knocked the ashes off the poker with his foot, and stood looking into the fire, idly revolving the knobby gold ring on his finger. The silence lengthened, broken only by the hiss of the glowing logs.

"And then?"

Ned turned, frowning. "Then what, Wink?"

"Then what *happened?*"

Ned shrugged. "Not much left to tell. I filed our claim to what turned out to be the biggest strike on the eastern slope of the Rockies. Down in a little side valley it was, hardly more than a steep ditch, with a little bitty stream running through that everyone else had passed by."

"Didn't you say your nugget came from there?" Flora prompted.

Ned held out his hand. "Syms found it wedged under a rock in that little stream." The firelight glinted off the irregularities in the surface of the gold knob on his finger. "Gravel-sized versions of this are what led Syms to the strike, just like the trail of crumbs to Hansel and Gretel's cottage."

Except that the birds ate the crumbs and the poor lost children ended up at the witch's gingerbread house. Since my urging Ned to tell his adventures had been intended to divert us from talk of witches and such, I saw no point in mentioning this unimportant inaccuracy, but I recall thinking it ironic that glittering trails of gold often ended, as did that fairytale path of crumbs, in loss: loss of family, of fortune and, too often, of life itself.

". . . had it made into a ring for me," Ned was saying, "in gratitude for my backing. Two days later he was dead. He'd been celebrating after we filed the claim, and forgetting it was too dark to see anything he took a lady friend out to the scene of his triumph. He took it into his muddled head to clamber down into the stream to find her a nugget, and that's the last she saw of him.

"Next morning I found him lying face down in a shallow little pool." Ned demonstrated with his thumb and forefinger just how shallow it had been. "My guess is that a rock had tumbled down after him and cracked him on the head. Didn't kill him, though; the water took care of that. Poor old Syms. I couldn't work the claim by myself, and I didn't trust anyone else." He shook his head. "As I said, they were a sorry-looking bunch. So I sold it. This ring's all I've got left from those days."

Ned fell into a contemplative silence.

"Not quite all," Rafe remarked from his seat near the windows, removed from the rest of us. "Not if you take into consideration the money you realized from the sale of the claim, without which, I seem to remember you saying in Paris, you wouldn't have been *emboldened*—the word was your choice—to propose to Rose."

Ned cocked a finger at him. "Right you are, pardner," he drawled. "I have my ring, I have dear Rose . . ." His eyes lighted with satisfaction. "And I have Brambledene."

Rafe eyed him speculatively. "You know, Poole, I can't quite see you grieving for long over the death of a partner you hardly knew, and who, from your own account of him, was little more than a drunken bum blessed with intuition." His brow knotted with what I was sure was pretended perplexity. "Are you sure your decision to recuperate at Lake Placid wasn't influenced by the possibility of courting a wealthy young lady while you were coming to terms with your terrible loss? Somehow your talents seem more suited to whirlwind romances than gold mining."

Ned abandoned his languid pose. "Why you—" He cocked his fists and lunged forward toward Rafe.

Freddie darted between them. "Now, now, no need for that, Neddy. Taliaferro can't be held responsible for his ignorance. How could he be expected to know how difficult it is to meet a girl at one of our old watering holes who *isn't* well fixed? My brother met his wife at Poland Springs and she's positively stinking, isn't that so Flossie?"

Flora nodded vigorously. "Carter never set out to make Marjorie fall in love with him," she said with an indignant glare at Rafe, "if anything, it was the other way around. In fact, they often tease each other about it."

"I may be ignorant of the finer points of American modes of recreation," Rafe responded cooly, "but I assure you I'm not the only one who senses the inappropriateness of choosing a seance for this evening's entertainment!"

He looked at me meaningfully, but I dropped my eyes. Although I agreed with him, I did not wish to be seen as taking his side.

"'Inappropriate' is it?" Ned sneered. "Vulgar is what you really mean! Maybe you don't know what Ada's been up to, filling Violet's ears with all manner of tall tales—taller and I guess a lot more awful than anything I could dream up." He turned to me. "Rose told me something of what Ada said to you in the conservatory, Vi. She tried not to let on it bothered her, but I could tell it did. Hell, it bothered me! So I figured it was time to bring it all out into the open."

Ned spread his arms wide, inviting our approval. "The worst Ada can do is make a spectacle of herself, and if she does, folks, you can bet Milo will put an end to her nonsense once and for all."

Ned's impassioned speech impressed me, and although my reservations about the seance remained, I found his forthright sincerity convincing. So, to my astonishment, did Rafe.

"You have a point, Poole," he conceded grudgingly, "even if I don't happen to agree with your idea of the worst that could happen. I just hope none of us has reason to end the evening regretting your choice of *divertissement.*"

CHAPTER FOURTEEN

"It will be ten o'clock in . . . seventeen minutes," Freddie announced after consulting the imposing gold hunter watch he pulled from his waistcoat pocket.

"Doesn't that weigh you down, Freddie?" I asked. "You ought to get yourself a wristwatch, like Rafe's. I understand they're all the rage in Paris."

Freddie shot a disapproving look in Rafe's direction. "That's all very well, Vi, but I have to think about how I present myself to my clients, don't you know."

I suppressed a smile. Apparently decadence came in many guises. I suspected Freddie would as soon wear yellow shoes as a wristwatch. "How long did you say we have?"

"Fifteen minutes, now. If you intend to powder your nose you had better scuttle."

And scuttle I did. Although at first undecided whether to rejoin my companions, I'm ashamed to admit that common and garden curiosity finally won out over disapprobation. I hoped Ada would be content with a straightforward bit of table-tilting—even Lily and I had been capable of that on occasion—or if not, that the mechanisms controlling her spirit manifestations would be clumsy enough to be obvious to everyone.

As I teased dark ringlets across my forehead I noticed a blister on one of my fingers, raised, no doubt, by one of the embers I had sent flying. I rummaged in my bag for the court plaster, salve, and gauze my father, ever the doctor, insisted I always carry with me to guard against the often serious consequences of a neglected blister or cut. I found the packet crumpled in a corner, abrasions not being a common occurrence in my unathletic adult life, and dutifully applied it as instructed. Just before leaving my room I tucked a strip of court plaster in my skirt pocket to wind around the shank of Ned's ring. It would be a shame if he lost a memento of considerable monetary as well as sentimental value.

I found, to my surprise, that only Ned had preceded me downstairs. Determined to take advantage of this brief moment we would be alone—I very much doubted that Rose would appreciate my fussing with her husband's belongings—I demanded the surrender of his ring.

Nick stepped back, obviously reluctant to relinquish it; but when I told him I only wished to ensure its safety, he smiled and plopped the ring off into my cupped hand. It was even heavier than I expected—all the more reason to secure it—and judging from the crude workmanship, I suspected the person who fashioned it was more at home fitting shoes to horses. I leaned close to the lamp on the table between the wing chairs and prepared to wind the plaster around the ring's shank. Inside, worn but still readable, was a single word engraved in simple block letters: *Eureka!*

I hesitated to apply the plaster, which would obscure it. Eureka was more than just Ned's partner's nickname; its original meaning in Greek, *I have found it!*, was the ideal phrase with which to commemorate the rich strike Ned's faith and financial backing had made possible. No wonder he treasured it.

I smoothed the plaster with my fingernail to close the joining as invisibly as possible, and suggested he take the ring to a jeweler to be sized at the earliest opportunity.

Ned extended his forefinger like an obedient child. I

favored him with an indulgent smile as I slid the ring home. "There now!"

Instead of returning my smile, Ned captured my hands in his, and looked at me with sad yearning. "You are so dear, so kind . . . and so very lovely." His hand slid around my waist and splayed against the small of my back, pressing me closer. "If only—"

"Please, Ned," I whispered, placing my palms against his chest. "As you said yourself, it's too late for us now." I gently pushed, but he pulled me closer still.

"That was before you reminded me how sweet it is to have someone care about me. Oh, Vi, how I miss being cared for! Why, that little strip of plaster means more to me than—"

We sprang apart at the sound of footsteps rapidly descending the stairs. The Latimer twins bounced in, followed closely by Wink and Iris. Moments later the clock struck ten, and just as we were about to give them up, we were joined by Rose, then Rafe, and finally Victor, who had come up from his room to wait for us at the entrance to the corridor.

As Victor waved us by, his face expressing the usual affectionate indulgence with which he favored his blossoms, I could not tell if he had witnessed Ned's and my short-lived embrace, nor could I even begin to guess what his reaction might have been if he had.

Except for Freddie and Flora, who bounded into the classroom wide-eyed and voluble with anticipation, the rest of us entered hesitantly, in huddled twos and threes, like naughty school children called before the head-mistress.

Ada Devlin certainly suited the part. She had changed for the occasion, and although the color of her dress was, as usual, black, it held no hint of her everyday garb's rusty undertone, characteristic of cheap dye exposed to bright sun on the washline. No, this black was as pure an absence of color as could be imagined. The fabric was heavy and faintly ribbed, bengaline I think. Even the braided velvet trim was black, and a jet and cut steel brooch adorned the ebony satin ruching at her throat.

She had none of the uncorseted Bohemian abandon of the medium my mother had engaged. In fact, as she stood before us, austere and thin-lipped, her hands clasped across her severely tailored bodice, all she lacked was a long thin whip with which to chastise her charges.

"Whew!" I heard Rafe say softly behind me. "The Witch of Endor."

I suppressed a smile. "I was thinking of something more along the lines of the Salem variety," I whispered back.

"True," he agreed thoughtfully. "Too bad we can't duck her in the Ashley to find out for sure."

The mental image of Ada Devlin bobbing in those icy waters like a soaked and very indignant black cat, released my laughter in a staccato splutter.

All eyes turned to me. Ada's unblinking stare, as cold and sere as a nighttime desert wind, withered my amusement and sent my gaze searching for less unsettling objects to fasten upon.

The lowest of the schoolroom tables, a round one, had been cleared of Valentine decorations and pulled into the center of the room. A dark cloth draped it and the circle of candles flickering in the center would, once the lamps had been extinguished, provide the only illumination. Behind the table I spied a makeshift curtain rigged upon a wire too light for the weight it was expected to support. I fancied that the faint billowing I detected betrayed the presence of an assistant, probably her brother; the maids were too silly to be of much use.

Judging from the amateurish setup, Ada Devlin was, for all her professed familiarity with arcane rites and demons, clearly a charlatan. I smiled as I imagined Jack Stark's clumsy manipulation of her hastily assembled paraphernalia, and anticipated her bluff being called with a certain mean relish. In her eagerness to curry Ned's favor, which her husband on more than one occasion had disdained to do, she had, I suspected, overreached herself.

Ada asked us to bring chairs to the table, and when we had done so—bumping together in the shadows after Ned had obligingly turned down the lamps—she instructed us to take our seats and link ourselves together by putting our right hands on the table and our left on that of our neighbor. When we had accomplished this to her satisfaction, although Rafe's hand resting on mine was not entirely to *my* satisfaction, she sat down in the chair she had placed for herself directly in front of the sagging curtain, just as I had expected.

At first, there was only the sound of our breathing, followed by restive resettlings into the upright and unyielding wooden chairs. Ada finally broke the silence to implore those of us hostile to psychic exploration to suspend our disbelief.

"Surrender your hearts as well as your hands," she invited in a low, pleading tone quite unlike her usual speech. "Please join with us in an unbroken chain of spiritual communion so that together we may provide the lighted path our loved ones are seeking." Her words and phrasing, which were far more eloquent than usual, made me suspect they had been memorized.

"I can feel them there, hovering, crying out in the dark," she continued in a rising voice, "but you must believe. *You must believe,*" she repeated. "*Believe! Oh, yes, believe!*"

I could hear Freddie's breath quickening beside me. His hand stirred under mine. "Believe!" he muttered.

"Believe," Flora echoed to the left of him.

Ada's hypnotic cadence soon carried the others with her. *Believe, believe, believe . . .*

My breathing shallowed. My eyelids fluttered shut. "Believe," I murmured, unable to resist. And then the taps began.

At first they were tentative, like those of a frightened child seeking entrance through an unfamiliar door. Then the taps became raps, first here, then there, gaining in strength and speed and culminating in an urgent tattoo that made Iris gasp aloud.

Victor hushed her. From his vantage point at Rose's left, who was seated across from Mrs. Devlin, it was apparent that the housekeeper had fallen into a dazed state.

"The woman's in a trance!" Freddie hissed, and indeed, much as I hated admitting it, that genuinely seemed to be the case.

"Can you open the door?" she called out. Her voice was high now, and her breathing thready. "Come in to us . . . answer our call . . ."

A humming sigh began to vibrate in the air. We all sensed it—I could tell from the quiver of Freddie's and Rafe's hands moving against mine. It seemed to emanate not just from behind the curtain, but from several distant sources. And then I heard a squelching, as if something wet were approaching. Something awful. *Ada's Old Ones . . .*

I fancied I could smell the lake's decay, the sweet, cloying odor of rotting weeds and algae . . . was *that* what I had smelled the night Lily had been strangled? *Oh, that dreadful, vile odor . . .*

Apprehension dizzied me. I told myself my morbid imaginings were a product of my own agitated senses, and indeed, Ada's very next trick proved how necessary an induced, shared propensity for self-delusion was to the success of her amateurish performance.

A muffled chanting issued toward us from behind the curtain, claiming to speak—in Jack Stark's unmistakable accent—for the spirits of Brambledene. The next moment, a pale glowing object accompanied by a strange barking sound moved jerkily across the room, like a large white bird trying to gain the air on injured wings. It looked rather like an owl . . .

Of course! My snowy owl! What could be a more appropriate choice for the spirits' go-between? But this one's body was made from painted cardboard, and the strangled hoots issued from Jack's, not a feathered raptor's throat.

I couldn't decide whether to be angry or amused. I leaned forward slightly to look at Rose, planning to take my cue from my hostess, and was dismayed to find her visibly distressed. Far from recognizing the manifestation as a hoax—and a clumsy one at that—she seemed on the verge of panic. Her brow was beaded with moisture; her cheeks were ashen.

Victor, on Rose's left, spoke to her soothingly in a low voice, but I doubt she heard a word he said. Ned, on her right, patted her hand reassuringly, but I saw her fingers bend into rigid claws as she stared unseeingly across at Ada.

"Lily . . . Lily Forrester . . . is that you? Come across, dear girl, your friends are waiting for you here . . ."

I was aghast! How could Ada, seeing Rose in such a state, continue with this malicious farce. Before I had a chance to protest, however, a sudden creaking at the schoolroom door distracted me, followed by the wuthering sound of a searching wind seeking entrance. Perhaps, I thought, the conservatory door has come unlatched. Perhaps . . .

My thought died unfinished. The door blew open, admitting a rush of frigid air that cut short Jack Stark's unconvincing response from the spirit world. The cold settled upon us, pressing us into our chairs like icy hands. Speechless with fright, we stared helplessly at one another. My teeth began to chatter; my cheeks and lips felt like congealed wax. The very ticking of the schoolroom clock seemed to slow.

It could have been hours or a mere heartbeat later that

a warm, springlike zephyr swept in to dispel the appalling chill. As it swirled around us in a teasing, sweet-scented dance, I sensed a haunting familiarity. My mind flashed a picture of Victor presenting his gifts of perfume to his beautiful blossoms. My nostrils flared with astonished recognition. The scent was, unmistakably, lily of the valley.

"Dear Lily!" I cried.

I did not realize I had spoken aloud until Rose sprang to her feet with a fearful shriek. Her cry released us like a flurry of suddenly loosed arrows from their bows, and in the ensuing commotion the insecurely fastened curtain tore away to reveal Jack Stark, gape-mouthed with apprehension, clutching a speaking horn in one hand.

Once he realized that he was the least concern in anyone's mind, Jack began a sneaking retreat toward the door, only to be recalled by a bark of command from Victor. Ned, who was as bewildered as Rose was terrified, stood shifting uncertainly from one foot to the other. The others, still dazed by the unnerving perception that neither Ada nor her brother were likely to have been responsible for the perfumed presence we had sensed, filed silently out of the room. I turned to follow them, but Ned beckoned me to stay.

"You were Lily's closest friend," he whispered. "You must convince Rose that you were mistaken . . . that you spoke without thinking . . ."

I hesitated, not because I was unwilling to help, but unsure if I could. Given her expressed hostility to me, Rose might well distrust anything I said; it could even make things worse.

"Please, Vi, say *something.*" Fear had flattened the light in Ned's blue eyes, turning them as leaden as a squall-threatened sea. "My God, look at her!"

Rose stood apart, as rigid as the stone angel in the Bramble; as white as the square of marble marking Lily's grave. She looked unreachable by me—by anyone.

"This could send poor Rose right over the edge."

Ned's expression, the droop of his broad shoulders and loose hang of his muscular arms eloquently expressed his regret.

He's very good at that sort of thing, I found myself thinking coldly, almost as if a stranger were looking out of my eyes at him, but I bit back the words that sprang to my lips, the harsh, blunt words that would have told him he should have thought of that before proposing such a risky entertainment.

A moment later, when I realized that Ned's charm had, for the first time, failed to move me, I felt older, sadder, and in no way grateful for whatever bit of wisdom I may have gained.

CHAPTER FIFTEEN

The fears for her well-being that Rose's trancelike state of mind had aroused were shortly dispelled.

Within minutes of Ned's agitated appeal to me, she quite literally pulled herself together: a shudder seized her slender frame and as it subsided her limbs relaxed and color returned to her cheeks. The words she addressed to Ada Devlin, however, were delivered like shards of ice.

"I will expect you and your brother to be packed and ready to leave Brambledene two weeks after my guests have departed. I will provide no references."

It was a harsh penalty, but Ada's gasp failed to win my sympathy. Milo, who would have little choice but to go with them, would pay the hardest price for her mischief. For him, Brambledene was much more than a place of employment: over the years it had become as embedded in his heart as the Irish countryside he had roamed as a boy. It would be cruel to cast him out.

"Please, Mrs. Poole, my husband had no part in this." Ada splayed her fingers in the direction of the pathetic hoard of props revealed when the curtain had fallen away: a cardboard owl, a pail of wet sponges, a set of crude wooden clappers. Misery sent her dark head swaying from side to side like that of a shackled circus elephant.

Ned extended his hand toward Rose, his palm turned up, his fingers unfolding in mute appeal. I was struck by the uncharacteristic subtlety of his gesture, perhaps intended to slow her rush to judgment. "My dear Rose, don't you think it a bit hasty—"

Rose cut him short, her face ablaze with scorn. "*Hasty?* How could you, of all people, say that? It's only been a year since Lily . . . We've only just begun to be able to live with . . . with what happened, and now these despicable people . . ."

One long stride brought Victor to her side. Rose turned her face into his chest, allowing herself only a few muffled sobs before collecting herself and returning to the matter at hand, her face tear-blotched but her chin at a determined tilt.

"I will provide Milo with the good references due him, Mrs. Devlin, but he must leave with you. Now if you will please—"

Rose attempted to skirt past Ada, but the distraught woman scuttled into her path and threw up her hands. Strands of her black hair, which had escaped its tight bun to trail untidily down her cheeks, framed feverishly glittering eyes. She had never looked more like a witch than at that desperate moment. But this time neither Rafe nor I were the least tempted to exchange humorous remarks.

"We wasn't up to idle mischief, Jack and me." Ada's formal mode of speech, revealed now as painstakingly acquired, had broken down under stress. "You see, Miss Rose, when we learned that you and Mr. Poole were meaning to spend more time here at Brambledene, I figured that maybe, if you and your friends thought . . . if you was helped to think that Brambledene . . ."

Her words trailed off; her mouth began to quiver. I don't think she realized the enormity of what she had been doing until the moment she began putting it into words . . .

"You wanted us to think not only that Brambledene was haunted," I supplied tersely, "but that whatever lurked here, be it ghosts or demons, meant to do us harm."

"I never!" She gulped. "*I never,*" she repeated under

her breath as if trying to convince herself.

"Come now, Mrs. Devlin, have you forgotten your telling me in the conservatory about the Old Ones and their lust for blood?"

"Good Lord!" I heard Rafe mutter.

Ada's eyes slid over me and fixed imploringly on Rose. "All we wanted was for you to change your mind, Miss Rose, about Mr. Poole's plans and all. It wasn't that I wanted to frighten you . . . I just couldn't think of any other way."

"Any other way to do *what?*", Ned demanded. "What possible interest can you have in my plans for Brambledene?"

"And why don't you want us here?" Rose added, more incredulous than angry now. "What on earth have we ever done to make our presence here so abhorrent to you?"

One of the candles on the table flared high before guttering out. The shadows pressed closer.

"It's like a tomb in here," Rafe muttered as he struck a match to relight the lamps earlier extinguished.

The warm light washed over Rose's face, delicately tinting her flawless complexion. Except for the dimple high on her cheek, which the flickering light lent the illusion of pulsing with emotion, her expression was as implacably impassive as a bisque doll's.

By now we had formed, unintentionally, a rough circle around Ada, whose eyes skittered from one to another of us like a trapped animal. I found no pleasure in observing her desperation. At length, she uttered a strange moaning sigh, and her twisting, twining fingers fell slack when she at last realized that the truth was her only refuge.

"We could never have any children, Milo and me," she began haltingly. "He always said it didn't matter, but I knew it did. Then, when you came back after your mother died, Miss Rose, I remember thinking how queer it was. But I didn't think anything more about it until Milo told me about the storm the day he and Miss Rosalind was out riding."

Ada paused. Her tongue darted out to wet her lips. "Your mother was a harum-scarum rider, Miss Rose. She'd head her horse straight at whatever took her fancy, with no thought of how high or wide it was or what might be on the other side, and she had many a bump along with whatever horse took her over. Her mother—your Grandmother Thornbush, Miss Rose—finally forbade her riding out without Milo to keep an eye on her.

"Led him a merry chase, she did, but no one can outride my Milo. He was something to see in those days! Tall and straight with eyes like a piece of the sky. When he began courting me—this was a few years later than I'm telling you about—I knew there wasn't a luckier girl in the Commonwealth, or in the whole world, when it comes to that. And that's all part of it, too, you see."

She paused again, her brow knitting. "Did I mention the storm? It came on sudden-like. One of those summer downpours out of a sky that's sunny one minute and black as a coal cellar the next. They sheltered in a barn, fallen into ruin now, the other side of the Ashley."

Ada sighed as if exhausted by the effort demanded of her. "They were soaked clear through and shivering by the time they reached it, Milo said. But the sweet hay, mown just that week, gave them comfort and Miss Rosalind . . . she just kept pressing closer." Ada gulped and plodded on. "'Twant Milo's doing, Miss Rose. Your mama was a mighty pretty girl and used to having her own way about things. Milo never meant it to happen, and he never put himself in the way of it happening again."

Rose stepped forward and stared up into Ada's face. "Are you saying that my mother and Milo . . . ?"

Ada nodded. "That's what I'm saying because I know that's what happened; I'm only guessing about her scheming to visit her sister before her parents were the wiser. She met the Count over there, isn't that so, sir? Married before you hardly had time to say how do, to hear tell of it. She never came back here to Brambledene, in life, again.

"But after she died *you* came, Miss Rose, and I thought it queer even then, though Milo hadn't yet told me about that stormy day. But you never came for long, and when your friend was killed, I thought maybe you, too, would never come again."

"You didn't just *think* it, Mrs. Devlin!" Ned accused. "From what you're telling us, I'd say you were counting on it."

"I even prayed on it, Mr. Poole! Yes, I prayed that awful killing would keep you away. By then, you see, Milo had told me about Miss Rosalind and him—he said he could no longer bear the burden alone. I think maybe seeing Miss Rose stirred something in him, but I kept my suspicions to myself." She laughed bitterly. "I knew the hornets set loose from that nest of secrets could sting me worse than anyone."

Her next words were addressed to Rose. "Then you and Mr. Poole got married, and when Milo told me you were coming to Brambledene to stay, I got scared of what might happen. I've never been so scared, Miss Rose, not even when my Dad raised his fist to me. My Milo's all I've got, and he's all I ever wanted."

"You got me, Ada," Jack muttered, slouching forward. "I always aim to look out for you, same's you did for me."

Ada turned to face her brother. She laid her hand on his cheek. "Oh, Jacky," she murmured, "it's not the same a'tall."

"Speak plainly, Ada!" Victor demanded. "What is it about my daughter that drove you to such preposterous lengths?"

"*Your* daughter, Count Stirbey?" Ada raised her finger and jabbed it toward the deep dimple placed high on Rose's cheek. "*Not likely!*"

Ada's exclamation generated a shock so profound it was almost palpable. As the silence lengthened, it all fell into place. No wonder Milo's similarly placed dimple had struck me as oddly familiar. That stormy afternoon in the hay barn had bred more than guilt and remorse: Rose was Milo's daughter, not Victor's, and Ada, the rough horse-breeder's daughter from Arkham, couldn't bear the possibility of being displaced in his affections.

I heard the hiss of Rafe's indrawn breath behind me. "My God! That certainly puts a different complexion on things."

I turned to look at him. "How is that?" I inquired in a low voice. "Brambledene descends through the maternal line, so it's only who Rose's *mother* was that matters as far as you're concerned. Who her father is has no relevance—except socially, of course. Does that bother you, Rafe?"

"How charming to be accused of being a money grubber and a snob in a single speech! I do believe you've outdone yourself, Vi, but I suggest you'd be better employed narrowing your eyes at Ned than me—"

"Hush!" I snapped, for Ada had begun speaking again.

"In time, seeing Miss Rose day after day, seeing that dimple on her cheek so like his own . . ." Her words trailed off. She stood there for a long moment, lost in thought, then slowly nodded her head. "In time, he would have guessed this pretty and fine young lady was his daughter, and what of my place in his heart then?"

I couldn't help feeling sorry for Ada. Despair dulled the light in her jet eyes, and the coarse strands of hair trailing untidily around her gaunt face seemed to symbolize the disintegration of her rigid self-control. Although her means had been crude, even cruel, she had fought her fears as best she knew how, only to have her effort come to naught.

I looked from the stricken woman to Rose who, next to Ada, was the one most affected by her revelations. To my bewilderment, the color had risen in her cheeks and her eyes fair sparkled. She reached out to Victor, and having clasped his hand drew it back to press to her dimpled cheek. Only then did she speak.

"Nothing can excuse what you did, Mrs. Devlin, but I am moved to reconsider your dismissal. Regardless of what your husband's relationship may be to me, what you have told us has reminded me anew that Brambledene was my grandparents' dream."

Rose's posture as she delivered her formal little speech struck me with awe. It may sound silly, but I felt for those few moments as a commoner must feel in the presence of royalty. Something had happened, quite aside from Ada's astounding revelations, to animate her. Whether it was something to be alarmed about, I was unable to tell.

"My grandfather brought Milo here with the hope he would one day rise to the position of manager," Rose continued in measured accents. "I shouldn't have presumed to tamper with an arrangement that has served their beloved estate so well for so many years. As long as I am mistress of Brambledene, your place here is secure."

"Oh, Miss Rose." Ada's acknowledgment could barely be heard, but the tears in her eyes attested to her gratitude. "And Jack, too?"

Rose gazed serenely into the older woman's beseeching face. Even though I guessed what she would say, I hoped Rose would not come to regret her generosity. Ada's actions had been motivated throughout by desperation, but Jack's treatment of me in the stable was mischief of the most malicious sort.

"Your brother, too," Rose agreed. "My . . . your husband will need him for the horses, whether or not I choose to take up residence."

Whether or not I choose to take up residence.

Rose's concluding phrase, casually appended, was said with a radiant smile at Victor, but it was Ned on who it registered with startling effect. His fists clenched convulsively at his sides and his face became livid, its lines accentuated by his waxen pallor. Seeing Ned thus, I realized how he would look in middle age, and I was disconcerted to find how much a part of his appeal was his youth.

Rose, who had started for the door, turned to speak. "Is Milo in your quarters, Mrs. Devlin? I think it time I made my father's acquaintance."

Ada darted ahead, Jack at her heels, eager to lead the way. Victor, who followed to join Rose at the doorway, seemed remarkably unaffected by his displacement. Ned, on the other hand, remained rooted to the spot. It pained me to witness this drainage of his jauntiness, but Rafe couldn't resist throwing up to him what lay in store.

"Your life appears to have taken another melodramatic turn, eh, Poole? One moment you have a member of the Balkan nobility for a father-in-law, the very next sees him displaced by the Irish manager of your wife's estate, a man with whom—correct me if I'm wrong—you're not even on very good terms. What's next, d'you suppose?"

"Damn you for a scheming snake, Taliaferro!" The cords in Ned's neck stood out, and a red flush suffused his face.

Rafe raised his eyebrows. "What have I to do with it?" he protested. "I was hardly out of the nursery when all this began in that old hay barn across the river. No, the next move is yours: all you have to do is persuade your loving bride to boot her newfound father out and resolve to spend the rest of her life here with you at Brambledene. Victor is good with horses, maybe he could take Milo's place—"

I stepped between them as Ned advanced on Rafe with raised fists. "Stop it, both of you! You're acting like children! Now, more than ever, Rose needs at least the semblance of support from those closest to her."

Rafe gave an exasperated snort. "I don't deny she does, but if you're expecting us to shake hands and declare undying friendship—"

"I'm not that silly!" I snapped, ignoring Ned's growl, "but you both could at least try to put on a civil face for the rest of our stay here—I assume you're returning to New York with us on Sunday, Rafe?" He nodded. I looked from one obdurate face to the other. "Two days! Is that so much to ask?"

Rafe shrugged and nodded. Ned's eyes slid away from mine; his shoulders hunched in a cramped, reluctant gesture of assent. He moved jerkily toward the door, like a marionette with ill-fitting joints. "Stay out of my way,

Taliaferro," he rasped from the doorway. "Just stay clear, understand?"

Rafe didn't bother to respond. His eyes flicked towards Ned's disappearing back, and returned as quickly to me. "Still his champion, Vi?"

I tried to overlook the smugness I detected in his tone. "I don't know. I don't know what to think about anything. He can't change what's happened," I offered, unsure whether I felt hopeful or resigned.

"Can't he?"

"No more than you!"

"Ah, but the circumstances have changed. Rose made it quite clear she was considering leaving Brambledene—why do you suppose she omitted any mention of Ned's plans, or for that matter any mention of him whatever? Her smile was for Victor, not her husband—what do you suppose that signifies?"

"I don't suppose it signifies anything at all." I found it easier to evade his question than apply serious thought to an opinion I might not care to admit. "Omission is hardly proof of anything, Rafe. If I had been Rose at that moment I wouldn't have known which end was up."

"She seemed fully in control to me."

"But that's just it, don't you see? She's not in control, and hasn't been for some time."

"Are you suggesting she's experiencing some sort of lull before an emotional storm?"

"I don't know," I cried, twisting my hands together, "but I do think Ned has ample reason to be angry and upset. If he loves her—"

"If?" He cupped his hand to his ear. "Did I actually hear you say *if?*"

I felt like slapping the arch smile off his face. "*Since* he loves her," I amended, "it's no wonder he feels hurt. And it's no wonder you wear that gloating smile. If their marriage fails it would serve your purpose very well."

"But not yours, of course." His smile cooled; there was a knowing look in his eyes.

I tossed up my hands in exasperation and swept out

into the dim corridor. He followed and grabbed my arm just above the elbow; then, as I turned to wrest it from him, he grabbed the other. The reflection of the schoolroom lamps from the corridor's creamy white walls was the only source of light, as wavering and uncertain as my sorely tried emotions. We stood face to face, locked in a bitter, silent struggle.

Inexorably, by virtue of his greater strength, Rafe backed me up against the rough plaster, then bent his mouth to mine. His kiss was hungry, desperate, and exciting. Yes! I admit it! How could I fail to be excited by this slippage, after all these years, of Rafael Taliaferro's urbane mask? Yet how could I not also be wary? It would take more than the excitement of his kisses to persuade me he was any less self-centered now than nine years ago when he played careless games with my affections.

His grip relaxed as his lips trailed along my jaw. Taking advantage of his momentary vulnerability, I pushed him away.

Rafe turned on me with a savagery far removed from his usual urbanity. "By God, sometimes I wish I'd left you in that damned menagerie!"

I gaped at him. "What on earth . . . ?"

"It all comes back to the same thing, doesn't it? No matter what our feelings may be for each other now—No! Don't interrupt! I'm not a fool, Violet, I can sense when a woman is attracted to me. What I don't understand is why you continue to punish me for my neglect of you all those years ago yet are all too ready to forgive—even reward—Ned Poole's much more recent ill treatment."

Rafe's plainspokenness shocked me into silence. As few as twenty-four hours earlier I could have protested his assumptions unhesitatingly, but now I felt unsure about many things once clear-cut and certain, including the LOPH friendships woven years before from the sturdy strands of trust and affection. Like Jack Stark's fragment of quilt, they, too, had started to unravel.

Long ago, while exploring the shore at a seaside resort in Maine, I had paused to admire the midnight blue sheen of mussel shells whose nacreous linings, emptied of their occupants, glimmered in the gentle tumble of the tidal pools. Alerted by a sense of motion close by, I turned my head to watch in horror as a marauding starfish pried apart and slowly consumed a living cluster. I was very young, and the helplessness of the mollusks seemed hideously unjust to me.

I recall running crying to my mother who, aside from a hug and a clean handkerchief, had nothing to offer but platitudes about God's plan. They had provided little comfort then and even less now. The cruel ebb and flow of the tides of my life were slowly, surely, devouring my youthful certainties and there was nothing I could do to prevent it.

"I'm sick to death of suspicion and disillusionment and unsettling surprises," I blazed, "but most of all I'm sick of your condescension. At least Ned knows how to laugh!"

"I regret the low opinion of me it suits you to express," Rafe drawled. "I'll not deny Ned Poole the gift of laughter, but I predict you'll be hearing less and less of it from him in the days ahead."

Taking refuge in silence, I watched him stroll up the corridor and disappear into the parlor beyond and the maelstrom of questions and speculation that probably awaited all of us privy to Rose's confrontation with Ada. Serve him right if he drowns in it, I thought meanly.

I sighed and wished—oh, how I wished!—I could be set adrift once more on those calm Adirondack waters, just dear, uncomplicated Wink and me and our little cedar-strip skiff, but Rafe's velvet rumble of a voice continued to echo in my mind: *the low opinion of me it suits you to express . . .*

Suits me? Rafe Taliaferro was more than just condescending; he was downright insufferable.

CHAPTER SIXTEEN

I awoke next morning with an aching head, resenting the early hour until I realized that a high, white overcast was responsible for the dim grayness I perceived through my unshaded window. Actually, as a squinty look at my lapel watch on the table next to my bed soon informed me, if I didn't get cracking I might very well miss breakfast.

The house was abustle with activity. Ada Devlin, her arms piled high with table linens, hurried by me on her way to the dining room. Rose sailed by in the other direction, a list in her hand. "Don't forget the flowers, Vi!" she called out gaily as we passed.

In view of Ada's revelations the previous evening, I found Rose's good spirits bewildering. As for the flowers, hadn't I already done that? So much had happened during the last few days the events had become confused in my mind.

Flora and Freddie emerged from the corridor carrying crepe paper hearts. "Happy Valentine's Day!" they chorused. And then I remembered. Although today wasn't actually Valentine's Day—that wouldn't be until the following week—it was the day of the party I so dreaded. The party planned, I now recalled, to announce Rose and Ned's happy union to the neighborhood. Good heavens, I thought. How would we ever make it through the evening?

As I passed by Ada in the dining room on my way to the morning room and breakfast, I fancied I heard her humming. Her reprieve had obviously improved her mood, and as her hum, unmistakable now, swelled like the purr of a contented cat I assumed she had escaped her husband's censure as well as Rose's.

I couldn't help wondering what the course of Rose's fateful meeting with Milo Devlin had been. As I entered the morning room, I saw Ned seated alone next to the window, but his halfhearted greeting discouraged any questions I might have been tempted to put to him. The room had not yet been cleared of dirtied breakfast plates—from the number of them it seemed I was indeed the last to appear—and the cold light seeping through the panes spread a gray film over the room's faded colors. It was a dispiriting scene made even more so by Ned's woebegone expression as he listlessly pushed at his egg with a soggy wedge of toast.

"Not much left, I'm afraid. The others descended before us like a cloud of locusts."

I lifted the cover on the platter of scrambled eggs, and spooned the remaining small congealed morsel onto my plate. I added a piece of cold toast from the rack. There was no bacon.

"At least the tea is hot," I sighed, wishing I could sit alone to collect myself, but knowing Ned would interpret it wrongly. I made a small ceremony out of pulling out the chair opposite him and settling in, but in the end I was still left not knowing what to say. I gave an uncertain smile, and began to eat.

"Thanks for not asking me how I am," he said wryly. "I don't *know* how I am; I'm not sure when I will. Rose is as chipper as a chikadee and I feel as if I'm wearing a cloak of invisibility."

"People sometimes react . . . oddly to momentous news, Ned. Give Rose time to come to terms with it. Give yourself time, for that matter. Milo is a good man, an honest man. I'm sure you'll be able to work out an acceptable accommodation with him."

"Honest? You haven't heard the latest, I take it," Ned said with a wry smile.

"I just came downstairs, Ned. I haven't had time to hear anything."

"Well, my dear Violet, it seems there's more to Milo Devlin than meets the eye. That dimple he shares with Rose? In the part of Ireland he hails from it's known as the Devonshire Dimple. Milo inherited it from his natural father." Ned heaved a tired sigh. "It's an Irish version of the sad old story of the innocent village girl taken advantage of by a highborn rascal. In this case, the scoundrelly gentleman was, if you please, no less a personage than the Duke of Devonshire, who had hired Milo's mother to assist his children's nanny when the family visited the Duke's estate on the Blackwater River."

"Good heavens!" I exclaimed, then fell silent, wishing I could avoid the question that begged to be asked. I couldn't. "Is there any proof, Ned? What I mean is, I'm sure Milo is telling the truth, but still . . ."

"Aside from the telltale dent, you mean?" Ned asked, screwing his forefinger into his cheek. "Ada says his mother's parish priest sent him a letter after she died that rambles on for pages about the wrongs done Milo and how grateful his mother was for the money he sent back to her. Apparently he was such a dutiful son that Milo and Ada couldn't afford to marry until his mother died. As for proof . . ." Ned shrugged. "Milo offered to let us read the priest's letter, but Rose claimed she was satisfied. She wasn't interested in hearing my opinion," he added with a tight smile.

"But why did Milo come to America? I would think he would have found ready employment on the Duke's estate."

"That exactly what I asked Rose, Vi! She said Milo told her that when the Duke learned one of his bastards had schooled the horses that were outjumping his, he tried to hire Milo as head trainer for the Devonshire hunting stables, but Milo'd have none of it. He told Rose he'd already had his fill of the whispers and sniggers his dimple caused wherever he went. Shortly after he refused the post, Roswell Thornbush passed through Lismore on the lookout for a clever lad to take back with him to Brambledene, and Milo jumped at the chance."

I shook my head. "Imagine all this coming out now! How many years is it since Milo first came here?"

"About thirty, I'd guess. According to Rose, all Ada knew until the priest's letter arrived was that Milo didn't like any mention of his dimple. He still doesn't, but . . . well, you remember what she said last night."

I nodded, recalling Ada's fear that in time, seeing Rose day after day, Milo would have been forced to face what his wife had already guessed.

"It can't be easy for him," I said.

Ned glared at me. "Not easy for *him?* What about me, Vi! Victor has taken to treating me in a distant and gingerly fashion, as if I were a potentially explosive device, and Rose's charming cousin ignores me altogether. If he could, I'd think he'd drop me in the dustbin. As for my new family, I find Milo a bit too full of himself, and I can't quite see myself walking arm and arm with Ada in the Easter Parade, not to mention that repellent brother of hers!

"Victor and Rafe took themselves off this morning on a neighborhood errand without so much as a glance in my direction. Fred was the only one to take friendly notice of me, but if he calls me Neddy and purses his lips at me in that wet way of his once more, I swear—" He broke off suddenly. "Just listen to me . . . Ned Poole, whimpering!" He gave a snort of disgust.

"Don't be so hard on yourself, Ned," I soothed. "As I said, it will take time for you—and them—to come to terms with all that's happened. Maybe when the party is over and the rest of us have gone . . ."

He smiled. A determined light appeared in his eyes.

"Yes, things will be different when the party's over." He reached over to place his hand on mine. His expression softened. "Thank you, Vi. I can always count on you."

I gently withdrew my hand to place my already drained cup to my lips. "Of course you can," I said. I rose to my feet and smiled down into his blue eyes. "And so can Rose. Apparently I promised to do something about flowers."

The conservatory no longer held horrors for me. The spirit Brambledene harbored had nothing to do with Ada Devlin's loathesome "Old Ones." It meant me no harm, of that I was sure. As I moved down along the aisles of benches seeking blooms appropriate for Valentine arrangements, I found myself regretting Rose's apparent decision to leave Brambledene. If she stayed, I mused, the brick floor and fountain might be cleaned of moss and slime and the wicker furniture refurbished. Even another bright, plushy Oriental rug might be brought in. A small one, easy to put to one side in case someone wanted to dance there, someone like Lily . . .

The scene wavered before my eyes. I seemed to see blond hair turned gold by lamplight, a pale lacy dress drifting across the bricks, swirling around the bright, white wicker chairs . . . and wasn't that distant laughter I heard? Laughter and a strain of music? The sweet sound of violins and the ripple of harp strings?

I blinked my eyes. The only music was the dry click of my secateurs as white carnations and red geraniums fell victim to their blades. I couldn't remember consciously selecting them; I felt as if I had, for the briefest of moments, been transported out of time. I glanced around me, dazed, seeking reassurance of the here and now: yes, the mildewed wicker remained piled in a cobwebbed corner, and the gray morning light I had noted earlier seemed colder and dimmer than ever. I rubbed the nearest fogged pane with the heel of my hand. It had begun to snow.

Gruff, unfamiliar voices greeted me upon my return to the main part of the house. There were a stamping of snowy feet, and an invitation from Rose to go in by the fire. Curious, I entered with my pail of flowers, and saw that the visitors were policemen. I felt the blood drain from my cheeks. Ned had said that Victor and Rafe had gone out together earlier—could anything have happened?

The taller of the two men turned. He removed his cap. That grizzled red hair and whiskers . . .

"You remember Sergeant Morley, don't you Vi?"

"Miss Grayson," he acknowledged with a stiff little nod.

Now I remembered: he had conducted the investigation, after Lily died. "Of course. How are you, Sergeant? Not bad news, I trust?"

"Depends on how you look at it, miss."

"Lily's killer has been found, Vi!"

Rose's expression was—there's no other word for it—ecstatic.

Bemused, I stammered only bits and pieces of the questions that thronged my mind. "Where . . . who . . . ?"

"That old tramp known hereabouts as the Raggedy Man, miss," the sergeant stolidly supplied. "Some boys were out during that mild spell exploring up in the hills. Playing at cowboys and Indians or some such. Stumbled over the old man's corpse in a cave." He gave a grim, toothy smile. "Those boys won't be playing up there again for a while, I reckon."

"His *corpse?*" I blurted.

"Dead as a doornail," his companion piped in cheerfully. "Has been for some time, eh, Sarge?"

"Seems that way. Won't know for sure 'til the coroner gets a look at 'im. We're on our way back now, before the snow gets too bad. Looks like we're in for it, ma'am," he said to Rose. "I suggest you ask Jack Stark to bring enough wood in from the shed to keep your fires going for the next day or two."

"What's that?" Rose seemed distracted, but happily so. "Oh, yes. Thank you, Sergeant, I'll do that."

The men turned to leave.

"Sergeant Morley?" I felt a fool, but I had to know. "I was wondering, did you happen to notice if the . . . the body had calloused hands?"

He looked at me expressionlessly, but I fancied I could hear him wondering if that didn't beat all. "I can't say as I did, miss," he replied stolidly. "Henry?"

His subordinate seemed similarly flummoxed. "Never thought to look, Sarge. No reason to!" he added defensively, as if accused of neglecting his duty. "But I 'spect he had callouses, right enough. Old Raggedy was a champion with a scythe." He vigorously pantomimed the sweeping motion. "When you think how much he done over his life, bound to leave a mark."

I nodded, satisfied to have that last niggling question put to rest.

I carried my flower-filled pail into the kitchen. Jessie and Agnes, the village girls Ada had hired on for the house party, were washing up the breakfast crockery. Ada herself was putting the finishing touches on an immense, many-layered heart-shaped cake iced in white. I watched, fascinated, as she deftly applied a red butter-cream frill to compliment the red arrow piercing Rose and Ned's curlicued names.

"Why, you're an artist, Mrs. Devlin!" I exclaimed.

She looked up at me, startled, wiped her hands on her apron to hide her confusion, then stepped back to inspect her creation. "D'ye really think it'll do?"

I surveyed her work judiciously. "I think it looks good enough to eat," I solemnly replied.

My feeble witticism all but collapsed Jessie and Agnes in giggles. Ada contented herself with a satisfied bob of her head.

I lifted and rattled the pail of flowers. "Please, don't let me interrupt you, but is there somewhere out of the way where I could arrange these?"

"Ooooh, aren't they pretty!" Agnes said. "Jessie and me's about done, miss. You can have the sink all to yourself."

"Thank you, Agnes. Let's see, I'll need a pair of shears for the stems and two . . . no, three bowls to put them in, preferably matching. One for the middle of the table and one at each end. The bowls shouldn't be too high, girls," I called as they rushed about opening and shutting cupboards. "We'll want to be able to see each other over the flowers without craning our necks like a gaggle of geese."

I was rewarded with another fit of merriment, which was flattering but not very helpful. Ada shortly put an end to it.

"There's a sack of potatoes yet to peel, Agnes, and Jessie, see to the dough for the rolls. It should be risen by now."

I busied myself at the sink while Ada selected bowls for me. I was dismayed to find that some of the geraniums harbored the same tiny insects Ada had deplored on my first visit to the conservatory.

When I brought them to her attention, she clucked and put the bowls down on the drainboard. "These aren't too badly infested," she said as she inspected the big red blooms. "A swish through a bit of warm soapy water and a rinse in cool should put them right."

Fifteen minutes later saw them, as she put it, right as rain. "I'll see to the rest of the plants in the conservatory this very afternoon," she said.

"Goodness, Mrs. Devlin, with all you have to do I'm sure that can wait a few days longer."

"It's not just them little bugs I'm worrying about,

miss," she said in a low voice, but before I could ask what she meant, Ned appeared in the doorway.

"Oh, it's you, Vi," he said. "I heard voices . . . I was looking for my wife, Mrs. Devlin."

"She's been that busy this morning, Mr. Poole, I can't tell you where she might be now."

"Sergeant Morley suggested she ask Jack to bring in more wood," I said. "Do you think maybe—" But I was never to know what Ned thought.

"Sergeant who?"

"Why, Sergeant Morley, of the Lenox police. You know, the policeman who came by earlier about the tramp who killed Lily."

Ned looked thunderstruck.

"I'm sorry, Ned," I said. "I assumed you knew."

The silence in the kitchen was profound.

"No, I did not know," Ned hissed. Grabbing me by the arm, he propelled me out of the kitchen before I hardly had time to tell Ada I'd finish the flowers later.

Ned hauled me down into the classroom and kicked the door shut behind us. The props used in the seance had been spirited away; only the makeshift curtain, carelessly heaped on one of the tables, remained.

I rubbed my arm where I was sure the imprint of Ned's strong fingers had left its mark. "You could have just asked me to come with you," I remonstrated.

"I'm sorry, Vi," he said, "but those girls' ears were flapping like rabbits. I didn't want our business going back into town with them. Now, what's all this about the police? What did they say?"

"They came to tell Rose the Raggedy Man had been found."

"Where . . . when?" he rasped. His hand reached out to clutch at my bruised arm again, but I stepped back just out of reach.

"Some local boys found him in a cave up in the hills. I'm not sure when—yesterday, the day before. I didn't ask."

"Did the police arrest him? What had he to say for himself?"

I had never seen Ned so tense. His bright eyes bored into mine like diamond-tipped drills.

"He wasn't capable of saying anything, Ned. He's dead."

Ned released a little whuffing sigh. His rigid limbs slowly relaxed, but the impression I received was that of a deflating balloon, its colors dulling as the animating air escapes. I would have thought he'd be glad.

"One year," he muttered. "Only one short year."

Only a year? To me it had seemed a lifetime. But I didn't have time to think about it. Ned stepped lightly toward me, suddenly reinvigorated, his blue-eyed smile as dazzling as a sunlit sea.

"The uncertainty of it all was driving me crazy, Vi. Good news, bad news, I can stand anything but no news. I think a celebration is in order, don't you?"

At first I thought he was referring to the party, but when he pulled me into his arms and began nuzzling my neck I realized he had another kind of celebration in mind.

To my bewildered astonishment, I found the longed-for touch of his lips on my flesh damply distasteful. I gently disengaged myself.

"There was a time, Ned, after Lily died, after those months in which we spent so much time together . . . I expected that something more than friendship might . . . I hoped that maybe you and I . . ."

My words faltered. It was so difficult, so *humiliating*.

Ned took my hands in his. His blue eyes gazed deeply into mine. "I know, Vi. I did too. But when I returned here to discuss with Rose the plans for Lily's memorial instead of our wedding . . ." He broke off, struggling in silence to regain his composure. "In some strange way it brought us together, and before I knew what was happening, Vi, things . . . my emotions . . . got away from me.

"It was so stark here, so dark and *dead*, even in April." Ned loosed my hands and gestured to indicate the dusty barrenness of the room in which we stood. "Rose was pale and distraught, and the urge . . . the *need* to help her bring Brambledene back to life, to erase its morbid image, overcame me." He ran a hand through his honey-gold hair. "Did I mistake my sense of . . . mission for love?" he said with a wry smile. "I don't know, Vi; neither am I sure what Rose felt—gratitude, perhaps. Victor was here, of course, but he wasn't involved in our emotional discussions of graves and monuments and shared memories."

Ned paused, perhaps recalling the memories we, too, had shared and discussed. "We thought we had fallen in love, Vi—it's only now that I realize how little I really knew about her." He swallowed hard. His eyes seemed to burn into mine. "It all happened so fast I didn't have the courage to tell you then, but things have changed. You know they have."

"Rose is still your wife and my friend, Ned."

"Well, well, what a difference a day makes. You weren't as noble yesterday in the library."

His smile softened his mockery, but I turned away to escape his reproachful gaze. I couldn't explain even to myself why I had resisted his embrace.

"I just hope Rose is a better friend than wife. You saw her last night after Ada Devlin let her cat out of the bag. She had eyes only for Victor. This morning it was even worse. Seeing the two of them together . . . it disgusts me. I don't care what their relationship is in law, it's unnatural. But ours, Vi . . ."

Ned again gathered me forcefully into his arms, but when I deliberately averted my face from his he abruptly released me and, grimacing with disgust, roughly shoved me aside.

"Damn you LOPH girls! Not a woman worth the game in the lot of you. Lily's the only one of you who knew how to live, and she's dead."

Ned turned on his heel. His abrupt, angry departure created a miniature whirlwind which swept up snippets of red ribbon and lacy white paper from under the schoolroom tables.

I looked out the window at the falling snow. The ground was completely covered. There was no wind to disturb the white batting that lay clustered along the tree banches within view. I imagined that the Bramble's hedges, which I could not see from here, must seem like icebergs rising out of an Arctic sea. I wondered if Lily lay warm under her white quilt.

I idly fingered the quilt heaped upon the table below the window. A foolish choice to hang on that light wire. Jack must have snatched it up at the last minute from the table of valentine decorations it had been covering.

If Ada had been a little less hasty about agreeing to the seance, and Jack a bit more careful about his choice of a curtain, then the wire mightn't have given way under its weight, and Ada wouldn't have been revealed as a fraud and forced to relinquish the secret that weighed so heavily upon her heart.

Good heavens. How did those lines go about the mischief that a little neglect can breed? "For want of a nail the shoe is lost, for want of a shoe the horse is lost, for want of a horse the rider is lost . . ."

I thought of the embrace I had rebuffed. *And for want of a lover? What then of the loss?*

CHAPTER SEVENTEEN

I remained standing in the empty schoolroom, staring out at the snow, lost in thought. The flakes were smaller now, falling as silently as secrets. It had snowed last year, too, on the day of the party; the day Lily had died.

For want of a lover . . .

I couldn't remember Lily ever wanting for much of anything. In fact, her bold assertiveness was one of the things I had admired most about her. She would certainly have never wanted for a lover, I thought enviously. Then, in a deplorable access of self-pity, I heard myself wondering aloud in a tremulous voice if I might die for want of one.

Nonsense! An overwrought response like that was all very well for someone like Shakespeare's Juliet—a rather silly girl I always thought—but a commonsensical young woman like me? There was nothing to be gained by waxing melodramatic about it. True, I sometimes despaired of loving and being loved in return, but I would survive. Father needed my services, and I had my little visits to the Metropolitan . . .

I sighed. My drab, solitary, spinsterish anticipations contrasted sadly with the delightful afternoon I had spent with Rafe searching among Brambledene's ugly duck furnishings for its few antique swans. It was the only time his company, his very presence, had not bred suspicion. And what of his demanding kiss in the corridor the night before? I vividly recalled—how could I forget?—the way his mouth fit on mine, the pleasing odor of his warm flesh, his quickened and uneven breathing . . .

My sense of his arousal had excited me then; the memory of it now turned the nipples of my breasts into hard buds and my betraying flesh to feathers.

I hugged my yearning body fiercely, as if to punish the yielding emotions women accepted without question as their lot. How wonderful it must be to choose rather than wait to be chosen! Resentful tears tracked down my cheeks. I rummaged in my pocket for a handkerchief. Empty.

I grabbed up a corner of the quilt on the table to dab my eyes. Its mustiness made me sneeze, and as I held it away from me at arm's length I realized for the first time that it was a crazy quilt, although of an uncommonly refined sort. Its subtle colors and elegant patterns put me in mind of the fragment Jack Stark had found under the hedges. I took it closer to the window. Yes, even the precise cross-stitched joinings were similar . . .

A hesitant knock at the door attracted my attention. "Yes?"

"It's Ada Devlin, miss. May I come in, please?"

"Come along, Mrs. Devlin."

"I'm looking for a piece of cardboard," she said, holding up squared hands to roughly indicate the size, "and a black crayon to make a sign for the conservatory. Mr. Poole has told me to go ahead with the fumigation; he says people going in there tonight might upset Miss Rose."

I looked up to see Ned standing in the doorway. He didn't say anything; he didn't have to, his blue eyes were liquid with remorse for his earlier display of temper.

"But need you go so far as to actually do it today?" I asked, thinking of her busy agenda. "Surely a warning sign should be sufficient."

"Huh." Ned's grunt was heavy with contempt. "You haven't met the local gentry, I see. Give them a bit of whiskey and it's unlikely they'll be able to read the sign, much less pay attention to it."

"If they're likely to barge in, sign or no sign, then why go to the bother?"

"Ah, but you see, Vi, the fumigation provides us with a second line of defense. Have you ever smelled formaldehyde?"

"Good heavens, no! I realize my upbringing has sheltered me from many of life's sober realities, but the embalming room is one I don't in the least regret missing."

Ned, at his disarming best, flashed a brilliant smile that melted away the last traces of my annoyance with him. "Formaldehyde is also used for fumigating. A glasshouse staple, Mrs. Devlin tells me. One whiff, and . . ." He waved the air away from under his nose. "Believe me, Vi, drunk or sober a man would go to great lengths to avoid it—even if it meant rejoining the missus in the parlor."

Ned winked at me to underscore his teasing and, I suspected, to arrest any suspicion of unmanly sensitivity. No matter what Rafe thought, or tried to lead me to think, Ned did care about Rose, even if he was no longer in love with her. Why else would he go to such lengths to put the conservatory off limits on the anniversary of Lily's death there?

Having found a dusty cache of drawing materials in a cupboard, Ada proved less adept with a crayon than her pastry tube, and her fidgeting and fussing led me to guess that the spelling of "fumigation" was beyond her. I offered to do the lettering to spare her further embarrassment, and produced in short order a sign formidably black and bold enough to give the most oafish of the Brambledene neighbors pause.

Ned offered to attach the warning to the conservatory

door. While we waited for him to return with tacks and a hammer, I showed to Ada the quilt Jack had used as a makeshift curtain.

She twisted her hands together agitatedly. "Oh, Miss Grayson, I should never have let Mr. Poole persuade me to try to call up Brambledene's spirits . . . I never meant—"

"All's well that end's well, Mrs. Devlin," I quoted tritely, anxious to deter what promised to be another lengthy exposition. I saw no point in letting on that I had been more upset by the tales she told me in the conservatory than her shenanigans in the schoolroom. "By the way, am I right to assume all *did* end well? Concerning Rose and your husband, that is?"

"Oh, yes," she said. "They still have a lot of catching-up to do, of course." She paused. "The queer thing is," she added, shaking her head wonderingly, "Count Stirbey doesn't seem to be minding much about it."

I appreciated Ada's bewilderment, but I could see no acceptable way to enlighten her concerning Victor's odd lack of disappointment about being displaced as Rose's father without betraying my having eavesdropped on a scene never meant to be overheard.

"About this quilt," I began briskly.

Once I had assured her that my interest in the quilt had nothing to do with her ill-fated seance, Ada was ready enough to talk about it. She said the piece I held was one half of a larger crazy quilt the Thornbush daughters had made long ago for their parents.

"Miss Rosamund—that's Mr. Taliaferro's mother, you know—had trunks of stuffs like this. Not lively enough for a proper crazy quilt in my way of thinking, but pretty enough in its way, and the stitching!" She drew it enviously between her hands. "Finer than anything I'd have the patience for, I can tell you."

"But it used to be one quilt, you say?"

She nodded. "Great big thing it was, too. I'm glad I never had to worry about the washing of it. After Mr. and

Mrs. Thornbush died in that accident I found it folded away in the wardrobe in their bedroom, that would be Mr. and Mrs. Poole's now. The fabric being so old and fine, it had given away at the seams in places, so I had a seamstress in Lenox make two quilts out of the best parts of it."

Shortly before this, according to Ada, Victor and Rose had come to New York to settle her grandparents' estate, and thinking it time Rose became acquainted with her native country, Victor had enrolled her at Miss Peebles. Although they lived in New York in the Thornbush house Rose had inherited, they visited Brambledene on occasional weekends, and for several weeks during a particularly long hot spell one summer they escaped there along with a variety of house guests grateful to share their retreat from the oppressive heat and dust of the city.

"We had those city folk coming out of our ears!" Ada confided. "Count Stirbey decided to outfit the tutor's room—the one he's in this weekend?—as a guest room," she amplified.

"That's when the original quilt was divided?" I asked.

Ada nodded. "Yes. Two narrow beds were moved in, and both needed coverlets. The following summer Miss Rose brought up new covers from the city made from stouter cloth, and since then these old quilts have been used here and there, wherever needed. Give me a minute and I'll tell you where this one's been, although why Jacky used it as he did I can't think."

I did, of course. Rose had borrowed it from the tutor's room to cover the table piled with party decorations, so it had been right under Jack's unattractive nose, so to speak. I had been in the tutor's room only once, and the memory of my brief unpleasantness with Rose there included only vague impressions of its furnishings, but one of them, perhaps because of my interest in textiles, was of a quilt folded at the foot of only one of the beds.

"And the other quilt?" I asked.

"Like I said, miss, they come and go." Ada obviously saw no point in my quizzing her on matters of interior decoration when she had so many things yet to accomplish. "Maybe a guest soiled it or tore it and, ashamed to admit it, bundled it away. Mr. Poole had some friends up a while back," she added with a disapproving frown.

She pointed to a place where the fabric had thinned and parted. "They wasn't in the best of condition to begin with. Maybe Miss Rose took it away, thinking to look in those boxes of fabrics her aunt left behind in the attic for pieces to mend it with." Ada relinquished the quilt to me. Having exhausted her maybes, and not really caring, she shifted restively. "If that will be all, miss . . ."

I nodded absently. Questions racketed in my head, vying for attention. I looked again at the quilt. Had I seen this one or its twin on Victor's bed? If this was the only one I had seen, where was the other? Was there any point in comparing this quilt to the fragment Jack had found under the hedges?

I looked out the window to see the snow falling harder than ever. A wind had risen; the branches had tossed off their shawls of snow. I had no wish to go out to the stables in this rapidly worsening storm. Truth to tell, I had no wish to match the quilt in my hands against Jack's fragment in any weather, foul or fair.

Even if they *were* a match, what would it prove aside from carelessness on the part of a Brambledene house guest? I smoothed the exquisitely patterned patches with my hand. Ada had mentioned boxes left behind in the attic by Rafe's mother. Perhaps one rainy afternoon a bored houseguest, exploring the attic's shadowed nooks and crannies, had brought down the only piece remaining of a similar quilt damaged long ago, only to discard it when the return of sunshine offered more appealing diversions.

There were any number of reasonable explanations, I told myself as I neatly folded the coverlet and returned it to the table. We already knew who had murdered Lily. I had seen the Raggedy Man that dreadful night with my own eyes, and all the quilts lost or found in the Berkshires could not acquit his corpse of that grim verdict.

Although satisfied I had at last achieved a fit for all the pieces of my puzzle, I felt unready to reenter the stream of activity flowing throughout the house. The likelihood that neighbors would be sending servants out into the storm to deliver their regrets added to my reluctance.

Despite Ned's unflattering reference to them, new faces would have provided a welcome addition to a group whose childhood ties had frayed and whose adult connections were tenuous at best. I hardly knew anymore what to say to Rose and Victor, and I found Rafe and Ned's unceasing conflict, not only with each other but within my heart as well, increasingly painful.

If only there were someone I could talk to! I would not find the objectivity the situation required from Flora and Freddie. Freddie disliked Rafe, and although I knew Flora thought him attractive, her allegiance, too, had long since been awarded to Ned. In any event, the norms of polite society so controlled their attitudes, a confession of my ambivalent feelings for Ned would garner little sympathy.

My dear Violet, I could hear Freddie saying with that new pomposity of his, *you simply must pull yourself together;* and from Flora a horrified, *But, Vi! Ned's married to Rose!* Dear sweet Flora. Her convention-bound sensibility would never allow her to entertain the possibility that although consideration of a person's marital status might determine one's actions, it had nothing whatsoever to do with one's feelings.

No, the Latimers would never do as confidants, and I could hardly spirit Wink off for a quiet chat without incurring Iris's displeasure. Not that he could offer much in the way of sage advice—he was too far removed from the worlds Rafe and Ned inhabited to sensibly speculate about their motivations—but at least he would not judge me, and his self-effacing steadfastness was in itself a comfort. Of all the LOPH's he was the least changed. He still had the innocence and keen, serious look of a youth who longed, bravely, to be given orders; I hoped Iris would resist taking advantage of it.

But there was more than my own needs to be concerned about: supposing I ran into Milo Devlin? What on earth would I say to him? Was he still an employee or had he become a host? What was Victor's status now that Milo had, in effect, displaced him? Shouldn't Ada, as Rose's stepmother, cease addressing her stepdaughter's guests in her accustomed, subservient fashion? The new relationships all but overwhelmed me, as they already had Ned. *Could Jack Stark really be Rose's uncle?*

I heard the sound of hammering out in the corridor. Grateful for the distraction, I opened the door to find Ned driving in the last tack affixing the sign I had made to the conservatory door.

I was amazed. I must have loitered in the old schoolroom longer than I had realized. "Don't tell me Ada has already been and gone!"

"That she has, Vi. The preparation takes only a minute; it's the effect that's long-lasting—long enough at least to keep nosy neighbors from intruding."

"I wonder how many of your neighbors will be coming. The last time I looked, the storm showed no sign of abating."

"That's another question altogether," Ned said, thrusting the remaining tacks in one trouser pocket and the hammer in the other. Its outline against his thigh under the tightly stretched fabric was shockingly suggestive.

Ned hooked his arm through mine. "What d'ye say we go in search of an answer together?"

The corridor being barely wide enough to accommodate two walking side by side, we were pressed rather closer than I would have chosen. Ned took advantage of the situation to slip his arm cozily around my waist.

"You can't blame a fellow for trying, Vi," he murmured.

"Not for trying, perhaps, but for persisting?"

"Faint heart never won fair lady."

"You've already won a fair lady, and unless you've converted to Mormonism I believe that's all you're entitled to have."

"Not if the fair lady you're referring to has other plans in my mind," Ned retorted sharply as we entered the parlor to find Rose and Victor standing side by side, talking with Milo Devlin. They were holding hands.

Rose turned. "Oh, there you are!" I was uncertain if she was addressing me or Ned. So, apparently, was Ned. "Yes?" we both said. It was an awkward moment.

Rose's brilliant smile emcompassed us both. "Milo tells us messages of regret have already arrived from two households, and he doubts the others will be able to make it through."

"Does that mean—"

"The party will take place as planned, Vi. You needn't worry about that! We LOPH's have never been in need of anyone else's company to ensure a good time—except for Victor's, of course."

As if to underline her concluding phrase, Rose began swinging Victor's hand, the coyness of the gesture contradicted by her defiant gaze. Milo appeared perplexed; Ned fumed. I could hardly blame him; Rose seemed bent on provoking him. But I was also worried. Not about the party, for I had anticipated the possibility Milo had confirmed. No, it was Rose herself who concerned me: her high color, her uncommonly bright eyes and spirits.

Remembering what Ned had told me, I wondered if she had been drinking; remembering what Rafe had told me, I was reminded unsettlingly of her mother's spiraling course to disaster. But whatever the cause, I had the strong impression of a shiny top spinning ever faster out of control. Coward that I was, I prayed Brambledene would see the last of me before anything untoward happened.

"Do you know where your cousin is, Rose?" Ned asked.

Rose raised her eyebrows, as well she might. "Rafe's in the library, taking refuge from the storm in a good book. You really should try it some time," she murmured. "Do you a world of good, darling."

"I had my fill of books at Yale. Sitting around on your duff just gives the other fellow a head start; it's action that gets a chap ahead in the world. Speaking of which, have you seen my sketches for the renovations we planned?"

"*You* planned, Ned, not I. Last I knew, they were in the drawer of one of the library tables. I suggest you leave them there."

"But Rafe is leaving tomorrow. I don't know when I'll have the chance—"

"I suggest you leave them there," Rose repeated softly, but her words had a steely edge.

They stared at each other for a long moment. "I will take your suggestion under advisement," Ned said woodenly. Then he turned and strode into the library.

As Rose watched him go a sly smile quirked her lips. "Poor Neddy can never leave well enough alone, can he Vi?"

"I wouldn't know about that, Rose," I returned evenly, becoming rapidly aware of how little I knew about anything.

She cocked her head consideringly to one side. "No, I guess you wouldn't." Then, for no reason at all that I could see, her eyes filled with tears. "Forgive me, Vi, things are—"

"Oh, good heavens!" I blurted. "The flowers! I never finished the flowers!"

I hurried out to the kitchen, grateful for a legitimate reason to flee Rose's sudden and confounding change of mood. For the next half hour, as Agnes and Jessie busied themselves sticking cloves in the glazed surface of a huge pink ham and grating sharp local cheddar cheese for the scalloped potatoes, their ingenuous chatter about the village lads they fancied offered escape from Brambledene's mounting tensions. My floral arrangements, when completed, gained their wide-eyed approval.

Lunch was both late and informal. The dining room table having been set and reset to accommodate the rapidly dwindling party, I helped Ada and the girls carry to the parlor platters of cheeses, freshly-baked rolls, and a cauldron of soup concocted from leftovers simmered for hours on the back of the big black kitchen stove.

Freddie helped himself to a bowlful and settled down in a chair well away from the fire, having no wish, as he put it, to be grilled like a sausage. Flora, on the other hand, dragged a cushion off the sofa onto the floor and pressed as near to the flames as she could. It was an incongruous scene, dark damasks and plushy velours being ill-suited to the establishment of a picnic atmosphere.

"Wink and Iris and I braved the storm to make a snowman," Flora announced, "but the snow covered him up as fast as we made him, so all we have to show for our trouble are cold toes and noses." She lifted her face to the flames. "Hmm-mm," she sighed contentedly. "Just like a camp meeting."

"Maybe so, but please spare us the campfire songs, Florrie," her brother teased.

Flora looked at him reproachfully. "Would that be so terrible? Iris, you know them better than anybody, why don't you lead off?"

Iris, eager to oblige, stepped forward, but Wink forestalled her with crockery and silverware. "Not yet, my little nightingale, not until you've stoked your furnace with some hot soup."

Wink's solicitude made Iris blush with pleasure: few men were big enough to describe her legitimately as a little anything. For my part, I silently blessed him for this temporary reprieve, intentional or not, from her off-key contralto. Perhaps I would have time to finish my lunch before bolting—at a ladylike pace, of course—to my room.

A moment later, Rafe and Ned's quarrelsome emergence from the library put an end to any notion of a campfire sing.

". . . No, I don't care what you say or Rose thinks," Ned was saying, "I want my own lawyer to review it."

"I say, old chap," Freddie said, responding to the word lawyer like a Dalmatian dog to a fire alarm, "can I be of any help?"

"It's this agreement that allegedly passes Brambledene down through the Thornbush line outside of any wills. Surely I, as Rose's husband, must have some rights in the matter."

Freddie looked alarmed. The injection of family business of this sort into a social gathering was quite outside his experience. "Oh, Neddy, I really don't think—"

"It's too late, Ned," Rose broke in. "It doesn't matter any more, can't you see that?"

"It matters to *me*," Ned said, jabbing his finger fiercely at himself. "And I can assure you the how and why of it will matter to a lot of others, too," he added ominously.

Rose paled noticeably.

"Isn't that line a bit righteous for a man more at home in gold town saloons than drawing rooms?" Rafe drawled.

Why did I have the feeling that Rafe and Ned were talking at cross-purposes?

"*My* conduct isn't in question here," Ned retorted.

"Watch what you say, Poole!" Victor had entered the fray. From the look of him, in another place and time his challenge might well have ended in a duel.

Rose looked in panic from one to the other—apparently I wasn't the only one confused—but instead of bursting into tears, as I fully expected, she announced she had had quite enough of this idiocy, and suggested we all go to our rooms and see to our costumes.

Flora stared at her as if she'd taken leave of her senses. "Costumes, Rose? But if no one is coming . . ." Her voice faltered. "Is the party still on, then?"

Rose's pretty chin tilted defiantly. "On? Of course it's on, Flora! Why shouldn't it be? We have food and drink enough for a dozen parties, and the LOPH's have never wanted for merriment." Her eyes had a glittery look. "We'll all die soon enough, God knows."

Under the circumstances I thought it a dreadful choice for an exit line. My expression must have betrayed my unhappiness, for when Rose left the room Victor took me aside to beg my support.

"Don't judge her harshly, Violet," he pleaded in a low, voice. "My poor Rose . . . if only you knew—" He broke off and ran his long hands through his silver-threaded hair. His hands had a betraying tremor; there were dark, aging smudges under his eyes.

I bit my lip. "I know more than you think, Victor," I finally said, hoping I would not regret my frankness. "More than I wish I did. You see, I overheard you and Rose in the stable yesterday. I am aware that your feelings for each other are . . . unconventional."

I tried to keep the distaste I felt out of my voice, but I could tell Victor sensed it. I also sensed that his initial shock had been succeeded by a measure of relief. For all the wrong he may have done Rose, I did not doubt that Victor was still a man possessed of some honor. Perhaps he was the sort of conscience-ridden wrongdoer who found relief in discovery.

Good heavens. They say that confession is good for the soul, but for all the good it might do Victor's, I fervently prayed he would not choose me to receive his.

CHAPTER EIGHTEEN

My prayer was ignored. No sooner had I sent it wafting heavenward than Victor fixed his fine dark eyes meaningfully on me.

Feeling unfairly put upon, rather like the unfortunate passerby stopped by the Ancient Mariner's glittering eye, I nevertheless resolved to attend patiently to what he had to say. I owed him—and Rose—that much, even though the attentions he paid his "beautiful blossoms" no longer seemed quite as innocently indulgent as they once had.

"Rose's mother was seventeen when I married her," he began. "She was a beautiful child, and remained one—willful and mercurial—to the end of her short, unhappy life. I had no reason to suspect she was with child when we were married—how thrilled I was when she told me I was to be a father!—and Rose was such a small baby, I accepted her "premature" birth without question."

After Rose was born, Victor said, Rosalind proved all but incapable of caring for her. Marriage had brought to full flower the sexuality unwittingly awakened by her father's handsome stableman. She feared nursing would spoil the pretty figure that drew admiring masculine glances, and the baby's cries of hunger served only to provoke tantrums from her mother. In desperation, Victor asked her sister Rosamund to engage a wet nurse, which allowed Rosalind to ignore her child for days on end except to dress her for occasional outings in the Paris parks.

"She would exchange one tiny lacy robe and cap for another, as one might when playing at dolls, and then grow angry when the poor mite protested.

"That is only one example, you understand. As Rose grew, I became more than just a father to her, and sensing the void in my life—although she did not yet understand it—she looked as best she could to my well-being. More than once I heard her piping voice take the cook to task for an ill-prepared dish." He shook his head sadly. "Is it any wonder that by the time of her mother's death, Rose had become more of a wife to me than her own mother?"

My expression must have given me away. Victor grasped my arms and shook me as if to physically dislodge the shock he saw in my eyes.

"No, no, Violet, not in the sense you're thinking! But somehow we must have known, have somehow sensed, that we weren't . . . that we had no blood ties . . ."

Blood ties . . . the phrase echoed in my mind. I stood as if frozen, staring at him, and when Rose reentered unexpectedly from the hallway, his hands were still grasping my arms.

"Déjà vu, I do declare! Silly me, come to tell Vi I've done the favor of laying out a costume for her on her bed, only to find she has once again taken advantage of my absence to solicit favors of her own."

I cautiously retreated from my determinedly advancing hostess only to come up against Ned, who had entered behind me from the library and received me in a protective embrace.

"Perhaps, my dear Rose," he drawled, "you'd better snap on Victor's leash before he plucks another of his beautiful blossoms."

Rose looked from Ned to me. A sneer distorted her pretty mouth. "Aren't you the pair! Meant for each other, wouldn't you say, Victor? Both of them ready to make the most of whatever situation presents itself. Well, you have my blessing!"

It was an ugly moment. I shrugged off Ned's arms and headed without comment for the stairs.

As I turned to enter my room, I saw Rafe wandering disconsolately down the corridor. His face brightened when he saw me, and despite my dread of the evening stretching ahead of us, which promised to become a mockery of the celebration originally, if unwisely, intended, I couldn't help but smile at the sight of him. He wore a voluminous black cape and atilt over his forehead was a floppy felt beret. A flamboyant mustache had been crayoned beneath his long nose. I began to laugh.

"This is the best I could come up with at the last moment," he protested. He spread his arms and bowed. "A starving artist, at your service, Mademoiselle. All I need is a half-clothed model on my arm . . ." He looked at me hopefully.

"I'm not sure yet what role Rose has in mind for me," I returned wryly, thinking of her reference to the costume she said she had left on my bed, "but I *am* sure that an artist's model *en déshabillé* is unlikely."

"Well, can I at least prevail upon you to do something about this blasted shawl around my neck? I'm all thumbs."

"Nonsense! It's just an ordinary scarf—well, not quite ordinary," I admitted as I adjusted the ends of a wide flowing length of scarlet silk before looping it in a loose, flamboyant bow. "There! You look splendid!"

As a matter of fact, except for the grease mustache, he did. The costume lent him an air of theatricality enhanced by his silver hair and olive-toned complexion. He looked romantic yet sinister, like a character out of one of Mrs. Radcliffe's Italianate Gothic novels.

"You're staring. Has my mustache smeared?"

"No. I was just thinking, I saw some paint brushes in

one of the schoolroom cupboards; there might be an artist's palette there, too—"

"But I've already found one," he announced smugly. "I think it may have belonged to my mother. It still has smears of paint on it, hardened and cracked of course, but it looks very authentic. Come see!"

I followed him into his room. The palette, of enormous size, was indeed the very thing. "Wherever did you find it?"

"I found it in the attic along with my scarf." He lifted the scarlet tip of it with his fingers. "It was Mrs. Devlin's suggestion."

The attic. Where his mother's boxes of fabrics had been stored. "Did you happen to see any quilts there?"

"Quilts?" He drew his dark brows together consideringly. "I don't recall any quilts . . . but there's so much up there, I might have overlooked one, or even two or three. It's like every attic you ever saw, dim and dusty and chockablock with old toys, discarded furniture, and trunkfuls of fabrics and clothes and linens and blankets—moth-eaten, most of them—of every description. Why do you ask?"

I traced for him my convoluted line of reasoning about the quilt Jack had used for a curtain, including my reservations about Jack himself.

Rafe listened attentively, frowning at some points; nodding at others. "But the police are satisfied this raggedy person was the culprit?"

"They appear to be, yes."

"Then I think Jack's quilt is the least of the things you need worry about, Vi."

We were seated side by side on his wide bed, the one Lily and I had shared. I suddenly remembered the hollow in the mattress that one or the other of us had kept rolling into. If one shared it with a lover, I found myself thinking, such a thing might prove more pleasant than annoying . . .

I bent my head to hide the pink I feared had risen to my

cheeks. "If you're referring to Ned, Rafe, please try to put your view of him into better perspective. You've allowed your dislike for him and your disapproval of his plans for Brambledene to affect your judgment of him in every regard."

Rafe looked at me. His eyebrows were raised in surprise. "Of course I have, as well it should."

"I admit Ned's schemes for Brambledene's renovation and enlargement are rather . . . ambitious—"

"Pretentious is more like it," Rafe muttered.

"But it's not as if Jefferson's Monticello had fallen into the hands of barbarians," I continued, as if he hadn't spoken. "For all the family sentiment about it, Brambledene is hardly a national treasure. Ned's wish to have an objective legal opinion about the document that reserves the estate to the Thornbush family strikes me as prudent. In his place, I would not only want, but demand the same protection."

"*Protection?* What does bully-boy Ned, of all people, need to be protested against? I would think it quite the other way around!"

Why was he so willfully obtuse? "Why, against Rose's increasingly unpredictable changes of mood! Against whatever complications the revelation of Milo's parenthood may inject into this already confused situation, and against your desire to have Brambledene for yourself! No! Let me finish! Unlike you, I'm not passing judgment, I'm merely stating Ned's predicament as it seems to me—and, I'm sure, to others of our friends."

"Ah, yes, the famous LOPHs! Epitomized by the ever credulous Fred Latimer, who persists in seeing Ned as a latter-day version of Buffalo Bill. You may be interested to know that your old boating companion isn't quite as admiring."

By now I knew Rafe well enough to guess that his use of "quite" in a context such as this was ironic. What he meant was that Wink had grave reservations. "Why would you say a thing like that?" I ventured cautiously.

"Because the day after he held you all in thrall with his colorful reminiscences, Wink told me Ned had written a number of his Yale classmates, including Wink's brother, proposing they take a flyer in a Colorado gold mine. He claimed that promising color had already been seen by his partner, a man who wore on his finger a huge nugget—'big as a pigeon's egg' is the phrase Wink repeated to me—that had led him to an earlier and very prosperous strike in Gunnison."

"I fail to see the point."

"Haven't you noticed how Ned likes to embroider his stories with convincing detail? In his letter to his prospective investors, he said that the ring had been made for his partner by the grateful backers of his Gunnison venture and inscribed with the nickname they had given him. 'Eureka,' I think Wink said it was. I wonder if we'd find a similar inscription on Ned's ring."

I avoided his speculative gaze. Although I knew he would, I found nothing in that to give me second thoughts.

"You're grasping at straws, Rafe!" I protested. "Surely there was more than one large gold nugget to be found in the Colorado gold fields. In fact, I think it more than likely Willard Syms decided to have a copy made of the ring he treasured as a way of thanking Ned for his faith and trust, and I find nothing reprehensible about Ned canvassing his college chums for funds to secure the claim. Since his partner's taste for cards and liquor invariably ate up whatever profits his nose for gold brought him, money would always have been in short supply. What you have said proves nothing."

"It proves that Ned had no money of his own to risk, and according to Wink, he had a devil of a time raising enough for even a modest stake. It seems that in New Haven he had a reputation for not paying his gambling debts."

"Good heavens, Rafe! How big could his debts have been? He was still a student and presumably dependent on his family—who have nowhere near the wealth of their Van Renssalaer relations—for his support. Besides, no young man worth his salt wants to be seen as fearful of taking a risk, and Ned has never been one to pay much attention to the odds."

"Not even when they might be reckoned as running against him?"

"Particularly then." I laughed. "In fact, that might be enough to persuade him to raise the ante."

"Part of his fabled charm, no doubt," Rafe said with a wry smile. "However, despite your flair for analysis, I fear you have allowed sentiment to sway you. A debt is a debt, and according to Wink, Ned's classmates thought him . . . unreliable."

Could that be why Ned hadn't been tapped for Bones? How petty! "Tell me Rafe, what of those he *did* persuade to invest? Did Wink say whether or not they had been repaid?"

Rafe looked at me sourly. "Yes."

"With interest?"

He scowled. "I believe so," he finally admitted. I could barely hear him.

I got up and walked toward the open door, then turned back to deliver what I hoped would be a withering final comment. Rafe sat slumped on the edge of the bed, disconsolately rubbing his jaw and in the process smearing his mustache. The curlicued, greasy black ends now trailed untidily below the corners of his mouth. He looked ridiculous. I opened my mouth to say just that, then thought better of it. There really was nothing more that needed to be said.

I quietly closed the door to my own room. The lamp on my bedside table had already been lit, and in the glow of it I saw a length of red wool on my bed. It was a cloak. A long, full, finely woven cashmere cloak, more luxurious than any garment I had myself ever owned, and beside it was a basket filled with pretty trinkets. I picked up the cloak by the shoulders. A hood fell back from its wide Pilgrim collar. *Of course! Little Red Riding Hood.*

I wondered what Rose's choice for me was meant to signify. Was I meant to infer that Ned and Rafe were wolves in disguise, to be pursued at my peril? Rose had certainly left no doubt that she thought me desperate enough to be in active pursuit of one or another of them, perhaps both.

Ned, from whom she was making a deliberate effort to distance herself, seemed the obvious choice, but Rafe could be seen as lurking on the sidelines awaiting an opportunity to have the custodianship of Brambledene transferred to himself. If Rose perceived a threat to herself from her cousin, it was understandable for her to think that anyone with whom he formed a close association might live to regret it. Rafe had cruelly neglected me once, who was to say it could not happen again?

I absently stroked the cloak's soft red folds. Even as a child I had thought Red Riding Hood remarkably obtuse. Certainly that long, hairy nose should have alerted her to the wolf's disguise long before his fangs came into view. But suppose it was her lover's identity that the wolf had usurped? And suppose that instead of approaching that woodland hut suffused with filial affection, her wits had been drugged by desire, how then could she have been expected to recognize in time the nasty, sharp-toothed surprise that awaited her in that roughly cobbled bed?

Was it Ned? He and Rose had become estranged, certainly, but wasn't that due more to Rose's perverse attachment to Victor than to anything Ned himself had done? No, much as my suspicions pained me, I knew it must be Rafe that Rose meant to warn me about. How could I forget those telling words from her own lips, those whispered words expressing her fear of the blood ties that would forever bind her . . .

I sighed and, pushing the folds of red wool aside, sank down upon the bed to inspect the contents of the basket.

A note was tied to its handle.

After I selected this cape for you, I thought it might be appropriate for you to distribute the party favors from this basket. I know you must be anxious to leave Brambledene and me behind, but please, dear Vi, let's pretend for a few hours longer that we're still "all for one and one for all."

I sighed again. Obviously, my analytical tendencies had this time led me, when combined with an imagination run riot, badly astray. Rose had thoughtfully found for me an enveloping garment in a color suitable for a Valentine Day costume, and the fact that it was a hooded cape had suggested the basket. Neither choice was symbolic of anything except Rose's generosity. The girlish role she asked me to play did not thrill me, but what choice had I? It was the least thing I could do to repay her hospitality, and judging from her note—which reflected my sentiments as well as her own—it might possibly be the last.

I fingered through the basket's contents. The men were to receive samples of a toilet water that, according to its Bond Street label, had been blended originally for the Prince of Wales. For the ladies there were the familiar crystal flacons of perfume Victor had once again ordered for his beautiful blossoms. Each was equipped with a silk-netted atomiser and tied with satin ribbons: Flora's flower-garden blend was accompanied by a swirl of pastel colors, Iris's orris scent with deep vibrant purple, and mine—my finger traced the Parma violets scattered on its label—with pale lavender. Rose's was bowed with a shade of pink as richly warm as the scent itself. I bent my nose to the stopper, and as I did so the well-remembered rose fragrance brought to mind an incident I had witnessed the night Lily died.

On that fateful evening, Victor had distributed the perfumes to his blossoms when the company gathered for sherry in the library, in case we wished to apply a fragrant drop or two to wrist and throat while dressing for the party. He had presented each gift with a few graceful words that made each of us in turn blush with pleasure, but even though the compliments were flatteringly personal, there was nothing in any of them to cause even the most conventional of eyebrows to arch.

The fellows had chuckled indulgently, and we dispersed to don our costumes in high spirits. Lily, impulsive as always, had paused at the foot of the stairs to throw her arms around Victor and kiss him soundly. Lacking a family of her own, she was enormously touched by this thoughtful gift given her by her friend's dashing father.

Rose, coming up behind them in the hallway, had wrenched Lily's perfume from her hand and hurled it to the tiled floor, smashing the crystal into a hundred glittering lily of the valley scented bits. Lily had stared open-mouthed at Rose, then, as tears of outrage spilled down her cheeks, she grabbed Rose's bottle and emptied the contents over her hostess' sleek blond head.

"There!" I recall her crying. "If you can't act as sweet as a rose, at least you can smell like one!"

How could I have forgotten that? Had the appalling tragedy of Lily's death induced me to idealize our friendships? Although Rose had never been as tolerant of Lily's boisterousness as the rest of us, I had failed to sense the unhealthiness of her jealous reaction to Lily's innocently affectionate display of gratitude. I wondered now if Mrs. Taliaferro's disapproving long-ago reference to an adult male taste for very young girls had been meant to apply, not to her absent husband, but to her brother-in-law's relationship with Rose.

Maybe that was why Rose had married Ned. She hadn't loved him at all; to the contrary, taking advantage of her blond resemblance to Lily to attract him, might she have intended their union to conceal the true nature of her relationship with the man she thought was her father?

But that seemed so cold, so calculating! I found it hard, even after all that had happened, to think so badly of Rose. To give her all possible benefit of the doubt, perhaps she had hoped her unnatural feelings for the man she thought was her father would be driven out by marriage to Ned Poole, whose roguish, virile charm was famously admired. Obviously, however, marriage had failed to effect the desired cure, and when Milo Devlin was revealed as her true father, the sooner she could dissolve a union whose forced intimacy had become distasteful, the better.

What, I wondered, could be harder for a proud man to face than the certain knowledge that his wife considered him an encumbrance? Indignation routed my earnest attempt to provide a sympathetic reading of Rose's motives. I no longer cared. Poor Ned! If anyone was a victim here it was he.

CHAPTER NINETEEN

Dinner was scheduled for half past eight. I waited until I had heard the others descending before following them down into the dining room.

The show, it seemed, was fated to go on despite the storm raging outside which had forced the loss of our entire audience of local gentry, not to mention the musicians who, if they had arrived at all, would have only the stationmaster to serenade. We would, in effect, be players playing to ourselves, and for that reason I was relieved when the sherry hour was cancelled. As far as I was concerned, this play had already gone on too long, and the celebratory scene we were about to begin seemed forced at best. I felt as if we had all been swept up in an inexorable flow of events whose final act I was loath to contemplate.

As I entered, Victor was touching a lighted taper to the clusters of candles in elaborately chased silver epergnes set between my arrangements of white and red carnations. The flicker of candlelight, the faint, ecclesiastical scent of beeswax and the gleaming silver set upon the heavy, creamy linen cloth generated an air of quiet opulence. The wavering shafts of warm light emitted by the fire crackling cozily on the hearth lent a healthy, sun-kissed glow to the faces that turned to greet me. For the moment at least, my misgivings were quieted.

"How splendid you all look!" I exclaimed.

Obviously the Latimer twins had, like Rafe, foraged for their finery in Brambledene's cavernous attic. Freddie was got up in yellowed ivory flannel breeches, high black boots, a white dress shirt and black tail coat, all somewhat too large for his short, tubby frame. A shiny top hat and black whip completed his impression of a circus ringmaster. Flora, eye-catching in tights, plumed cap, and a borrowed bathing costume swagged with satin trimmed with a variety of faded artificial flowers, posed demurely by his side. All she lacked was a trapeze.

Wink was a lumberjack. His rough garb of suspendered and broad-belted red and black checkered trousers, stout laced boots and red flannel shirt with sleeves rolled to reveal muscular, auburn-furred forearms, would have suited any number of manly outdoor occupations, but the great axe over his broad shoulder was worthy of the ill-fated Harry Dale himself. As I looked at his strong, kind face I prayed his supervisory job in the family timberlands would keep him out of harm's way, although his skill with axe and saw was probably the equal of any logger in his employ.

Flanking him was Iris, skirted in vivid blue, who looked the very spirit of Lady Liberty thanks to the broad red, white, and blue striped sash that stretched from shoulder to waist across her impressive, white-shirted bosom. Her handsome features had an exalted look, and I forebore to question the suitability of using the American flag, the staff of which she clutched in her hand, as a costume accessory. My patriotism, although sincere, was not up to quibbling about the finer points of flag display etiquette with such a determined-looking bearer.

Rafe's black-caped form, lit fitfully by the fire he stood to one side of, looked like a figure in a Rembrandt painting: somber, contemplative, shrouded in mystery. He had dispensed altogether with his grease mustache. A wise decision, I thought, for his haughty, fine-featured face did not lend itself to caricature.

Ned, grinning broadly, called to me from across the room. "Damn me if that red cloak doesn't set off your black hair and pearly skin to perfection," he exclaimed, seeming to jingle as he turned, open-handed, to invite agreement from the rest. Unlike Rafe, he was a man made for flamboyant gestures.

His white shirt, open at the throat, was tucked into blue Levi trousers belted with a broad, flashy, silver-mounted leather strap and topped by a bright yellow, leather-trimmed waistcoat. The fringed ends of a loosely knotted red, white-figured bandanna trailed over his shoulder, and on his tawny head sat a wide-brimmed Stetson hat of fawn-colored beaver fine as velvet, cocked low to one side.

The jingle came from the wickedly roweled spurs on the newly burnished square-toed, high-heeled leather boots that had a way of transforming his stride to a cocky, swiveled-hip strut, one sight of which would persuade a prudent mother to lock her daughters up.

"You deserve the blue ribbon for your getup, Neddy," Freddie said admiringly. "No question about it. I swear I can smell the sagebrush."

Ned laughed. "That wouldn't be fair, Fred. What I have on is an ordinary cowboy's workaday garb, not really a costume at all. Like Victor, I cheated, but I'm certainly not in his class. He looks every inch the nobleman he is. I ask you, who could resist him?"

Ned's expression was guileless enough, but I inferred without hesitation the answer to his rhetorical question: *not Rose!*

Victor, who had just lit the last of the candles, looked up frowningly. In elegant contrast with his guests' motley garb, his immaculate evening dress fitted his tall, spare figure to perfection, the only touch of color a dark red and purple rosette on the black silk revers.

The taper he held in his long thin fingers guttered out. A trail of blue smoke eddied up to blur his gaunt face, and as it did so, Rose emerged out of the shadows behind him like a conjuring trick.

Her billowing white satin dress had a large neck ruffle above a close-fitting bodice buttoned with large red-painted wooden hearts, whose shape and color were repeated by smaller versions on her wrists and fingers. Framed by the red-dotted netting with which she had looped up her blond, loosely curled locks, her face wore an expression of unearthly serenity. I gasped.

"Do you recognize it, Vi?" she asked as she pirouetted slowly down the room toward me. "Ada gave our Lenox seamstress the two Pierrot costumes, and voilà! One Columbine."

I stared at her aghast, unable to say a word. At last year's party both Lily and Rose had dressed as white satin-pantalooned Pierrots. Of similar height and coloring, their faces white-powdered and lips and cheeks brightly painted red, they had dispensed with the traditional black masks. It had been Lily's idea, and although their quarrel before the party had prevented them from collaborating as fully as planned, their costumed similarity caused several amusing instances of confusion as to their identities, and by the time I had last seen them together—while Lily was still alive, that is—she and Rose were again on speaking terms.

"Cat got your tongue, Vi? Or perhaps I'm invisible! Columbine is supposed to be invisible to mortal eyes . . . isn't that so, Ned darling?" Her tone was openly mocking. "Surely even you had a smattering of literary history at Yale."

Ned looked at her. I could not read the expression in his eyes. They seemed strangely opaque, as if blue painted shutters had swung shut over their brightness.

"'Fraid your reference escapes me, Rose," he said lightly. "I'm not much of a reader, you know." Far from taking offense at Rose's barb, the indulgent tone of his reply struck me as suitable for a willful child or a hysteric. Curious about her reaction, I glanced back toward Rose.

She stood beside Victor, her billow of white satin in sumptuous contrast to his austere formal dress. Her saintly expression, illuminated flickeringly from below by the candles he had lit, had not altered in the slightest detail. She had not made herself up in white face this time, and the frightening artificiality of her uplifted, unmoving wide blue eyes made me fear for the balance of her mind.

I knew by now that Rose had more strength of character than her fragile form and delicate features suggested, but was a strong character sufficient to rescue her from the tendency toward cruel despondency that had destroyed her mother?

Rose slowly turned her head, puppetlike, and as I watched in horror, her face began to slide. A gagging sound escaped me—I could not help it!—before I realized that her hideously slipping face was in fact a painted mask.

"Columbine was Pierrot's sweetheart, isn't that so, Violet?" she asked. "So I decided to let her wear in his place the mask that according to tradition Pierrot uses to hide his true emotions."

"But Pierrot's mask is black," I blurted, "and covers only the upper half of his face."

"Bravo, Vi! Miss Peebles would be proud of you!" She made an elaborate curtsey, spreading her satin skirt like great white wings. "But I've decided to break with tradition: what you see before you is a little of the old me and a lot of the new."

"You're not making a particle of sense, Rose," Iris said plaintively. "I haven't the faintest idea who of you is which, or which of you is who or whom or . . . oh, bother!" Her full mouth twitched petulantly. "This house party isn't at all like the ones I remember."

"Poor Iris!" Rose said. "I'm afraid it's not been like

what any of us remember. Nevertheless," she continued with ghastly forced sprightliness, "I'm counting on all of you, my dearest and oldest friends, to help poor Ned decide whether I'm more like Pierrot," she raised the mask to her face, "or Columbine." She whisked it away again and darted behind Victor. "You see?" she said, "I can vanish at will!"

"You are whoever you wish to be, Rose," Rafe said gently. "No one can decide that for you." His simple, quiet words had a ring of conviction that arrested me. "But please," he continued in a lighter tone, "can't we put this metaphysical discussion to rest long enough to enjoy the wonderful meal I'm sure Mrs. Devlin has prepared for us?"

Much as it pained Freddie to approve of anything suggested by Rafe, he did so now. "As far as I'm concerned, we can put it to rest forever. It's enough to give a fellow indigestion."

Freddie's gruff pronouncement broke the spell Rose's strangely buoyant variety of contentiousness had cast. Released from its thralldom, we scurried around the table seeking our place cards as if our very lives depended on it.

"Here you are, Wink! Here, next to me!" Iris caroled joyfully upon discovering a seating arrangement that came as no surprise to anyone else.

"Violet?" Flora called, "We're over here, with Rafe between us, *mais je ne parle pas français, Monsieur,*" she added coyly as Rafe held her chair for her.

"In that case, I will not be tempted to say unsuitable Gallic things, will I, *mon petit chou?*"

Flora eyed him doubtfully. "Vi! What did he say?"

I laughed. "He called you his little cabbage, Flora."

"I'm not sure I like that . . . what d'ye think, Vi, should I be cross?"

"My dear Flora," Rafe responded, "I don't know you well enough to call you 'my little darling' in English."

"Well, in that case I shan't be cross at all."

Flora blushed, Rafe smirked, and I laughed again, a

little tinkly sound as artificial as all the other attempts at airy conversation taking place around us. I excused myself to distribute Rose and Victor's gifts from my basket.

During my playing at Lady Bountiful, I became achingly aware of the visual memories I was capturing of these dear old friends assembled here tonight, perhaps for the last time. Like the swift stroke of an artist's pen, my eyes recorded the characteristic toss of Flora's strawberry-blond curls and the gleam of Wink's teeth, as big and white as piano keys, as he leaned to share a laugh with Ned. As I passed behind Victor I rested my hand lightly, briefly, on his shoulder. No one else would ever address me with sweet affection as his beautiful blossom. He did not notice my touch; his fine eyes, pouched now with fatigue and worry, were fastened unwaveringly on Rose and Freddie's earnest exchange. As he listened to something Rose was saying, Freddie's lips pursed in the way he had lately affected, and I fancied I could see him in a judge's robes one day, balding perhaps; plumper, certainly.

The images I hoarded were unimportant ones: a joke shared; a shadowy face caught in a moment of solitary reflection; a man's strong hand, Rafe's hand, extended in a quick, fluid motion to either underscore a point or grant one, I had no way of knowing which. Images which goad us with their familiarity: unforgettable, yet never quite remembered; the trace of a passing moment, like the bird whose flight is sensed from the corner of an eye.

As I dispensed the pretty bottles from my basket one by one into eagerly receiving hands, the ribbons, labels, and colors were minutely observed and compared and exclaimed over. Plainly, my charity by proxy had offered a new and safe topic of conversation to be mined, and by the time Jennie and Agnes began serving the meal, I thought we were home free.

I put the tissue-lined basket down next to the fireplace before taking my seat, and as I did so a bottle rolled out from under the varicolored papers. Puzzled, I picked it up. I was certain I had given a bottle to every member of our party. The label was printed in pale green on white, difficult to read in the dim light. I held it closer to the flames.

Lily of the valley.

I hadn't meant to read it aloud, but an anguished, choking cry told me I must have.

"If this is your idea of a joke, Vi!" Rose scraped back her chair and got to her feet. Her red-painted mouth and cheeks were like gashes against her livid face; the big wooden hearts on her fingers bobbed as she clutched at her wide collar.

"*My* idea! Good heavens, Rose, how could you—"

Victor placed a restraining hand on Rose's arm. He looked miserable. "I fear I'm to blame, darling girl. I never stopped to think . . . it's what I had always ordered, you see; the shop had no way of knowing. When you asked me to put the bottles in the basket, I didn't think to look—"

"Neither did I, Victor," I offered. "I saw no reason to . . . it never occurred to me . . ."

I faltered; I seemed merely to be compouding Victor's error. Without thinking, I held up the little crystal bottle. "How Lily loved the perfume you gave her, Victor!" I blurted. "Perhaps in the morning I'll take it out to her grave and—" I broke off in dismay as Rose, balling her hand against her mouth to stifle her sobs, fled from the room.

For a long moment the only sound to be heard was the hiss of glowing embers. Mrs. Devlin and the serving girls had stopped in their tracks like children playing at statues. A log popped loudly, making everyone blink. Rafe cleared his throat.

"Would someone mind telling me what this is all about?"

I sensed all eyes turning to me as I leaned down to place Lily's perfume back in its nest of tissue. I straightened up with a sigh and gazed into the flames, seeking a moment's respite in which to gather my forces, but all I could see were those wooden rings on Rose's fingers.

"Will someone try to enlighten Rafe, please? I think I had better see to Rose."

Ned threw his napkin on the table. "I'll go, Vi! You seem to forget—all of you do!—that Rose is my wife!"

I held up a restraining hand. "Please, Ned, not yet. She needs another woman now . . . will you allow us a little time alone together?"

I could tell from Ned's scowl he didn't much like it, but he nodded curtly and waved me from the room.

Truth to tell, I wasn't at all sure that Rose needed or wanted a female confidante, and even if she did I doubt she would have chosen me, but it was the kind of generality that if said with sufficient authority men are unlikely to dispute. We had a few things to put behind us, Rose and I, and I might never have another chance.

CHAPTER TWENTY

I knocked on the door to Rose and Ned's room and entered before Rose had a chance to tell me to go away.

She was seated, her head bowed, on the edge of a handsome netting-draped Empire tester bed. Her wan fairness set against the room's subtle, dimly lit colors put me in mind of the mannered elegance of a painting by Watteau. The shadowed folds of her crumpled satin skirt gleamed against the gauzy hand-embroidered peach bedspread; her pretty slippers, their ribbon ties in disarray, lay discarded nearby upon a pale Kirmanshah carpet swirled with vines and arching floral sprays. Seeing her thus, palely lovely and vulnerable, it was easy to see why Ned might have fallen in love with her; harder to understand why he wondered now if he really had.

Rose glanced up at me. Her grave expression conveyed no sign of the glittery-eyed agitation that had earlier alarmed me—although her twiddling of the wooden rings on her fingers betrayed a certain restlessness—and if she had been drinking, she had been at pains to conceal the evidence.

"Rose? Can you believe me if I swear to you I have no designs on either your husband or your . . . on Victor? Even if Ned were free, I'm not sure . . ."

My words trailed away as tears swelled in her eyes, spilling over like great pale pearls upon her cheeks. "Rose," I began again, even more gently, "is there something you wish to tell me?"

She began to sob, her tears falling unheeded onto her satin bodice. "It was an accident Vi. A terrible accident."

"I'm sure it was, Rose." I reached into my pocket for a handkerchief and gently blotted her wet cheeks. Not having the least idea to what she was referring, I smiled at her encouragingly.

"The night of the party last year; the night Lily was— She stopped abruptly and took a deep shuddering breath. "Lily asked you to deliver notes to me and to Victor . . . you do remember, don't you, Vi?"

Rose grasped my hands; her tear-reddened eyes searched mine intently.

Her urgency made me frown. What could be so important about notes I could barely remember? She and Lily had had that foolish quarrel over Victor, then later, while we were dressing for the party, Lily told me how much she regretted pouring Rose's perfume over her head. "Even if she did deserve it," she had added with a characteristic little jab of her forefinger.

Knowing how hard it was for Lily to admit to mistakes—"never explain; never apologize"—I had suggested she write them brief notes expressing her regret. "That way you can put the whole foolish business behind you, Lily," I had said.

My tone must have been sterner than I intended, for I recalled now the astonished expression on Lily's face, followed in rapid succession by a defiant uptilt of her chin, a thoughtful frown, and a sly little smile. *That sly smile* . . . I should have known something was up, but at the time I took her next action at face value.

I remember her rummaging in the drawer of the little desk in our room for notepaper, then sitting down to scribble off a few lines, her white satin Pierrot pantaloons ballooning around her. She had slipped the sheets into envelopes, sealed them—a precaution I had not appreciated, considering I was supposed to deliver them—and handed them to me with a flourish. If I had suspected then, as I did now, that I would thereby be setting cats among the pigeons, I would have refused.

"It was my understanding," I ventured cautiously, "that what I delivered to you and Victor were notes of apology."

Rose laughed, but there was no mirth in it. "Not quite that, Vi. They merely set a time for a meeting. It was to be in the conservatory after dinner, when everyone would either be busily arranging the parlor for dancing or playing that game of Ned's you're all so fond of, the one he said was inspired by the protective coloration of some of the insects he'd seen out west."

"Chameleon, you mean?"

Rose nodded. "But the notes weren't signed by Lily, you see. She signed my name to Victor's note, and Victor's to mine, but in my note she set the time of the meeting ahead by five minutes."

Rose got to her feet and began to pace restlessly, her fingers clutching at the folds of her satin skirt. Her distraught expression made me apprehensive. I wished suddenly that I could seal her lips; stop her story there.

"When I arrived, I didn't see them at first," she continued. "They were in that little ferny glade where Lily liked to sit and read. I remember thinking how lovely it was to come into that warm enclosure smelling of damp earth and flowers with snow falling just the thickness of a pane of glass away. Then I saw them. Lily was in Victor's arms, looking at me over his shoulder with a look of triumph on her face." Rose's voice was choked with emotion; her hands gathered the satin folds into creased wads.

"Not triumph, Rose!" I protested, "never that! It was mischief—ill-conceived mischief, to be sure—but she meant no harm by it."

Rose gestured impatiently. "You always were ready to give Lily the benefit of the doubt, Violet. Not that it matters any more *what* she intended; all I know is what I saw. Victor tried to tell me he mistook Lily for me: he went on and on about the dimness, our similar coloring, our identical costumes and make-up. It made sense, I know that now, but I wouldn't listen to him and then Lily began to laugh. And when she laughed . . . oh, Vi, when she laughed I hit her. I hit her very hard and she slid down onto the bricks, hitting her head a glancing blow on the nearest bench as she fell."

Rose, who had crossed to the window, turned toward me. I could sense from across the room an appeal for understanding in her eyes, but I could only stare at her uncomprehendingly. *Rose had struck Lily? Hard enough to knock her down? How could that possibly be!*

"I stood there, Vi, staring down at her," she was saying. "It all happened so fast! I remember thinking what a shame it was that her pretty costume had become slimed with algae. Victor tried to rouse her, but she just lay there, crumpled, her eyes half open, only the whites showing."

She came back to sink down on the bed beside me again. "Later, when I came to my senses, I wanted to tell what had happened, but by then it was too late. We were trapped, all three of us, by ghastly circumstance. And I'm still trapped, Vi! Trapped in a marriage with a man I don't love, trapped by my emotions, trapped by feelings of guilt I can no longer endure. My life is a lie, a shameful, unendurable lie."

Rose's overwrought words and slumped posture alarmed me. Her wooden rings clacked dully as her fingers twisted around one another like snakes. Those crude wooden rings. They could have caused the bruises on Lily's throat. Jealousy and rage can lend murderous strength to even a girl's slender fingers, especially if the victim is already unconscious . . .

I grasped Rose's shoulders roughly and forced her to meet my eyes. "After Lily fell, Rose, did you . . . did you touch her? Shake her, perhaps? Did you feel for the pulse in her throat?"

Rose stared at me. Her eyes were glassy with remembered horror. "Did I?" she whispered. "I don't remember, I can't . . ." She slumped again and began to sway.

I shook her. *"Did you touch Lily after she fell?"*

Rose shuddered. She raised her head; her eyes regained a more normal focus. She shook her head. "No. I was angry, but I never meant . . . No, Vi, I didn't touch her."

"Then listen to me, Rose. You must try to put this behind you. No matter what you did or didn't do, as far as the police are concerned the case is closed. You heard Sergeant Morley say so yourself. What happened between you and Lily was an accident; what happened between her and the Raggedy Man was murder. He must have been passing through the storm on the way to one of his secret shelters—he may have had one in the Bramble, for all we know—but however he got to the conservatory or why, I saw him with my own eyes, Rose! Why not leave it at that? No one else need ever know what you have told me here tonight. Lily was impulsive and headstrong and sometimes, as she was that night with you and Victor, unthinkingly unkind, but she wouldn't want you to continue punishing yourself like this. I know she wouldn't."

Rose's face contorted with despair. I had clearly failed to convince her. Her hostility toward Lily had twisted in her mind over time until she had become convinced she had actually done what she only wished to do.

I watched in helpless sorrow—sorrow for Lily as much as for Rose who rocked back and forth beside me, clutching herself as if that were the only way she could keep herself from flying apart.

As if she had read my mind, Rose suddenly got to her feet and resumed her restless pacing. "You said no one else need know, Vi," she said brokenly, "but I know, and Victor knows. How can we live in peace knowing that old derelict was accused of a crime he didn't commit?

"Ned knows, too," she added in a confiding whisper, "but if you ask him he'll tell you—"

"He'll tell you that murderous tramp is dead, Rose," Ned said from the doorway. He strode into the room, and as he neared Rose he opened his arms to embrace her. With a despairing sigh, she rested her head on his shoulder. Her hair had escaped its netting enclosure, and Ned gently stroked the blond locks loosed on Rose's shoulders. They looked like characters in a romantic novel: Rose in her billow of white satin and Ned in his yellow-vest-topped Levis. The princess and the cowboy. A desperately unhappy princess, I told myself, as I caught a glimpse of Rose's tear-stained cheeks.

"These fantasies of guilt are making you ill, dear Rose, but I promise to help rid you of them, and I will keep you safe always."

Rose peered at me over Ned's shoulder. His encircling arms seemed like a cage, I thought, and Rose more like a captive than a loving and submissive wife.

"And Lily knows," she whispered, completing the statement Ned had interrupted. "That's why she came back, isn't it, Vi? That shining shape in the schoolroom was hers, its warmth and sweet fragrance meant to lull me into thinking it meant me no harm."

After what she had already said, it came now as no surprise that the mysterious and wondrous manifestation the night of Ada's seance had served to confirm Rose's sense of guilt. The subsequent revelation of Milo as her true father had merely, I realized now, postponed this hour of dreadful reckoning.

"Shhh-hhhsh," Ned hushed in a rhythmic, soothing tone.

Rose's eyelids drooped. "She's out there somewhere," she muttered, "waiting to wrest the sin from my soul."

Ned was right: she *was* making herself ill. I rose to my feet, planning to assist Ned in undressing her and putting her to bed, but as I moved toward them Ned motioned me to the door with a flick of his head. "Thank you, Vi," he said quietly, "I can look after my wife myself."

His resolute dignity both touched and impressed me. I wondered how many men were as ready as he to fulfill his wedding-day pledge "for better or worse, for richer and poorer, in sickness and in health?" He had rallied to Rose—as Freddie assured me he would have to Lily once her impoverishment had become known—and I respected him for it. I had been charmed by Ned, amused and excited by him, I had even fallen in love with him, but I had never before respected him.

I nodded and left the room, closing the door softly behind me. It had been a disquieting scene. Poor Rose! She was unhappy in a marriage that Ned, despite its problems, seemed determined to preserve, yet if Rose chose to abandon him for Victor, what kind of life awaited them? Despite Milo having been revealed as Rose's real father, society would not tolerate their relationship. I was sophisticated enough to know that happy unions were not as usual as I had once thought, but Rose's must surely be uniquely accursed.

I hesitated at the top of the stairs. I would have much preferred to retreat to my room, but I owed it to my hosts to return to the others and see what I could do to help salvage what was left of the evening. A distraction was in order—for me as much as anyone else—and despite Rafe's distaste for it, I decided I would organize a game of charades. Yes, that was the ticket! I began descending with a firm step, but faltered when I became aware that Rafe was awaiting me at the bottom.

I told myself I would not be dazzled by his smile or dizzied by the silver eyes fixed upon me, but despite my resolve I found myself unsteadied by the intensity of his regard.

"Like pansies," he murmured.

I stared at him. *What on earth . . . ?*

"Your purple eyes, Vi." He stepped closer. "They're like huge velvet pansies. A man's cautions could drown in their soft depths."

I stepped back up one stair tread, swallowed hard, and clasped my hands primly at my waist. "I've just come from Rose," I said, deciding to ignore his provocative remarks, which was made easier by looking down on him from my artificially achieved height. "I think you should know that you were quite wrong about Ned. He's sincerely concerned about her welfare."

He smiled, more in response to my retreat than my statement. "If that is the case," he said soberly, "nothing could make me happier—although I wonder if the same holds true for you." He held out his hand to me. "I'll make you a bargain, Violet: I promise I'll try to think better of Ned, provided you try to think better of me." He waggled his fingers. "Come now, my girl, what could be fairer than that?"

I hesitated, then reached down to seal with a traditional shake of the hand the pact he offered me. I intended to do no more than grasp the tips of his fingers, but the moment my hand touched his, a merest glancing graze of flesh, I knew I was lost.

Did I walk down the step that separated us? I felt as if I had floated into his arms, and for a long delicious moment all that mattered was the warm urgency of his mouth on mine.

"I already know one thing Ned was right about," Rafe whispered. "That red cape against your black hair and fair skin does indeed combine to ravishing effect, but tell me, how should I think of you? As Red Riding Hood or my valentine?"

"I would say that depends on whether I decide you're my King of Hearts or the big bad wolf."

"When will you decide?" His warm lips brushed along the sensitive rim of my ear.

"I haven't decided *that* yet, either," I murmured.

"Perhaps you need additional evidence . . ."

My eyelids fluttered closed as he bent his persuasive lips to mine, but hurried footsteps made us spring apart.

"Violet? I thought I recognized your voice." It was Victor. "Isn't Rose with you? *Is she all right?*"

"She's a bit anxious and very tired," I said, moving to block his access to the stairs. "But you needn't worry, Victor. Her husband is with her. I really don't think she needs you now," I added pointedly. "Ned is putting her to bed; I'm sure she'll be ready to rejoin us in the morning."

I spoke with more confidence than I felt and, judging from his stricken expression, my briskly optimistic assessment failed to quiet Victor's fears.

He sighed and passed a shaking hand across his brow. He seemed to age ten years in as many seconds. "You know nothing about it, Violet," he muttered. "Nothing at all." He smiled wearily. "Come along, then, we might as well join the others in the library. They're just about to start playing a favorite LOPH game."

"Not charades, I hope," Rafe protested. "I loathe playacting."

Victor arched a dark eyebrow. "Do you, Rafe? You needn't worry then; it's a game of Ned's devising. Chameleon, he calls it. When it became obvious the storm would keep all our neighbors at home, Ned thought it might keep us occupied. That's why we cancelled the sherry hour, to give him time to make the necessary preparations."

"Chameleon?" Rafe said. "An odd name for a game."

"I understand it's based on the principal of protective coloration," Victor said, "which, come to think of it, is itself a form of playacting—as are the lives many people choose to lead, even here at Brambledene."

Rafe eyed him narrowly. "Why do you say that?"

"Unlike the leopard, people can change their spots quite easily to suit whatever company or circumstance they find themselves in. It's safer that way." His laugh had a biting edge. "The truth is often so hard to accept."

An uncomfortable silence followed Victor's pronouncement. Were his words meant as a warning or an accusation? Rafe looked as unsure of his intent as I.

The sound of a throat being cleared on the landing above us made us start. It was Milo Devlin.

"Count Stirbey? Is Miss Ro . . . is Rose downstairs with you?"

"She's retired for the night, Milo. Is there anything I can do for you?"

"I was wondering about your guests' plans for tomorrow. Are they still hoping to take the afternoon train to New York?"

"I'm still planning to leave, Mr. Devlin," I said. "Depending on your ability to get me to the station, of course. This dreadful storm . . ."

"The wind has shifted, Miss Grayson. I expect the snow will slacken by morning, and Jack is a grand hand with a sleigh! It would take a big push of weather to keep him off the road, but he should know whether to hitch up the big sleigh or the cutter."

"I'll be leaving, too," Rafe said. "I think everyone will, except for the immediate family."

Victor paled.

"*Mon dieu!*" Rafe muttered when he realized the implication of his careless words.

"Count Stirbey," Milo blurted, "I—"

Victor held up his hand. "Please, Milo, we'll sort this all out in time, but for now . . ."

"Of course, sir, I understand." Milo's brilliant blue eyes looked directly down into Victor's. The deep dimple in his cheek seemed almost disfiguring from this angle. "I am that sorry, sir."

"Nothing to be sorry for, Milo. You're a good man, I know that." He smiled tiredly. "Rose could do much worse."

The two men didn't go so far as to shake hands, but I sensed a strengthening of the strange bond circumstance had imposed between them. I couldn't help wondering how that bond would fare once Milo became comfortable with his newfound paternity. No matter how understanding a man Milo Devlin might be—his tolerance of Ada's peculiarities was certainly a case in point—his old country upbringing undoubtedly had its limits, and I suspected Rose and Victor's relationship would fall far beyond them.

"Shall we join the others in the library, Vi?" Rafe said, cupping his hand under my elbow.

"What? Oh, yes! Yes, of course," I said in response to

the gently urging pressure of his fingers. "You'll let us know in the morning if the sleigh will be going, Mr. Devlin?"

"As soon as ever I can, miss. It should be a fine treat jingling through the countryside dressed all clean and white in new snow."

A cold treat, too, I imagined. As Rafe and I turned toward the parlor I saw Victor look longingly up the stairs, "Are you coming, Victor?" I asked. "I imagine Rose is asleep by now. I think it best we not disturb her."

"The dear girl's not feeling poorly, is she?" Milo inquired anxiously. "Should I ask Ada to have a look at her, d'ye think?"

Victor frowned. "I think not," he said. I could not tell whether his answer was prompted by my rather stern statement to him or Milo's awakening paternal feelings. Whatever the cause, by denying Milo access to Rose, he had in effect denied it to himself as well. As this realization belatedly presented itself to him he bade a curt good evening to Milo, then resignedly joined Rafe and me.

"Well! It's high time you showed up! It's a bit difficult to play a game when the players keep disappearing, you know."

"You have every right to be miffed with us, Fred," Rafe admitted.

"Miffed? I'm not miffed. I've never been miffed," Freddie muttered in a decidedly miffed tone of voice.

"Annoyed, then, or irritated or provoked or—"

"You needn't review Roget's entire list of synonyms, Taliaferro." Rafe's placating smile seemed to have compounded the offense Freddie perceived. "Rose and Ned coming?"

"'Fraid not, Freddie," I said. "Rose is . . . exhausted. Ned's putting her to bed."

"That shouldn't take all evening," he protested.

"Oh, for pity's sake, Brother, stop fussing!" Flora exclaimed. "Ned left the list of objects he hid with Wink, and since the game was his idea he wouldn't have been able to play anyway. Besides, there's no required number of players for Chameleon."

"No-o-oo," he conceded reluctantly, "But the more the merrier."

Freddie's cross expression was so at odds with his words, we all laughed. Wink's anxious face relaxed, and he and Iris began passing out the copies of Ned's list they had made in our absence.

"Now remember," Iris said, wagging an admonishing finger. "No peeking and no collaborating."

"How about explaining?" Rafe asked.

We looked blankly first at him and then each other.

He threw his arms wide. "Must I remind you again of my status?" he implored. "A stranger in LOPH land?"

"We're not likely to forget, old man," I heard Freddie mutter under his breath.

"Oh, it's great fun, Rafe!" Flora exclaimed. "I'm sure you'll enjoy it." Then, recalling his dim view of charades, she added doubtfully, "at least I hope you will."

Rafe, no wiser than before, turned to me. "Violet? Enlighten me, please?"

I took pity on him. "You'll be given a list of objects, all of which are hidden in a defined area, in this case the library."

"There are more than usual this time," Wink continued. "Twenty-four altogether, but they aren't hidden in the ordinary sense—"

"In fact," I broke in, "they're not hidden at all. The trick of it is to match like to like . . . for example, if I wished to 'hide' a penny, I'd place it on a copper tray."

"Assuming they had a similar degree of brightness or tarnish," Freddie amplified.

"And there are two dozen such pairings in this room?" Rafe asked.

"In plain sight," Wink confirmed.

Rafe scratched his ear. "Doesn't seem much of a challenge to me."

Freddie exchanged a knowing smile with me. "If you'd been as royally hoodwinked by Ned as the rest of us, you wouldn't say that."

Rafe raised his eyebrows. "If I had been, Latimer, I wouldn't be as ready to admit it, either." His lazy smile made it clear he was not just referring to the game under discussion.

Freddie's jowls quivered with indignation. "By George! I resent your implication!"

The two seemed almost ready to square off. Victor stepped forward, ready to step between them, when Iris, who, busy with the game's preparations, had been oblivious to the flare of tempers, peremptorily called us to order with a schoolmarmish clap of her hands.

"Your attention, please! Does everyone have a list and a pencil? You have exactly one hour—Wink, dear, will you please act as timekeeper? On your mark, get ready, set . . . go!"

Lists in hand, we scurried around the room. Save for Victor, who retreated under the spiral stairs to stare out at the falling snow, our energies were bent toward spying out Ned's clever concealments without betraying our successes to the others.

Freddie, knowing his twin would be unable to suppress her yips of delighted discovery, trailed in his keen-eyed sister's wake until Iris, incensed by his subterfuge, declared him *persona non grata*, a characterization to which Freddie took loud exception.

By the half-hour mark, I had checked off only eight on my list, and Rafe's superior air had been replaced by a frown of concentration that to judge from Freddie's smug observation of it compensated for his dressing down by Iris.

By game's end, Flora was the winner by virtue of having found twenty of the objects Ned had concealed. She had even spied the gold pen nib, which eluded the rest of us, snugly attached to the narrow rim of brass banding the library table drawer.

After our lists were compared and exclaimed over with cries of, "How could I have missed that?" and "I never thought to look there!", I was inordinately pleased to hear Rafe admit to Freddie that the game had indeed been more of a challenge than he had expected. Mollified, Freddie conceded that Rafe had made a respectable showing for a beginner.

"It takes a degree of concentration," Freddie pontificated, "to outwit a master of the game like Ned."

A gleam flashed in the depths of Rafe's gray eyes. He opened his mouth to reply, but contented himself with a nod of his head, apparently thinking better of the provocative riposte he had in mind.

I smiled gratefully and moved toward him. As I did so, there was a tap at the library door. Asked to come in, Ada Devlin appeared in the doorway. The basket from which I had distributed the party favors was in her hands.

"Miss Grayson? I was about to put this away in the cupboard in the old schoolroom, but there appears to be a bottle of perfume still in it . . . I thought maybe you would know what Miss Rose wants done with it."

The perfume meant for Lily. I recalled dropping the bottle back in the basket after Rose's tearful departure from the table. My heart gave a sad little lurch. To this day I can never see or smell lilies of the valley without thinking of her.

"Thank you, Mrs. Devlin," I said. "I'll take care of it.

Rafe reached out his hand toward me. "Violet?" he inquired in a low voice.

But the moment had passed. I shook my head and moved quietly toward the door. For now, all I wanted to be was alone.

CHAPTER TWENTY-ONE

The lively sound of chatter in the library receded behind me as I crossed the parlor with the basket looped again over my arm. By the time I reached the second floor landing I was struck by the pervasive sense of quiet.

As I entered my room, I cocked an ear toward Rose's room. Not a sound could be heard. She must be sound asleep by now, I thought with relief. Poor Rose! With or without Ned, the future she faced was blighted.

I wondered if Ned was still watching over her. It was unlike him to forego the company of like-minded fellows and girls. Especially admiring girls, preferably pretty girls, but where was the harm in that? Contemplation was as foreign to Ned's nature as the craving for society was to mine. Perhaps that was why I had always found him so attractive: Ned, who had a talent for making light of the dark, and a way of bringing me out of myself. Rafe thought him shallow and devious; I thought him . . . I groped for appropriate adjectives, failed, and mentally shrugged. Ned was too mercurial to pin down with a facile phrase. He was just . . . Ned. An original. One of a kind and as elusive as a firefly . . . or was he? Recalling his stalwart support of Rose in their room when she was on the verge of succumbing to her dark despair, I prayed she might see him as I did before she made any rash decisions.

Rose's relationship with Victor would never be countenanced by the circles of New York society that claimed them as their own. A divorce and Rose's acknowledgment of her estate manager as her father would be bad enough, but Rose and Victor living openly as lovers? No, she would be set adrift to make her way as best she could with an aging consort embittered by their isolation from the only world he knew. One might hope Victor would display grace under such cruel pressure, but what if his emotional reserves proved as threadbare as the title he bore?

I closed the door to my room quietly behind me and tiptoed down the stairs. As I crossed the parlor to return the basket given me by Rose to the old schoolroom, I heard a groan followed by laughter issuing from the library. The game players I had left behind must still be trying to locate the objects that had eluded us during the course of Ned's most inspired effort to date. I smiled as I recalled one of them: the tip of a fern frond. There was so much olivey-green in the library, the feathery snippet would probably not reveal itself until it turned brown from lack of moisture.

The corridor was dark, but as I neared the end of it I spied a glimmer of light seeping through the crack between the wall and door, which was slightly ajar. My heart began to pound. I knew—I don't know how or why, but I knew without a doubt that Ada's amateurish seance had not brought Lily to us; she had brought herself. Had her need now become so urgent that the unifying bond created by her friends' clasped hands and willed suspension of disbelief was no longer required to clear the way for her passage?

As I moved cautiously forward, step by hesitant step, I heard a shuffling sound. The light dimmed, then brightened as if someone or some *thing* had flitted across in front of it. Taking a deep breath, I pushed the door with the tips of my fingers. It swung slowly open to reveal a tall, slim-hipped figure whose wide-brimmed hat sprayed droplets of water as he spun to face me. It's hard to say who was the more astonished, Ned or I.

"What on earth brings you here, Ned?"

"After Rose fell asleep I grew restless. I never could sit still for long, you know. I thought I might find a book in the schoolroom to take back up with me to while away the time."

I smiled. "I imagine all you'll find here are fairy stories and juvenile cautionary tales."

Ned bared his teeth in a forced grin. "Just the ticket for a simple fellow like me, wouldn't you say?"

I belatedly recalled Rose's deprecating remark at dinner about Ned's lack of literary appreciation. Smiling brightly, I told Ned he should have joined us in the library. "Your game was a great success! We never did find everything you concealed, and if you ask me," I confided, "you put Rafe's nose quite out of joint!"

The satisfied chuckle I expected from Ned failed to materialize. "I needed to stretch my legs. Get a bit of fresh air in my lungs."

I stared at him. "You went out in this storm?"

His mouth thinned. "For God's sake, Vi, a little snow never killed a man. I'm more apt to come to grief when Ada sees my wet footprints."

"I didn't see them, and the Devlins are snug in their quarters by now. Besides, since when have you cared what Ada Devlin thought? I grant you she's intimidating when she puts her mind to it, but you're the master here at Brambledene no matter what Rose's relationship to Milo may be."

Ned stood quite still for a long moment, then drew himself up, his blue eyes lighting with pleasure. "Master of Brambledene," he murmured. "By God if that doesn't have an agreeable ring to it!"

As he continued to stand there, as if transfixed by the grand-sounding status with which I had presented him, I noticed a shiver run through his lean frame. I looked at him more closely. His clothes were decidedly damp. He shivered again.

"Good heavens, Ned!" I exclaimed. "The snow might not kill you, but pneumonia could."

I looked around the room for something to rub some warmth into him. My eyes fell on the crazy quilt that still lay folded on the table where I had left it earlier in the day.

As I reached up to take off his hat and throw the quilt around his broad shoulders, I became aware of an unpleasant odor wafting toward me from Ned's clothing. Was it the wool in his fuzzy yellow vest? Puzzled, I stepped away. Ned began to blot himself, and as his body warmed, the odor strengthened. *Why did it seem familiar?*

I swallowed hard, willing myself to ignore it. Ned's body had relaxed into a graceful slouch, one knee slightly bent, and he smiled lazily at me as he wiped beads of moisture from the wavy ends of his hair. The drying honey-colored strands, wisped at his brow and back-lit by the golden lamplight, shone like a halo, and the exquisitely fashioned quilt enveloped him like an Old Testament robe. Joseph's coat of many colors, I mused fancifully.

"Give us a hand, will you, Vi? My back could use a good rub up, there's a good girl."

I felt a flash of resentment at this assignment of me to the role of complaisant handmaiden, praising me as one might a fawning sheepdog. On the other hand, why should he think of me otherwise? Hadn't I always been quick to defend him and even quicker to respond to his charm?

And yet that very afternoon I had rebuffed this man whose touch had so recently had the power to turn my limbs to water. I had used Rose, piously citing his marriage and my friendship, to justify my reluctance to accept his once longed-for embrace, but I suspected that when strong emotions conflicted with codes of morality, the code was usually the first to show the white flag. I had, after all, experienced no similar qualms with Rafe, who had given me far more reason to distrust. But try as I might, I found myself unable to determine the cause of my unease about Ned: was it that wretched polo game that had ended so badly? Rafe's oft repeated insinuations taking their toll?

I sighed. It was unfair of me to make Ned suffer for my unsettled state of mind and confused emotions. As I dutifully rubbed the quilt over his back, I was again struck by how like Jack Stark's fragment it was. I fingered the precisely stitched joinings of the irregularly shaped patches. I knew from what Ada had said that there was a twin to this one somewhere, and the chances of there being *three* such quilts . . .

My rhythmic motion slowed.

"Don't stop, Vi," Ned crooned softly. "It feels delicious."

I resumed my gentle massage. Rose's Columbine costume had been fashioned from the two Pierrots she and Lily had worn; Ada had commissioned two quilts from the one the Thornbush sisters had made for their parents. It made for an ironic sort of reverse symmetry, I reflected. But how on earth had the Raggedy Man obtained the twin quilt from which the piece Jack found had been torn? I no longer credited the possibility of a *third* quilt, either whole or half-completed, having been discarded and found, fragmented, months later under the hedges. Coincidence had its limits. Yet having decided that, I was left with no alternatives to explain the tramp's possession of the one I had seen him wearing.

I could make no sense of it, and yet . . . What was it Rose had said to me about the poor old derelict being accused of a crime he had not committed?

Rose had denied touching Lily after she fell, and I was convinced that was the truth as she saw it, but suppose guilt and horror had blanked out the memory of what *really* happened that night? Suppose her tortured conscience refused to allow her to recall bending over Lily's unconscious form, clutching at her throat with jealous fingers?

No wonder Rose had taken refuge in drink! *We were trapped, all three of us, by ghastly circumstance,* she had said. Rose and Victor, of course, but who was the third? Lily? The Raggedy Man? He *was* there. I had seen him, *but where had he found the quilt?*

Ned knows, too, Rose had whispered, and I recalled Ned coming into the room just about then and stating firmly that the case was closed. My hands slowed as I recalled the note of warning in his voice.

That wretched quilt. All along it had been the sticking point; resolve that, and everything else would fall into place. I stepped away from Ned. Suddenly it all seemed quite clear.

"Rose was telling the truth, wasn't she Ned? But it wasn't the Raggedy Man I saw in the conservatory that night, it was *you.*"

Ned stiffened as if he had been struck a fearful blow. He slowly turned. His face was ashen; his mouth sagged open.

"You must have unexpectedly come upon them. Were you looking for Lily? You knew how she loved the conservatory, had you hoped to join her in a private waltz amidst the ferns and palms? Instead you found Rose and Victor standing over her, dazed and distraught. Rose didn't even know what she had done, did she? It was too late to save Lily so you did what you could to save Rose. No one else but you would have been so rash, so heedless of the consequences!"

Ned regarded me solemnly. "All for one and one for all"—hasn't that always been our motto, Vi? As you said, it was too late for Lily; I just did what I thought at the time needed to be done."

I bit my lip. I had always suspected Ned of secretly mocking our youthfully earnest loyalties, and I resented his using the LOPH motto to justify his action.

"We're no longer children, Ned. If Rose was responsible for Lily's death she cannot be allowed to entirely escape responsibility for it."

Ned stepped toward me. He rested his hands on my shoulders, his eyes searching mine. "You talked with her tonight, Vi. You've seen for yourself the desperate straits she's in; how can you possibly think she's escaped being punished for what she did?"

I gently disengaged myself and turned away. It was hard to think clearly under his bright blue-eyed gaze. He was right, of course. Rose, haunted by guilt, had locked herself into an emotional cell from which she might never be released.

I sighed. "If Rose is not to end like her mother you will have to continue to protect her, you know. The courts will probably appoint you as her guardian. I don't know what rights Rafe may have or claim, but surely the ties created by marriage count for more than . . ."

I broke off. All along I had assumed the ties of blood I had overheard Rose lamenting were familial ties. But suppose the blood she referred to was Lily's, and the blood ties hers and Victor's to Ned? Was Ned the loving protector I assumed him to be? Could he be instead a conspirator?

I backed a step away from him. "Your marriage to Rose was a sham from the start, wasn't it? When I think how hurt I was when I learned you and Rose were to be married! We had grown so close after Lily's death."

"Too close, Vi," Ned said. "It was a closeness grounded in grief. It wasn't healthy."

I laughed bitterly. "Surely healthier than the basis of the bond between you and Rose! Graves and memorials. I find that positively morbid."

"I've already confessed I was unsure that what Rose and I felt for each other was love," Ned said reproachfully.

"Oh yes!" I said dryly. "You had your sense of—what did you call it?—sense of mission. Very high-minded of you. And Rose, I suppose, was trying to escape—unsuccessfully, as it turns out—her obsession with Victor. She never much cared for you, you know."

Ned's eyes flashed indignantly as he opened his mouth to protest.

"No, it's true!" I cried. "She was the only one of us who found your charm unpersuasive. At the time, of course, none of us suspected that Rose had long ago placed her heart in Victor's keeping. But what about you, Ned? Rose was never more than a pale copy of Lily; I would have thought that once your good deed was accomplished you would have been glad to put it behind you; Rose even more so. Death and deceit is an unpromising foundation for a marriage."

Ned gestured impatiently. "By God, if that isn't just like you, Vi! Forever analyzing. Can't you just this once accept the obvious? Rose was enormously grateful, and I felt . . . obligated."

"Good heavens, Ned! For the rest of your *lives?*"

Ned hitched up his Levi's with his thumbs and glared at me belligerently. "It wasn't easy to pull off! There was a lot more to it than you might think."

Was that a note of braggadocio I detected in his voice? Surely not! Only a year had passed since Lily's death. They had been planning to marry. He had *loved* her!

"For one thing," he continued, "I had to find a way to disguise Rose's perfume. The conservatory reeked of it."

"That's because Lily dumped a bottle of it over Rose's head, after you and Freddie had gone to the tutor's room to change into your costumes. Rose furiously accused Lily of flirting with Victor, and Lily's response was, as you might expect, rather forceful. Where Victor was concerned, Rose was always quick to take offense, but even at the time her jealousy seemed . . . irrational."

Ned nodded. "As I said, the aroma of roses was pervasive, but as luck would have it, a bottle of the formaldehyde Ada uses for fumigation was right at hand. I remembered my father reeking of it sometimes when he came from the hospital, so I was familiar with its penetrating odor. Persistent, too—I recall my mother rushing about opening windows. Just the ticket for hiding a sweet floral scent."

Ned's expression had relaxed, and his stance radiated assurance. I was reminded of the night he held us in thrall with his tales of the Colorado gold strike he had taken a winning gamble on.

"I assumed that smell was the Raggedy Man's body odor."

Ned hooted. "I doubt if even the unwashed ever smell *that* bad, Vi!"

He seemed amused, and he *was* bragging. Clearly, Ned no longer doubted my willingness to condone the year-old conspiracy.

"Poor Lily!" I breathed.

"At least she died thinking she was rich as Croesus."

His insensitivity deeply offended me. As if Lily would have chosen riches over life! "Surely you and Lily needn't have worried about money."

Ned looked at me blankly.

"Your gold mine, Ned. Didn't you say you sold it after your partner died? I assume you invested the proceeds."

He blinked. "Of course! That's just what I did. Lily knew I would provide for her."

I frowned. "But you just said she died thinking she was rich."

"I may have." He shrugged. "What does it matter?"

It mattered to me. As Ned had earlier and irritably implied, I was the sort of person who liked her i's dotted and her t's neatly crossed. In fact, all at once I knew it mattered very much. "Just to indulge me, Ned, can you try to remember when you first learned that Lily's fortune was gone?"

Ned slanted a wary look at me and rubbed his jaw. "I don't know as after all this time I can rightly—"

"Rose told me *she* found out when there were burial arrangements to be made and no money available to pay for them."

His brow cleared. "There you are! I'm sure Rose—"

"But Freddie said he told you before we arrived for the house party. He said you swore you would look after her. He was impressed by your commitment, but then it doesn't take much effort on your part to impress Freddie, does it? No one ever had a more loyal defender."

I cocked my head thoughtfully to one side. "I think I know now why your marriage was doomed from the start, Ned. Although she denies it, and probably doesn't even remember it, after Rose knocked Lily down, she throttled her. I always assumed those bruises I saw on Lily's throat were caused by hard callouses on the Raggedy Man's hands. For a time, after seeing the ropy scars on Jack Stark's hands, I suspected him—until both you and Rafe talked me out of it. But tonight, seeing again those wooden heart-shaped rings on Rose's fingers . . . Heart-shaped, Ned! What an irony!"

Ned advanced toward me. "We've been over this ground already, Vi. What are you trying to say? Come on, spit it out! It's not like you to pussyfoot."

"*Rose* killed Lily; you helped conceal her crime. I think that at first your motive was as selfless as you claim. You may have married Rose with the best of intentions, but Rose is very rich, and there's no such thing as too much money, is there? Later, when you realized she would never come to love you, you decided to turn your guilty knowledge to your advantage, and you must have pressured Rose and Victor into this fiasco of a party to consolidate your position. I wondered from the beginning how they could countenance such a thing."

Ned scowled. "Be careful, Vi. Blackmail is an ugly word."

"I doubt you ever thought of it in such stark terms, although in a court of law . . ." I shrugged. "But it will never come to that, will it? You were Rose's good Samaritan, the only difference being that you decided to exact a fee for your services." I smiled. "You've always been a high-flyer, Ned, your plans for Brambledene bear that out, and even churches expect offerings for their good works, after all."

Ned's eyes narrowed. My sarcasm had not escaped him. "Well, thank you very much for that small token of good faith! But tell me, Vi, where was the real harm in it? Lily was dead; nothing any of us could do—you, me, Rose, Victor, or the police—could bring her back. Rose never meant to kill her, surely you grant that?"

"I do, Ned, but the fact remains that the person accused of killing Lily, didn't."

"That filthy old man is dead!" he stormed, his patience at an end. "Forget him! Rose will in time, I'll see to that. As for Rose and Victor, what they share is unnatural, Vi. It confuses her, even scares her. He's old, Vi! Old and juiceless. I truly think there's still hope for us, Rose and I . . ."

Ned's tirade drifted into silence. When next he spoke, his voice was low and his words measured. "Even if I fail to win her love, I will not abandon her. Nor will I let Taliaferro get his hands on her inheritance no matter what injustice he thinks may have been done his mother by his grandparents." His tone was lofty, as befits a knight in shining armor, and his guileless blue gaze was as clear and warm as a cloudless June sky.

"But the only way Rafe can inherit," I argued, "is if Rose divorces you before she—" I stopped short.

Ned, sure of my sympathetic complicity, had strolled back to the table and perched himself on its edge. He crossed one long leg over the other; his booted foot swung idly back and forth. As I was speaking, he reached for his Stetson and smoothed its pale pelt with a swipe of his forearm. The gesture caused the quilt to slide from his shoulders, and as he clutched at it, his hat tumbled to the floor. He crouched to retrieve it from under the table. "Before she what Vi?" he prompted, looking up at me. The quilt had flopped over his head, hood-like, just as it had the night he had masqueraded as the Raggedy Man.

Before she dies, I completed in my head. But suppose she dies first, what then? Rose had no intention of staying married to Ned—hadn't she hinted as much to me in her room? Now that Milo had been revealed as her real father, she and Victor were free to do whatever they pleased, regardless of the social cost.

Ned passed his thumb over the toe of his boot, stained by the melting snow. "And after I went to the trouble of polishing them," he muttered, rubbing his hand briskly across the watermarked leather. The lamplight glinted off the lumpy irregularities in the gold nugget perched on his finger.

Oh my God. Oh my good God! It had been *gold* I had seen glinting at Lily's throat, not steel, and it had been Ned's bruising, murdering hands I had seen pulling away from Lily's throat. What better way to insure falling from one well-feathered nest into another? And if his easy prosperity was threatened a second time?

"*It was you!*" I murmured, shrinking back. "Rose may have knocked Lily down, but it was you who choked the life out of her! You let Rose and Victor think that glancing blow on the head killed Lily; no wonder Rose was confused when I asked her if she had touched Lily after she fell. She didn't know about the marks on Lily's throat; I never mentioned them to her, why should I? It was only tonight, when she unburdened her conscience, that her wooden rings assumed any importance in my mind.

"Thanks to the evidence you painstakingly arranged for me to see, the police readily assigned the blame to that poor old tramp. Unfortunately, as you keep reminding me, I have this habit of analyzing everything, and I never stopped worrying about that glint. Rose's rings and the Raggedy Man's callouses would have accounted for the bruises, but the glint? *That nagging, maddening glint!* Could it have been a small knife? I asked myself. Perhaps the one I saw a few days ago in the conservatory, the one that Ada uses for pruning? Except it wasn't steel I saw, it was gold!" I shook my head wonderingly. "Who could guess a little detail like that could be so important?"

Ned stood up, stretched, and approached with that lazy hip-swivelling gait of his as if he hadn't a care in the world. He pulled the quilt from his shoulders and tossed it carelessly back toward the table. The smell was stronger now. That same vile smell. Formaldehyde! But how . . . ?

I recalled the sign I had lettered for Ada, meant to bar accidental access to the conservatory during its fumigation. According to Ned, she used formaldehyde.

"*What have you done with Rose?*" I demanded.

Ned smiled. "Why, nothing, Vi. She's done it to herself. You see, the sleeping draught I gave her wasn't quite strong enough to keep her quiet through the night, and I had already disposed of the liquor she had hidden so craftily. Poor, troubled girl! Deprived of the means to quiet them, her anxieties overwhelmed her."

I stared at him, aghast, as the glib half-truths rolled forth. Suddenly it all became chillingly clear just how carefully Ned had constructed his web of deceit. Rose was troubled, yes, but it was Ned who had made her so. Sensing the threat their deepening estrangement posed to his long-term enjoyment of her wealth, what pains he must have taken to nurture Rose's guilt over Lily's death and strengthen his role as her protector. The notion of a seance, rising naturally from our dinner-table conversation that ill-fated night, must have seemed heaven-sent! In addition, knowing I knew of her mother's fate, Ned had persuaded me that Rose, too, had fallen victim to alcohol. How solemn his expression, how convincing his distress when he told me she used her perfume bottles to conceal her supply! The revelation of Milo as Rose's father, which released Rose and Victor from the curse of incest, merely speeded the twisted train of events he had already set in motion.

"You've locked Rose in the conservatory, haven't you? You knew we'd be engrossed in your game—no wonder you concealed more objects than usual! The storm kept the neighbors away and stranded the musicians, so you had to find another way to keep us occupied. You drugged Rose, then whisked her down the stairs and out the front door to minimize the chances of anyone seeing you. That's why I didn't see any wet footprints in the parlor; there weren't any to see!

"You must have taken her outside and in through the side door, and then returned alone from the conservatory's corridor entrance. There was no need to lock it; you knew the sign would keep us out. But *why*, Ned? Lily loved you—and you loved her, I know you did!"

He shrugged. "You said it yourself, Vi. I'm a high-flyer; not the type to settle for a dear little rose-covered cottage. I knew before we came here last year that Lily's fortune was gone. Good old Freddie thought I should know. He was sure I'd do the right thing by her, and I would have, but that damn gold mine fell short of what Syms had led me to expect. Even with his share added to mine, it brought only enough to set myself up in a way to lull fears about my being a fortune hunter."

"Lily once told me I would find it difficult to keep up with you," I said slowly, hardly able to credit what I was hearing. "At the time, thinking she meant that I *couldn't,* I was quite resentful, but perhaps she was hinting that if I knew you as well as she did, I might not choose to."

Ned laughed. "It wouldn't surprise me; Lily was no fool, and she was a high-flyer, too, in her own way. I know she had doubts about that oily voiced guardian of hers," he added admiringly. "Too bad events proved her right."

I felt numb. "Did you dispose of the inconvenient Mr. Syms, too? That nugget ring you're wearing was his, wasn't it? And to think how concerned I was about your precious memento sliding off your finger!"

"Willard managed to fall off that cliff all by himself," Ned said reproachfully. "Drunk as a lord, he was. All I did was roll him into the trickle of a creek he drowned in.

The way his head looked, I doubt he would have survived the fall anyway." Ned held up his hand and waggled his ring finger. "I thought the part about the ring being a gift was a nice touch. He *was* grateful for my backing, after all."

"Rafe once commented on your flair for convincing detail; it's a pity I didn't pay him more heed. When I think of the hours you spent with me, comforting me, encouraging me to cry on your shoulder . . ."

"Wasted hours, as it turns out. Sorry to put it like that, Vi. It wasn't all duty. I'm very fond of you . . . always have been, but that 'steely glint' you kept mentioining worried me."

"And until just now, that's how I remembered it." I began to feel hysterical laughter bubbling up in me. "I never associated gold with the ragged old derelict Milo had described to us." My laughter burst forth in a senseless cascade. "Why, it's just like your game, Ned! I saw what I expected to see, and who would ever expect a homeless tramp to be wearing a gold ring as big as a—" I broke off, what was it Ned had written Wink's brother about the nugget his partner wore on his finger? " 'As big as a pigeon's egg!' "

I wiped my streaming eyes with the handkerchief I pulled from my pocket. When I next looked at Ned, there was a disquieting look in his eyes. I edged closer to the door.

"I didn't plan it," he said quietly. "I was looking for Lily—you were right about that part of it—and I knew how much she loved that little glade in the conservatory. Then, when I came upon Rose and Victor standing over her . . . She was so deathly pale, Vi, and the blow on her head looked so nasty—I assumed she was dead, just as they did. Rose and Victor were so helpless, well, it just seemed made to order: all I had to do was cover up Rose's part in it to earn her lifelong gratitude."

I shuddered. "Off with the old, on with the new?"

Ned frowned. "It wasn't like that, Vi. I've told you it

wasn't—what do the police call it?—premeditated. I sent Rose and Victor back to the party and told them to give me ten minutes before sending you off in search of Lily. Freddie and I were assigned the tutor's room last year, so I nipped in to grab the quilt off my bed in the hope of passing myself off as the old tramp Milo had told us about. I tied it on, hooding my face as best I could, and waited for you in the conservatory. The light was dim; when you appeared, all I had to do was rise up near Lily's body and make a run for it out the side door.

"It never occurred to me Lily might still be alive. By the time I heard her groan my mind had already raced ahead to the sweet life awaiting me with Rose, so I just . . ." Ned's hands clutched the air. "As luck would have it, you chose that moment to appear as my made-to-order witness." He smiled regretfully. "I'm sorry if my attentions afterward misled you, but you see I had to be sure you hadn't seen anything that might later incriminate me. If the circumstances had been different . . . I've always found you attractive, you know."

I stared at him in horrified disbelief. "You murdered my dearest friend, and all you can think of to tell me is how . . . *inconvenient* her revival would have been for you? Have you no decency?"

"Decency is a poor man's virtue, Vi. I can't afford it. To get on in this world you have to seize opportunities as they come along, just as Rose will have seized this chance to rid herself of another rival for Victor's affections. Poor Rose has gone quite mad, you see. She'd rather die than let anyone else have him. I've already planned the heartbroken little speech I'll make regretting having fallen asleep, which allowed Rose to escape my vigilant protection and waylay you. I'm sorry you won't be able to hear it."

I became aware too late of how close Ned had come to me. Before I could open my mouth to scream, he drove his fist into the point of my chin. When I regained consciousness a moment later, I found he had torn his bandanna in two to bind my wrists and gag me, reducing me to kicking my slippered heels against the dusty floor in muffled, impotent rage.

Ned inched open the door and peered down the corridor. Satisfied that the household had retired—our voices had been too low to alert anyone, even Victor next door—he unceremoniously slung me over his shoulder and carried me the few steps to the conservatory. I didn't waste my strength in futile struggle. He would only hit me again, and unless I was conscious when he locked the door behind me, I feared I would have little chance of survival.

I took a deep breath just before Ned dumped me inside, but there was no escaping the burning, choking fumes of the formaldehyde, whose appalling odor made my stomach heave. The heat was stifling and the darkness so complete I felt as if my streaming eyes had been masked in black cotton. A moment later, the sharp click of a key securing the lock served notice that the possibility of retreat through the door into the corridor had been foreclosed.

My bound hands made it impossible for me to regain my feet, and as I squirmed blindly along the moss-slimed bricks with no sense of the building's plan to guide me, I lamented my inattention to detail during my earlier visits there.

My tortuous progress came to a dead end against a barrier of what felt like basket-woven reeds. It must be the pile of wicker furniture, I reasoned despairingly. No escape there. My breathing became ragged as I laboriously turned in the narrow space to crawl between the high benches in the opposite direction, praying this would be the route to deliver me to the outside door and the clean, fresh air beyond.

I bumped into a mound of slick-surfaced softness which stirred against me. It was Rose! Resisting my instinctive impulse to try and rouse her—I doubted I could, given my bound hands—I inched my way over and beyond her like some huge wounded caterpillar. The door must be somewhere near, I assured myself, but wherever I turned I encountered resistance: bench legs, clay pots, discarded wooden flats. Hopelessly disoriented by the impenetrable dark, my strength gone, I was ready to surrender my ebbing consciousness to this lethal Garden of Eden.

I sighed and resignedly rested my cheek on the mossy bricks. Then, as my eyelids slowly closed, I became aware of a glimmer high above me. I blinked and forced my burning eyes to focus. *Could it be moonlight?* Yes! Stronger now, it shone down through the glass roof where the intense heat, rising, had caused the snow to slide from the steeply pitched panes. The storm had passed.

The light grew even brighter. I became aware of it sparking off a bit of shiny metal on the edge of the bench above me. It was Ada's pruning knife! Last year, a metallic glint of another kind had signaled Lily's death; perhaps this time it would provide Rose and me the chance to survive.

I maneuvered my back against the bench legs. Fighting waves of dizziness, I shouldered my way up, inch by laborious inch, until my hands could grope behind me along the bench's surface. My fingers blundered through pot shards and spills of potting soil before finally closing hard around the sought-for wedge of sharpened steel. Ignoring the stabbing pain and warm trickle of blood, I awkwardly edged it into a crack between the bench top's roughly cobbled boards. Wobbling on unsteady feet, I began sawing the cloth that bound my wrists against the precariously balanced blade.

Despite my determination to take as small breaths as possible, the exertion made me gasp and the air entering my tortured lungs seared like molten lava. As the ties on my wrists parted, my consciousness wavered and dimmed, but my freed hands, acting independently of my dulled brain, grabbed up the knife and hurled it at the glass wall beyond.

The sound of the shattering glass was blessed music to my ears. Wrenching the gag from my mouth, I leaned close to the broken pane to inhale the pure cold air pouring through. Each hungry gulp afforded me an uncanny surge of purposeful strength. I fancied I could hear my blood singing in my veins: you must survive, it seemed to be humming. *You must survive: for Rose, for yourself, and for me . . .*

There was no time then for the analysis Ned found so tiresome. My eyes fell on the flat of carniverous plants Ada had brought from the Arkham bogs and tended so lovingly. I felt a flare of rage. How like Ned they were! Devouring those who ventured too near, attracted by the snare of sweetness that he, like the sundew, exuded. Without stopping to consider the size and weight of the box—it was only later I marveled at it—I seized it with both hands and lifted it high over my head to hurl with all my miraculously regained strength through the glass wall. After it, I threw anything and everything that came to hand: empty pots, pots filled with flowers, even bricks scrabbled out from beneath my feet, until walls, roof, and all came cascading down around me.

Galvanized by the alarming clangor, the entire household, in various states of undress, came running to find Rose lying under a blanket of glass, while I, standing in the midst of the chaos I had created and bleeding from countless tiny cuts, greeted them with arms outstretched in joyful thanksgiving. "Look!" I cried, "the snow has stopped! Isn't the moonlight lovely?"

It wasn't until much later I learned that the snow had, in fact, been falling faster than ever, starring my dark hair with its tiny crystals, and until the rays from Milo's upheld lamp searched Rose and me out, the darkness in the ruined conservatory had been absolute.

CHAPTER TWENTY-TWO

"Come, Violet." I felt a strong arm encircle my shoulders. "Come along with me, now."

I looked up into quicksilver eyes. "You've come back for me," I murmured gratefully. "Everyone else has left and the animals—" I broke off, confused. Where were the trees whose lengthening shadows had shrouded the menagerie in darkness? Why had the night-prowling beasts fallen silent? *Where was the moonlight?*

"Oh, Rafe," I cried, "What's happening to me? I'm so frightened!"

He held me very close. The heat of his body seemed to inflame the very air. "Come, Violet," he said again, his voice gently urging, "we must go inside."

As I drifted with him toward the open door I felt something splinter beneath my feet. I looked down, bemused by the glittering carpet of glass. I became aware of icy droplets on my skin and white stars on my sleeve. Snow? In Paris in springtime, when only the petals of horse chestnuts drifted white along the avenues?

"Rafe? What is this place?"

"We're at Brambledene, my darling, and there's a lovely fire waiting to warm you in the parlor."

Brambledene. Of course! I stared at the double door yawning wide before us. How could that be? It had been locked. I had heard it being locked, closing us . . . *us?* A burly figure brushed by us carrying a limp bundle wrapped in white satin. I clutched Rafe's arm as my blurred memory began to clear.

"Rose." I whispered. "I couldn't rouse her . . . I didn't have time to spare to rouse her. Oh, Rafe! Will she be all right?"

"Shhsh-shhh. You roused the rest of us, Vi, that's what's important. Otherwise, both of you . . . I'll never understand how you managed it, but you have nothing whatever to be sorry for."

We passed the door to the tutor's room. I could see a sprawl of stained white satin on one of the beds and Rose's blond head on the pillow. She looked as still and pale as the stone angel in the Bramble graveyard. Victor kneeled beside the narrow bed, rubbing one of her small hands in his; Milo stood guard above them. My steps slowed, but Rafe urged me ahead.

"There's nothing you can do, Violet. Mrs. Devlin will see to her, and besides, you have yourself to worry about."

"Me?" I was astonished. "But I'm fine, Rafe, I—"

"Oh my poor Violet!" Flora exclaimed as we came into the parlor. "We must do something about those cuts. Keep her here, Rafe, I'll get Mrs. Devlin."

Rafe led me to the couch that had already seen duty as a sick bed for Wink, then turned his attention to the fireplace close by that had earlier been banked for the night. The dry, splintery kindling he added soon caught fire from the slumbering embers, and its exuberant flames ignited in turn a trio of stout birch logs.

A returning wave of dizziness impelled me to sink down on the wide couch. I took a deep breath to steady my wavering vision; then, curious to discover what had distressed Flora, I splayed my hands up in front of my eyes. Tiny trails of blood oozed from a myriad of small cuts. Tentatively, I fingered my face and the skin exposed by my modestly low-cut neckline. I winced. "I must look as if I had been rampaging through the Bramble," I said, raising questioning eyes to Rafe.

His sleek silver-laced hair fell in a boyish shock across his forehead. The anxious crease between his brows eased as he smiled and sat down in the vee-shaped space framed by the crook of my legs. "You've looked better," he admitted, "but you must be *feeling* better if you can laugh at yourself."

I frowned. I had not meant to laugh, not even at myself. Somehow I felt sure there was nothing to laugh about. I sensed that something had happened, some significant thing or things my weary, fogged brain refused to relinquish. If only I could remember . . .

I sensed movement beyond the circle of firelight. "Rafe? Who's there, out in the darkness?"

"I've brought you some salve for your cuts, Miss Grayson." It was Ada Devlin. Her tall spare frame, muffled in flower-sprigged flannel, loomed above me. "It's made in Arkham from my granny's herbal. You won't find anything more healing."

She held out a small, crude pottery crock. Recalling the loathesome sundew plants that also came from Arkham, I shrank back.

"Milo swears by it, miss, for himself and the horses, too."

Knowing Milo would never use anything that might harm the horses in his care, I smiled weakly. "Thank you, Mrs. Devlin. It's very kind of you."

She nodded, then turned to Flora and gave her a packet of cotton wool. "Just soothe it on evenly, but not too thick, mind. We want to help the healing, not smother it. If that's all, Miss Grayson, I'll be getting back to Miss Rose."

"How is she, Mrs. Devlin?"

"Unconscious yet, but her breathing's steadier and her color's good." She paused. "Almost too good, if you ask me. I'm wondering if that cherry pink's a sign of fever. No telling what those formaldehyde fumes do to a body, or how long she'd been there breathing the awful stuff. All we can do is keep her warm and try to get a doctor up from town in the morning."

"But she'll live?"

"No reason to think otherwise, miss." Ada's lips thinned disapprovingly. "Although she might not thank us for saving her, poor troubled girl."

Flora gasped. "Mrs. Devlin! Surely you're not suggesting that Rose . . . that she tried to take her own life!"

"Sad to say, I am, miss. Like mother, like daughter."

Flora whirled on Rafe. "Can that be true?"

Rafe nodded. "I'm afraid so, Flora. When it was learned Milo was Rose's father, Victor thought the Devlins should know the truth about her mother's death."

"But there was never so much as a whisper!"

"Pains were taken to prevent such whispers."

"We should have been told, Rafe," Flora said accusingly. I winced as her application of Ada's salve to my cuts became harsher, unconsciously reflecting the severity of her criticism. "If we had, we all could have kept watch over Rose. After that idiotic polo game I knew something was wrong—we both remarked on it, remember, Vi?—but I never imagined . . . Could she have locked herself in the conservatory while we were playing Ned's game? Those dreadful fumes! Oh, how perfectly awful! Ned must have fallen asleep in their room and she slipped out—"

"It wasn't like that, Flora," I cut in harshly. "It wasn't like that at all."

But before I could begin to tell what had really happened, a tramping of feet diverted Flora and Rafe's attention. Wink and Iris and Freddie hustled in from the corridor brushing snow from their robes, and began jostling for space in front of the fire.

"Feeling more yourself, Vi?" Freddie asked. "Can't think why you thought the moon was out. Black as pitch out there. We thought of trying to save some of the plants, but since there was no place to put 'em, we decided to save ourselves from frostbite instead. That little stove out there was blazing away like billy-o, but even that didn't help much with all the glass gone."

"Good thing you girls got out when you did, Vi." Wink chimed in. "That shaky chimney had somehow come undone at one of its bends, and what with all that charcoal gas pouring in . . ." He shook his big auburn-thatched head. "Many's the logger who's come to grief in winter thanks to a leaky stove pipe in a tight cabin."

It happened in many a New York City flat, too, according to my father. Cherry pink, isn't that how Ada Devlin had described Rose's "healthy" color? And wasn't that the color my father said was characteristic of carbon monoxide poisoning? Had Ned intended the formaldehyde to do no more than he had freely admitted: to keep others out by virtue of its nauseating odor? Of course! It was the gas that had been meant to do Rose and me in, and so easily accomplished! All it would have taken was a smart rap on the stove pipe joinings with Willard Syms's heavy, all-purpose, gold nugget ring.

"By the by, had anyone seen Ned?" Freddie asked. "Surely he didn't sleep through all that commotion!"

"When I came down I found the front door open." Iris said. "Maybe Ned decided he'd get to the conservatory faster if he went around to the side door instead of adding to the crush in the corridor. Do you suppose he could have slipped on an icy spot and hurt himself?"

As these old friends exchanged worried looks of consternation about the whereabouts of another old friend, I wished—oh, how I wished!—it had not fallen to me to reveal to them his villainy. Perhaps because of that pained reluctance, my words were harsher than they needed to have been.

"Ned isn't asleep, Freddie, and I can assure you, Iris, that he had no interest in reaching the conservatory first—or if he had, it wouldn't have been to save us. Quite the contrary. He meant to kill us, you see. And the man in the quilt I saw bending over Lily's body last year?

It wasn't the Raggedy Man, it was Ned."

Rafe, readier to accept Ned in the role I had cast him than the others, took one of my hands in his. I folded both against my heart.

"Your insane jealousy does you no credit, Violet," Freddie said. There was no trace of bluster in his voice. "Perhaps Rose was righter than she knew; perhaps spinsterhood has already sent you 'round the bend."

"Oh, Fred," I said, "I wish for your sake you were right. I know how fond you are of Ned."

"*Fond?* It goes beyond fond, Violet. Damn girlish kind of thing fondness is, anyway. I know no one believes in heroes anymore, but Ned Poole—" Fred turned his back on me. "C'mon Wink, Ned may be lying out there in the snow, hurt. I say we get dressed and make a search before . . ." He turned back to glare at me. "Dash it all, Vi! There's no rhyme nor reason to it!"

"It was the money," I said quietly. "Rose was going to divorce him." Where should I start? It was all so complicated! "It began last year, with Rose and Lily's bitter quarrel the night Lily died."

"What quarrel?" Freddie demanded. "I don't recall anything of the kind!"

"I do!" Iris exclaimed. "It was after the sherry hour. Maybe you had already gone to your rooms to dress for the party, Freddie. Rose was furious! Quite unlike her. And there were bits of crystal all over the tiles in the foyer." She shrugged. "I think it had something to do with Victor and the perfume he gave us."

"Lily thought Rose had insulted her," I said, "and unfortunately she decided to carry the quarrel a step further. The hows and whys of it no longer matter, but there was another outburst between them in the conservatory, again over Victor, who was again an innocent bystander. Rose struck out at Lily, knocking her to the ground. Her head hit hard against the edge of a bench as she fell, and from the look of her as she lay sprawled on the bricks, Rose and Victor thought she was dead. Ned came upon the scene of this tragic accident—for that is all it was at the time—and offered to divert suspicion. Remembering Milo's story of the tramp who dressed himself in old quilts, Ned grabbed a quilt from the tutor's room—"

"We shared the tutor's room last year," Fred said. He frowned. "Not much warmth to those quilts as I recall. Jaggedy bits of thin old stuff stitched together every which way."

"Crazy quilts, Freddie, one of which Ned belted around himself and waited for a witness."

"Oh, Vi!" Flora whispered, "that was you!"

"Yes. Although it could have been any one of us, really. Ned has admitted to me that while he waited he began thinking of the fortune Rose had inherited."

Rafe turned to look at me. "Blackmail, Vi?"

"Not yet, Rafe. It didn't start out like that. At first it was just pleasant dreams of the good life Rose's gratitude might provide. Then he realized how even more pleasant it would be if they married. Nothing stood in the way of it now that poor impoverished Lily was dead. It must have been an increasingly happy resolution to contemplate, until he suddenly became aware that Lily *wasn't* dead, not quite. Not until Ned extinguished that inconvenient little spark of life with his grasping hands.

"That's when I arrived," I told my mesmerized audience. "Just as the 'Raggedy Man' was pulling his hands away from Lily's throat. It was an ugly detail I mentioned to the police, of course, but never to Rose. If I had, she might have been saved a year of punishing guilt."

"He was going to take care of Lily!" Freddie exclaimed. "He told me he would, and I believed him." He looked around at us, challenging us to find fault with the trust he had placed in the person he admired above all others.

"Dear Brother!" I heard Flora murmur, her hands fluttering in confusion as her natural sympathies warred with the shock that had assaulted her sensibilities.

"Of course you did, Freddie," I said. "He was your friend." His haggard, distraught expression persuaded me it would be cruel to berate him for his indiscretions. I was sure he would never make the same mistake again.

"Friendship allows one, indeed it demands one, to overlook and forgive a great deal, Latimer," Rafe said. "Your loyalty does you credit. But Ned was never my friend, and I saw much I could not like."

Freddie thrust out his chin belligerently. "I wouldn't expect a foreigner—"

Rafe waved his hand impatiently. "It had nothing to do with his flamboyant American ways. I could have found that . . . colorful. No, it was his moral judgment I found wanting. Ned and Rose were guests in my mother's Paris home during the two weeks before the wedding. Not having a daughter of her own, and a son who showed no signs of matrimonial inclination, she was quite looking forward to the attendant . . . how do you put it? Hustle and bustle? At first, Mother was charmed by Ned's dash and his devotion to Rose; after a week of it, she found it tiresome, and by the time of the wedding Rose's unenthusiastic reception of her lover's attentions had aroused her suspicions.

"I had reasons of my own to question his devotion, for by then several *boulevardiers* of my acquaintance had much to tell about his midnight excursions to that infamous stretch of the city from the place Blanche to Saint-Georges, from the rue Pigalle to the rue des Martyrs."

"Not your style or mine, perhaps," Freddie protested, "but who are you to deny a lively chap like Ned a last fling before smothering his instincts in the marriage bed?"

Iris looked at him reproachfully. "Fred Latimer! What a dreadful thing to say!"

"Hardly a last fling," Rafe said evenly. "More like indiscriminate wallowing, to hear tell of it. And considering the incidence of disease in such districts, my innocent cousin could have unknowingly received a very ugly bridal gift from her groom. It seemed to me a risk that a man genuinely in love would not court.

"Be that as it may, neither my mother nor I were happy about Rose's choice of a husband. I had already decided to, as they say, 'seek my fortune' in America; our concerns about Rose merely hastened my departure. I just wish I had not allowed myself to be swayed by your LOPH loyalties. As it is, all we can do is pray for Rose's recovery."

"And for Ned to be found." Wink added. His grave tone implied acceptance of the guilt I had assigned.

"That, too." Rafe agreed.

Freddie paled, but didn't speak. His shoulders slumping, he turned toward the stairs, tiredly waving Flora back as she scurried in his wake offering little bleatings of comfort. "Not now, Florrie, there's a good girl."

Flora watched helplessly as he mounted the steps with a slow, heavy tread, then looked back at us with tears in her china-blue eyes. Iris and Wink flanked her protectively, and the three of them, after being assured we would let them know of any significant change in Rose's condition, followed Freddie upstairs.

Despite the blaze of heat from the fire and the comforting warmth of Rafe's embrace, I shivered.

"My poor Violet! Would you like a cup of tea? A glass of warm milk?"

My formaldehyde-abused throat rebelled against the very thought. "There's a down coverlet in the chest at the foot of my bed, Rafe, would you mind—"

He was off before I could finish. A moment later I heard a fearful banging on the front door, and before I could call out Jack Stark came hurtling in matted with icy clumps from the top of his hatless, uncombed head to his thick-soled flapping boots, whose untied laces trailed untidily through rapidly widening puddles of snow melt.

"He's back, miss! I saw him in the stable, wrapped in his old quilt. The Raggedy Man's back and Milo's got to know. Came in to take Billy, he did. I shot at him, but he got clear away. Beggin' your pardon, miss."

With an apologetic duck of his head, Jack scuttled purposefully toward the stairs, just as Rafe came down, coverlet in hand.

"I've got to see Milo," Jack pleaded. "It's the Raggedy Man, back again, and up to no good."

"Jack!" I called, "Milo's not in his quarters. He's down in the tutor's room, off the corridor that leads . . . used to lead to the conservatory. He's with Mrs. . . . Miss Rose. There's been . . . an accident. And it wasn't the Raggedy Man you saw. He's dead, you know."

Jack looked at me, his mouth agape with astonished disbelief. "Why would you be telling me that, miss? I saw him, quilt and all!"

"His body was found two days ago. The police came about it—didn't your sister tell you?"

"I saw the *quilt*, miss!" Obviously Ada hadn't.

"It wasn't the Raggedy Man. It was Mr. Poole."

"Mr. Poole? Why would he be wearing a quilt like that? No, I wouldn't be shooting Mr. Poole!"

Rafe draped the coverlet over the back of the couch. "I'll get Milo for you, Jack," he offered, putting an end to our frustrating exchange.

While we waited, Jack shifted restlessly from one sodden booted foot to the other. His long sallow face lighted with relief as Milo entered the parlor, but rapidly dimmed as he took in his brother-in-law's grim expression.

"What's this I hear about Ned Poole stealing off on Billy and getting shot for his pains? I pray you didn't miss him, begod." Milo began pulling a stout coat on over his sweater, grunting as the wool of one garment resisted the wool of the other.

"It was the Raggedy Man," Jack persisted doggedly, looking as if he might burst into tears. Poor confused Jack. Unpleasant as he was, I couldn't help feeling sorry for him.

Milo waved his arms impatiently. "You're dead wrong

about that, Jack. As dead as that poor old tramp and as wrong as the rest of us. Ned Poole killed that poor girl last year and if it hadna been for Miss Grayson's quick thinking both she and my Rose would be victims to his villainous schemes." His voice hoarsened to a growl. "If ever I get my hands on that—"

"Is Rose conscious, then?" I broke in.

"Only since the last quarter hour, miss, but enough to know she'll be coming back to us—good as new most likely—and more than ready to sound the alarm about that husband of hers. She's hazy about the particulars, drugged as she was when he carried her down like a sack of potatoes into the conservatory, but she sensed what he was up to right enough." He turned to his brother. "D'ye think your shot hit him?"

"I don't rightly know, Milo. Bruno was barking and rushing about the way he does—it was him that woke me—and by the time I got down the ladder into the tack room and loaded your revolver, the Ragg . . . I mean Mr. Poole already had Billy out of his stall. By then the horses were stamping and whinnying as if judgment day was on 'em, and it was dark as the bottom of a well, so I just shot blind as he went rushing by. I think I heard 'im cry out, but what with all the animals in such an uproar . . ."

Milo snatched a muffler out of his coat pocket and wound it around his neck. "Hitch up the cutter."

"But the storm, Milo—"

It was like trying to put a cork in a cannon. "Hitch it up, Jack!"

Jack's shoulders sagged. He turned, opened the door, and trudged out into the driving snow without another word.

"Do you really think this is wise, Milo?" Rafe asked.

"Wise or not, each of us has to hammer out his own road. Brambledene was put in my care by your grandfather, Mr. Taliaferro. To my understanding that includes the people, and the creatures, it shelters."

Creatures like Sergeant-Major, I realized. "And

Rose?" I asked gently, hoping to divert this stalwart soul from the vengeance he seemed driven to seek.

"Count Stirbey and Ada are looking out for her, miss; there's nothing more I can do here until morning."

Our eyes followed Milo's departure out into the night. As the door clunked shut behind him, a gust of wind skittered in to coil icy fingers around my ankles. Seeing me pull my feet up under my skirt, Rafe drew the down coverlet over me. I gazed up at him as he plumped a pillow and tucked it behind my shoulders. Words escaped me. A simple thank-you seemed ridiculously inadequate; to say what was in my heart . . . I contented myself with reaching up to gently comb back with my fingers the wayward lock of hair on his forehead.

I cleared my aching throat. "Your robe is very handsome," I rasped. I didn't really care; I doubted if Rafe cared, either, but at the moment it was the most neutral comment my addled wits could produce.

Rafe looked quizzically first at me and then down at his long, well-tailored dark red robe as if he had never seen it before. "Yes, I suppose it is. A gift from my mother. She said hotel living requires a gentleman to present a well-dressed appearance at all times."

I smiled. "One must always be prepared for unexpected emergencies, like fire," I said in a lecturing, parental sort of voice.

"Or flood," Rafe added.

"Or, should you happen to be traveling west, an Indian raid on your wagon train."

His gray eyes flashed with alarm. "Good God, Vi! Surely that's no longer possible!"

I laughed. "Hardly," I assured him, "but Europeans—or as Freddie likes to say, 'foreigners'—prefer to think so."

We smiled at each other. I dropped my eyes for fear the entanglement of my gaze with his might rival the blaze on the hearth. I was not ready for that. Not yet.

"You haven't a place of your own, then?" I inquired politely.

"I thought it prudent to wait until I had a place of employment. There is a neighborhood much to my liking, though. Washington Square, it's called. Are you familiar with it?"

"Oh, yes! It's out of the mainstream of fashion now, of course—"

Rafe slanted a speculative look at me. "One of its principal charms, I thought."

"Oh, yes," I agreed. Why were we in such pleasant agreement all of a sudden? "At which hotel are you staying?"

"Holland House. I've taken a suite there; it's of modest size, but quite pleasant. Friends suggested I move to the Waldorf-Astoria when it opens next year, but I have no wish to make even a temporary home in a commercial palace whose public rooms are sure to be crowded with gawking tourists."

I stared at him. The Holland House was very grand, and to judge by the advance publicity, the Waldorf-Astoria would be the most opulent hotel in the country—perhaps in the world.

"Have I said something to offend you?" Rafe asked.

I blinked. "Not at all," I assured him. "It's just that . . . you see I thought . . ."

"Out with it, Vi. Surely we needn't have secrets between us. Not now, after all that's happened."

"I thought you were poor," I blurted. "I assumed you had lodgings in a boarding house—in a respectable one, to be sure—but instead you have rooms at the Holland House, and are apparently well able to consider the Waldorf-Astoria!"

Rafe laughed. "What on earth gave you the idea I was poverty stricken?"

"Ned suggested you might need the fee you would get for drawing up his schemes for Brambledene; need it enough, in fact, to induce you to offer a family discount and compromise your design standards."

"I imagine he assumed that because I was temporarily unemployed I was also out of funds. Happily that is not the case."

"But you told me your mother was more interested in storing up gold against her old age than adding to her collection of textiles."

"Mother is more Parisian than American now, and all true Parisians are more interested in saving than spending their gold no matter how much of it they may already have. Besides, Mother has decided that devoting serious study to what she already has in her collection is worthier of her attention than continued accumulation. It is an intellectual development my father fostered before his death, and that I continue to encourage." He made a deep, self-deprecating bow.

"Your parents were still married when your father died?"

Rafe looked astonished by my surprise. "Of course! Why would you have thought otherwise?"

"When we stayed with you all those years ago, I saw no signs of a man in residence. There were no pipes or boxes of cigars—"

"Father was a connoisseur of fine wine. Smoking would have dulled his palate."

"No walking sticks or man-sized umbrella in the foyer—"

"My father was too forthright a person to bother with the folderol the fashionable use of a cane requires; as for a brolly, you're thinking of London, not Paris." Rafe sat down again in the nook created by the crook of my legs. "Imagine all that going on behind those great purple eyes," he mused aloud. "Your habit of analysis is nothing new, I see."

"Neither is its fallibility," I admitted wryly. "I'm glad to learn that one of the Thornbush sisters remained content with her choice of a husband."

"They adored each other. Many women would have found Father's style alarming—his making and losing of fortunes in a matter of months alarmed *me*—but Mother found it exhilarating."

"He was a high-flyer, then, like Ned."

"Oh, not like Ned, Violet. Father made his own fortunes; Ned is merely a user of others. Mother made that distinction early on. That's why she asked me to keep an eye on Rose, even to the point of making that list of the fine pieces of furniture here at Brambledene. Mother wanted Rose to have it in case Ned attempted to sell them off and pocket the proceeds."

"Is that why she signed her interest to Brambledene over to you?"

"Yes. She suspected Ned had some kind of hold over Rose, and she wanted me to be able to act rapidly if it became necessary."

"You mean in case Ned tried to coerce Rose into assigning her interest to *him?*"

"Exactly. I'm not sure that such an assignment would have held up if challenged in court, but it would certainly have complicated matters. I asked Rose to sell her interest to me—remember our meeting in the library while the rest of you played cards?—but she refused. Not because she was unwilling, but because of Ned's probable reaction. The accident on the polo field had just happened, and although she wasn't as yet fearful for her own safety, I imagine it frightened her."

"With good reason, as it turned out," I said slowly. "Oh, Rafe, when I think now how I misjudged you!"

"As I said to Freddie, loyalty to a friend does you credit."

"Not blind loyalty!" I protested.

"You're forgetting, Vi. Ned was more than a friend to you."

His voice was very low, almost hesitant. I hastened to erase the question I saw in his eyes.

"Not for some time," I said, recalling my distaste for

Ned's long-desired kisses. "I finally realized that my feeling for him was only an echo of past yearnings; a residue of my schoolgirl infatuation mixed with gratitude for the comfort I thought he had given me after Lily's death."

"His reason for comforting you may have been false, Vi, but the benefit you received was not. You can be grateful for that at least."

I cocked my head consideringly to one side. "In your place I would not be so generous."

He grinned. "I'm not, really; I just thought it would be nice to get credit for it."

I smiled, then yawned as the warmth of the fire, the down coverlet, and Rafe's body close to mine combined to overwhelm me with sleepiness. "I'm afraid I can't keep my eyes open much longer."

"No need to try," he murmured. "Now, if you'll just scoot over a bit, there's plenty of room—"

My eyes flew open.

"I don't want to leave you here alone and unprotected. Besides, we're not in your bed, Violet; we're merely resting together on a couch in the parlor. Perfectly proper. I'll have, I hope, a lifetime with you for the other."

I found it hard to focus my scattering thoughts. I wasn't quite sure what Rafe had in mind for us, or whether or not it, too, could be considered "proper," but I heard myself asking, "Why me, Rafe?"

His clear gray eyes sought mine; this time I did not look away. "It's always been you, Violet, even though I haven't always known it. Now, if your eyes had changed color, or you had forgotten how to laugh—" He tugged my chin up with his crooked forefinger. "You haven't, have you?" he asked sternly, searching my drowsy eyes.

"Only temporarily," I murmured.

"Good!" he muttered in a gruff, satisfied voice. I felt the tip of his finger softly brush my eyelids shut. "Sleep, little one. I fear daylight will come all too soon."

* * *

I awoke to find myself alone on the wide couch. The fire had ebbed to a gentle simmering glow. I started to pull the coverlet closer around me when I heard a scuffling sound in the shadows. Heart pounding, I peered above the couch's high back and caught a glimpse of a red-robed figure, Rafe's, and Milo's burlier frame crossing behind me toward the corridor.

"Any news?" I called hoarsely.

Milo turned. The dimple in his cheek deepened in response to the downcurved stretch of his mouth.

"Not very good, I'm afraid," Rafe replied.

"Not for Ned Poole, leastways," Milo added, "but I'm sure we'll all be having our own opinions on the matter."

He came over to stand above me. His square, broad face was red with cold, a patch of white on his nose hinting of frostbite. "It wasn't hard to follow Billy's tracks, miss. I don't know what was in Poole's head. Nowhere near the road, he was. I held up a lamp for Jack to steer by, and the tracks lead straightaway down the hill toward the river and a little spring that bubbles up strong and clear right through the coldest days of winter.

"It was almost as if he were being led there, through drifts and all, like a dog on a rope," he said, blinking his eyes in bewilderment. "Jack thought he was heading for the old haybarn t'other side of the Ashley, and maybe he was, but as we came down upon him he was leaning low over Billy's neck like a man too hurt to know where he's at, and above him, miss, twisting 'round his head . . . wisha, I don't know what it was!"

He scratched his thatch of white hair. "Jack thinks it was a breath of steam from the spring catching the moonshine breaking just then through the clouds, but it was more gold than silver. Like a swarm of fireflies, only paler, as if a mist had come up between it and us."

Lily. I knew it was, but I held my peace. There were some secrets, extraordinary secrets, grave and mysterious secrets, best kept to oneself. I had learned that much from Ada.

"And then?" I prompted.

"And then Billy screamed, miss. Not in pain or brute rage as a horse will sometimes do. No, he was pure afraid he was . . . not that I blame the poor beast! That swarm had settled down around him, like a snare of sparks. Begor, how he plunged, first this way, then that, kicking up great white clouds of snow. When it finally settled we could see Billy making his slow way up, almost foundering in the drifts, but the swarm had left him, and the rider, too.

"I guessed what had happened, mind you, but I had to make sure. Jack tied Billy to the back of the cutter while I went down to the river, as close as I dared. There was a hole in the thin ice around the spring, with edges cut smooth and even like a hot knife through butter, and big enough for a man to slip through into the water below. The Ashley runs deep and fast at the bends. It could be days before . . ."

I nodded acknowledgement as his words trailed off.

He cleared his throat. "I'd best be telling Count Stirbey, and then try and get some sleep before the day breaks. Will you still be wanting to leave tomorrow? I can promise you sun."

I looked at Rafe. He squeezed my hand reassuringly. "We all will, save for Rose and Count Stirbey," he said, "She'll want time to herself to recover."

"Wanting and needing it, sir, after all that's happened." Milo shook his big head regretfully. "I sometimes think that when God made man he may have overestimated his ability."

The new day dawned fair, as Milo had predicted. The sunlight slanting through the mullioned windows cast dancing shadows on the plaster walls, relieving somewhat the parlor's customary gloom. Rafe and I had breakfast with Rose and Victor in the tutor's room. What I had to tell her was not easy for them to hear—I doubt she would soon return to the bed she and Ned had shared—but Rose's relief at learning she was not responsible for Lily's death more than outweighed her distress. I did not, however, mistake her gratitude for my saving her life as signaling a return to our girlhood relationship. Emotionally, we had already gone our separate ways; our gallant LOPH motto—"all for one; one for all!"—had become, for all of us, our envoi.

As I stepped out into the corridor—Rafe had some family matters to discuss with Rose—I saw Freddie leaving the old schoolroom. He had Ned's pale Stetson in his hands. He stopped short at the sight of me, stepped back, then came toward me, nervously revolving the wide brim in his pudgy hands.

"D'ye think it would be all right if I kept Neddy's hat, Vi? I can't believe he's . . ."

He gulped, and I stared down at the hat, unable to meet Freddie's imploring eyes. I had no idea how much he knew; I had no intention of asking him. Let him cherish whatever illusions were left to him of his idol a little longer.

I reached out to pat his arm. "Take it, Freddie. I can't think of anyone Ned would rather have it."

As Freddie trailed disconsolately by me toward the parlor, my eyes were drawn to the conservatory door ahead. The warning sign Ned had tacked up hung aslant; the casing was splintered. Ned had no doubt intended to steal back to unlock the door once he was sure Rose and I had succumbed to the gasses seeping from the chimney, but this plan, too, had gone awry.

I took a deep breath and turned the knob. The extent of the destruction that met my eyes made me gasp in dismay. Glass mixed with snow carpeted the bricks; only shards, sharp as daggers, remained in the bent frames. Pots and flats had been flung as if by a malignant child's hand; the brilliant sunlight casting rainbows through the bits of colored glass set in the conservatory's crown, seemed to mock the blackened flowers and ruined greenery.

How beautiful it had been! How lovely the friendships that time and events had altered beyond redemption!

As I stood there, huddled and forlorn, I sensed the approach of a pulsing presence. It brushed against my ankles, catlike, then wound warmly up and around to glide across my shoulders as gently as a silken shawl.

I lifted my hand wonderingly, but my questing fingers were not quick enough to capture the spirit kisses that mischievously darted and glowed, like a sunbeam through a prism, upon my brow, my cheeks, the tip of my nose.

Lily . . . ?

I felt a heady burst of effervescence, like bubbles rising from champagne, just before the warmth slipped away like smoke on a rising draught of air, soon lost in the dazzle of the midday sky above.

"Here you are, Violet! I've already put your bags in the sleigh."

I felt a rush of pleasure at the sound of Rafe's voice, and yet I hesitated. My eyes once more searched the sad remains of Althea Thornbush's pretty folly, but the presence I had sensed here was gone now beyond recall.

I pray you find peace, my well beloved friend . . .

"It's time to go, my darling."

I turned. Rafe's smile was tender, and as I moved joyfully toward him, his arms opened wide to receive me.

EPILOGUE

From Violet Taliaferro's journal: January 1, 1900

A new year and a new century! The automobile parade up Fifth Avenue last fall, despite the ridicule with which it was greeted, seemed to symbolize the extraordinary era that awaits us. I hope, therefore, these journals kept for my own amusement will prove to be of more than passing interest to my children and their children after them.

I must confess at the outset, however, that although the horseless carriage may be cleaner than its predecessor, the honking of brass horns indulged in by their drivers, multiplied by thousands, might require the poor pedestrian to wear ear muffs year 'round! Two steps forward, one step back—isn't that always the way with progress? Even the lately fashionable "rainy-daisy" skirt, for all its boot-top-length practicality, has its scandalized detractors. Alas, I fear Mrs. Grundy will follow us into our brave new world!

Enough of generalities. My children will already know much of what I am about to write, but theirs may not. If so, my as-yet-unborn darlings, command your parents to supply the missing bits and pieces:

Taliaferro and Taliaferro will start work on its first commission this very week. It was Bradford Lee Gilbert's generous gift to his departing, most promising associate.

Rafe decided to strike out on his own as a specialist in domestic architecture, hoping to woo forward-looking clients with the same sort of innovative approach Bradford brings to his designs for commercial buildings.

The second Taliaferro is me. Clients often require guidance in furnishing their homes to complement the architectural design, and since this formidable task is usually left to the client's wife, Rafe thought the process might seem less intimidating if the schemes were developed in partnership with another woman. "Men have this regrettable tendency to expound," he said, "when tactful suggestion is really what the situation requires." I tactfully forbore from pointing out to my dear husband that he occasionally erred himself in this direction.

My poor house-bound father continues to expound on the subject of tight-lacing, although fashion has quite passed him by. Rafe and I have kept our silence on that score, of course. So, too, has the admirable woman who has more than filled my shoes as housekeeper and amanuensis and whose generous wage eliminates any need for the put-upon air I fear I too often wore. Father's health continues to decline, but slowly. The principal difference I see is a lessening of the reserve that marred our relationship, which has allowed him to become a doting grandpapa to our darling son, Marco.

We have seen neither Wink and Iris McEldowney nor the Latimer twins since leaving Brambledene four years ago this February. Iris and Wink live in a huge log lodge in Maine with their two little boys, and although Flora wrote at Christmas that a third child is on the way, Iris allows nothing to interfere with her new vocation: fly-fishing. How I laughed when I read that! I knew that Wink, too, enjoyed the silent stalking of the wily trout, and this shared enthusiasm will not only bring them pleasure, but allow Wink relief from Iris's demanding contralto while in pursuit of it.

Flora added a sad postscript to her letter. Last fall, a

visiting nephew "who thinks all closed doors a challenge" discovered Ned's Stetson tucked in the back of Freddie's closet. When Freddie arrived home for a late tea, he had no sooner settled down before a small desperado whooped in to demand his money or his life.

Flora wrote:

> Freddie turned quite pale. He snatched the hat off little Georgie's head and gave him such a look! It shook me as much as the child, Vi. Without a word to either of us, he went out with it into the garden and burned it. Not that he told me so, but when he came back in and closed himself in his study, I crept out to find a small pile of embers and a bit of charred felt that had escaped the flames. He's Fred now, by the way, even to me; less trusting than the Freddie you knew, but maybe, for a lawyer, that's not such a bad thing.

Maybe not. And yet, if Rose and Rafe had not decided to place implicit trust in Milo Devlin . . .

Rafe is in closer contact with Rose than I. She and Victor, married in a private civil ceremony in New York, live in Paris with their baby daughter, and Rafe's mother, bless her, has been able to swallow her misgivings enough to provide the maternal comfort Rose sorely needs.

To all intents and purposes, Brambledene is now the Devlins' home, held in informal trust for our children—you, dear readers, the Thornbush descendants. Rafe returns occasionally to ride the splendid horses Jack and Milo breed and train there. I visited once, in May of '97, to place the stone ordered many months earlier to mark Lily's grave, but I had already said my good-byes and had no wish to linger. The conservatory, what remained of it, has been leveled. In its sheltered place is an extensive herb garden planted by Ada. "Would that she cared for me as tenderly she does her precious herbs," Milo joked.

Most of the plants luxuriating there were brought as

cuttings from Arkham, Ada told me. I do not know, nor did I wish to ask, if sundew lurked in the boggy spots I spied near the rainspouts, luring passing insects with its sweet entrapments. Ned Poole's body was retrieved from the river's dark waters after ice-out, in early April that cold year. I do not know the place his family chose to bury him, nor, like the sundew, have I any wish to seek it out.